"A bleak, lyrical tale that evokes Cormac McCarthy's *The Road* . . . the dystopic picture it paints is dreadfully plausible – a eurozone nightmare brought to life on the page"

JAMES LOVEGROVE, *Financial Times*

"Longo is a superb writer and every sentence drips intelligence and humanity. He creates of the soft apocalypse as complex and meaningful as Cormac McCarthy's *The Road*, but far more approachable . . . *The Last Man Standing* is set to be one of the novels of the year" DAMIEN WALTER, *SFX*

"After reading this, life in Ireland under austerity seems a nonstop frolic . . . The depiction of civilisation's end is terrifyingly convincing"

MARY FREELY, *Irish Times*

"A novel in which precision of language is as crucial an element as the steadily accelerating tension . . . We can only hope that Longo's visionary diagram of our possible future remains on the printed page" BARRY FORSHAW, *Independent*

"A complex and compelling investigation of the behaviour of survival" TADZIO KOELB, *Times Literary Supplement*

"*The Last Man Standing* has been likened to Cormac McCarthy's *The Road*, an accurate comparison in its style and foreboding. Yet this is a totally unique novel that blends despair with hope and angst with serenity so well that it deserves to be held in similar esteem"

CHRIS HIGH, *We Love this Book*

"With mesmerising con̶ ̶ ̶ ̶ ̶ ̶ ̶ ̶ ̶ ̶ ̶ ̶ ̶ ̶ ̶ ̶ ̶ ̶ ̶ale that will leave readers with ̶ave put it down" ̶ ̶ ̶ ̶ ̶ ̶ ̶ ̶ ̶ ̶ ̶ ̶ ̶ ̶ ̶ ̶ ̶ning Post

DAVIDE LONGO

THE LAST MAN STANDING

Translated from the Italian by
Silvester Mazzarella

MACLEHOSE PRESS
QUERCUS · LONDON

First published in the Italian language as *L'Uomo Verticale*
by Fandango Libri, Rome, 2010
First published in Great Britain in 2012 by MacLehose Press
This paperback edition published in 2013 by

MacLehose Press
an imprint of Quercus
55 Baker Street
7th Floor, South Block
London W1U 8EW

A CIP catalogue record for this book is available
from the British Library.

ISBN (MMP) 978 085738 629 8
ISBN (EBOOK) 978 0 85738 630 4

10 9 8 7 6 5 4 3 2 1

Designed and typeset in Scala by Libanus Press, Marlborough
Printed and bound in Great Britain by Clays Ltd, St Ives plc

To Emma

THE LAST MAN STANDING

Part One

Leonardo pushed back the curtain and took a long look at the courtyard where three cars were parked, one of which was his own. The open space was surrounded by a metal net three metres high with barbed wire at the top. The previous evening, though blinded by the light the guard had shone in his face, he had noticed the outline of the little tower, but he now realized it had been skilfully constructed from old advertising panels, sheets of metal, sections of railing, a shower cubicle and a fire escape. One of the two searchlights above it was pointed at the courtyard and the other directed at the desolate emptiness beyond the fence.

He looked out at the flat fields covered with low bushes where the road stretched into the distance, with occasional bends despite the fact that nothing seemed to be in the way to make them necessary. The sky was a monotonous unmarked grey for as far as he could see it, reminiscent in every way of the last few days.

A man appeared in the courtyard.

Leonardo watched him slowly make his way to the cars and walk round them, peering through their windows: he had a leather jacket and trousers with big side pockets. He could have been about thirty, with the compact physique of a rugby player.

Why not tonight? he thought, watching the man stop in front of the boot of his Polar.

The man took a screwdriver or knife from his pocket and with a simple movement flipped open the boot.

For a few seconds he studied the jerry cans inside as if trying to work out what might be in them, then unscrewed the cap of one and sniffed. When he was quite sure of its contents he replaced the cap, grabbed a can, closed the boot, and went away just as he had come.

Leonardo let the curtain fall back and went to the bedside table where he had put his water bottle. Taking a sip, he sat down on the bed. He could hear steps from the corridor, and the noise of something with wheels being pushed towards the stairs.

That evening he had hesitated for a long time before deciding whether to leave the cans in the car or take them to his room, but after thinking the matter over for a long time he had come to the conclusion that all in all he had done the right thing, or at any rate the least wrong thing, and that if the cans had been in his room it would have been worse.

He went into the bathroom, took his washbag from the shelf and put it into the holdall he was packing on the bed. He stowed the vest and pants he had been wearing before he showered in a side pocket, then slipped on his jacket and went out of the room, leaving the key in the door as he had been told to do.

Passing down the corridor he glanced at the pictures on the walls: dead pheasants on big wooden tables, baskets of fruit and pewter pots. There was the still the pervasive odour of boiled vegetables he had noticed the previous evening, and after the rain that had fallen in the night the fitted carpet smelt of damp undergrowth.

An elderly woman was clutching the handrail on the stairs. When he asked her if she needed help, the woman, wrapped in a most unseasonable tailor-made wool costume, looked at him with total indifference as though he had been nothing more than the sound of a closing door, then turned her face to the wallpaper. Leonardo apologized, pushed past her and went on down to the hall.

The surroundings, despite their gesso statue, artificial plant and carpet covered with cigarette burns, had clearly had quite a different appearance only a short time before. He could see marks where shelves and brackets had been roughly stripped from the walls, and big lead pipes ran the length of the ceiling. The door to the courtyard was protected by a heavy grille, through which the cars and the entrance gate were visible. Occasional circles were spreading in the puddles, and he could sense that the air was already heavy and sultry.

"Have the dogs been bothering you?" the man behind the counter asked without looking up from the papers spread in front of him. He was no longer wearing the green sweater he had had on the previous evening when he had demanded payment in advance and shown Leonardo how to use the hot-water token for the shared bathroom.

"There are packs of dogs all round the enclosure at night. We've tried poisoning them, but it doesn't help."

Leonardo watched him sign a paper in a sloping hand. His shiny head looked as if he were in the habit of greasing it with fat and polishing it with a woollen cloth every morning. A lot of postcards showing places which were now inaccessible had been clipped with clothes pegs to the metal frame of a bed propped against the wall behind him. On the counter you could still see where objects, now vanished, must once have stood. One space looked as if it might once have held a computer. A telephone had survived, even if no longer attached to any cable.

"I think something's missing from my car," Leonardo said.

The man turned to detach a couple of fuel tokens from the metal net and copied their code numbers into a register. When he had done this he took a pack of cigarettes from his shirt pocket and lit one. He took a puff and looked at Leonardo through the smoke.

"Are you sure?"

"Yes."

"Certain?"

"Absolutely."

The man dropped ash into a saucer with a picture of a saint on it. He had a leather armband round his wrist and his right ear looked as if it had been chewed. Leonardo imagined these two facts must be connected in some obscure way which would have required time to work out.

"The guard was in the watchtower all night," the man said. "No-one could have got into the enclosure."

"Yes, I'm sure that's true."

The man studied Leonardo's thin face and long, mostly grey, hair. He was probably reflecting that the man before him did not work with his hands and was physically inactive.

"Then you must suspect the other guests," he said.

Leonardo shook his head.

"No, not at all."

The man took in Leonardo's frank gaze, then puffed out his cheeks as if this would help him to think. His eyes were the colour of glass bottles that had spent years in a dark cellar.

"Denis!" he shouted loudly, then picked up his cigarette from the edge of the saucer and bent his bald head over his papers again.

A moment or two later a door opened behind him and the lad Leonardo had seen in the courtyard emerged.

"My brother," the man behind the counter said without looking at either of them. "He looks after security."

Seen close up, the lad looked younger than thirty. He had thick wool stockings and the side pockets of his trousers were full of short cylindrical objects.

"This gentleman says something's missing from his car," the bald man said.

The boy considered the tall body and narrow shoulders of Leonardo in his linen jacket, as if bewildered by a utensil which must have once been useful but had now become obsolete.

"I was on guard all night," he said, "and we haven't opened the gate yet this morning."

There was no shadow of defiance on his face. Only the boredom of someone compelled to go once again through an over-familiar rigmarole.

"I don't doubt that," Leonardo said, "but I also know that someone's forced open the boot of my car."

"What have you lost?" asked the boy.

"A can of oil."

"Motor oil?"

"No, olive oil."

"Was it the only one you had?"

"No, I had four."

The boy was silent, as if all possibilities had been covered. His brother stopped writing.

"If you like, we can call the police."

Leonardo thought about it.

"How long would they take to get here?"

"We use a private security firm and they don't much like to be called out. Once we had to wait two days."

Leonardo looked at his own hands pressing on the desk: they were long, thin and emaciated. The man continued to stare at him.

"Maybe you only had three cans and are making a mistake," he said.

Looking up, Leonardo saw the boy's back disappearing through the door he had come in by.

"I'm glad we were able to sort out this misunderstanding," the man said, lowering his bald head over the counter. "You'll find breakfast in the dining room."

The room Leonardo entered had been divided by a plasterboard partition, from the far side of which kitchen and laundry noises could be heard.

The old lady Leonardo had met on the stairs was sitting at the table nearest to the door, while a fat man of about forty breakfasted by the window. He was apparently a commercial traveller, with two black cases leaning against either side of his chair. On a round table in the middle of the room were a pot, two Thermoses, some bread, a few cups, a rectangular block of margarine and a bowl of jam of unappetizing colour. A clock on the wall showed ten past eight. No staff could be seen.

Leonardo poured himself a cup of coffee and took it to one of the three free tables. He put his bag down and took a sip: real coffee diluted with carob.

It reminded him of a conference on the circularity of Tolstoy's writing many years before in Madrid, and the dinner that had followed at a restaurant whose unmarked entrance had seemed like the way in to an ordinary block of flats. The chairman had been forced to spend the whole evening dealing with invective hurled by his wife against enemies of bullfighting. Most of those present must have been used to the woman's heavy drinking and aggressive defence of this spectacle outlawed only a few months earlier by the government, and they seemed not to be bothered by it. Then, at the end of the evening, with the restaurant nearly empty, a young woman – probably a student in the company of some lecturer whose more or less official mistress she was – had sung a song she had written in which she maintained that love was nothing more than a means to an end. None of those present had either the strength or enough reverse experience to contradict her. The coffee they had then drunk, each imprisoned in his or her own guilty silence, had been like the coffee he had before him now, except that at that time you could still find decent coffee everywhere.

As he lifted the cup to his lips again Leonardo became aware that the old lady was looking at him. He nodded to her, but she continued to stare without responding. Her sparse hair had been built up into a gauze-like structure through which light weakly filtered from the skylight. Her fingers were covered with jewels and everything in her appearance seemed calculated and tense in some way about which it might almost have been blasphemous to speculate.

Leonardo took a book from one of the side pockets of his holdall and leafed through it till he found the story he was looking for.

It was a story he had read many times since the age of twenty-two, and for which he had always felt unconditional love. Both in moments of utter despair or fierce hope the story had always adapted itself to his mood, revealing itself for what it was: a perfect piece of design. He had always advised his students to read it, both those with literary ambitions and those who imagined that a man in his position must be able to offer them useful pearls of practical wisdom. Many years had passed since the last time anyone had expected any such thing from him, but if it ever happened again, now or in years to come, he was certain that his answer would have been the same: *A Simple Heart*, he would have said.

When he had finished reading Flaubert's description of Madame Aubain, for whom Félicité was so ably performing her duty, he took another mouthful of coffee and it tasted better. The sun had come out in the courtyard and through the window he could see it reflected from the car windscreens. The incident of the oil can seemed remote and thus of little significance.

"I'll be home by this evening," he told himself.

Raising his eyes for a moment as he turned back to his book, he met those of the old lady, who had silently approached him.

"Please sit down," he said, removing his holdall from the free chair.

The woman skirted the short side of the table and sat down. The skin between the few deep creases on her face seemed strangely young and taut. She had carefully outlined her lips with deep scarlet.

"I'm sure no-one has recognized you," the lady said.

Leonardo shut his book. The woman nodded severely.

"I couldn't fail to. You've been one of the great delusions of my life."

"I'm sorry."

"I was so naïve. I spent years in the arts and should have realized better than anyone the huge gulf between the artist and the shabbiness of the man."

Leonardo took a mouthful of coffee.

"What was your own field in the arts?"

The woman checked the architecture of her hair with her left hand.

"Opera. I was a contralto."

Leonardo complimented her. The man at the other table was watching them; his heavy hands restless, the rest of his body motionless. Leonardo imagined he must be having ignoble thoughts.

"May I ask you a question?" the woman said.

"Please do."

"After what happened, did you continue writing?"

"No, I stopped."

The woman screwed up her eyes, as if reliving one of many memories.

"I could not sing for nearly two years when my daughter was born because of her health problems. I nearly went mad. And I don't say this out of empathy with you. The situation I found myself in was very different from yours. I had done nothing wrong."

Leonardo finished his coffee.

"Then you started again?"

"Of course," the woman exclaimed. "One engagement after another. Not many contraltos can boast of singing till the age of fifty-two, but I had a voice other women could only dream of. I was on stage two days after I lost my son. Have you any idea what it means to lose a son and two days later find yourself singing *Rigoletto* in front of a thousand people?"

The fat man got up from his table and passed them on his way out.

"Goodbye," the woman said.

"Goodbye," he answered.

Leonardo followed the man with his eyes as far as the door. Rembrandt without the beard, he thought.

"An arms dealer," the woman said. "Stays here two nights a month."

Leonardo would have liked more coffee.

"Do you come here often?" he asked.

"I've been living here for a year. If that's not often, I don't know what is."

The sound of the commercial traveller's car attracted their eyes to the window. He manoeuvred his luxury off-road vehicle and went out through the gate which was being held open by the man from reception. The two acknowledged each other, then the bald man closed the gate and padlocked it, slung his rifle over his shoulder and slowly walked back.

"His car's bulletproof," the woman said. "That's why he's able to come and go as he pleases."

Leonardo nodded and removed some perhaps nonexistent speck from his shoulder.

"Where did you live before you came here?" he asked.

"In P.," the woman said. "But when this business with the outsiders started, my daughter persuaded me to move in with her. After a few months my son-in-law was called up for the National Guard and my daughter decided it would be safer to move to Switzerland. So I told her to go and find a house, then come back for me. She knew this place and brought me here so I'd be alright in the meantime."

The old woman said no more, as if that was the end of the matter. Leonardo smiled weakly.

"Will you be staying here much longer?"

The woman gave him a sharp look.

"Where else should I go?"

"But I thought your daughter was waiting for you in Switzerland."

"She's not in Switzerland anymore," the woman said, removing a crumb from the table. "When her husband died, she married again, a German. Now she lives in Germany. She has suffered, but for the better: her first husband was an inconsistent man. He died at V., so far as we can understand from whoever writes those official letters. But the one she has now seems a lot better, altogether another kettle of fish."

"Why don't you join her?"

The woman looked at him as if he had just wet himself.

"Don't you ever watch television? Have you no idea what's happening? When the lines were still working, my daughter used to call me every day and beg me, I'm not exaggerating, beg me to let her come and fetch me. But I always said no. That it wasn't worth the risk. I'm ninety-two, I lack for nothing here, and she's the only child I have left. You have a daughter too, if I remember rightly?"

Leonardo lifted the cup to his lips, regardless of the fact that he had finished his coffee.

"Yes."

"Does your wife allow you to see her?"

"No. I haven't seen her for seven years."

"So I thought."

For a moment they studied different corners of the room in silence.

"Now I must get on with my journey," Leonardo said.

"Where do you live?"

"At M."

"Is that the village where *The Little Song of Tobias the Dog* is set?"

"Yes."

"So you've gone back to your childhood home?"

"Yes."

They heard a horn. A small tanker had stopped in front of the gate. There were two men in the cab.

"Not that I wish it for you," the woman said, "but perhaps sooner or later you'll want to start writing again."

Leonardo smiled and shook his head. They watched the bald man open the gate and the driver bring the lorry into the courtyard. Once out of his cab, the driver put on work gloves and attached a thick ridged pipe to the tank while the bald man opened a manhole cover fastened to the ground by two locks. Both men had a pistol in a holster under their jackets. Leonardo stared at the ochre countryside and a sky the colour of curdled milk.

"I really must be on my way," he said.

He picked up his holdall. The woman fixed her eyes on the yellowing lily of the valley in the centre of the table and waited till he had reached the door before calling him by his surname.

"The best possible interpretation is that you did something stupid," she said. "But no-one can ever forgive you for what you did."

Leaving the hotel, he drove north on the same secondary roads as he had come by. The *autostrada* would have saved him several hours, but he had heard of fake checkpoints at which travellers were robbed, and for this reason he preferred a less obvious route well away from the larger towns.

He drove with the window down, the hot, clammy wind filling his shirt; from time to time he took a mouthful of water from the bottle beside him. Since starting out three days before he had passed about a dozen cars and several military convoys. The villages he passed through were mostly deserted, with only an occasional old man sitting in a doorway, a boy on a bicycle, or the face of a woman drawn to her window by the sound of the car.

About noon he stopped to fill up with petrol. When he sounded his horn a man came out through the gate to the service station while another stayed in the doorway with his rifle lowered. Leonardo got out of the car, let himself be searched and said how much petrol he wanted. The man, who might have been about fifty, and wearing a rock band T-shirt, got into the Polar and drove it into the enclosure. Leonardo tried to check through the grille how much was being put in, but the back of the car was hidden by the prefabricated hut where the two men lived, and where a young woman with dark skin and curly hair was leaning out of a window. Leonardo imagined she must be tanned from working all summer in the open, unless she was an outsider who had got in before they closed the frontier.

The man in the T-shirt brought the car out again.

"See you later," Leonardo said as he paid.

"Take care," the man said, turning away.

Leonardo pulled over a couple of kilometres after the service station. Before getting out of the car he had a look round. The countryside was flat and the yellow grass, mostly unmown, was bending over in the hot wind. A long way off was a hut and the ruins of what must once have been a kiln for making bricks. Then a line of mulberries and some electric pylons disappearing into the distance in the direction of an almost invisible group of houses.

Leonardo listened to the silence for a while, then got out of the car and checked that the cans were in place. He opened them and sniffed to make sure the contents had not been replaced while the car was being filled up, then he closed the boot and mopped the sweat from his forehead with his handkerchief. He became aware of an acid stench of decomposition.

He looked into the ditch separating the road from the fields. There was a dog lying in it, its belly swollen, a swarm of flies whirling round its eyes and open mouth. A black labrador killed by another dog or poisoned.

He was about to turn back to the car when he heard a whimper.

A few metres from the dead dog the ditch disappeared into a small tunnel no wider than a bicycle wheel. He understood at once what was going on.

He returned to the car, started it and moved off. He switched on the radio, but the preset came up with nothing, so he switched it off again and drove for several kilometres without slowing down until he was forced to stop at a crossroads.

Checking to make sure that there was no other car with right of way, he noticed a group of men not far off in a field. There were six of them, armed with rifles, and they seemed not to have noticed him: two were using a long pole to explore the ditch that bordered the field, while the others were following them with their eyes on the grass.

Leonardo put the car into gear to drive on but, as he engaged the clutch, six, ten, perhaps twenty dogs jumped out of the ditch the men were searching and all began to run in the same direction. Taken by surprise, the men hesitated, then started yelling and shooting at the tapering shapes racing through the grass. The dogs had almost reached a water channel that would have given them protection, when, for no apparent reason, they turned at right angles so offering the wider target of their sides to the hunters. Leonardo saw one or two roll over in the grass, others vanish as if swallowed up by a hole, yet others explode into reddish puffs of air. Then the shooting stopped and the men spread out to comb the field. An occasional isolated shot followed, then total silence.

Leonardo realized his foot was still on the clutch. He put the car in neutral and took his foot off. The engine struggled, but did not stall.

The men went back to the irrigation trench from which the dogs had come. Leonardo saw some of them go down into the ditch and throw out what looked like small soft bags full of earth. After a few minutes there must have been about thirty of these, piled in a heap.

Then the men scattered across the field and dragged the carcasses of the dogs towards their puppies, and when this was done one of them took a can from his knapsack and poured the contents over the heap.

Leonardo closed his eyes, his chilled sweat-soaked shirt sticking to his chest. When he opened his eyes again a column of black smoke was rising in the air. He stared, paralyzed, for a few moments with the acrid smell of burned fur coming into the car through the window, then he engaged the gears and did a U-turn. Moving away, he thought he could see in his rear mirror the men waving their arms to attract his attention, but he continued to accelerate.

He recognized the place near the ruins of the kiln. He drew up and, while dust from the verge of the road enveloped the car, he went to the ditch. Lowering himself in, he slithered down it until he was lying on his face in the earth, a few centimetres from the dog's carcass. Disgust forced an inarticulate sound from him and when he touched his bare arms he realized they were dirty with yellow slime. He wiped them on his shirt, got up and walked quickly to where the tunnel passed under the road.

No sound was coming from inside it; all he could hear was his own laboured breathing and the rapid beating of his heart.

Bending down he looked inside. The tunnel was blocked by filth, stones and refuse brought by the water. But nothing moved or made any sound. He smacked his lips. There was no response.

Leaping up again he checked the road: the pyre was no more than a couple of kilometres away and he could not be certain the hunters would not follow him.

Kneeling down he stuck his head into the tunnel and thought he saw a movement. He reached in, and as if he had been breaking a membrane, was struck full in the face by the smell of death. Suddenly what he was doing seemed just as incomprehensible to him as when, years before, after one of his books had just reached the bookshops, he had been unable to explain to himself how he had spent three years of his life writing a complicated poem in a difficult and antique verse form, which many of his readers, and most of his critics, had already dismissed as an affected minor work.

He lay face down on the ground so as to be able to stretch out an arm, but also because his twisted position was making his head spin. His hand touched something soft and cold. Pulling it towards him, he saw it was a dead puppy covered with ants. He threw it behind him near to the body of its mother and when he heard the thud as it hit the ground he retched, as if his gesture had validated the existence of a hidden part of himself that had now emerged into the light with pangs like childbirth.

Reaching into the tunnel again, he felt something tepid and let it slide across the palm of his hand like a baker collecting a loaf from the far end of the oven.

He pulled the puppy out. It instinctively hid its muzzle between his fingers. It must have been the first time it had seen the light. It was wet with urine and yellow liquid had dried round its half-closed eyes. Leonardo climbed out of the ditch and sat down in the shadow of the car. Grabbing his water bottle from the seat he took a long drink, poured some water into his hand and tried to wash his arms and neck, then tried to get the puppy to drink from his hand, but the animal seemed stunned by sleep or hunger and did not react. Even when he cleaned the incrustation from its eyes, the dog continued to keep them closed. It was black and its ears were hanging sideways, giving it an air of resignation.

He put it down long enough to take off his shirt and stretch it over the seat. He settled the dog on top and was about to get into the car when he was stopped by a sudden pain in the pit of his stomach. With long strides, his naked thin torso marked by large moles, he ran towards the edge of the road, and was only just able to drop his trousers in time before a gush of diarrhoea emptied him.

Gasping for breath and bent double, he got back to the car door and took a toilet roll from the inside compartment. He wiped himself carefully, wetting the paper with a little water.

Sitting down in the driving seat, he took a casual shirt with horizontal brown stripes from his bag, and began searching on the map for a road that would help him avoid the crossroads where the pyre would certainly still be burning. He found one that would not take him too far off course: it was a case of going back about ten kilometres and crossing the river. His wristwatch said a quarter past three. To the north blue mountains closed the horizon. By eight it would be dark, but if he couldn't get home by then at least he would be on a familiar stretch of road.

He drove slowly, taking great care at corners as if his new passenger must not be disturbed. The dog never moved, and every now and then Leonardo reached out a hand to check its little heart, which beat rapidly under his fingers. Towards five it urinated, and when the light started to fail, it began lolling its head and emitting little blind whimpers. Leonardo stopped the car and cleaned its eyes which were encrusted again, then held a piece of the cheese he had eaten for lunch to its mouth, but the dog seemed not to recognize it as eatable and turned away in irritation.

He went off to urinate in the shelter of a clump of acacias, then got back into the car, put on his jacket because the air was getting fresh, and took the dog in his arms.

He looked down at the plain from the height of the first foothills. With the dying of day the sky had cleared and now the sun was sinking behind the mountains, the vault of heaven a deep unshaded cobalt.

It won't eat and tomorrow it'll be dead, Leonardo thought, holding the dog close.

Far off the lights of A. and one or two other villages were shining softly, with the lights of some factory prominent among them. For several months now the minor roads had no longer been lit, the football league championship had been suspended, and the television closed down after the evening news at ten, not starting again until the news at ten the following morning.

He smiled at the swarm of lights and the beauty of several fires burning on a hillside to the east. The dog's breathing had relaxed and the heat of its body through his shirt was warming his chest; it had the smell of things which are new to the world and still have no name. Like the smell of a birthing room or a cellar where cheeses ripen. Or a paper mill. A smell of transition.

"I won't give you a name," he said, stroking the puppy's head with his finger.

When he arrived in the square the church clock was striking eight.

He opened the door of the hardware shop. Elio looked up from a newspaper he must have salvaged from some packaging. The last newspaper had reached the village four months before. Leonardo went to the counter and put down the two cans he had brought in, then wiped his brow with his handkerchief.

"Only one more in the car," he said.

Elio neither nodded nor shook his head. He and Leonardo were distant cousins, but their friendship had nothing to do with blood or books or with other passions that can link men like hunting, the mountains and sport. It was seven years now since Leonardo had come back to the village but he was still a town man, while Elio belonged as much to the hills as any man could. He spoke the dialect, he knew what was going on, he had tried the women and played in the Sunday football matches against other villages. In the days when there were still summer tourists, he had spent long periods sitting with the other local twenty-year-old boys on the low wall that bordered the square, studying the German and Dutch girls at a distance, before taking them in the evening to the vineyards, to the river and up into the highest hills from where he had convinced them they would be able to see the sea. When he was called up for the National Guard, he had done the usual thing and given a big party, then disappeared for three days without anyone knowing where he was. He had served two years at the frontier until, in the winter of '25, he had been hit by the bullet which now saved him from being called up again. As soon as he was demobbed he had taken over the hardware business from his father and married the woman who had been his fiancée since he was nineteen: a woman with strong thighs and few frills; a type more likely to bore him than break his heart.

"What shall I say about the missing oil?" Elio said.

Leonardo raised his shoulders.

"Tell them it was stolen from me. That's what actually happened. Tomorrow I'll bring the money for you to give back."

Elio fixed him with his calm eyes. He was not yet forty, of a reflective temperament and Leonardo's only friend.

"What's happening out there in the world?"

Leonardo put his handkerchief back into his pocket. The mud had dried on his trousers in a dragon-shaped pattern.

"Yesterday some soldiers stopped me before L.; they told me to go back the way I'd come and sleep in the car because the road was closed until the next day to let a convoy of armoured vehicles through."

"Were the soldiers from O.S.R.A.M. or from the Guard?

"O.S.R.A.M."

"Then there was no convoy: they were just sweeping up. According to the television most of them have stopped coming, but a few groups have managed to get through."

Leonardo looked around the shop. Most of the shelves were empty, and despite Elio's efforts to make what little was left go a long way, one had an impression of well-concealed desolation. A passer-by unaware of the situation would have imagined the shop had been hit by floods, or that the proprietor had liquidity problems and was on the verge of going out of business.

"I've checked the vineyard for you over the last few days," said Elio. "If it doesn't rain, you should be able to harvest the grapes in a couple of weeks."

"Good."

"How do you plan to do it?"

"How do I plan to do what?"

"Harvest the grapes."

Leonardo brushed hair from his brow with a gesture he had used since childhood.

"Lupu and his people," he said. "As usual."

"You think they'll come?"

"I'm sure they will."

Elio shook one of the cans and watched its contents move about until they settled again, then looked out at the square where two silhouettes were passing silently under the only functioning street lamp.

"Even if they do come you'll be wrong to make them work."

"What do you mean, wrong?" Leonardo said with a smile.

Elio lifted his handsome shoulders.

"It's two years now since anyone has brought in outsiders for harvesting, and those who were linked in one way or another to local firms have not been reemployed."

"Lupu and his family have permits and they all came in before the borders were closed."

"Permits or no permits, it may have been alright last time round, but this year there's bound to be some problem."

Leonardo propped his long slender pianist's hands on the counter. He had never played the piano, but several women had told him he had the right hands for it. Only one woman had ever said he had 'a writer's hands'. A girl he had met on the train to Nice. When they got out at the station they had shaken hands and he had never seen her again. But that had happened long before he had married Alessandra. After his marriage he had never allowed any woman to come close enough to him as to comment on his hands. Apart from Clara that is, and such a thing would certainly never have occurred to her.

Suddenly he felt very tired. There was a pain in his leg: sciatica.

"Let's not discuss that now," he said, "we're tired. Just come and get the other can, because I want to show you something."

They went out into the fresh night air. The village was sleeping peacefully; like a child with an ugly scar on one cheek, who has fallen asleep pressing the scarred side against the pillow. The window of the hardware shop, bright with metal tools, was like a Nativity scene. Leonardo opened the door of the Polar and the internal light revealed the dog huddled on the seat. It was sleeping quietly, revived by the fresh air or the little water Leonardo had finally succeeded in getting it to lick from his cupped hand.

"Did you find it or was it given to you?" Elio asked.

"Found it."

Elio, short-haired and with an aquiline nose, looked at the dog as one might look at a car damaged in an accident that will either need work to make it roadworthy or have to be scrapped. Leonardo said he had tried to get it to eat some cheese, but without success.

"There are always Luca's baby bottles," Elio said. "But if Gabi finds out you're using them for a dog . . ."

He considered the problem, drumming his fingers on the roof of the Polar. The sound rang out clearly all over the square and up the narrow streets leading to the upper part of the village, the castle and the stars shining above it.

"I'll give you a rubber glove," he said. "You can fill it with milk and make a hole with a needle at the end of one finger."

"When they stole my she-goat and I had to feed her kids, it worked. It won't cost you anything to try."

"Alright," Leonardo said.

The dog was sleeping with its back turned away from them, showing the pink skin of its stomach. It had a few light-coloured hairs, wet with urine, round the point of its penis. One of its eyes had begun weeping again.

"I've heard there are packs of dogs on the plain that attack people," Elio said. "I hope he's not from one of those."

"We travelled together a good few hours and he hasn't attacked me yet," Leonardo said with a smile.

Elio shifted his weight to the other foot.

Leonardo's home was a modest little farmhouse, but on the better side of the hill and secluded. His father had died when he was six and his mother, to make ends meet, had sold the half facing the village to a surgeon from T.

During his years as a university student, when he came home to see his mother at weekends, Leonardo often travelled with the surgeon's family who liked to escape the city in search of a little tranquillity in the hills. The wife, many years younger than her husband, was an intelligent woman who wore high-necked jerseys over her enormous breasts. They had two sons: one born at six months who suffered from dyslexia, while the other was a brilliant chess player. When the surgeon was killed in a road accident, his wife no longer felt like making the journey to the house and telephoned Leonardo's mother to tell her so. Both had wept at great length. Two weeks later the wife had sent a removal firm to take away their furniture, and from then on that part of the house stayed empty and unsold.

Leonardo parked the car under the lime tree, hoisted his holdall onto his shoulder and carefully lifted the dog who was still asleep. On the veranda floor were two letters; no surprise and he did not bother to pick them up. The fridge was empty apart from a small amount of milk left in a glass bottle; he sniffed the milk, and finding it acceptable, poured it, before doing anything else, into the glove, pierced the point of the little finger with a needle and put it to the puppy's lips. But the animal ignored it.

Leonardo sat on the sofa for a while, one hand on the puppy's hot body, wondering whether rescuing the dog had been wishful thinking. An irrational gesture that had put him at risk and in the end would benefit neither of them.

Going into the bathroom he undressed, put his clothes into the washing machine and looked in the mirror. On his pale chest he had a deep red mark he must have acquired while crawling into the tunnel. He shuddered at the thought of what he had done and for a moment thought he could smell the nauseating stench of the dead puppy and its mother on himself.

Without waiting for the water to warm up, he got into the shower and roughly scrubbed his body and hair, reflecting, as he had not done for some time, that everything leads to ruin and that in his case this had happened to him in utter solitude. He felt extremely tired, but even more empty and discouraged.

When he was dry, he put on some periwinkle-blue underpants and went back to the sofa, where the dog was sleeping in the same position as he had been left. The kitchen was equipped in a functional manner. None of the furniture had belonged to his family: he had never cared for *arte povera*, and when he moved away he had sold everything to a junk dealer. He had then bought himself furniture in African teak, basic and without any fancy design. He had added plates, glasses and other necessary kitchen equipment from the catalogue of a major store and had everything delivered.

At the time he had attributed his choice to his haste to get organized and to the disorder of the time, but when he thought about it he soon convinced himself he would have done the same anyway. Throughout his life the objects he worked with, chose and gathered round himself had always been a matter of indifference to him.

He found some crackers in the cupboard and sat down at the table to eat them, by the light of the small neon tube above the cooker. The house he had been living in for the last seven years was one that, in the days when architectural magazines still existed, would have been worth photographing. He had had a large window put in facing the vineyard and the veranda where he could sit and enjoy the sunset behind the chain of mountains that closed the horizon like a zip. On the western side of the house was a strip of meadow, and on the other side of the courtyard was an outhouse, its ground floor kept as a storage area and its upper floor reconditioned so as to be able to accommodate a dozen people.

Leonardo finished the crackers and continued to gaze at the night through the great window.

Maybe better warm, he thought.

He heated the milk for a few seconds in a small pan, then poured it into the glove again. When he approached the dog with it, he moved his eyes behind closed lids, nothing more. When Leonardo squirted a little milk on his muzzle the puppy instinctively licked himself. Leonardo repeated the action until the dog realized where the milk was coming from and timidly began to suck the rubber finger. In the end they both stretched out exhausted, side by side on the sofa. The clock showed eleven-twenty.

"Bauschan," Leonardo said.

Bauschan was the dog protagonist of a story by Thomas Mann, a story Leonardo could only vaguely remember, but which had taught him that familiarity can develop between a man and his dog; something he had never experienced himself, having never had an animal of his own.

"Beddy-byes now," Leonardo said, placing the dog on the carpet to prevent him from falling in the night.

The air on the veranda was chilly. Leonardo picked the two letters up from the floor and glanced at them long enough to recognize the 'return to sender' stamp, before going back into the house to his bedroom where he opened the wardrobe and took a box with coloured stripes from under his jackets. Lifting the lid, he slid the two letters in on top of the others which were now almost filling the box to the top. Taking off his bathrobe, he pulled on a pair of white linen trousers and matching shirt, then went back into the bathroom to comb his hair in front of the mirror, cleaned and filed his nails, took the book he had started reading that morning from his bag, and went out.

He walked round the house to the west side, which had two small windows on the second floor and an arched door. He opened the door with a key he had taken from a nail before leaving the house, and went in.

When he was a child this room had been home to a dozen casks: his father and his grandfather had known every virtue and defect of each cask at least as well as they knew the individual combination of courage, patience and malice in each of their children.

His family had been wine producers for many generations, but in his last years his father had given up the work, selling the grapes to some local wine grower. Nevertheless the casks had remained in place until, seven years before, Leonardo had sold them together with the rest of the furnishings of the house. Then he had filled the space, about ten metres by four, with bookshelves he had had made to measure and fixed to the walls by a carpenter. Apart from thousands of books there was nothing but an armchair and a standard lamp on a carpet in the middle of the room. The floor was exactly as Leonardo had found it: earth trodden down so hard that you could not even scratch it with a pointed object.

Leonardo contemplated his books, which he had missed constantly, almost physically, during the four days he had been away, then lit the little standard lamp and sat down in the armchair. Twenty minutes later he had finished the story of Felicité for the umpteenth time and carefully replaced the book in the shelf reserved for the French nineteenth century.

He woke about ten, and realizing the time, ran into the kitchen where he found Bauschan collapsed on the carpet. He's dead, he told himself, but when he touched the puppy and called him by name, he raised his muzzle towards the warm breath of Leonardo's mouth. Then Leonardo noticed traces of faeces about the room and realized that the dog had been exploring during the night. So, after washing the animal's pus-encrusted eyes and giving him a little more milk from the glove, he took him round the house.

As he did so he became convinced the best place for the dog at night would be the studio. This square empty room had nothing in it that could be destroyed. It contained only an office chair and a coarse wooden table under its big window.

It had been an attempt to reproduce the conditions in which he used to write in his studio in T., a pied-à-terre off an internal yard in one of the city's main squares, where he had never wanted a telephone or doorbell or even his name on the door. But this project had been shipwrecked and the romance interrupted by the tumultuous events that had overturned his existence, and he had never got beyond the line he was writing when the telephone rang and started the massacre.

He looked at the little white portable typewriter abandoned in the dust on the table. It had been a present from Alessandra so he could write on trains and in hotels. He had punched out two novels on those keys, expending many hours of his life on them at a time when writing was indispensable to him for defining himself to himself and to others. Then suddenly his writing had vanished, just as stadiums and competitions and training and sponsors can vanish from the life of an athlete when he inadvertently severs his Achilles tendon by stepping on a piece of glass while playing on the beach with his six-year-old son. This was exactly how writing had disappeared from his life, and it had become a different life;

and all this only a few years before his publisher went bankrupt and the newspapers and magazines he used to write for closed down and reading became something comparable to the final extravagant request of a condemned man.

"The room's very well lit," he told the puppy. "When you open your eyes you'll see for yourself."

Leonardo washed his ears carefully in the shower and examined and disinfected the wound on his chest. Its lively pink colour reassured him and, since the pain of his sciatica had subsided, he decided to cycle into the village. He searched for a shirt with a large pocket and a square foulard to go round his neck, then put on the linen trousers he had folded on the chair and went out.

The distance from house to village could easily be covered even by a cyclist as unfit as he was. The dog, his head sticking out of the pocket, enjoyed the fresh breeze downhill and hung his head on the uphill bits as if helping to pedal. When he reached the first houses, Leonardo left the asphalted road for an unmetalled track that cut through a luxuriant hazel grove, ending in the yard of a large, neglected but busy farm.

"Ottavio!" he called.

Two very dirty and mischievous-looking sheepdogs emerged barking from the back of the farmhouse. Leonardo offered them a friendly hand, but they kept their distance and continued to bark.

"Who's there?" someone shouted from the cowshed.

"Leonardo."

The dogs for some reason went quiet and moved off, going to lie down in the shadow of a tractor. The yard was a mess, with sacks of animal feed, buckets and agricultural implements all over the place. Under cover in one corner was what might have been an ancient estate car or hearse. Leonardo was studying it when Ottavio emerged from the cowshed.

"What's this?" he asked.

Ottavio wiped his hands on his trousers.

"A hearse."

"Yours?"

34

"Of course, do you think I clutter up my yard with other people's stuff?"

It was covered by two old sheets sewn together. On its small roof was the pointed shape of a cross.

"What are you going to do with it?"

"Not much you can do with things of that kind."

"Then why did you buy it?"

"The funeral director at D. has moved to France. He'd been in debt to my mother for as long as I can remember so he paid up with what he had. He was an honest man, he could have left without a word. What's that in your pocket?"

Leonardo looked down; the dog had turned round and all that could be seen was the end of his tail sticking out of the pocket. Leonardo extracted him carefully and showed him to Ottavio.

"How old would you say he is?"

"Ten days," Ottavio said, after a cursory examination. "Maybe crossed with something useful for herding cows. Do you want to keep him?"

Leonardo looked at the dog, who seemed to be struggling to open his eyes.

"I think I do. Can you sell me any milk?"

Ottavio stared, his face red and sweat in the hair round his ears.

"Have you come here on purpose to annoy me?"

"How do you mean?"

They went into the cowshed past the immobile haunches of some twenty cows, about ten animals on each side, then passing through a metal door found themselves in a room tiled to the ceiling, in which a fan was stirring air charged with disinfectant. Ottavio took off his outdoor shoes and Leonardo did the same, placing his sandals in a small wardrobe. Both put on coloured clog-like rubber shoes. There were two large zinc vats in the room, and shelves with cheeses of various sizes. Ottavio uncovered one of the vats. It was full of a yellowish liquid with what looked like thin metallic plates floating on the surface, and it smelt like shoemaker's glue.

"What's this?" Leonardo said.

"This morning's milk."

Leonardo stepped back from the overpowering smell. Ottavio closed the vat and went to a window facing the back of the farm, which Leonardo knew to be where he kept his heifers and orchard. Ottavio parked his elbows on the windowsill and contemplated his property.

"Do you hear the planes going over at night?"

"Sometimes," Leonardo said. In fact, being a heavy sleeper, he had heard nothing at all. It had always been like that. Once he slept for five hours in an armchair at Lisbon airport, missing all the flights that could have taken him home. Returning to his hotel he had got in touch with Alessandra, who had no difficulty in believing him, then gone to bed to watch a bit of television, but without being able to keep his eyes open to the end of the film.

"When the planes go over, the cows play this trick on me. A few months ago it was only now and then, but now for a whole week I've had to throw away all the milk. The big producers add powdered milk, but I don't want that on my conscience. I don't even give this stuff to the pigs."

Seen from behind, Ottavio was a short stocky figure with no sharp edges; veins bulging on his arms even when he was not lifting anything heavy. He was five years older than Leonardo but looked five years younger.

"Can you trust a married man?" Ottavio said.

Leonardo said yes and thought of Elio. Ottavio nodded.

"Then just ask him about women's periods. My daughter hasn't had one for two months but can't be pregnant. And my wife, who hadn't had a period for years, has started getting them again."

Leonardo looked at the ascetic white of the tiles. Someone was singing a song somewhere accompanied by the regular beat of something like an old pedal sewing machine.

"I think," Ottavio said, pausing to add emphasis to what he was about to say, "that those planes are dropping something; something to calm us all down, because if not we're all going to go mad."

They went out into the yard where a light wind from the mountains stirred scraps of straw and blew hair about. The two dogs watched them closely from under a bench by the wall. As he mounted his bicycle, Leonardo could feel the puppy's hot urine running down his chest to his trouser belt. He pretended it was nothing.

"They've seen those two in the woods again," Ottavio said, "and they've also found a fire and the bones of a goat."

Leonardo swept his hair back from his brow.

"Must be campers," he smiled.

But Ottavio fixed Leonardo's pale greenish eyes.

"It's not the time for that kind of crap, Leonardo, can't you see how the wind's blowing?"

Leonardo looked down at his foot on the pedal. A nail had gone black where the old woman, sitting down at his table in the hotel, had accidentally placed the leg of her chair on it.

"Have you done anything for the dog's eyes?" Ottavio said.

Leonardo looked straight at him.

"What can one do?"

Ottavio shrugged.

"If you want my opinion, wash them with his own pee; he won't like it, but if you don't he'll never open them again, because they're full of parasites."

At Norina's grocery shop he bought some tinned tuna, a couple of dairy products, some sardines, two packets of rusks, jam and a pack of pasta, then got the baker to give him a French loaf and some *baci di dama* biscuits. There were no customers in either shop and the proprietors simply served him, took his money and called him professor when they said goodbye.

On the other hand the woman at the pharmacy, one of those waiting for oil, asked him how his journey had been as soon as she saw him come in. Leonardo said it had been fine and asked if he could have some cotton wool and sterile gauze. Before he left the woman complimented him on the dog and remarked that they would meet again in the evening when the oil was distributed. Leonardo said Elio would see to everything.

As he made his way to the bar pushing his bicycle, he remembered a painting by Balthus of a young girl – who could have been the pharmacist when she was young – and the way she had not yet lost her adolescent confidence in the sensual gesture of raising her arms and doing her hair. It was said that nearly all women born with that quality lost it when they grew up, while those who had it later in life had nearly always picked it up along the way, not having originally possessed it. This to him seemed to reward hard work rather than talent, something that hardly ever happened in nature, and the thought generated a surge of good humour in him.

Pulling his shirt out of his trousers and checking that the smell of the dog's urine was not too powerful, he went into the bar.

"Our professor!"

The postman was leaning against the ice-cream freezer with another man who did not live in the village, but was there to see his invalid mother. They were in the corner of the shop where it had once been possible to leaf through a national daily or local weekly and sports magazines. Now the fridge was silent and back numbers of a hunting magazine were stacked on it. Danilo, the proprietor, and three other men were sitting round a table playing cards.

"Good morning," Leonardo said.

None of the four looked up from the cards to answer his greeting.

Leonardo went to the bar and stood at an angle to it, so as to be able to keep an eye on the bicycle which he had left outside with his shopping bags slung from its handlebars. The postman whispered something to the man beside him who smiled, revealing very irregular teeth: he was dressed for fishing and a thick white beard under his chin linked his ears by the longest possible route. The postman, in contrast, had a freshly shaven face; he was separated from his wife and it was several months now since he had given up explaining to people why letters were not reaching them or were arriving weeks late. In any case, the explanations he offered came from a ministerial circular which, as everyone knew, meant that they had only a limited connection with truth.

Danilo slammed down his last card, then got up and went behind the bar, and without Leonardo saying anything made him a cappuccino without froth. When it was ready he put it down on the bar and, giving an expressionless glance at the dog's snout sticking out of Leonardo's pocket, went back to his cards. His companions had totted up the score and dealt the cards for the next hand. All four looked contrite, as if only playing to punish themselves.

"But I think," the man with the postman said, "they must be found. We have to know what they look like and find out what they plan to do."

Leonardo looked down at Bauschan's smooth head. A fly had settled on one of the dog's ears; he smiled and blew it away.

"I'd like to know what the professor thinks," the postman said.

Leonardo looked at him. In the first months after his return, the postman had come every morning to deliver letters from the solicitor, the court, the publisher and readers offering either support or expressing disappointment at what had happened, but with the passing of time the only letters that kept on arriving were written in his own hand and returned by the woman to whom he had sent them. A correspondence that made sure Leonardo and the postman still met roughly once a week.

"About what?" Leonardo said.

"We know you're just back from a trip. You must have some idea what's going on."

"The professor has other things to think about," said one of those at the table. "Unlike the rest of us."

No-one laughed, but the men near the fridge exchanged glances with the card players. Leonardo took a sip of coffee and wiped his lips with a napkin from the dispenser.

"I saw nothing unusual," he said.

The postman drank from the glass of white wine he had on the freezer.

"You must have been lucky," he said smiling. "To listen to this lot it seems they're everywhere."

An alarm went off. Danilo pressed a button on his big wristwatch and the alarm stopped, then he went to the counter and used a remote control to switch on the television in the corner of the room. The other players had already put down their cards and turned their chairs to face the screen. After the music introducing the broadcast, a woman newsreader with an expensive hairdo commented on images of an encampment in the middle of a wood with shacks of cardboard and sheet metal hidden in luxuriant vegetation. The camera showed men in uniform circulating among these rudimentary shelters with their camp beds and improvised pallets, blankets, gas cookers and other objects.

Finishing his cappuccino, Leonardo walked towards a wall with two doors, one leading to the toilet and the other marked "Private". A man with a shaved head was sitting on the floor in the space between two video poker machines. His sharp, serious face was like a tool used for prising open doors. His eyes were black but not at all malicious.

"Will you come to supper with me, Sebastiano?" Leonardo asked.

The man looked up but did not move. His legs were drawn up to his chest, hiding his mouth.

"Please come, we'll make some pasta," Leonardo said.

It seemed to take Sebastiano a long time to get to his feet, and he made Leonardo, himself more than one metre eighty tall, look tiny. Sebastiano was as thin as a rake. He had large bones and hairy legs sticking out from a pair of Bermuda shorts stained with fruit. He looked like nothing so much as an enormous prehistoric bird.

"Can I pay?" Leonardo asked, turning to the bar.

Without taking his eyes off the television screen, Danilo placed the palm of his hand on a black book beside the till to indicate that he had marked it down. Now the newsreader with the expensive hairdo was giving the latest news about the eastern front, while a small panel was showing images of a road block where three National Guards armed with machine guns were forcing several unkempt and very dirty people to get out of a car.

Before he left the village, Leonardo gave Elio the money he should have repaid him the evening before, then he and Sebastiano set off for home, pushing the bicycle. It was mid-September, but the one o'clock sun was hot on the asphalt, making it shimmer in the distance. Leonardo asked Sebastiano to walk on his left, so as to give shade to the dog asleep in his pocket.

Lupu and his family arrived early in the morning.

Leonardo, woken by the sound of cars, came out onto the veranda in pyjamas and raised an arm in the grey light of early morning to greet them. They did not have the van of previous years but two cheap second-hand cars, and they were not wearing their usual dinner jackets over white singlets, but T-shirts with slogans in English and well-worn trainers.

"I've been waiting for you," Leonardo said.

Lupu stood beside his car staring at Leonardo, as if trying to make out something he should have been able to see even at that distance. Despite his tanned skin and powerful arms, there was an unfamiliar fragility about him. His cousin, who had got out of the second car, was looking at the vines sloping down beyond the low fence of the yard. All the others had stayed inside the cars.

"Come in," Leonardo said, "I'll make you some coffee."

At a nod from Lupu, his wife got out of the red car with their small son and older daughter and Lupu's two brothers, both similar to him, even if different in build. The daughter was seventeen now and already a woman who had learnt to show herself off to her best advantage, while her mother had grown thinner in the face and broader in the hips. In the second car were Lupu's cousin's wife and a teenage boy Leonardo had not seen before. This boy had different eyes from all the others; uncertainty seemed to have produced something sharp and fearless in him. None of them were wearing gold on their necks, fingers or wrists.

They sat on the veranda and accepted the coffee Leonardo had mixed from real and ersatz coffee, then put their cups on the floor and watched the rising sun dispel the grey from the vineyard and the forest beyond the river.

Bauschan was gnawing at one of Lupu's wife's sandals. Leonardo called him and the dog sprang over to him. His eyes had been open now

41

for a couple of weeks, turning out to be a silvery light blue. Ottavio had established that he was a cross between husky and some sort of hound with his pendulous ears, plus a touch of setter in his back and gait. There were broad black patches on his ash-grey coat.

"That's a dog who will follow you even if you throw yourself in the river with a stone round your neck," Ottavio had declared before launching into a long speech from which Leonardo understood that the dog would grow to medium size and would be incapable of excelling in any of the special qualities of his ancestors, but would preserve a decent dose of each.

"Now go and have a rest," Leonardo said. "You can settle in over the store like in previous years."

He took the cups to the sink and washed them, then looked out of the studio window. Lupu and the others were standing in the middle of the yard, holding plastic bags and old triacetate sports bags with the logos of firms, banks and sponsors that no longer existed.

The teenager was the only one not carrying anything; he was talking to the others in an excited voice. He could have been sixteen, but was probably one of those boys who long retain the traits of adolescence only to lose them at a stroke from one day to the next. When the adolescent had finished speaking, Lupu said a few words. The boy lowered his eyes as if they had suddenly grown heavy and they all moved towards the storehouse.

During the morning Leonardo reread *The Death of Ivan Ilyich*. By eleven o'clock he had come to some conclusions he thought he could develop, but by eleven-thirty they already seemed odd to him. The sun beat down relentlessly; none of the few distant wisps in the sky could really have been called a cloud. Since they had retired, Lupu and his family had made no sound; the guest rooms – that was the name Leonardo used these days for the rooms above the store – seemed as empty as ever, apart from an orange towel spread over a windowsill.

"Let's go for a walk," Leonardo said to the dog.

He and Bauschan crossed the yard, but when they reached the vineyard the dog stopped. Turning to follow his gaze, Leonardo saw Lupu at the door of the store in shorts and work shoes.

They descended the headland together and halfway down entered one of the rows of vines, following it until the vineyard ended in a field of parched grass. The vines were heavy with grapes, the bunches a powerful violet under a thick coating of dust. Lupu let a bunch slip into his hand as one might lift the breast of a woman who was no longer young, but to whom one feels an enormous debt of gratitude.

"This winter at the workshop I worked nights so no-one would know they'd taken me back. I'd go in at the back after dark and find a note telling me what needed to be done. For a while Tashmica was able to do a few hours cleaning there too, but then they did not ask for her again."

Lupu delicately picked a grape, dusted it on the sleeve of his shirt and put it into his mouth.

"No-one even trusts official papers. The man who took us on for the peaches had problems and had to ask us to go. We've spent the last month near the mountains with a relative."

Bauschan was tormenting a large lizard. The reptile seemed stupefied by the sun and made no attempt to get away. Leonardo watched its tail, detached from its body, writhing on the ground.

"What will you do after the grape harvest?"

Lupu thrust his hands into his pockets and looked over to where the haze was growing denser and the sky was turning opaque with heat. He seemed to be listening for a far-off noise.

"I don't know whether to go back to the town. Mira's afraid of going back to school. Before we left we took everything to my sister's; it's not safe to leave stuff in an empty home, those people come in and steal and smash everything."

"Who comes in?"

Lupu shrugged.

"Gangs. People say they're searching for outsiders, that they're every-where and that it's not true the army has dealt with them. I haven't seen them. I did see two bodies on the pavement, but they weren't outsiders."

Leonardo picked a ladybird from a leaf and watched it walk on his finger. It was a pale orange and extremely elegant. In the heavy midday silence he imagined the sound of its footsteps.

"When you've finished, you can all stay on here," he said.

Lupu nodded without conviction. Bauschan, sitting in the shade, was watching the final twitches of the lizard's tail. The main body of the reptile, a few centimetres away, was interested only in soaking up the heat it needed to keep its tiny heart beating.

"How long will the harvesting take, do you think?"

Lupu looked at where the vineyard ended and the hillside began. A ditch had been dug and the strip of meadow beyond the ditch turned to forest further up.

"Four days. There's two less of us than last year."

Leonardo removed a fragment of earth from one of his sandals.

"Starting tomorrow?"

"As soon as possible." Lupu gave a half smile.

"That can't be too soon," Leonardo said with the other half of the smile.

At the end of the first day of the harvest they ate in the courtyard on a board propped on two trestles, after which the women carried the plates to the wash house behind the store, while the men sat watching the smoke rise from their cigarettes and disperse before it could reach the starry sky.

For a while Leonardo studied their gaslit faces, unable to read either doubt or exhaustion on them, then wished them goodnight and went indoors to undress, clean his teeth, rub cream into his sunburned arms and neck, and get into bed.

He would have liked to fall asleep instantly to wake again free of the constant pain in his arms, legs, back, ankles and hands, as well as in the stomach muscles he had forgotten he had since the year before. That had been the last time he had found himself thinking the same thoughts in the same bed.

Until he was twenty-five he had been a good long-distance runner and every evening, summer and winter, had covered a fifteen-kilometre course along the river and out of the city before returning to the old centre. But after taking his doctorate he sacrificed sport to his university duties and work on his first novel. In a few years his longer muscles grew slack and the occasional outings he attempted in shorts after that led to cramps and a massively discouraging exhaustion.

During the last thirty years his shoulders had curved and narrowed while his legs grew thin and his stomach got bigger even though he had always been a moderate eater and never drank alcohol. He now had the body of a man of fifty-two dedicated to books, intellectual speculation and conversation. Not much use in the world now unfolding before his eyes.

With these gloomy thoughts, Leonardo got out of bed and went into the kitchen in the dark. He poured a glass of water and went to the large window: there were no lights on in the guest rooms and the building was silent. Moonlight seemed to have covered the courtyard gravel with a thin layer of water.

Seven years since I last made love, he thought.

Bauschan had dirtied the parquet in two places and was now asleep on the carpet with his head between his paws, probably drunk. He had spent all day eating windfall grapes fermenting in the sun; seeing him stagger about, Leonardo had thought it best to shut him indoors.

He crouched down and stroked Bauschan's neck. The dog seemed to smile in his sleep.

Taking pen and paper from the drawer, he sat down at the table. When he had finished writing, he put the paper into a buff envelope, addressed it and put it on the dresser, planning to post it next day when he went to get the money to pay Lupu. Going back to bed, he fell asleep immediately and dreamed about a hotel room he had known many years before.

"You really want the money now?" the cashier asked, looking over her spectacles at him.

"Yes," Leonardo smiled. "Please."

The woman touched her breast. Clearly her mind was somewhere else.

"I realize it's not very professional of me to mention it, but you took out a considerable sum only last week. I have to say this because this new withdrawal could cause a problem of liquidity."

Leonardo understood from the woman's expression that a tediously practical complication was about to come into his life.

He had known for some time that most people had emptied their accounts down to the last cent, hiding the money in their homes or goodness knows where, so as not to have to worry that they might one day be told at the bank that their money was no longer there. He had also known that it had been devalued or burned, or simply that money transfers no longer existed so that it could not be moved from one place to another, but Leonardo had never been sufficiently interested to get the idea into his head that one day his money might simply disappear. His only shrewd move had been to choose that particular bank because it had its central office in A. and no apparent ties with the major banks which had in the past closed down because of scandals, the mortgage crisis or the fall in exports. He had deliberately chosen this particular bank because it raised money locally, kept it in the form of cash in a safe, and redistributed it in the same area.

"When will it be possible for me to withdraw my money without causing problems?"

The woman pursed her lips to indicate that she could not answer that offhand. The two of them were alone. The bank's grey marble walls dated from the Fascist era, erected like the rest of the building in the middle of the village a century earlier. Only one of the building's three doors was open; the others had been masked with opaque paper to prevent anyone seeing through to the other end of the hall. This despite the bank's proclaimed motto: "Territory and Transparency".

"I'll be frank with you, professor," the woman confessed in a low voice. "We've had no contact with head office for a week and no couriers have come."

"Are you trying to tell me you don't think any more money will get here?"

The woman moved her mouth without speaking; her eyes shone as she shook her head.

"I know it's not your problem, but I haven't been paid myself for three months."

Under the vertical light waiting for him outside the building, Leonardo was seized by consternation. What should he do? That morning he had woken refreshed and unexpectedly vigorous and, before going down into the village, had worked for a couple of hours, ignoring the sharp twinges of pain running through his arms and legs. Now that energy was a distant memory: he felt exhausted and soaked with sweat.

At the post office he handed in his letter, slipping it under the glass window as lazily as the assistant took it and put it in the receptacle for outward post, then he returned to the square. The sky was a cloudless white, the sun covered the village without producing any shadows. The buildings, the two trees in the square and the metal octagon of the old news-stand seemed insubstantial objects with no density. Everything seemed about to evaporate.

It was then that he saw the teenage boy materialize from a side street. With his short black hair and pointed chin, he was heading for the bar with studied indifference, wearing the same clothes as in the vineyard, though he had rolled up his shirtsleeves to reveal a tattoo on his right shoulder.

Leonardo told himself that Lupu would never have dreamed of sending him to the village, and decided his presence there was no good sign. He raised an arm to attract his attention, but at that moment the boy turned his head to take a quick look at his reflection in the windows of the bar, and a second later was inside.

When Leonardo followed, he found the boy standing in the middle of the main room, watching the four men playing cards at the only table. Making up the game that morning with Danilo, the postman and the man with the beard was an insurance agent who had once been the local *pallapugno* champion and the owner of a tobacconist's shop.

"Got any cigarettes?" the boy asked.

None of the players lifted their eyes from their cards. The boy took a couple of paces towards them and stopped a metre or so away.

"I'd like some cigarettes," he repeated in a calm, firm voice.

Danilo looked up.

"We don't sell cigarettes," he said.

"So what's them over there then?" the boy asked, indicating a dozen packs on the shelf behind the counter.

Once in a London theatre Leonardo had seen a show with a young actor who was famous on television. Every evening he attracted an audience of adoring girls who would have liked him as their boyfriend, as well as ladies of a certain age who would have liked him as their son or lover. In order to prove he was not just a petty small-screen celebrity, the actor had chosen an extremely complicated script and was applying himself to his performance in a spirit of frank self-denial. So much so that, when in the third act his jacket was supposed to have vanished from its clothes hanger, but unfortunately was in fact still there for the whole audience to see, he had turned to the clothes hanger and the supposedly blind and pregnant actress who was playing the part of his woman, and asked her, as if the words were part of the script: "Where's my jacket? Who's taken my jacket?"

Since the blind woman was not supposed to be able to see the jacket, the actress had swallowed her cue, hoping for assistance from the actor who, far from helping her, had headed with great strides for the clothes hanger and, running his hands round the jacket without touching it said, "But I left it just here." At that point Leonardo had heard a woman behind him whisper to the friend beside her: "What a love! He's going blind too!"

Danilo played the four of hearts. The man with the beard took it with the six, then turned to the boy.

"You heard what he told you?"

The boy smiled and Leonardo realized that, young though he was, he was in perfect control of the situation.

He also understood that what was happening in that room was the result of fear, but he himself had grown so far from his former self that he hid his awareness. He knew he was the only one among those present to have this feeling and he felt humiliated by it as on every other occasion.

What was paralyzing his legs and constricting his throat was exactly what he felt when watching a climber clinging by his fingers to a rock face, or listening to how a man had thrown away all his possessions on a mere whim. Acts he could have easily proved to be pointless and stupid, as he had during a symposium on the extreme that he had taken part in once in Oslo, but even so such things had always filled him with a profound sense of inferiority.

It was a truth that he had painfully been forced to acknowledge for some time, at least to himself: that the creative force in life was extravagance rather than tightfistedness, gambling rather than calculation, and that every true creative act was born of risk taking, without which nothing better than sterile repetition was ever possible. History and the march of civilization had been a long and successful attempt to reassure the meek and cowardly, constantly disguising in new clothes a terrible hypocritical reasoning in favour of logic, morality and beauty. He with his profession, his books, his long slender body devoid of malice, was merely the ultimate development of this trend, like a fussy piece of lace worked with great skill for the sole purpose of lying covered with dust and compliments on some aunt's bedside table.

He noticed the card players were staring at him.

"The boy's working for me," he said, trying to smile.

Danilo stared at him. He was young and bald and it was said he had many lovers in the district though not actually in the village, because this was a pact his wife had extracted from him after they had quarrelled for years.

"If you must bring these people here," Danilo said, "keep them at your own place."

Leonardo nodded, afraid he would not be able to control his voice if he spoke.

"Let's go," he said to the boy who stuck his hands in his pockets, apparently entirely at ease.

"You'd best listen and keep out of the way," the insurance man said.

"Let's go now, please," repeated Leonardo.

The boy took a few steps towards the door, then stopped, turned and gave the four players a smile.

"You're all dead," he said, his words sounding terrible yet at the same time as mild as a verse from the Apocalypse recited by a child; after this he vanished into the light beyond the door.

Leonardo caught up with him in the middle of the square and for a while they walked side by side in silence. The boy, calm and indifferent, barely lifted his feet from the ground. Leonardo occasionally turned to make sure they were not being followed. He was conscious of a pulse in his temples and his feet were cold.

They passed a building on whose façade an ivy leaf had once been drawn so accurately that it still looked real from a distance, and several jerry-built blocks of flats, after which the road passed fields and clumps of hazel. Leonardo looked at the boy; there were drops of sweat among the few soft black whiskers on his upper lip. He remembered his name was Adrian and that he had always known this.

"Once at school they made us read one of your books," Adrian said.

Leonardo had no intention of getting involved in a discussion about his work. His stomach was in turmoil and all he wanted was to get home to his bathroom.

Even so he asked, "Which book?"

"The one about the dog."

Round the corner they could see the gate. And among the rows of vines the straw hats of the grape pickers.

He wondered if he should tell Lupu what had happened. And whether he would do this for the good of the boy or only in the secret hope of having him punished.

Adrian kicked a stone into the dead grass at the edge of the asphalt.

"What's the use of a book like that these days?" he said.

"Books are always useless," Leonardo said to close the subject, "even when what's happening now isn't happening."

The boy sighed and Leonardo believed he had given him something to think about, but soon noticed they were no longer together and turned.

Adrian had stopped and blood was pouring from his nose down his chin and soaking his shirt.

"Lift your right arm," Leonardo said, searching in his pocket for a handkerchief.

The boy gave a broad smile, his perfect teeth stained with blood.

"I really believe you won't survive," he said, and leaped away into the hazel grove at the side of the road.

The store caught fire that night and burned completely in less than an hour, giving off great spirals of grey smoke.

Leonardo had stayed up till late in the book room and once in bed had not been able to get to sleep. At two o'clock he became aware of variations in the light between the shutters on his window. At first he thought it was the moon, but when the glare began dancing and turned a magnificent shade of ochre, he ran from his room, his throat tight with bitter foreboding.

On the veranda, he was assailed by cold smoky air; the flames lighting up the yard like daytime had already eaten the left side of the building. Lupu and the others, lined up at the edge of the vineyard, were watching the blaze without moving. He counted them; all were there. Their faces were entirely calm, as if what was burning was not the beds where they would have woken next morning if the fire had not consumed them.

"Anyone hurt?" he asked, walking towards them.

Lupu shook his head. The little child was sleeping on his mother's shoulder. On the ground were the few bags they had managed to bring out.

"We realized in time," he said, still staring at the building.

Like the other men he had nothing on but his underpants. The women, on the other hand, were fully dressed. Only the daughter was weeping, tears pouring down her sunburned cheeks like drops of brass.

Leonardo had never been so close to a fire before. Contrasting with the moving light, smoke and heat was an extraordinary silence. The fierce flames were stretching towards the rafters of the roof like the fingers of a rock climber reaching for a higher hold. The almost imperceptible sound of the flames was reminiscent of teeth being ground in moments of extreme effort. He wondered if the flames might attack the house, but seeing how calm the others were and judging that they must know the ways of fire better than he did, he stopped worrying about it.

When the glass in the windows shattered, everyone took a step back and the little child raised his head: he glanced at the vineyard where the light was projecting the long shadows of his family, then buried his face in his mother's shoulder again and closed his eyes. Columns of black smoke were issuing from the windows of the store: the plastic baskets used for the harvest were burning.

"Tonight you'll sleep in the house," Leonardo said. "Tomorrow we'll sort things out."

Lupu looked at him without expression.

"We're leaving," he said.

Then Leonardo read in his eyes something that must have been clear to everyone from the start and had nothing to do with the question he did not ask himself.

"They poured petrol under the door," Lupu said. "Luckily my brother was on guard, or we'd all be dead."

In that moment Leonardo understood the edgy expression in their eyes the day they came into his courtyard. Their eyes had been saying, "This place is not safe, and the reason it isn't safe is that now there is nowhere we can feel safe any longer." This animal instinct had led Lupu to set up turns of guard and had allowed him to save his family. Leonardo, in his pyjamas with their slender vertical stripes, was fully aware of his own inadequacy. Part of the roof collapsed raising thousands of sparks that lifted gently into the sky where they were gradually extinguished.

"I'll make some coffee," Leonardo said. "Come inside."

He put the large coffeepot on the gas, then sat down at the kitchen table and studied his own hands against the wooden surface. No-one came in or went to the veranda. When the coffee was ready, he poured it into a dozen cups without counting if there were too many and carried them out on a painted wooden tray. Lupu and his family were still standing where he had left them. They had all covered themselves with something, leaving only Adrian without shoes.

They acknowledged the coffee with an inclination of the head and drank it. The store was now burning peacefully.

"Are you sure you want to leave tonight?" Leonardo asked.

"Best for you too."

"Where will you go?"

"Back to the mountains."

Leonardo went back into the house. Bauschan was sleeping on his rug in the studio and had not noticed anything.

"You really are my dog," he said, then opened a drawer in the desk. Inside was rather less than he should have paid for the four days' work planned and rather more than what was due for the two they had done. He put the banknotes in the pocket of his pyjama jacket and closed the door behind him to stop the dog following.

Lupu and the others had loaded the cars with the little they had saved from the fire and were waiting at the back. The upper floor of the store had collapsed and the flames had regained a bit of strength, but the darkness was winning back space and everything they did or said was now happening almost entirely in the dark.

He handed Lupu the money and they shook hands, then the cars processed out of the courtyard to the subdued sound of crushed gravel.

Left on his own, Leonardo went back into the house, urinated and put Bach's suites for unaccompanied cello on the stereo, before going out again to sit on the veranda steps with the dog in his arms. For a while Bauschan licked his right thumb, then dozed off. By now the burning store was crackling quietly and the air was filled with a good smell of resin and hot earth. It was a smell that made Leonardo think of Humanism and a baker's window facing a lane with the light on all night.

They stayed like this till first dawn, when the building that had once been a store and lodging for guests appeared in the weak new daylight like an empty skull with thin threads of anthracite smoke emerging from it.

Then the dog, followed by Leonardo, got up and went into the house, both of them exhausted, as if they had just had a long lesson from a master.

The first to hear the news had been the teaching faculty, then their families and the literary world, and only after that the newspapers and the students.

Leonardo had been one of the last it had reached among the lecturers, before the rest of his family. The telephone rang at six in the evening and the level voice of the rector at the other end of the line begged him, despite the unusual hour, to come as quickly as possible to the university since only he would be able to throw any light on an unpleasant event that had occurred.

The meeting had taken a couple of hours while a dozen of the most senior and influential teachers in the faculty had gone in and out of the office. No-one had claimed to take seriously what was written in the letter that had accompanied the video and the photographs, but no-one had asked Leonardo to vouch for the truth of those images either, still less the reasons for his relations with the girl.

The next day he had stayed at home: his lecture cancelled because of sickness, the rector had suggested. Leonardo spent the morning in the studio with his computer turned off, listening to Alessandra on the telephone in the next room discussing her monthly schedule of exhibition reviews with the arts magazines she worked for, until finally at lunch, over a salad of prawns and avocado, he had decided to face up to what had happened.

At first Alessandra had shown no reaction, suspecting it was some kind of game, but becoming aware of Leonardo's pallor and trembling lips, had asked her husband to tell her frankly whether he had really had sex with that piece of trash, and to tell her what the video and photographic material actually showed.

Leonardo had very calmly told her the whole story and Alessandra, equally calmly, had shut herself in her study for a couple of hours to reflect. Then a storm of insults and the hurling of objects had been unleashed, accompanied in the evening by the defacement of all his books in the lower part of the bookshelves.

Humiliated and impotent, Leonardo had witnessed this crescendo of violence against his books, condemned as "false intellectual shit", then had retired to sleep in his daughter's little bed while she, in view of the situation, had spent the night at her grandparents' home.

The next day, from nine in the morning, when the video and photographs had been accessible on the internet to anyone capable of keying in the three codewords, his home telephone had never stopped ringing and the shouting of Alessandra, Alessandra's mother and Alessandra's father had alternated and been superimposed on one another until Leonardo decided to go away for a few days while the storm blew over, to an anonymous hotel outside the city where in fact he remained for the next seven months.

The first person he heard from, once the story had appeared in the press, was not one of the two or three friends he imagined he had among his fellow writers, but a university colleague of about fifty, a stalwart figure of mediocre ability, with whom he had never had any contact apart from exchanging the odd word at meetings.

For this reason he had been suspicious of the man's suggestion that they meet for a coffee; he had been put on his guard by his publisher and by many requests from both quality and other newspapers for a well-paid interview, in which he would have been able to put his own version of the facts. Yet the oppressive sense of loneliness he felt during those days had overcome every fear, persuading him to accept this meeting which had been organized in a bar next to one of the city's minor railway stations, opposite an open space that the Council had tried to improve by building an enormous fountain that terrified children and depressed the old by reminding them of the war.

Renato, a Sociology lecturer, was waiting at a little corner table well away from the window. With his short hair, broad swimmer's shoulders and his tanned face despite it being autumn, the man was the very image of health and hunger for life. He looked like one of those winged lions on the end of banisters in blocks of flats where no expense has been spared on the marble. They shook hands, sat down, and ordered freshly squeezed orange juice and barley coffee.

"You and I are both people of superior intelligence," Renato had started, "So I'm sure you won't mind if I skip the 'I'm so sorry' and 'I can imagine how you must be feeling'."

Leonardo nodded in the most macho way his lanky figure allowed him.

"I'm not here only for myself," Renato went on, "but on behalf of many of your colleagues, most of whom, I must say at once, will not have the courage to support you in public, but share my esteem for you and believe that what has happened cannot be other than the logical consequence of things."

Leonardo waited, but the man seemed to have nothing more to add.

"What things?" he felt forced to ask.

The man smiled, like an experienced skipper warned by a radio station of bad weather at sea.

"Most of the girl students," he said, "are tarts and use their bodies to try to get what they want, then yell rape if for some reason they can't have it. As though any man who cares for culture must be a eunuch! A castrated man stuck behind the lecturer's desk to entertain a gaggle of female idiots showing themselves off for their own amusement, in the certain knowledge that the teacher wouldn't know what to do with them if he had them."

Leonardo studied his coffee: it had delicate verdigris reflections, striking if entirely inappropriate, and tasted of boiled cabbage. He had never drunk barley coffee before, but then he had never spent three nights in a row without sleeping either.

"I'm grateful for your moral support," he started, "but—"

"Our support is unconditional," Renato interrupted, a fragment of orange hanging from his lip making him look even more deeply committed. "And we'll bring pressure within the university to have this business set aside. The fact that you are also a writer doesn't make things any easier, but many of us have passed the same way and could tell you that what in the morning may seem to have been a storm, almost always turns out by evening to have been nothing more than a gentle breeze. But I would advise you not to try to extricate yourself just by fencing with a mere foil. You must reply with the same weapons used to attack you. You don't know it yet, but you have much more to lose than to gain. The sooner you make that clear, the sooner you will be able to take a milder view of things."

Leonardo realized the pointlessness of any attempt at explanation. Taking his silence for tacit agreement, the man placed a hand on his shoulder.

"Here's my mobile number," he had said, "give me a call."

Leonardo took the card he offered. The man got up.

"I won't hide it from you, but I always thought you were probably a bit of a queer. A man with lots of brain, but not much in the balls department. I have to admit I was wrong. You even deceived me." Then he squeezed Leonardo's hand, paid the bill and went out, offering him a final smile from the other side of the window.

Leonardo had never seen or heard of him again, but a year later, by which time he had already lost his job at the university and any chance of seeing his daughter again, he had noticed his name in the pages of a daily paper to which Renato had begun contributing a column, commenting and explaining the ins and outs of current affairs.

Six months later the daily closed down. By that time Leonardo had moved to M. and heard nothing more, good or bad, about Renato or any other of his former university colleagues.

He spent the afternoon sitting on the veranda, staring at the rows of vines on which the grapes had started to wither; the air full of the constant buzzing of bees attracted to the ruins of the store by the smell of cooked grapes.

The hot weather continued and the vegetation on the far side of the river took on a ferocious yellow hue. Clouds above the mountains hinted at autumn, but for the time being the wind confined them to France.

It was already evening when Elio came into the yard on his bicycle and stopped a little way from the steps. He was wearing a white shirt with the sleeves rolled up and blue striped trousers. His folded jacket was clipped to the pannier rack. Drumming his fingers on the handlebars as if describing the scene in Morse code, he stared at the pile of blackened rubble.

"Well, look at that," he said.

Leonardo picked up his glass from the African wood table and drank a mouthful of water. It tasted good. At the time he had decided to move to M. the excellence of the water had come first in the list of advantages he had looked forward to. This list had been one of the last ideas suggested by his psychoanalyst. In fact, after a month of telephone calls, the man had told him he could do nothing more for him unless he came to the surgery by car. Leonardo had promised to think about it, then done nothing. So, from one day to the next, what he had thought of as an essential lifeline had been cut off. And this had been the second point on his list.

"Would you give me a hand to finish the grape harvest?"

Elio looked at him as one might look at someone on the bridge of a ship heading to a place from which he was unlikely to return.

"You must be joking."

Leonardo shook his head.

"If you don't, in a few days the grapes will have to be thrown away."

Bauschan came out onto the veranda and sat down beside Leonardo. He had a slipper in his mouth, but his serious eyes were fixed on Elio. Apart from a shambling gait and huge paws, there was almost nothing left of the puppy with the round stomach he had once been; he seemed more like the miniature version of an adult dog.

"Even if we did harvest the grapes, what could we do with them?" Elio said. "The wine growers haven't even harvested their own."

Leonardo drank more water. Far off, beyond the river, he thought he could see movement amid the yellow stubble. It turned out to be two men carrying jerry cans down to the waterside. The sky was clear, but the heat made the atmosphere transparent.

"Maybe I can give them to the cooperative," he said.

"Do you think they'll be getting orders anymore?" Elio snorted. "Most of the wine used to be exported to northern Europe and America. Have you noticed it's been nearly a year since the last lorry passed on the main road?"

Leonardo went back to contemplating the point where the hill met the river. The two men had stopped on the bank; one was filling a container, while the other was watching the road which touched the edge of the river two hundred metres lower down before regaining height with a couple of sharp bends.

"Anyway, if you could spare a couple of afternoons to give me a hand I'd be grateful," he said.

Elio set the bicycle on its stand and took a few steps towards the veranda. Leonardo heard him go into the house, take a glass, fill it with water, drink, rinse it and put it back in its place. When he came back out he placed his hands on the back of the empty chair.

"The people who started the fire were not the ones you think," he said.

Leonardo watched the men on the other side of the river carry their containers across the last open stretch of field and disappear into the forest.

"Who was it then?" he said.

Elio put his hands in his pockets.

"The schools are still shut and the boys are hanging about all day with nothing to do. The other day four or five of them had a few words with that young man who was staying with you."

Leonardo rubbed one of Bauschan's ears between his fingers. It was like silk. The sun was sinking and the shadow of the blackened walls of the store was reaching the edge of the veranda. Elio put his hands back on the back of the wooden chair and studied them, as if he suspected they might have changed colour while in his pockets.

"Gabri's in touch with her sister in Marseilles. She says they're going to close the frontier and these may be the last good days for crossing it. I'd like her to take the children, but she doesn't want to go alone."

Bauschan barked twice at the hazel grove near the house and a few seconds later a stocky shape emerged from the thicket. The wild boar looked fearlessly at them, then grunted and three striped piglets came through the opening it had made.

The little family filed past the veranda at a gentle trot and disappeared behind the remains of the store. When they had gone Bauschan sniffed the scent of forest in the air and lifted his head to see what the two men might have to say about it.

"There seems to be some petrol at C.," Elio said. "Shall I get you some too?"

Leonardo shook his head. The sun had half disappeared behind the mountains; the sky was turning red and a few clouds that looked like ginned cotton were appearing in the east. The buzzing of the bees had stopped.

Adele's house was neither a farmhouse nor a modern home but one of the few buildings built in the seventies of the last century, when the hills were about to become a pilgrimage destination for tourists from the Nordic countries and America.

Coming into the yard, Leonardo was greeted by cries from the geese in the poultry pen. There were three of them, one male and two female, and they usually scratched about freely, hurling themselves at anyone who ventured on their territory. After their most recent ambush, the postman had taken to leaving the post in the fork of a pear tree a few metres from the gate.

Hearing the noise of the geese, Adele came out of the house, her hair thrown roughly back, as if she had just been walking against the wind on a pier in Normandy. She was wearing a flowered dress under her apron and her legs were enclosed in brown tights. Her shoulders were those of a woman who had done a lot of swimming in her youth, but she had the hips and legs of an elderly peasant woman. On her feet were a pair of flip-flops.

"*Ciao*, Adele. Do you have time for a treatment?"

"Time's the only thing I do have," the woman answered.

The kitchen was cool and full of cheap furniture. On the mantelpiece several vases with medicinal herbs were lined up and a yellow clock was ticking on the wall. The walls badly needed a coat of whitewash, but the total effect of the atmosphere was somehow Greek and restful. The table was set for two.

"We can do it another day," Leonardo said. "It's nearly dinnertime, I forgot."

Adele dropped a leek into the pan boiling on the gas, then rinsed her hands.

"If it hadn't suited me I'd have said no," she said, drying her hands on her apron.

They went into the room where she kept her massage bed. Leonardo took off his sandals and lay down.

It was a small room with walls of a gentle yellow. No posters, pictures, shelves or books, just a small table holding a jar of ointment, a wristwatch and a notebook.

Adele sat down on the stool, took a little ointment from the jar and began working it with her thumbs into the soles of Leonardo's feet. She did this for about ten minutes without a word from either of them. Her fingers moved quickly as if running over a pattern they knew well but that sometimes needed to be explored with careful precision. Through the only window Leonardo watched the she-ass grazing in the field behind the house.

"Have you heard what happened yesterday?"

Adele nodded and the little oval she wore round her neck with the portrait of her husband moved against her wrinkled chest. When Leonardo was a boy, the man had toured the Langhe district in a small lorry selling viticultural products. He was of Ligurian origin and it was said he had been a billiard player when young, good enough to compete in serious championships, but in his free time doing the rounds of the fairs to relieve the farmhands in the bars of the money they had earned working with animals.

Adele first met him at the railway station in Genoa. She was just back from South America where she had been living for six months with a shaman, and the man had been in Viareggio and reached third place in the national championships.

Before she agreed to marry him she had made quite clear what he already knew, that championships were fine but fleecing people at fairs must stop. In any case, cheating people out of their money involves constant travelling; you cannot do it to the local people where you live. The men, blinded by pride, may allow themselves to be milked for years, but sooner or later their women will find a way of getting their own back on you.

He was a man known for good sense and discretion, and would not have wanted to argue. Leonardo had once seen him dominating the billiard table in the bar, but when a stranger challenged him he had handed the cue to someone else, saying his wife was waiting for him at home.

"Do you think I ought to do something?" Leonardo asked Adele.

"What would you like to do?"

"Go and talk to the people who started the fire."

Adele went on working on Leonardo's thin feet. Her hands were barely warm, like ashes disturbed hours after a fire has gone out.

"Last year Laica had six puppies, but the next day there were only five. Bitches sometimes notice one of the little ones is too weak and eat it to make sure there's enough milk for the others."

Leonardo locked his hands behind his head and looked up at the flowered lampshade, noticing the black shapes of dead flies inside the ridged glass bowl. One was much longer than the others: a huge wasp.

"Is that a metaphor?" he asked.

"Don't use words like that with me. You being a professor doesn't interest me in the least. You don't even know how to light a fire without matches."

Leonardo let his head fall back and dozed off. He was woken by the cracking of his own feet as the woman squeezed them between her hands. He had no idea how much time had passed.

"There," Adele said.

Leonardo got off the bed and slipped on his sandals. The woman looked at the notebook where she had divided the pages in two columns.

"You've already paid," she said "Last time I hadn't any change to give you."

They went back to the kitchen where the pan on the gas was spreading a good smell of boiled vegetables and rosemary. Beyond the misted windows there was little light, but he could make out a pile of firewood and the white of the birches that formed a crown round the courtyard.

"Is Sebastiano at home?" Leonardo asked.

Adele took a piece of cheese wrapped in greaseproof paper from the refrigerator and put it on the table.

"He's upstairs. Tell him supper's ready."

Leonardo climbed the stairs and went along the corridor that led to two bedrooms and the bathroom. Sebastiano's door was closed. Leonardo knocked and looked round the door. The room was tidy with nothing but a single bed, a wardrobe with two doors, a writing desk and a bookcase. On the walls were a crucifix and a poster of Machu Picchu. Sebastiano was standing by the window. Leonardo knew that the night before he must have seen the glare of the fire.

"No-one was hurt," he said.

Sebastiano turned, showing his hollow cheeks and humped nose. He was ten years younger than Leonardo, but a bald head surrounded by thin hair made him look older. An African totem pole in a tracksuit.

"I need a hand with the grape harvest," Leonardo said. "Can you help me?"

Sebastiano nodded, parting his lips to show extra-large teeth.

"Thanks," Leonardo said. "Your mother's waiting. See you tomorrow then."

As he closed the door, Sebastiano turned back to the window. Leonardo went downstairs and back into the kitchen. Adele had served the soup.

"Will you stay?" she said.

"Thanks, but I'm tired. I think I'll read a bit and go to bed."

"You should always go to bed early and get up early. But you sleep too much, walk too little and are always reading. If you were a man who works with his hands it would be alright, but people like you need to do a lot of walking."

"I could always become someone who works with his hands," said Leonardo, smiling.

"You're too old now to be any different. And you've done too much studying."

The courtyard was dark and there was a faint smell of fruit in the air. Leonardo went to the bicycle, which he had leaned against a wall. Adele watched from the doorway.

"When the time comes, you should take Sebastiano with you," she said.

Leonardo put down the leg he had raised to mount the saddle.

"When the time comes for what?"

"When the time comes to go."

"But I've no intention of going anywhere," he smiled.

Adele touched first one eye and then the other to indicate either exhaustion or far-sightedness. On her cheeks was a complicated pattern of wrinkles and veins.

"But that's what you should do all the same."

Leonardo accidentally touched his bicycle bell and its trill spread through the courtyard. The surrounding silence was so complete it seemed the sound would radiate away to infinity without meeting an obstacle. He felt a great need for his own armchair, with a cup of coffee in his hand and a book on his knee.

"Ever since he was a child Sebastiano has talked in his sleep," his mother said. "I often go into his room to listen. He talks to people who are no longer alive and others who are yet to come. Take him with you, he'll be useful to you."

Sebastiano could be heard coming down the stairs. He passed behind Adele.

"You're right to finish harvesting the grapes," the woman said, looking up at the sky where a modest moon was shining.

"It's not good to let grapes rot. A sign people are going mad. Like not combing your hair or washing yourself. People sometimes come to me with dirty feet and when they realize it they apologize by saying 'No wonder with what's happening!' But your feet are always clean. You haven't gone mad yet."

Suddenly the geese began honking for no reason and Adele shut them up with a cry Leonardo had heard Mongolian shepherds use to make dromedaries run, then indicated he could go and went back into the house.

Leaving the yard, Leonardo cycled down the pathway as far as the road and once on the asphalt started in the opposite direction to the village. After ten metres or so he braked sharply and, laying the bicycle on the ground, took a few quick steps into the field by the road, opened his fly and released a powerful jet of urine. It was the effect the massage had on him.

Going back to the bicycle he noticed something among the lights on the plain that was full of life yet at the same time deeply saddening.

A great fire burning under the nearest hills was sending up an enormous column of smoke. It must have involved a whole group of houses or a large factory because the flames were coming from such a wide base.

Seven years earlier, on the same day and at about the same hour, he had been sitting at the desk in his study about to read an essay on *The Outsider* by Camus written by a student called Clara Carpigli; at that moment all he could have said of her was that she was a young woman with fair skin and raven-black hair who used to sit near the front at his lectures. It was the last piece of work he planned to correct before going into the dining room where Alessandra was waiting with their supper.

At the end of the essay a piece of paper was clipped to the page with three lines on it written in ink between inverted commas.

Starting from that moment, delicate glances, a couple of notes and a coffee, gradually transformed Clara Carpigli into a face, a way of walking, an increased heartbeat and an expectation. He knew well that many of his teaching and writing colleagues were in the habit of making the most of their status as "*maestri*" with dinners, weekends and nights with women students or lecturers, but though he never moralized, he had always liked to think of himself as different.

Then a month later he left home for an out-of-town restaurant where a girl twenty years his junior was waiting for him with no legitimate reason for meeting him anywhere other than in the lecture rooms of the university.

Three days later, by midday, the grapes had been harvested.

Elio drove the tractor he had borrowed from his uncle into the yard, loaded with the final baskets, and they went into the house for a bite to eat. Leonardo had avoided the village since the night of the fire and there was nothing left in the larder except pasta and tins, but Gabri had given her husband a pan to heat up containing vegetables, anchovies and bread-crumbs.

They sat down at the table and began devouring the food in big spoon-fuls while Bauschan watched from the corner where he was lying, half closing his eyes from time to time like an employer not quite trusting his workforce.

Elio was wearing shorts and a shirt marked with one or two stains of varnish, while Sebastiano was in a mechanic's overall that must have belonged to his father. His hands, after three days of work, were white and unmarked. The weather was mild and the sky covered with flat, incon-sistent clouds hinting at the blue behind them.

As they ate, Elio told the story of a man from a nearby village where Leonardo had never been. This man, known to all by the name of Nino Prun, lived in an isolated ruin and several years earlier had bought himself a coffin that he kept in his bedroom. Apart from this eccentricity and a somewhat shabby style of dressing, everyone knew him to be mild, celi-bate and reserved.

Two weeks earlier Nino Prun had gone down to the priest's house-keeper to arrange for the curate to call on him the following day. Although the woman knew that the man had never been a churchgoer, she passed on the message and the next day the priest climbed up to the man's house in hopes of a late repentance. Instead he had found Nino Prun in his coffin, stiff, washed, combed and ready dressed for burial. All the priest had to do was administer benediction and order the lid to be nailed down. The man had left his few belongings on the dresser in two supermarket bags, one marked with the name of a prostitute from C. who by then had no longer worked for a number of years, and the other with the name of the Association of Alpine Mountaineers.

They talked of this and other things just as in earlier years when Elio's shop had been full of customers, and when it was possible to see people in trains and on benches with one of Leonardo's books in their hands. Sebastiano shifted his eyes from one to the other as he followed the conversation, but it was as if his silence were concealing thoughts unrelated to what was happening round him. A medieval Japanese poet might have described his figure as combining the strength of a centuries-old tree with the ephemeral wonder of a chrysalis.

"We could try Gallo," Elio said as they put the dirty plates in the sink.

They lay resting on the veranda floor for half an hour, then loaded the filled baskets on the trailer and set off for the village. Elio took the driving seat while Leonardo and Sebastiano made room for themselves among the baskets. The air was tepid as the light faded and the smell of the grapes caused them a slight dizziness. Bauschan watched the passing countryside from his owner's arms. Leonardo wished he could travel like this for ever.

"Guido, if only you and Lapo and I," he quoted in a murmur, *"could be enchanted and put into a ship with the winds carrying us across the sea to your heart's content and mine, so that neither destiny nor any other bad weather could impede us, but that on the contrary, united by a common desire, we would feel an ever-increasing need to keep together."*

They passed the carabinieri station. The windows were barred and crocuses and wild spinach were growing from the steps. It was a year now since the men had been either diverted to the National Guard or transferred to a larger base. The nearest of these was at A., but no-one was in a position to say whether there were any carabinieri there anymore, since the Land

Rover that used to come every two days and park in the village square was no longer to be seen.

When the road divided they took the route that climbed the hill in gentle curves. The vineyard was at the top of the knoll with its entrance marked by a great red iron gate without any surrounding fence; all round it the vines sloped away like waves in a geometrical sea, to far-off churches and towers still lit by the sun. A clock in the village struck five.

Elio drove the tractor straight into the courtyard. The two-storey house, neat as a biscuit, had its laboratory and cellar in an annexe. The balconies on the upper floor were luxuriant with geraniums, and apart from some fifty or so cardboard boxes piled in the yard, everything seemed in perfect order.

Elio switched off the motor and headed with Leonardo for the portico, where Cesare Gallo was sitting on a white leather sofa; Sebastiano and the dog stayed in the trailer. Gallo was wearing leather boots and over his shirt collar was one of those leather ties that a hundred years earlier herdsmen on the other side of the world used to put on in honour of the Sunday sermon. Everyone in the district knew that in his basement dining room he kept one of those mechanical bulls that used to be found at fairs.

"Do you want me to laugh?" he said, even before the two men reached the steps. "We only picked our own because the thought of the harvest rotting away broke my heart."

Elio and Leonardo looked at the yellowing boxes in the middle of the yard: five years earlier they would have been full of bottles that would have been quite inadequate to satisfy constant orders from Russia and the East. A swarm of swifts was circling the yard even though it was not the right season for them.

"Do you know anyone who might want the grapes?" Elio said.

Cesare picked up his glass from the ground and drank. What Leonardo had taken for a cardigan flung on the sofa moved and he realized that it was a grey short-haired cat.

"If you want a friendly word of advice," Cesare said, "go to the river and chuck the lot in, then go back home and get drunk like me."

There was a short silence while each stared at the shoes of the other, then a lad emerged from the shed with a large birthmark on his cheek and hair that looked as if it had been cut by someone who had got bored halfway through the job.

"Allow me to present the last employee of the house of Gallo," Cesare said.

Leonardo and Elio acknowledged the boy who responded briefly.

"I've turned on the fans," he told his boss. "Will you see about turning them off again?"

Cesare nodded. The boy stuck his hands in his pockets and headed for the gate. The green of his overalls seemed to become darker before he vanished among the hedges lining the drive out of the estate. To Leonardo, it was like reading the last page of a South American family saga. A light breeze stirred a couple of lemon trees under the portico. Then Cesare got up and gestured to them to follow him.

The terrace at the back was piled with a haphazard collection of furniture, children's toys and other objects. It looked as though several rooms had been emptied according to some criterion connected with the size of their contents. Below this, beyond the parapet, the plain extended in regular geometrical shapes defined by the fields and roads that linked the villages. It was a magnificent view. Far off the foothills of the mountains were hidden by a layer of mist that left their summits free.

"Look at the main road to C.," Cesare said, offering them a small pair of binoculars from his pocket. "That's how it's been since this morning."

Elio looked first, then passed the binoculars to Leonardo who took several seconds to find the road. Both lanes were jammed with a continuous queue of motionless vehicles.

"My family left at seven," Cesare said, "and at midday I could still see them. They'd gone five kilometres, more or less."

"Are you the only one staying behind?" Elio asked.

Cesare nodded.

"After what happened at C., Rita couldn't be persuaded. So we loaded the lorry last night. They're off to our house in Nice."

"What was it that happened?" Leonardo asked.

"Haven't you heard? They committed every kind of obscenity and set

69

fire to the village before leaving. This morning Stefano Pellissero ran to see if his sister was alright. He said all you can do is tear your hair out. It's like war's passed through."

"Were they outsiders?" Elio asked.

"It seems so, but people say some of them spoke Italian."

Going back to the front of the house they found the tractor abandoned. Neither Sebastiano nor the dog were to be seen. The setting sun had transformed the courtyard into a uniform grey lake on which the tractor and its trailer seemed to be floating.

"Did you know he was unfrocked because of a woman?" Cesare said.

Leonardo did know but said nothing.

After seminary, Sebastiano had taught in the Faculty of Theology, but after several years asked for, and was given, a parish in upcountry Liguria. There he had got to know a woman whose man was often away at sea. The relationship continued in secret for nearly a year, then Sebastiano abandoned his work as a priest to be with her. But at this point the woman decided to stay with her earlier companion. Everyone said the disappointment had deprived Sebastiano of his senses and speech.

"You have to know how to control women," Cesare said. "I've known Rita for thirty-six years and there's nothing in her I could possibly complain of, but if one day she stuck a knife between my ribs I wouldn't look at her with astonishment as I died. It's not a question of malice or bad faith. Women can just wake up one day with a new idea in their heads. It's their nature. If you can't accept this possibility, it's better not to get involved at all. Let alone risk losing your speech!"

They heard the door behind them open. They turned to see Sebastiano on the threshold: he was holding the dog in his arms and had draped a cowhide round his shoulders, fastening it at the throat with a curtain cord.

"Hey!" Cesare said. "That's my bedroom carpet!"

Sebastiano passed between them and made for the trailer. His cloak smacked against his heels like a whip. It was a dappled cowhide, but in some places so threadbare that the animal's skin was visible.

"Can you let him have it?" Leonardo asked.

Cesare shrugged, picked his glass up from the floor and took a swig.

"Are these Barbera grapes?" he asked, indicating the trailer.

"Yes," Leonardo said.

Cesare scratched his chin; he had not shaved that morning.

"I let Rita take all the cash," he said, "but if you like, we could do a deal."

In half an hour they had unloaded the grapes and replaced them on the trailer with a crate of potatoes and another containing cauliflowers, carrots, chicory and a large pumpkin.

On the way back Leonardo hugged himself: a cold wind was blowing from the mountains and moving the tops of the trees. A few gloomy black clouds were floating round the moon and the countryside seemed full of unknown things. Once home, they unloaded the cases and Elio went back to the village. Left on their own, Leonardo and Sebastiano looked at the river: the water was shining like a strip of pewter against a black cloth. Bauschan sniffed the cowhide. Sebastiano bent down to stroke him.

"Nothing that goes from outside into a man can defile him," he said.

Leonardo looked at him; his voice had passed through his body without leaving any trace as if through an empty pipe, but the silence round them had been completely transformed.

"Does that mean we should prepare ourselves?" he asked, but got no answer.

When Sebastiano had gone, Leonardo went into his book room and looked in St Mark's Gospel. He read: "*Nothing that goes from outside into a man can defile him. It is what comes out of a man that defiles him. For from inside, out of a man's heart, come evil thoughts, acts of fornication, of theft, murder, adultery, ruthless greed, and malice; fraud, indecency, envy, slander, arrogance and folly; these evil things all come from inside, and they defile the man.*"

He tore out the page, folded it and put it in his wallet. It was the first time he had heard Sebastiano speak. He was sure he would never hear him speak again.

*

Throughout the whole of October the line of cars continued to move slowly through the valley towards France, without ever thinning out. It was not easy to find out what was happening: the national radio had not been broadcasting for weeks and the only stations you could pick up were independent ones broadcasting music programmes. Both landline telephones and mobiles were silent, and the internet had been the first thing to crash. The only remaining source of information was television, which for several days now had been transmitting classical music concerts. A journalist made an appearance late one evening to read a government communication that claimed the situation was stable and urged citizens to be vigilant. Practical advice was also available about food and water, collecting rubbish and the precautions to be taken by anyone planning to travel.

Halfway through the month a delegation went to the valley to interview the queuing travellers. The picture they brought back was schizophrenic. Many maintained that the north-east of the country was in the hands of plundering gangs who took everything they could lay hands on, and that although the National Guard controlled a few cities and major routes of communication, otherwise all law and order had broken down. Others, however, reported that things were near normal. They complained of a shortage of petrol and other necessities, but insisted they had seen or heard nothing of assaults or other violence. One man from T. said that in the city the market was crowded, the shops open as usual and the streets well protected by the military. When asked in that case why he was taking his family to France, he answered "To be on the safe side".

The consequence, in any case, was that the country began emptying. The first to leave were those who had relatives or friends beyond the frontier, also families with children. Those who stayed behind were the old, people who were waiting for somebody, and those like Cesare Gallo who would have stayed even if bombs had been falling.

Leonardo spent the month reading on the veranda or in the book room. Elio had closed his shop and passed by most days for a chat, updating him on who had left and on the general state of affairs. When the weather was fine they would walk as far as the hill of Sant'Eugidio. There was a small Romanesque church on top of it, surrounded by an English-style churchyard, in which the most recent grave was a century old. Bauschan loved this walk for the river, the stretch of woodland and the bushes from which he could make the thrushes rise.

When he ran out of provisions, Leonardo was forced to go into the village which he had avoided since the night of the fire. Only Norina's grocery, the bar, the baker's, the chemist's and the butcher's were still open. All the other shops had drawn their shutters with no notices to say why they were closed or for how long. Apart from a knot of old people leaning on the balustrade of the belvedere and commenting on the length of the queue of cars down in the valley, the square was deserted. The narrow streets were full of the stench of the grapes rotting in the vineyards.

Waiting his turn at the grocer's, Leonardo noticed the only subjects of conversation among those who were left were medicines, petrol and cigarettes since no-one knew if or when any of these would arrive. When he bought a loaf of bread, he told the three women who ran the shop that he would be going down to A. on business and would find out all he could about the availability of these goods; they looked at him as though he were a young blond volunteer sticking his head out of the window of a train heading for the front.

The next day he settled Bauschan on the rear seat, started the car and drove through the village under the sceptical eyes of the old men on the belvedere. During the eighteen kilometres to A. he only passed two cars and one small lorry going in the opposite direction. Many of the houses along the route had their windows barred and the fields looked neglected, but apart from this, the hills had a gentle autumnal air while the Dolcetto vines were already a vivid yellow, the Barberas turning wine-red and the Nebbiolos still green.

Things gradually changed the nearer he came to the town. It seemed as if everything had suddenly grown old: shop signs, warehouses, super-markets, even the roadsigns: everything seemed faded and cold. The petrol pumps looked like archaeological relics, and the lorries and car transporters cluttering up the open spaces were like tanks from some ancient war waiting to be overgrown with ivy and rust away.

He felt better when he saw several people walking along the station approach with shopping bags, pushchairs and overnight holdalls. Bauschan watched the coming and going of the town without much interest and from time to time yawned with boredom.

They parked in the central square and Leonardo took from his pocket a rudimentary lead he had made the evening before from a piece of cord, a clip and a piece of sticky tape. Bauschan accepted this philosophically and walked without testing the fragility of the noose. The shops were open, but few of the passers-by showed any interest in what was left in their windows. The tables outside the bars on the main street were empty.

The bank was on the ground floor of a building from the Fascist era, originally an agricultural cooperative and later a school. The entrance was protected by a National Guardsman with a submachine gun, bulletproof vest and helmet. The young man demanded to see his papers and read the details into his transistor radio, asking Leonardo to be patient for a few minutes while his identity was established. The man's cranium was like a crudely hewn block of marble.

Once approved, Leonardo was allowed inside, where another soldier, who was smaller in size, checked his documents again.

"Go ahead," he said when he had finished.

The young cashier at the window was thorough. Leonardo still had just over ten thousand lire in his account and, as was made clear to him on a circular with an annexed table, customers were permitted to draw out in cash up to between 10 and 20 per cent of their total deposit, depending on its size. The rest would be available at a monthly rate, but in order to state this the young man looked away from Leonardo and fixed his gaze on the pen tied by a little chain to the marble surface of the counter.

Leonardo established that the sum in his account allowed him to take out 13 per cent of his deposit and, while the young man was counting out the one thousand three hundred lire, Leonardo asked him for the latest news of petrol, medicines and cigarettes.

The young man could not have been older than twenty-five.

"We are not qualified to give such information," he answered.

Leonardo studied his red hair and the freckles that covered most of his face. He could easily have been one of the children forced to thieve in the muddy streets of London by the crafty Fagin.

"I understand," he said.

The boy asked him to sign a piece of paper which he placed on a pile reaching from the floor up to his elbow; then gave him a serious look.

"After a theatre reading two years ago," he said, "you autographed a copy of *The Roses near the Fence* for me. You won't remember, but I told you about a novel I was writing. You shook my hand and told me to keep at it."

"I'm sorry, I don't remember. And did you keep at it?"

The boy looked across at the girls moving between desks cluttered with papers and large registers on the other side of the great hall. For the first time, he seemed aware of where he was.

"No."

"You're very young, you can easily begin writing again."

The bank clerk shook his head.

"I'm twenty-seven, but that's neither here nor there. May I give you some advice?"

"Please do."

"Don't count on the money still in your account."

Leonardo placed a hand on the marble counter and realized it was not cold.

"Thank you very much. Thanks to your sincerity I think I have an exact picture of the situation."

"So far as is possible," the young man added placidly.

"So far as is possible," Leonardo agreed.

Leaving the bank, he walked through the town in no particular direction.

He spoke to a policeman, a priest who was painting a side door to the church, and a woman selling household objects from an improvised stall.

He learned that the little petrol still available was reserved for security, hospitals and the local services, while medicines could only be obtained from the hospital and a couple of authorized pharmacies, with the available drugs all requiring prescriptions which only doctors were allowed to issue for the most serious emergencies. As for cigarettes, the woman said he would have no problem finding these in the district round the race-track.

On his way back to the car, he saw a group of teenagers standing in front of a bar. Some had shiny quilted jackets and others singlets or T-shirts with slogans in large letters, but all were wearing shades, tight-fitting trousers and white trainers, and were talking in loud voices, their bodies nervous with unpredictable energy.

He crossed the road. Sitting on the steps of the bar were two girls in heavy make-up who seemed to be waiting for some sort of response before deciding whom they were destined for. As they waited they seemed entirely at ease.

Hearing a whistle, Leonardo decided the boys were trying to attract the attention of the dog, but immediately afterwards the first insults reached him. He quickened his pace without turning round. He still had about twenty metres to go to the end of the block, where he would turn the corner and be out of their sight.

As he calculated the distance something small and hard hit him on the neck. For a moment he was stunned, but kept going. Other coins struck the wall beside him and fell to the pavement; the dog, attracted by the noise, stopped abruptly and snapped his lead. Leonardo hurriedly bent to pick him up, but on straightening up again was hit by a fierce pain in his back.

He struggled on, bent double and with tears in his eyes, terrified that at any moment a hand might grab hold of his jacket. His loud breathing drowned out every other sound, and he became aware that a thread of dribble was running from the right of his mouth.

Rounding the corner he still felt unsafe, and made his way to the next corner where a small group was waiting in front of a large door. He passed them without looking up and rounded another corner, then leaned on a wall to get back his breath. Very soon he felt his legs give way and collapsed. He stayed like this for several minutes and saw the feet of two men pass him. Neither stopped to see how he was. Bauschan stared at him in despair, now and then licking his lips.

"It's nothing," he said to reassure the dog.

But it took him an hour to reach the square where he had parked the car.

When he got there the clock was striking one. He slaked his thirst at a small fountain in a little public garden where a woman was sleeping on a park bench.

He sat in the car and mopped the sweat glueing his hair to his forehead. After a few minutes his breathing steadied and the pain in his back became less intense. He gingerly took off his jacket: his sweat-soaked shirt had turned a light greyish-blue, but he had nothing to change into. Bauschan watched him, wagging his tail from the seat beside him.

"Home now," he told the dog, then remembered the cigarettes. He did not feel like waiting for the shops to open again for the afternoon, or walk about in the hope of picking up more information, so he decided to drive round the area the woman had recommended, only stopping if he noticed a tobacconist's still open. It was a district that had grown up at the end of the last century round the old motor-racing circuit: streets of detached houses and modest blocks of flats for the middle classes, a large hypermarket, a bank and a health centre with sauna and swimming pool.

The last time Leonardo had been there, six months before, the health centre was already closed and the hypermarket had been transformed into a depository for ironmongery, but the houses still looked attractive with well-kept gardens, windows decorated with vases of flowers and brightly polished brass doorbells. Everything had given an impression of serenity and quiet living.

As he approached, he began to be aware of the coming and going of people walking and cycling at the edge of the road, all carrying a wide variety of objects. A kilometre further on the first stalls appeared, and the throng of buyers and sellers grew until the road was completely blocked.

Leonardo drove into a field that must once have been a football pitch, where hundreds of cars had been parked higgledy-piggledy. He left Bauschan in the car – the lead was broken and he was afraid of losing him in the confusion – and continued on foot.

He moved through the mob with tiny steps because of the pain in his back. People were pushing and shoving as they struggled to get a view of stalls displaying clothes, furniture, electrical goods, lamps, alcoholic drinks in bottles, plates, tablecloths, curtains, sanitary appliances and every kind of household goods.

At the beginning of their relationship, Alessandra had sometimes dragged him to villages and small towns where dealers in used goods and simple ransackers of cellars and attics displayed their merchandise, amusing themselves by haggling and claiming emotional links with horrible paintings and ancient chamberpots of every description. But what Leonardo saw now was quite different. Many of the sellers looked as if they were trying to make a little money by offloading things they would not be able to take away with them. The bargaining was fast and ferocious and coloured the proceedings with a dismal air of misfortune and speculation.

In front of the racetrack gates were several armed guards who seemed to be neither from the police or the National Guard, but from some sort of private militia specially created for the occasion. They were distinguishable by their orange caps and badges.

He crossed in front of their arrogant gaze, and passing through a tunnel, came out on tiers of steps. A huge crowd was circulating among tables displaying merchandise, producing the same indistinct buzz or hum as a swarm of insects.

Dizziness forced him to lean against a wall and like a drowning man he grabbed the nearest arm. The man jerked himself free and began moving away, then changed his mind and turned back. Leonardo apologized.

"I'm looking for cigarettes," he said.

The man smiled, showing a gold tooth.

Half an hour later Leonardo was driving towards the hills, the town now behind him. On the rear seat were four cartons of cigarettes for which he had paid more than two hundred lire, an excessive price even allowing for the fact that they were foreign, possibly Turkish; they were undoubtedly remainders stored long past their sell-by date, but he believed the village's smokers would welcome them just the same.

He left the cigarettes with Elio, telling his friend to sell them at whatever price he could get; it would be enough if he could get back what he had spent on them. Elio, noticing he was having difficulty with the steps, asked him what had happened and Leonardo said he had strained a muscle getting out of the car and needed to lie down for a bit and close his eyes.

When he got home he found his most recent letter, posted a month earlier, had been accurately returned to sender, evidence that for some bizarre reason the post was still working, at least in his case. Somehow the familiar disappointment comforted him and his backache seemed less painful.

As he prepared Bauschan's lunch, he hummed Brahms's song *Gestillte Sehnsucht* and then, while the dog ate, collapsed on the sofa and closed his eyes.

When he woke up it was dark. He had no idea of the time, but looked neither at the watch on his wrist nor the clock on the wall. He simply stared at the night through the glass door of the veranda, a fragment of sky in which two very bright stars were shining, and wept for at least a quarter of an hour.

He remembered the last time he had wept like this, eight years before.

His relationship with Clara had been going on for several months, but they had never slept together. Leonardo had not felt like taking her with him on his trips to attend conferences and give lectures, and when he was in the city, family demands prevented him being away at night. On this particular occasion, Alessandra had gone to Paris to review an exhibition by an American artist who constructed perpetual-motion machines out of refuse, and Lucia had been excused school for two days to go with her.

That evening, after dining in Clara's little flat, they had gone to bed and Clara had made sure he came on her stomach. Then they had examined the shape of the pool of semen on her belly and invented resemblances as one does with the shapes of clouds. Then she had taken a pen from the bedside table and asked him to draw its outline on her before she went to the bathroom. He continued to lie there gazing at the large rose on the ceiling, meditating on the gift of love this young woman was presenting him with. Then, aware of being in the presence of some form of perfection, he had wept, the way an old man can weep when he recognizes in a child a turn of speech or gesture that had been his own in his youth.

Leaving the bathroom, Clara had come back to lie down naked beside him, her belly still marked by the ballpoint pen.

"Shall we always do it?" she had asked.

Leonardo had said yes.

The next time he had been on the point of tears had been seven months later, when the polaroid photographs of the drawings had been shown in court by Clara's lawyer as evidence of the deviant sexual practices to which the well-known writer and university lecturer had subjected the young woman, with the threat of interrupting her career at the university as well as her doctoral degree.

Leonardo got to his feet and moved slowly towards the bathroom. The sight of himself in the mirror disturbed him.

There seemed to be new wrinkles round his eyes and his cheeks had sagged to reveal sharp cheekbones. His body was drying up; soon he would be nothing but a husk, an old man in a world where speed and determination were necessary.

Why had he not faced up to those boys? He should have stopped and told them off. They were nothing but badly brought-up children and he was a man of fifty who could have been their father.

In the gentle middle-class world he had inhabited until a few months before, his timidity had always been mistaken for moderation; the mediocre music his instrument played joining with others in an uninspired orchestra, but now everything was changing and there would no longer be any melody for him to harmonize with.

He rubbed painkilling cream into his back and dried his hair; the weather had changed and he was afraid that the cold air might bring on a migraine; then he put on his pyjamas and went to bed.

Just before he fell asleep he felt for the first time that he was beginning to understand the true dreadfulness of what was happening. It was the beginning of a new age, a naked age that seemed likely to last and whose key word would be "without", just as the key word of the previous age had been "with".

But even the black glue paralyzing his thoughts could not keep him awake.

On the first Thursday in November a car came into the courtyard, and after describing a slow half moon on the gravel, stopped with its bonnet towards the way out.

Leonardo was sitting in one of the armchairs on the veranda with a fleece over his knees. He lowered the book he was reading and watched the woman who got out of the car as though she were merely a couple of hours late, whereas in fact he had not seen his wife for six years.

Alessandra walked towards him. She was slim and looked hardly any older, yet many things about her, starting with her hairdo, spoke of a woman who had made radical alterations to her scale of personal values. For all Leonardo knew this could have happened as soon as they separated, or only yesterday. But the decisive air with which she climbed the steps and stopped a few paces from him made it clear that this would not be a subject for discussion.

"*Ciao*, Leonardo."

Leonardo got up and took a step towards her but stopped, hampered by the cover which had slipped down between his feet. In the car were a girl, and a boy of about ten. The pair were watching them through the blue-tinted windscreen. It was a high-powered car and extremely elegant. But its hubcaps had been taken off, as had its front grille and mirrors.

Leonardo looked at the girl and her long smooth hair.

"Is that Lucia?" he asked.

As he spoke he realized he had not pronounced her name for many years. The little girl he had taken to the cinema and the puppet theatre and spent the hottest summer months with in a little house in the Ligurian hinterland, the two of them alone, making up stories in rhyme, going for long walks in the morning and bathing only after four.

"Yes," Alessandra said. "But first I need to talk to you. Can we come in?"

Leonardo made his way to the kitchen where everything smelt of smoke. The tanker that usually passed in October to fill the cistern with methane gas had not come and in any case Leonardo no longer had the money to pay for it. So he had pulled an old stove out of the cellar and collected some firewood in the forest. His first attempts to light it had been pathetic, but for a few days now he had been able to heat at least this part of the house.

They sat down facing each other at the table.

"Have you got a dog?" she said, noticing the bowls under the sink.

"A puppy."

She moved her hands on the table as if drawing something that would help her say what she had come to say. Thinking it might require summing up many years in a few words, Leonardo kept silent.

"I remarried four years ago."

"I didn't know."

She said that was just how it was.

"I met Riccardo a few months after we separated. We went out together for a year going here and there, then after our marriage Lucia and I moved to C. We have a villa by the lake. Riccardo's a communications engineer. The boy in the car is Riccardo's son; his name's Alberto."

Leonardo studied the woman who had once been his wife and now was another man's wife. Her expression, her shoulders and her small breasts still had the attractive nervousness of the days when she had worked and talked and been ironical and spent many hours flying to see exhibitions by painters desperate to impress her. Even so, Leonardo could not help noticing that the old warmth had gone from her body. She was much sharper now, like a poker kept beside the fireplace to stir up the fire.

"Last year Riccardo was called up," she went on. "The army was working with new communications systems and his expertise was indispensable. At first he came home once a fortnight, then less often. Now I've heard nothing from him for four months."

Alessandra spread her hands on the table. In addition to her wedding ring, she was wearing several rings set with small stones – none of which Leonardo recognized.

"Would you like something to drink?" he asked.

"A glass of water would be great, thanks."

He went to the sink, filled two glasses from the tap and returned to the table.

"I want to go and look for Riccardo," Alessandra said, "and in the meantime I'd like the children to stay with you. Riccardo's mother is very old and I have no-one else; most of our friends are abroad. If I don't find him within a week, I'll come back and collect the kids. We have a pass for Switzerland. The last thing Riccardo sent us."

Leonardo wiped a drop of water that was running down the outside of his glass.

"Tell me about Lucia," he said.

Alessandra stared at him expressionlessly.

"What exactly do you want to know?"

Leonardo smiled. His back was still hurting.

"Does she get on well with her friends, what subjects does she like best, has she thought yet what she might like to study at university?"

Alessandra tucked some hair behind her ear. She must have had it dyed blonde, but now it was returning to its natural brown. Her eyelids were vibrating with tiny electric shocks entirely unrelated to tears.

"In September," she said, "in front of your daughter's school, they hanged a Pakistani couple, a husband and wife, who had been in service with a family we knew. Our friends had been found dead two days earlier and it seems the Pakistanis had been seized in revenge. They were left hanging for a week, in the hope of discouraging other criminals. But it didn't work like that. The assaults continued. Gangs of stray kids, goodness knows from where. No-one can say how many there are of them. They do horrible things then vanish, and no-one knows where they've gone till they come back, they or others like them."

Alessandra touched the water in her glass and massaged a temple with her wet fingers. Her lips were marked with small cracks.

"All people can think of is getting out. They abandon everything they can't get into their cars, including old people and animals. I know what I'm saying is hard to believe, but I have no reason to tell you lies. I just want to find Riccardo and take the children away. The only reason I haven't already gone is that once I've left the country they won't let me back in."

A shuffling sound distracted them. Turning, they saw Bauschan staring at them from the door. They heard a car door opening in the yard. Alessandra jumped to her feet, made her way round the dog and went out onto the veranda. Her black crew-neck sweater perfectly matched the grey sky. She was also wearing a pair of claret-coloured trousers. Her head stood proudly on the long neck she had inherited from her horse-riding ancestors, but he noticed her breasts were lower than before.

"Get back in the car, Alberto."

"But there's a dog!"

"I know, but get back in the car."

"I want to touch it."

"Later, now get back in the car. I'll tell you when you can come out."

"But I'm thirsty!"

"There's a bottle of water in the bag. Tell Lucia to give it to you. I'm coming in a minute."

Leonardo heard the door shut again. Alessandra stepped over Bauschan as if he were nothing more than a pair of slippers someone had left on the floor, and sat down again.

"O.K. if I smoke?" she asked.

Leonardo fetched a saucer from the dresser. Alessandra took a packet of Marlboro and a lighter from her bag. Bauschan followed their movements with apprehension. Alessandra lit up and blew smoke from the side of her mouth. Before turning back to Leonardo, she stared for some time at the volume of Lorca's poems next to a plate of boiled *zucchini* on the dresser.

"Alberto's not an easy child," she said. "He's suffered during this last year from the absence of his father, but I've talked to him and he's old enough to understand. And Lucia knows how to deal with him, she'll take care of that."

Leonardo understood from the way her fingers were working with a fragment of ash that had fallen on the table, that no matter what happened she was determined to be somewhere else before dark.

"Has Lucia ever asked about me?" he asked.

Alessandra quickly raised the cigarette to her lips.

"There was a time, during her first year in upper school, when she asked me a lot of questions. Maybe she'd found an old newspaper or someone had talked about it at school. I told her what had happened without hiding anything. Since then she's asked nothing more. I know that she's looked out for your books in the library and read them, but she has never asked to see you or talk to you."

Leonardo fixed his eyes on a crumb on the table.

One September more than twenty years before he and Alessandra had gone to the sea together.

They had known each other for two weeks and had caught a mid-morning train, lunched in a restaurant at the port, then walked as far as the town boundary. The sun was sinking, but the day was still open and luminous. Alessandra had suggested a bathe, but he had excused himself because he had no costume and had sat with his hands on his knees, watching the slow movements of her arms rising and falling in the water, raising weak soundless splashes of spray. During that half hour, he had had a chance to measure his own inadequacy compared to this woman who had travelled, worked in Germany and known the daring, cultivated and ambitious men whose names frequently came up in their conversations.

Seeing her emerge from the water in her one-piece costume, her skin suntanned and ribs prominent under the close-fitting cloth, he had experienced a fierce urge to possess her, a primitive need to make her body his property. An entirely amoral egoism.

They had spent that first night in a pension out of sight of the sea, methodically exploring each other's bodies. By morning Leonardo had known that Alessandra's sacrum stuck out in an altogether unusual way and that her right breast was smaller and more sensitive than the left, though he did not have the experience to judge whether the fact that her clitoris stiffened and relaxed with almost mathematical regularity like the breathing of a tiny lung was a special quality in her or a trait common to most women.

Alessandra crushed her cigarette against the saucer. There had been a time when, far from annoying her, the processes of Leonardo's mind had seemed to her to have the seductive power of a closed box. But that time was past.

"I must have an answer," she said.

Leonardo moved his glass in a little circle.

Part Two

November was a thoroughly wet month, lashed by a cold wind that deposited white sand on the windowsills. Something more typical of summer.

Great flocks of birds traced patterns with changing contours all day from north to west in the windy sky. Their passage was noticeable even at night, like an endlessly moving curtain in a dark room.

Halfway through the month several handwritten notices appeared, summoning residents to the elementary school gym on the evening of the 22nd. They were signed by the deputy mayor and the only remaining member of the council.

On the evening of the meeting, two hundred people gathered in the building. Some had brought greetings with them or permission to vote by proxy from relatives who had not felt like coming out, but even so the general impression was one of great distress; a year earlier the village had had more than a thousand inhabitants.

The most striking thing was the grey, discouraged faces of those who gathered in the hall. Each person's despair seemed to reflect that of the others, and soon a timid initial buzz of conversation was succeeded by a deafening silence. The deputy mayor took the chair and, using an amplifying system borrowed from the local tourist office, read out the agenda.

First there was the problem of petrol, medicines and heating. Discussing this did not take long, because no-one knew anything that had not already been common knowledge for some time: all they could do was confirm that there was no petrol left, and that medication was only obtainable from the hospitals, which would only help the most pressing cases. As for heating, as things were at present there was no point in hoping for a supply of fuel oil or methane. Anyone with a wood-burning stove would be able to face the winter calmly, and those without had permission to take wood-burning ranges and stoves from abandoned homes. The deputy mayor, a short man whose remaining side hair was long enough to have been combed not just once over his bald head but back again as well, stated that the regulation requiring a chimney at least a metre high for the discharge of smoke was suspended, and anyone could arrange a chimney pipe in any way he liked.

The second item on the agenda dealt with the presence of outsiders in the area.

Many had seen strangers in the forest or on the river bank and smoke rising every day from the hills as evidence of the increasing numbers of people camping there. Then there was the theft of fruit from orchards and the danger that the intruders, whether outsiders or not, might become so numerous and bold as to approach inhabited areas. Someone mentioned what had happened in A., where the supermarkets had been taken by assault, and in V., where inmates had escaped from the prison. Definite information was supplemented by rumours, inferences and fears. It was decided that several volunteers would patrol the district the next morning and drive away anyone who had no good reason for being there. Two squads were formed, each of about a dozen men, mostly hunters with rifles. A third squad would stay in the village to protect it, since neither the local police nor the carabinieri were any longer in a position to do so.

But the most controversial item on the agenda was the last one, the change of hour from daylight-saving summer time to standard time. With both radio and television off the air, no-one could be sure that this had actually happened, and in some neighbouring communities the clocks had not been put back. When the shouting began the parish priest Don Piero, who had been silent until then, spoke up in favour of standard time – *Ut natura fecit* – and stated that if anyone decided otherwise he would stop the mechanism that regulated the church clock.

When the meeting broke up, several groups continued the discussion for several minutes in the unlit square, until faint but chilly rain dispersed even the most heated disputants.

Leonardo and Elio waited for the square to empty, then walked as far as the belvedere and looked down at the plain beneath: few lights were moving on the road, and they belonged to freight escorted by the National Guard. The long line of cars had disappeared a few days after the frontier was closed.

"We'll be leaving in a few days," Elio said. "Gabri's sister has got us passes. We'll pay whatever we have to. It seems some people in the mountain crossing points have been waiting for days even though all their documents are in order."

Two shadows passed in the street: a couple who lived beyond the petrol station. The woman turned and saw them but offered no greeting. When they passed under the solitary street lamp their breath formed a fluorescent halo. It made Leonardo think of the soul.

"You and the children could come with us," Elio said when the couple were some distance away. "It's going to become more and more difficult to get away."

Leonardo nodded, then remarked that by spring things would be better.

Elio lit a cigarette. His father had been a heavy smoker, but he himself hardly smoked at all. He drew on his cigarette a few times in silence. Only three lighted windows could be seen anywhere near; the rest were all dark or barred.

"In the Frontier Guard," he said, "we were divided into two squads. One to control the frontier, the other to operate a few kilometres further on in the valley."

He stopped as if searching with his tongue for some small object caught between his teeth. The rain was lightly touching the umbrella over their heads.

"When unauthorized groups turned up, the first squad would demand payment to let them through, and if they had no money would ask if they were prepared to lend their women for an hour or two. If they refused they were sent back and if they agreed they were let through. Then the other squad would intercept them further down, pack them into a lorry and take them back over the border. The squads switched places once a week. I always wanted to stay in the valley. One day, while we were loading people on the lorry, a man who had paid started shooting. That's how I got a bullet in my lung."

Leonardo studied his friend's profile, then went back to watching the plain: a sea on which few lights were moving. Now there were no vehicles passing it was hard to believe there had ever been a road there at all.

"Have you nothing to say?"

Leonardo placed a hand on the parapet.

"When you're young you can do fine things or terrible things. Either can easily happen."

Elio closed his lips round his filter.

"They'll make us pay for everything we've done to them," he said.

Four people passed through the square sheltering under two jackets and an umbrella. One was Don Piero. The jackets vanished into a doorway in the square. The umbrella accompanied Don Piero as far as the sacristy, then went on alone.

"Last month I was nearly lynched by a gang of boys," Leonardo said.

Elio looked at him.

"Why?"

Leonardo shook his head. All that existed for him at that moment were the square, the church, the campanile, the houses and a wet street leading nowhere.

"Perhaps we went wrong much sooner than we think," he said.

Elio took two more pulls at his cigarette, then threw it over the parapet;

it drew a brief glowing arc, then landed and went out. With the hand that was not holding the umbrella he searched his jacket pocket and pulled out a bunch of keys.

"In the store you'll find some tools and kerosene and two gas stoves though the cylinders are finished. Take anything you can use."

Leonardo pocketed the keys.

"I'll leave you a can of petrol too. But don't let it stay there too long; I wouldn't like it to disappear. Here's the address of our cousins in Marseilles. The telephone number too."

Leonardo put the slip of paper in his pocket with the keys. The church clock struck one. The light in one window went out and the night crept forward a few metres, stopping at the first rows of vines. Beyond that point there could have been anything.

"I'll be off now," Elio said.

"Say hi to Gabri for me."

"Shall I leave you the umbrella?"

"I've got my hat, thanks."

"Take care then."

"You too."

On the road home Leonardo noticed the rain getting heavier. He began walking faster. The night was closed, leaving no crack for escape, and no smell was rising from the asphalt. Rounding the last bend he recognized the lighted window of his kitchen. That had not happened since he was a child.

"Papà?"

"Yes."

"Have I woken you?"

"No, just resting my eyes a bit."

"Have you finished your book?"

"Nearly. It's excellent."

"Do you really mean that?"

"Yes, I really think it is. What have you been doing?"

"Translating a bit of Latin, but I need a walk now. Would you like to come?"

"Alberto?"

"He's in his room. Shall I ask him?"

"Yes. See what he says."

He heard the door slide back and Lucia's footsteps moving through the house. The sky was a ragged white and puffs of mist were floating over the forest, just touching the tops of the trees. He stretched his legs, trying to shake off the sluggishness that had come over him immediately after lunch. A bird was still singing in the clump of acacias behind the storehouse. He had always admired writers who understood flying creatures and trees, not to mention those who were capable of writing knowledgeably about trails of animal droppings, but he had never managed to master such knowledge himself, and for his own books had trusted the series *Know Your Plants*, *Know Your Herbs* and *Know Your Animals*. The last one was divided into three volumes and dedicated to large mammals, small mammals, and insects, which in the end turned out not to be animals at all. It had been enough for most of his readers to think of him as a wise man profoundly symbiotic with nature.

He heard the door behind him open, then close. Lucia passed him and went to lean against one of the roof supports.

"Did you tell him he can stop and play at the river?" Leonardo asked her.

"Yes, but he'd rather stay in his room with his game."

They gazed at the river, swollen by the rain of the last few weeks. It was flowing slowly towards the valley, carrying on its brown waters large branches and stains of scum. The unknown bird had stopped singing either because it was tired or because it was satisfied.

"Did I like having a bath when I was little?" Lucia asked.

Leonardo looked at her back: under her cream-coloured top it formed a perfect triangle, divided into two exactly equal halves by her long tail of hair. Her grandmother, Leonardo's mother, had had the same shining black hair and clear skin. It was not unusual in those hills and someone

94

said it was a result of the Arab invasions. Lucia nearly always kept her hair gathered into a ponytail by a red rubber band. The only times Leonardo had ever seen it loose was when she had washed it and was sitting by the stove to let it dry. As she did so, she read a novel written a few years before by an American folk musician who had been a baseball player and a tireless traveller. Someone had called him the heir of Bob Dylan just as the young Bob Dylan had been the heir of Woody Guthrie, and several coincidences made it clear this was no meaningless idea.

Bob Dylan as a boy had gone to see Guthrie in the sanatorium during the last days of his life and had sung his own songs to him, and in the same way the young Isaiah Jones had been to Bob's house several times in the months before Dylan's death. Many claimed those meetings had ensured the passing on of the great popular American narrative message. This had struck Leonardo at the time, and he had written about it in a daily paper. He had admitted in his article that what had most attracted him in Isaiah's songs, as in Dylan's and earlier in Guthrie's, had been a sense of wonder he did not understand but intuited. Like seeing a perfect naked body through frosted glass. A vision full of promise for the future. When he listened to their songs he understood how the first readers of the Bible must have felt, when there was a kingdom to be conquered and still the chance of spending long nights forging the swords for the battles ahead. The songs of those three gave hope.

"You had some rubber dolphins you liked to have in your bath," he answered. "I used to sit on the floor and read out their names: there was the bottlenose dolphin, Hector's dolphin and the spinner dolphin, the common one. You used to look at the pictures in the book and divide them into families on the edge of the bath. The one you liked best was the beluga."

"What's that?"

"A white dolphin from the northern seas. Did Alberto enjoy having his bath at home?"

Lucia shook her head. Leonardo moved the book that had been lying open on his stomach while he was asleep to the little table; for a moment its silvered cover reflected the sky. A few drops landed on a metal sheet in the ruins of the store. In the vineyard fallen leaves had formed a mush the colour and consistency of polenta.

"One day I'd like to talk about it," Lucia said.

"About what?"

"About what you've done."

Now the rain was beginning to fall in a tired manner, almost as if engaged in work it no longer felt up to.

Leonardo looked at the mountains: a blue deprived of light, as if painted by someone who has just lost a war. Lucia's gaze passed over her father's trousers, his patched pullover and the long grey hair that reached to his shoulders.

"We could do it this evening," she said, smiling weakly, "after Alberto's asleep."

His face was open and full of gentleness. There were no hidden reasons why this should be so, just as there are no reasons on a windless day for the lake facing you to be completely still. Something uncommon, but hiding no secrets.

"Alright," Leonardo said.

Lucia tucked some loose hair behind her ear.

"I'm going in now," she said.

"Fine."

"And you?"

"I'd like to finish my book."

"You don't have to, if you don't like it."

"But I do like it."

"Sure?"

"Sure."

"O.K."

For supper they boiled three eggs and half a red cabbage and heated some leftover soup on the stove, to which they added a little fine pasta, and then, when it was all ready, Lucia filled a plate, took a spoon and fork and disappeared into the corridor. She came back a minute later without the plate or cutlery. Then she picked a C.D. from the many available, put it on the stereo and joined Leonardo at the table.

"Where's this music from?" she asked, putting the first forkful of cabbage into her mouth.

"Mali."

"Where's that?"

"Northwest Africa."

"Did you go there before it was closed?"

"No."

"And to Africa?"

"Once."

"Mamma's been there many times."

"Yes. She's been to lots of places."

Bauschan let out a sigh from the rug next to the stove where he was dozing. For a couple of weeks now he had started leaving the house to patrol the environs. He ranged further afield every day and Leonardo was sure that that afternoon he had seen him trotting about among the beeches on the hillside at the front of the house.

"The apples smell good," Leonardo said.

Lucia looked at the pan on the stove where they were cooking.

"I put in a little of Adele's honey. The sugar's nearly finished."

"That was a good idea."

After Elio's orchard had been plundered, the only fruit they had been able to find had been these bitter wild apples.

"Why does Adele's son dress in that cowhide?" Lucia asked.

Leonardo said he did not know, but that it was a recent development. To her next question he answered that Sebastiano wasn't dumb, but had just decided not to speak. They heard Alberto leave his room for the bathroom. Neither of them made any comment. Soon they heard the toilet flush and the steps of the child going back to his room.

"Did you go to Africa because of your books?" Lucia asked.

"No, for a demonstration."

"What sort of demonstration?"

Leonardo looked at the egg he had just cut open. It had boiled too long and the yolk had a greenish tinge.

"At the time of the closing down a singer organized a meeting in the Congo, a sort of sit-in protest, and invited directors, musicians, painters and other such people. Flights were forbidden but those who had private planes made them available. We chartered a plane from Italy."

"Cool!"

"It wasn't bad."

"And what did you all do?"

"The programme was made up of a series of meetings, concerts, processions and documentaries, which everyone would have later found some way to project in his own country, but I only attended the first session, after which I fell ill with fever and had to stay in the hotel."

"For how long?"

"A couple of weeks. The others left because their governments were threatening not to let them back in, but I had a high temperature and wasn't allowed on the flight. They were terrified I'd caught some tropical illness. Your mother wrote to the papers and moved heaven and earth or I'd have been stuck there."

"What a crazy story!"

Leonardo nodded.

"The person playing on this recording was my doctor. He gave me the C.D. as a present before I left."

"Really?"

"Really."

"But what language did you speak with him?"

"Colin spoke both English and French extremely well."

Lucia moved her fork automatically from the left to the right of her plate, keeping her eyes fixed on Leonardo's face.

"And you've never seen him since?"

"No. We wrote to each other for a time, but then the net was blocked. The last I heard was that he had moved to South Africa."

Lucia put a forkful of cabbage into her mouth.

"My literature teacher had lots of books by African writers. He used to photocopy parts of them and we would read them, but some of the parents didn't like it. He could have lost his job."

"That would have been a pity."

"One of the stories was by a woman. I think she was called Jasmina."

"Jiasmina Tofi."

"It was about a boy who was desperate to have a pair of sunglasses, so while his mother was visiting her sick sister, he sold the well in the courtyard to a wandering pedlar in exchange for a pair of Ray-Bans. By the time the mother got home, the man had put up a tent near the well and wanted to be paid for the water. In the end the boy died in a brawl in a disco and his mother married the pedlar, who wasn't as bad as he'd seemed to be."

Leonardo nodded. "She's a good writer. Do you want some more?"

Lucia shook her head.

Leonardo went to pour what was left of the soup into Bauschan's bowl. The dog watched but did not move. When Leonardo started clearing the table, Lucia vanished into the corridor, reappearing soon afterwards with Alberto's plate.

"Has he eaten anything?"

"The egg. He's left all his greens."

Leonardo shook the tablecloth out of the window even though there had never been any crumbs on it since they had run out of bread, then poured hot water from the water heater into the sink and started washing the plates. Lucia sat down on the sofa. The C.D. had finished.

"Is there any more African music?"

"Yes, put on anything you like."

Lucia calmly studied the C.D.s arranged by geographical origin, period and type: there were up to a thousand of them, mostly classical, and she chose one with a green cover. Then she went back to sit down with her knees drawn up to her chest. The light from the only lamp lit up the kitchen leaving the area of the sofa and stove in shadow.

"That's from Senegal," Leonardo said. "Do you like it?"

Lucia stared at a point in the floor where the floorboards changed colour. Years earlier there had been a leak and an area of the parquet had been soaked with water, but in the deceptive light of the lamp it looked more as if the room was on two different levels separated by a small stair. Bauschan had gone to his bowl and was eating peacefully.

"What's the time?" Lucia asked.

"After nine."

"Then I'll be off to bed."

"Yes."

When the girl had left the room, Leonardo finished the washing-up, then moved to the studio where he put on his cashmere evening pullover. Since the children had come he had been keeping his things there, thus freeing the chest of drawers and wardrobe. Then he picked up the pillow, his washbag, bedclothes and pyjamas piled on the desk and went back into the living room.

He cleaned his teeth and washed his face in the sink, opened the divan and prepared his bed. When his sleeping place was ready, he sat down and studied the night through the window: everything lit by the moon looked mute, magnificent and cold. The C.D. had finished and the crackling of the stove was the only sound dividing him from the silence. It seemed that to get up and put on more music would be a huge undertaking. He scratched his shoulder, then his ear, then his shoulder again.

He had no idea what might be passing through the head of that ten-year-old boy barricaded in his room all day. He had never seen him wash, weep, shout, be afraid, sleep or even look sleepy. He had never heard him ask about his father or wonder aloud what would happen if Alessandra did not come back. Leonardo knew nothing of the boy's likes and dislikes. Of what upset him or comforted him. Whether he slept on his stomach or whether his hair had always been the same length.

Though he had not heard Lucia speak for seven long years, he had immediately recognized her language, while the boy remained an inde-cipherable hieroglyph. An idiom invented by goodness knows who to express goodness knows what. A box closed from the inside.

In a dream the night before, Leonardo had found himself in the middle of a desolate expanse with no vegetation, sitting in front of a man with strange marks on his skin. The countryside round them was flat, without mountains or trees, or even a church tower or the outline of a building; there was no dust or stones or fragments of anything that could ever have existed: the earth was an immense expanse of solidified amber. Eventually the man opened his hand to show a little object unlike anything Leonardo had ever seen before or that he had ever heard anyone speak of. Then after saying a single word the man let himself slip to the ground, turning into burned paper which was immediately blown away by the wind. Leonardo was left alone with the little object in his hand and that one incomprehensible word to define it, and small marks began appearing on his skin.

Feeling cold, he went to put another log on the fire to make the flames climb the chimney again, then closed the door of the stove. Going back to the divan, he stroked Bauschan between the ears, and the dog rolled onto his back to show where he wanted to be scratched. Leonardo obliged. Ever since he had given his bedroom to the children, the dog had taken to spending the night with him in the living room, curled up beside the stove. He had been of a mild and meditative nature from the first. His eyes were like blue steel buttons on a shabby military tunic.

"Here I am," Lucia said.

They made some herbal tea and sat down at the table.

Leonardo talked for twenty minutes without any interruption from Lucia and by the time he had finished the tea was cold.

He drank it all the same, in small sips, while Lucia contemplated the night beyond the veranda, her face expressing a subtle disappointment, as if she had just discovered that the heavy rucksack she had been carrying for so long was only half full of food, but otherwise contained nothing but rocks and useless knick-knacks she could have got rid of long ago.

"Mamma won't ever come back, will she?"

Leonardo stopped lifting his cup to his lips and put it back down on the table.

"I'm sure she will come back," he said.

Lucia went on looking out at the darkness beyond the window. She had a small beauty spot above her lip and an extremely graceful neck.

"She said one week and now four have passed."

"Sometimes you have to stay where you're safe. I'm sure that's what she must be doing. As soon as things settle down a bit, she'll be back on the road."

Lucia looked at her cup, identical to her father's but yellow.

"I must tell you something I haven't told you before," she said.

"You don't have to."

"Yes I do, Mamma said I must."

Leonardo waited in silence. Lucia looked up, pale and serious.

"She said if she didn't come back in two weeks, to give our permits to you and tell you to take us to Switzerland."

Leonardo touched his shoe. He had an idea the laces had worked loose, but that was not so.

"Even so, I think it's better we wait for her here," he said. "With the money she left we can buy all we need. The important thing is to keep warm and not get ill."

Lucia looked down at her cup again. A fly that had been walking on the middle of the table flew away.

"Mamma told me you talk like this."

"Like what?"

She raised a shoulder.

"Like everything's always fine. She said she couldn't stand it."

The two men were caught a few days later in an isolated house on the main road not far from the village.

The proprietors, a couple with a three-year-old son, he a central-heating and plumbing engineer and she a nurse, had left at the beginning of September with the idea of getting to Marseilles and taking a flight to Canada, where they had relatives. The house, hidden behind a line of acacias and an ancient elm, was no sooner empty than it was raided by thieves who had first removed everything of any possible value and subsequently what was utterly worthless too.

If they had resisted the temptation to light a fire, in all probability the two men would have been able to stay there for weeks, perhaps even for months, without anyone noticing. But the cold and the absence of cars on the road must have convinced them that the risk of detection was minimal. Then Giampaolo Sobrero, on his way to R. on his Ape three-wheeler to barter a cylinder of gas for a kerosene stove, noticed smoke from the chimney.

Returning to the village, he told his friend Massimo Torchio and they went together to the bar where the men whose job it was to watch over inhabited properties were warming themselves. They all agreed something had to be done, but not knowing who or what they would find in the house, they decided to wait for the patrol. This had already been in action for a couple of weeks with meagre results; all they had been able to find was a shelter made from branches and scraps of nylon behind a wall of tufa rock. There had been footprints, excrement and rabbit bones round it, but nothing to suggest the shelter was still in use.

When the squads came back, it was getting dark so it was decided to put the expedition off till the next day. They took advantage of the wait to sum up their view of the situation: in the last few weeks rabbits, firewood and poultry had been disappearing from the more isolated farmsteads and Vigio from the Marchesa farm had lost a calf. Giovanni Alessandria's eldest daughter claimed she had been followed by a man on her way back from the orchard. She had not been able to see his face clearly, but he was an outsider and had made off only when she reached the first houses and called out in a loud voice for someone to come out. Everyone knew Rita was not a woman to be easily scared and still less to invent stories. She had had a boyfriend from Luxembourg who had got up to all kinds of tricks but eventually she had got out of the relationship with her house and cellar intact and her head held high, while he ended up as a door-to-door salesman for a big frozen-food chain on the Côte d'Azur.

The next morning some twenty men armed with hunting rifles took the road for R. When they reached the house indicated by Sobrero they surrounded it. No smoke was coming from the chimney but there was a strong smell of firewood and burned hides.

The director of the local tourist office, Vincenzo Maina, yelled out for the occupants to surrender and come out with their hands up, but there was no sign from the house. Norina's husband then fired his rifle twice into the wall, dislodging a piece of plaster the size and shape of a cello. As the fragments fell they raised a little cloud of blue dust immediately dampened by the drizzle and a few crows took off from the roof. A few moments later a shutter on the second floor squeaked and a hand emerged waving a shirt the colour of sugarcane.

The two men were forced to kneel in the middle of the courtyard while the leader of the patrol searched the house. The rooms were empty and the furniture had been broken up and burned, as had the upholstery and parquet. The only room with its floor intact was one on the second floor where they had rigged up a cast-iron stove and a couple of mattresses. By the wall were bags of fruit and vegetables, a can of water and a suitcase full of clothes, among them a fur and a coat. Three rabbit skins had been stretched out on a line to dry.

Once the search was over the outsiders were interrogated: Where are you from? Why did you go into the house? Don't you know you shouldn't trespass? Where did you get your vegetables, fruit and clothes? Did you steal a calf from Vigio at the Marchesa farm?

The two men said nothing, their eyes fixed on the nearest patch of ground.

Someone repeated the questions in French, but the prisoners still said nothing. The rain had glued their clothes to their thin bodies and their beards and shaggy hair shone as if they had low voltage bulbs inside their heads. On the way back the party was swollen by people who came out on to the road to see the two prisoners, then the procession climbed the street to the centre of the village and the school. Reaching the red gate, they all realized there was no good reason for them to have come so far and no-one knew what to do next. So they sent for the priest.

While they were waiting for him, Fausto Conterno, who had worked as school caretaker for twenty-five years, suggested using the little room next to the gym as a cell: it had a window with iron bars and a door that could be locked from the outside. It was the nearest thing the village had to a prison, apart from the secret parts of the ancient castle which no-one dared to suggest, so the two men were taken to this lumber room and shut up there amidst gymnastics mattresses and footballs.

When Don Piero arrived it was past two, and he was furious to find Pietro Viglietta guarding the door alone with nothing but his rifle and bandolier. Pietro explained that when they had not seen Don Piero coming, the others had gone to lunch and would be back at four o'clock. The priest, calming down, asked Pietro to explain what had happened; Pietro, who had not been on the expedition because of his bad hip, passed on what he had been told. Don Piero asked if any water had been left with the two men. Fausto said he thought so.

At four the party reassembled in the main hall of the school, some twenty metres from the cell.

Assuming it was certain that the two men had been responsible for thefts from the unprotected orchards and houses, the villagers were now faced with the problem of deciding what to do. They could not hold a trial without any lawyers or a judge or at least a representative of the Council. The three lawyers with homes in the district had all gone abroad, the deputy mayor had also gone and none of those present had any wish to assume any such responsibility. Nor did anyone want to go to A. to pass the problem on to the police or the magistrates' court; even if there still were offices capable of taking on such things, they must be up to their eyebrows in similar problems. Even worse was the fact that it was impossible to communicate with the prisoners and find out who they were, where they had come from, and whether there were others like them in the district. They were certainly not Romanians or Slavs or even Africans, but apart from this no-one had the faintest idea of their origin. At this point someone thought of Leonardo.

When he heard the car come into the courtyard Leonardo jumped out of his armchair hoping it might be Alessandra, but when he opened the door the light of a torch shone straight into his eyes.

"I'm alone here!" he protested, terrified.

The three men confronting him restricted themselves to explaining why they had come. As soon as he recognized Norina's husband, Leonardo calmed down.

"Someone must stay with the children," he said.

The shortest of the men said not to worry, he would do that.

So Leonardo said, "Please come in," and going to tell Lucia he would be away for half an hour, put on his raincoat and left.

When he came into the hall the twenty or so men who by this time had been there for six hours looked at him as though Leonardo was not exactly what they had had in mind. Even though the central heating was off, the air was warm and fragrant.

"We've tried French," the pharmacist said, "but it was no good."

He was the only one with his rifle on his shoulder. The rest had propped their weapons against the wall under the blackboard. The prisoners were sitting on two children's chairs on the other side of the room. The voices of women waiting for the outcome of the interrogation could be heard from the entrance hall.

Leonardo spoke to the men in English, then German and finally his very basic Russian, but the two continued to stare at their own feet. The older man could have been about thirty, the younger one not much more than twenty. They had black curly hair, which had been given an auburn gloss by a combination of dust and humidity. One could easily imagine them landing from a Phoenician ship which had been on the high seas for months, or descending from a mountain range perpetually covered with snow. Their eyes were vigilant yet expressionless, like the eyes of goats.

"Would someone please get an atlas from the library?" Leonardo said.

While they waited, time seemed suspended. The rain continued dripping silently on the windowsills. Further off, the roofs of a few houses could be seen, also a lamp post, and the tower of a church deconsecrated many years previously. When Fausto came back with the atlas, Leonardo opened it in front of the two outsiders. The older man looked at a map covering a double page, then at Leonardo, then back at the map and pointed to an area south of Russia.

"Where are they from?" someone asked.

"Azerbaijan." Leonardo said.

The two men did not react in any way to the name of the country. The elder rearranged his hands on his knees. The younger never moved at all. They were wearing winter trousers, in one case a women's pair.

"How long has it been?" Leonardo asked them.

The two men looked at Leonardo; they had not understood. Leonardo pointed to his watch which was still on his wrist even though its battery was dead. The elder lifted two fingers.

"Two years?"

"Perhaps he means two months," someone said.

"Two years?" Leonardo persisted.

The man shook his head as if to say either he did not know or did not understand or it was not important. At that point Leonardo noticed the younger man was weeping, shedding great tears that slithered down his cheeks and fell to the floor. He wept, Leonardo thought, in a very feminine way, musical and full of dignity. The elder man, perhaps his relative or a person who was in some way responsible for him, touched his knee to encourage him to stop. There could have been ten years between them, but the skin of the younger man was very smooth and his teeth perfect, whereas the weathered face of the elder had creases that shifted when he opened his mouth, but were all bitter. He was wearing a red waistcoat over a green jumper. The other had only a rollneck sweater whose sleeves were too long; and a woollen cap hanging out of his trouser pocket.

"Why did you come here?" the pharmacist asked.

The man slowly passed a hand over the atlas as if sweeping crumbs away from his own country and towards Europe.

"What does that mean?" Don Piero asked.

"I don't know," Leonardo said. "Perhaps they were forced to move."

At a quarter past ten the two were taken back to the room with the footballs. Leonardo asked if they had had anything to eat and everyone looked at each other in silence. A man went into the hallway where the women were waiting, and before anyone could ask anything, told his wife to talk to the other women and arrange something to eat for them.

"But what do they eat?" Leonardo heard the woman ask. The man returned, shut the door and went back to sit where he had been before. At this point there was an exchange of views on what should be done. Someone suggested taking the two men away and letting them go on the understanding they must not set foot in the district again, but it was explained to him that there could be no guarantee that they would do what they were told. They might just as well be given one of the abandoned houses and a piece of land to cultivate to stop them going about thieving. But if news of this got about, it might attract other strays to the area.

When the clock struck eleven, Leonardo, who had expressed no opinion and had not even been asked for one, said he must go home. The others too agreed they were all too tired to reach a decision: for the moment the two men must stay in the little room, and over the next few days there would be time to decide calmly what should be done with them. But by now it was clear to everyone that the only solution would be to expel them from the district.

The destiny of the two men changed course on the last day of the month, when Cesare Gallo was found on his back on the floor of his sitting room with his head smashed in. The chemist said that he must already have been dead three or four days, since his blood had been completely absorbed by the parquet and his body, despite the cold, had begun to decompose. Jewellery, money and clothes had disappeared from the house and the corpse had been stripped of its boots. The killers had come on foot, and after killing Gallo, had searched the house and eaten in the basement dining room. The mechanical bull was stained with blood, a sign that they had set it going for a while. The footprints suggested two or three persons.

Because of the body's condition, the funeral was held the same evening and next morning the two outsiders were shot against the wall of the handball court.

Three men volunteered for the firing squad, and three others were chosen by lot from the twenty-five who had voted for the death sentence. The assembly had contained thirty members, none of them women, and Leonardo took no part in it. Execution by firing squad was chosen because no-one had any experience in preparing a noose, and hanging could have caused problems. It was reported that the assembly had proposed loading two of the rifles with blanks so that everyone could think it might not have been him to fire the fatal shots, but no-one in the village had any blank cartridges so the suggestion came to nothing.

Leonardo heard the shots from his book room and stayed staring for a long time at the same page without thinking of the book or of what had just happened only a kilometre away. When he went back into the house he found Lucia sitting on the divan. She was wearing a tracksuit and looked as if she was listening intently to music, but the stereo was not on.

"Something ugly has happened in the village, hasn't it?" she asked, watching him slipping off his jacket.

"Yes, very ugly."

"Like what happened to the Pakistanis where we were?"

"Something like that."

Lucia pulled her knees up to her chest, freeing half the divan. Leonardo, on his way to the table, hesitated, then sat down. He touched the palm of his right hand with a finger, as if looking for a spot where he had hidden something under his skin.

"What did you tell Alberto?"

"That they're hunting wild boars."

"Did he believe you?"

"I think so, he wanted to know how much a wild boar weighs and how you go about skinning it."

Lucia stretched her legs and put her feet in his lap. Leonardo took them in his hands. It seemed to him the first beautiful such thing he had done for many years.

*

As Christmas approached it got colder and the earth froze. In the morning the sky would be clear, but in the afternoon slow clouds without distinct outlines would be drawn down from the north by the dusk. By nightfall they would have taken over the sky. This raised the temperature a few degrees making it possible to sit on the veranda watching a great unbroken black cloth descend beyond the fence. During the night, though no wind could be felt, the clouds would disappear and by morning the ground would be covered with frost. The sky, before the sun had fully risen, would reflect this pure white as flocks of large birds headed for the south.

Leonardo would be the first to wake. Putting on his slippers he would take Bauschan as far as the edge of the vineyard and bend to study the tiny crystals that looked as if they had been set there by an army of watchmakers. While the dog raised his leg against the fence, Leonardo thought of cathedrals, illuminated books and other products of limitless and patient intelligence, asking himself whether anyone would ever again be able to devote himself to such laborious but inessential work. There had been a time when he had felt himself to be one of those who believed in art for art's sake. Only such people would ever understand such things: a simple piece of wood cannot know why nails and hairpins leap towards a magnet.

When Bauschan had finished his patrol they would go back into the house and Leonardo would return to the book he had fallen asleep over the evening before. He would be able to read for a good two hours or so before Lucia emerged from her room. It was good that she and Alberto both slept late at this time when there was nothing special to do. Sometimes they managed to get Alberto to the river before lunch, where he would play with pieces of wood carried on the flooding river, throwing them back into the icy water in the hope that Bauschan would retrieve them. But the dog would not listen to the boy and never came nearer to him than a metre or so, as if by some form of intuition or foresight.

Alberto was tall for his age, but even so his head seemed exceptionally large.

His face was pale and covered with small freckles, and like his grey adult eyes was in no sense naïve. His whole personality seemed constructed round his eyes, as if to protect and mask them. His auburn hair had grown in the weeks since he had arrived and was now down to his shoulders. He had long bones, to which his flesh seemed to stick like paper, and it was easy to guess that he would be a tall man. But at the moment his walk and his hands were awkward and clumsy.

Lucia often threatened to leave him on his own and take away his video game if he didn't come with them to the little church. Alberto said he did not care and that he would either stay where he was or go home. Leonardo stood aside to let them argue it out. The thrust and parry would last about ten minutes; a conflict whose rules, controls and counterbalances were well tested. Usually Lucia had the best of it and Alberto would follow them along the lane in resentful silence.

When they got to the church, Leonardo and Lucia would lean against the low wall and watch the hills disappearing all round while Alberto would wander among the graves in the little cemetery. When it was time to go they would usually find him staring at the tombs of those who had died in Russia. Leonardo had told him about that interminable retreat in the snow and how so many had died of cold and hunger, while Alberto, impressed by the size of the massacre, constantly demanded more details. It was the only time he would ever approach Leonardo; otherwise he kept himself to himself and avoided close contact even with his sister. He had never once had a bath since his arrival. Sometimes the other two heard him running the water and apparently having a shower, but they both doubted it was really happening. There was a shadow round his neck and his hair had become dark with dirt. He always wore the same clothes and boots. Despite the fact that Alessandra had left two suitcases full of suits, socks, shoes, shampoo, bubble bath, bathrobes, slippers, tubes of toothpaste, soap and a leather briefcase that Leonardo had not seen again, but which presumably contained their permits and some money.

They would spend the rest of the day at home. Sometimes Leonardo would go out to look for firewood, or to exchange a few words with Adele and buy some honey from her. At such times he would leave the children on their own, but never for more than an hour.

Once a week he would go into the village to buy bread, a couple of small cans of food, and some pasta and tomato sauce. Apart from milk and cheese this was all that was available; meat had become very expensive and fish could not to be found at all, even deep-frozen. The only shops still open were Norina's grocery store and the bar. The chemist had moved all his medicines to his home where he was available to customers every morning between ten and midday. The proprietors of the shoe shop and the hairdresser had done the same. The village streets were fragrant with the smell of burned wood and even though the dustcart no longer operated, the litter bins were empty. Cars were hardly ever heard and the only voices came from the church during services or from the bar, where the circle of regulars had grown since hardly anyone now had any work, agricultural or otherwise. Conversations tended to be brief and nearly always ended in silences full of questions. Only ersatz coffee was now served; the real thing had run out. And despite the fact that it was nearly Christmas, no-one had put up decorations.

For Christmas Eve they asked Adele and Sebastiano round.

They arrived with five eggs, a pan, a basket of vegetables and a large parcel. The table had been laid with care and a half candle was burning in the middle of it.

While waiting for the rabbit and potatoes to heat up on the stove, they dipped the raw vegetables in the last of the olive oil. From now on they would have to make do with other edible oils. As they ate, Adele told a story from when she was a girl, of a hornbeam growing near their house that her father had wanted cut down to make room for a shelter for the tractor. One evening while she was feeding the chickens, the tree had told her it was ready to go, but only if moved to a precise point that it indicated. That evening Adele explained this to her father but he told her that the next day the builders would come, the tree would be cut down and the garage for the tractor would be built, and that was all there was to it.

But the following morning her father seemed less sure of himself. At breakfast he looked exhausted, as if he had had no sleep.

"I had a bad dream last night," he told his daughter.

Adele had then interpreted the dream for him in detail as if she had dreamed it herself, and her father had lowered his eyes in shame because it was not the first time he had put his daughter's talent to the test. When the builders arrived, Adele showed them the place they must move the tree to, and without asking too many questions they got to work. That very night, with the leaves of the tree rustling outside the window, Adele's father had dreamed of a blackbird whistling a tune and the next morning, beside his cup, he found a black feather that his daughter had left for him before going to work.

Several times, Leonardo surprised Alberto and Sebastiano staring solemnly at each other while Adele was speaking, as if something had happened between them that the others were not aware of.

After dinner, Adele made a *zabaione* that turned out rather bitter because she had to use Fernet rather than Marsala, but they ate it all the same, and then unwrapped the presents.

Leonardo gave Lucia an edition of the *Odyssey* which had been printed in Florence in 1716. For Alberto his first thought had been a book by Salgàri, then, thinking he would not have much use for it, he had added a small box of tools with a little tube of glue for woodwork, pincers, hammer, pliers, nails, some oakum for trimming, and two batteries found in Elio's shop. The idea was that Alberto could use this to build something. He gave Adele a book of gems of Islamic wisdom given to him many years before by a friend who translated from Arabic. Adele gave three knitted scarfs and balsamic drops against coughs and sinusitis and to discourage lice. Sebastiano gave no presents but got a cap from Leonardo, which turned out to be rather too tight. Lucia gave Leonardo a collection of ten poems written in her own hand and bound in a firm cardboard cover cut from a box of detergent.

A little before midnight, Adele and Sebastiano went into the village to Mass; by now Alberto had been in his room for some time. Lucia and Leonardo decided to have herb tea on the veranda. The sky was overcast, but if you stared at it for long enough you could sense the moon's path behind the clouds. The cold was very dry.

They did not feel like discussing what the future might or might not hold, so simply listed little events that can brighten a day. Unimportant things, just to be able to share the sound of their own voices in the darkness. To Leonardo, Lucia's voice sounded like the swish of water in a metal basin.

It was very late when Lucia said she was sleepy, and it would have been entirely natural if before going in she had bent to kiss her father goodnight on his cheek, but she did not do so.

Left alone, Leonardo was touched by the memory of mornings when he had woken in the great double bed at Via B. to hear Lucia breathing beside him. Holidays when her nursery had been closed and Alessandra had already gone off to some engagement, and the light was pouring serenely through the shutters and projecting oval shapes throughout the room. At such times he had liked to lock his hands behind his head and stare up at the chandelier, immersing himself in the story he was writing at the time: the characters, the course of events, the places where they lived and the things that were making them happy or sad. At such times he felt he understood the pleasure a horse must feel when given a huge field to roam in, with the grass tickling its stomach and nothing to be heard but the beating of its own heart. Reaching out his hand he would touch Lucia's little calves, as perfect as a ship in a bottle. The little girl's eyes would be closed and slightly puffed up with sleep. She was four or five years old at the time, and during the night her long hair would have formed little knots that would be troublesome to disentangle.

As he slipped into the divan that had become his bed, he thought of this as the happiest of all his memories, and asked himself what he would feel if Alessandra's car came into the courtyard a second time.

Alberto spent the morning making a harpoon by fixing a fork on the end of a stick, and after lunch said he wanted to go down to the river.

Once they had reached the shingle of the bank he spent at least an hour trying to spear a trout darting about in the middle of the riverbed, where a strip of water was flowing, gentle and dark, through the ice.

Leonardo and Lucia, sitting on a large smooth rock, discussed Achilles and Aeneas. Leonardo had once read an essay that maintained that Aeneas had been the first epic hero to hesitate before killing an enemy, the first to see death as a subjective choice and not as an action of destiny like an eruption or a conception. Alberto launched his harpoon with a cry that sounded like a twice-repeated German word. On the other side of the river, Bauschan was inspecting the edge of the forest. When Alberto got tired, Lucia asked him if he would like to go up to the little church to see if any animal had been digging up the bones of the dead.

It was after three by the time they reached the cemetery, where they sat on the low wall enjoying the weak sun on their faces and on their gloveless hands. Alberto asked Leonardo to repeat the story of the Alpine troops preserved in the ossuary. He then asked a few questions about the Aztecs and cruel things done in antiquity. A Nordic fluorescence lit the sky while an insubstantial mist oscillated in little waves lower down.

It was not easy to climb back up the vineyard below the house: the rising temperature had turned the earth to sticky mud.

As they struggled up the the final stretch, Leonardo noticed the veranda door was ajar. He tried to remember whether he had been the last to come out, then stopped and summoned Bauschan in a whisper of a kind one might have used to attract the attention of a relative at the other end of a bed as one kept watch beside a dead body: neither a whistle nor a word, but sharing the quality of both.

"What is it?" Lucia said.

Leonardo beckoned the others, then bent double and followed the line of vines to his right. When he came to where the briers were thicker, he knelt down and the children did the same.

A young man with his hair combed in a curious quiff was coming out of the house carrying a bag of food and a bag of clothes. He went down the steps and disappeared round the corner. They heard the door of a car open and close.

"They're stealing our things!" Alberto said.

The man reappeared. He was in a leather motorcyclist's jacket of the type with showy padding on the elbows and back. This made him look hunchbacked, which he was not, even if something about his body and legs suggested rickets. As he climbed the steps a woman in a hat came out of the veranda and offered him the bottle of Fernet that Leonardo had opened for the Christmas *zabaione*. They talked for a minute or two, passing the bottle backwards and forwards between them; when it was empty, the man threw it into an armchair and they went back into the house.

"You've got to do something!" Alberto said.

Leonardo merely held Bauschan close and kept his eyes fixed on the house. Alberto, a few centimetres away, stared at his pale thin well-shaved face.

"Let's go and call someone," he said, pulling Leonardo by the jacket.

"No!" Leonardo said. "Let's wait for them to go."

"But they've taken over the house!"

"Shut up!" Lucia said.

By the time the door opened again the church clock had long since struck four and the sun had set behind the mountains. A flat, almost rosy haze had shut off the sky to the north. Two men and the woman brought out bags and suitcases. The older man was wearing Leonardo's camelhair coat and leather gloves. His hair was an unnatural grey as though ash had fallen on his head. The plump young woman at his side was in a T-shirt. Under her arm was Lucia's vanity case and a bag containing a packet of biscuits and a bottle of wine. The younger man, the one in the biker's jacket, was carrying the stereo. They went round the house to the back. Leonardo and the children heard the sound of an approaching engine and a few seconds later a grey car slipped through the gate and disappeared behind the mulberry trees skirting the road.

They stayed kneeling in the mud for another minute or two, then Leonardo released Bauschan. The dog moved a few metres away and urinated at length, at the same time giving Leonardo an afflicted look as if unsure whether he had passed whatever test he had been set.

"Bravo, Bauschan," Leonardo said to reassure him.

Every drawer in the kitchen had been pulled out and turned over on the floor. Leonardo moved towards the table where the intruders had left a pan covered with tomato sauce, a bottle of coffee liqueur and a few eggshells, then turned towards Lucia who had stayed close to the door. He stared at the plates, cutlery and C.D.s strewn across the floor amid flour and detergents.

"Let's tidy up a bit," he said to her.

She said nothing but wept in silence. Leaning against the doorway, her face at a slight angle, she was like a seventeenth-century Madonna with skin as impalpable as moonlight yet enthralling the viewer's gaze. Behind her, Alberto was holding back Bauschan so he would not cut his paws on the broken glass.

Going down the corridor, Leonardo glanced into the bathroom: among the bottles and containers emptied at random he thought he could also see plaster rubble, but did not go in to check. In the bedroom there was a suffocating smell of urine, and the clothes the raiders had not taken away were lying slashed and piled up in a corner in a many-coloured mountain someone must have pissed on.

"What would they have done if we'd been here?" Lucia asked, looking into the room.

Leonardo noticed the bedcover was stained with blood. Not a large patch with sharp contours, but more as if something had been rubbed against it. He said nothing but opened the window, then went to Lucia and gave her a hug.

"Let's go," he said. "I'll sort it out."

They were careful not to tread on the small eighteenth-century maps lying on the corridor floor among fragments of frame and glass. In the kitchen Bauschan was licking something. Leonardo lifted the dog's head to check what it was but realizing it was peanut butter, let him continue. Alberto was neither there nor on the veranda.

Leonardo found him in the studio with his hands behind his back. He was looking through the window, towards the vineyard and hillside, now indistinguishable in the dusk.

"All O.K.?" he asked.

Alberto went on staring at whatever he was looking at. There was a terrible stench in the room. Someone had defecated on the desk and scattered Leonardo's collection of letters over the floor. The walls were stained with the bloody imprints of hands that had taken on the colour of the brickwork.

The woman was menstruating, Leonardo thought, and she must have coupled with one man in the bed and with the other here against the wall.

Such thoughts slipping so easily into his mind frightened him. A year ago such stains would have made him think of Basquiat's paintings or the caves of Lascaux. A year ago such an image of entwined bodies would never have sprung so vividly and realistically into his mind. And he would never have thought of words like "menstruation" and "coupled" to describe it. Perhaps this was what barbarism was, he thought: a new vocabulary gradually taking over with new images. The first word was the Trojan horse. Which polluted the well and reproduced itself. Sickness. Cholera.

He looked at Alberto and gave him a smile.

"Let's go out," he said.

The boy took a few paces towards the door as if to do so, but instead stepped up to Leonardo and unleashed a punch at the base of his stomach.

Leonardo doubled up in pain and Alberto punched him again, this time on the nose and in the left eye. During the few seconds this took neither of them uttered a sound, then Alberto left the room.

Leonardo prostrated himself on the floor like a beggar about to start his day's work.

His testicles were throbbing and pain was spreading through his whole body. Even his buttocks had gone rigid, perhaps from some sort of muscular contraction, and he could not breathe because his whole body seemed to have petrified round the pain. His first breath was like the first breath taken after birth and he imagined it must have been taken with equal desperation. He studied his slightly trembling hands. Like the hands of a pianist told that from now on every piano will be destroyed and he will need his hands to extract all his food from fields that until then had simply been somewhere to walk while thinking out a more subtle interpretation of a prelude by Chopin.

No living creature had ever before deliberately hit him to cause pain; he had never fought as a child and his parents had never slapped him to punish him. Now, at fifty-three, he had been called to account and found wanting.

He could hear Lucia in the kitchen telling Bauschan not to do something, then her footsteps came in his direction. When Leonardo tried to stand he was stopped by a sharp pain in his testicles.

"Are you looking for something?" Lucia said.

Without turning he moved a few of the pieces of paper on the floor. A drop of blood fell on one.

"Something I wrote."

"Would you like me to help you?"

"No. Stay with Alberto."

"They've taken his electronic game."

Leonardo nodded without looking up from the floor.

"Wait outside, both of you. Take Bauschan with you."

There was no sound of the girl's shoes moving. Leonardo began rummaging among his papers again. Blood was pouring from his nose and he realized his eyes were full of tears.

"Papà?" said the girl after a little.

"Yes."

"They've taken all the sanitary towels."

"Don't worry, we'll find some more."

"But it's difficult!"

"We'll find some, I promise, now please go away. I'm trying to do a bit of tidying."

Leonardo heard her footsteps move into the living room. When he was certain he was alone he took his handkerchief from his pocket and blotted his nose. The box of letters was by the wall. Some had been opened, perhaps in search of money, and then torn up, but most seemed intact. He collected them and put them back in the box together with the torn pieces, then picked the box up and carried it into the kitchen. His nose had stopped bleeding and the pain in his testicles seemed to have dulled and spread into his belly. He could hear the children's voices in the yard trying to keep the dog outside.

He put the box of letters down on the divan and took a brush, dustpan and refuse sacks from beside the sink. He decided to start with the bathroom.

The fragments of plaster had come from the wall above the toilet. The intruders must have been attracted by a loose tile and, suspecting a secret hiding place, had smashed a few more to uncover it. Finding nothing, they had perhaps defecated in the bath out of sheer spite. They had certainly taken razor blades, scissors, the electric shaver, shampoos, the hairdryer, toothpaste and medicines. Perhaps even more, but with such a mess it was difficult to say.

Leonardo opened the window, swept up the rubble and broken glass from the floor, cleaned the bath and put everything in a plastic bag.

When the bag was full he realized it was too heavy to be lifted without tearing and tried pulling it along the floor, but the pieces of broken glass in the corridor ripped it and its contents came out, getting mixed up with the rest of the filth.

He stood for a minute staring at the part of the kitchen cut off by the door, then turned abruptly and went into the bedroom. Near the upended bedside table he found the keys he was looking for. He picked them up and put them in his pocket.

Hearing the glass door open, Lucia and Alberto turned and Bauschan lifted his head. When Alberto met Leonardo's eyes he looked away.

"I've put a suitcase on the table," Leonardo said. "Take what you need for the night and put it inside. We'll come back for the rest tomorrow."

"Where are we going?" Lucia asked.

"To Elio's house."

While the children were getting ready, Leonardo went to his book room. The door had been forced. He went inside with Bauschan and turned on the light. Now that the bookcases had been overturned the room seemed bigger. There was a strong smell of petrol in the air.

He walked up to the mountain of fallen books in the middle of the room. He had once seen a similar installation in a major museum in New York, though the pile had been crowned by a wax Moses with an enormous wick coming out of his head.

The jerry can Elio had left for him was lying empty in a corner. Petrol had been poured over the books but for some reason the pile had not been set on fire. He told himself he would never know why, and this seemed more seriously disturbing than anything else.

When he closed the door and left the room he knew he would never go in there again. He had eight books under his arm. He could have taken more, but he decided eight was right.

Snow was falling outside when they woke the next morning, and after breakfast with some camomile Elio's wife had left in a cupboard, they waited, each in a different room, for the snow to stop so they could go back and collect what had been left in the other house. Lucia had taken over the double bedroom, Alberto the child's room, and Leonardo the divan in the kitchen. From the window he could see large slow snowflakes drifting obliquely down into the square. On the roofs opposite the snow was now as thick as a dictionary. The few passers-by on their way to the grocery store would look up at the lighted windows. When they did this Leonardo waved to them. The only sound in the house was the crackling of wood on the kitchen stove.

At midday, as it was still snowing, Leonardo put the chains on the Polar and they drove out of the village. The driver's side window had been smashed by the thieves, but Leonardo had patched it with an opaque sheet of nylon.

When they got to the house Leonardo told the children to look especially for food, medicines and clothes; they would be able to come back for the rest later. To save Alberto from having to go into the rooms with excrement and blood, Leonardo set him to collecting what could still be eaten from the kitchen. The boy made no comment but got to work.

There was no longer any bad smell in the bedroom and studio after a night with the windows open, but the rooms seemed contaminated by something obscurely connected with excess. When he went into them Leonardo felt dazed as though just waking from a dream in which he had done something contrary to his usual moral code. The whiteness and orderliness of the countryside outside the windows was confusing. Bauschan, as though aware of Leonardo's bewilderment, kept close to him all the time.

When the boot of the Polar was full they went back to Elio's house, having listed the things they had not found: the computer, the stereo, eggs, biscuits, pasta, vegetable oil, many of the medicines, bedclothes, gloves and scarves. Alberto did not mention his video game and Lucia said nothing about the sanitary towels. Leonardo made no reference to money.

They entered the storeroom from the back and took only a few minutes to unload what had taken nearly two hours to collect, since Lucia suggested it might be better if they stayed there long enough to sort the stuff out. Leonardo realized she did not want to go back to the house again and said it was a good idea to divide the jobs that needed doing. By the time he went back into the yard the snow had stopped. He decided to take a short walk. The white blanket was soft and dry, the river below him a line of Indian ink.

He walked for half an hour without any particular purpose or in any particular direction. Bauschan stayed a metre or two ahead, diving into the snow and occasionally raising his eyes not to the sky, but towards something immediately above the hills. The light seemed to be coming to them through heavy air and appeared exhausted on arrival. There's a mournful beauty in all this, Leonardo thought, a beauty he should make friends with, since from now on no other friend would be possible.

After another tour of the house, he took a piece of paper, wrote on it where they would now be living and fastened it to the door with a piece of wire he had found among the ashes of the burned-out store building.

They spent the next day washing, mending and storing what they had saved. Lucia looked after the clothes, putting them in the washing machine and setting them to dry on the rack before the wood-fired cooking stove. Leonardo sorted out the little food they had rescued and went out to buy more with the money that had happened to be in his pocket when they had gone out for their walk. Alberto took charge of dishes, matches, detergents and other utensils.

The activity did them good and no-one referred all day to what had happened. At lunch they ate pasta with margarine and, for supper, polenta and cheese. Leonardo, who had been wondering whether to hold Alberto to account for his aggressive behaviour, finding him more cooperative than usual decided to let it go and treat the whole episode as no more than an attack of nerves. In any case his testicles were hardly hurting any longer and the same could be said for his nose so long as he did not try to blow it.

The only person he told about the incident was Norina, the proprietor of the grocery. She showed no surprise; rather that they should think themselves lucky that they had not been in when the house was raided unlike poor Cesare Gallo, and that it had been irresponsible of Leonardo to keep those kids isolated out there. Since before Christmas not even the armed patrol had gone out and everyone had moved to abandoned houses in the centre, where they could feel safer. Outsiders, vagabonds and refugees had taken over the hills and nothing could be done about it any longer. Better to concentrate on defending their homes and shops. Norina knew this because her husband, a former National Guard officer, was responsible for organizing the local guard-duty roster. Two years earlier, when the frontier problem had reached dramatic proportions, he had asked to be recalled to the military despite being more than sixty years of age, but the ministry had simply rejected him with a letter of thanks.

Passing Leonardo a bag of cauliflower across the counter, Norina asked him if he had a gun.

"No," Leonardo said, "we have no guns."

"If you'd like one, I think I could arrange it."

"Thanks, but I think I'd rather not."

Norina took his money and put the banknotes into the cash register.

"Pay attention to a woman who has never had the advantage of education," Norina said, pushing his change across the counter. "Please do get a gun. It won't be a waste of money."

That evening, playing about with the radio, they hit on a station broadcasting fairly recent Italian pop songs interspersed with commercials for furniture manufacturers and department stores which had probably long since gone bankrupt or been plundered. The songs and recorded voices sounded mocking in light of the present situation, but they stopped to listen all the same. Lucia had heated a huge panful of water and taken it into the bathroom to wash her long black hair. Now she was sitting in front of the stove with wet hair down to her shoulders as she listened to those voices from what seemed an unbelievably distant past. Leonardo, also listening, felt an agonizing pang of nostalgia for those hypermarkets, furrier's shops and beauticians he had never been to, which had once even opened on Sunday mornings. Some of his writing and teaching colleagues had always been ready to rant furiously against those temples of consumerism while others preferred to see them as phenomena to be monitored, analyzed and classified. Leonardo had never inclined to either view because he had never held opinions about the matter. On the occasions when he had set foot in any of these places he had never really felt at ease, but the same could be said of his visits to the opera. But he had noticed that no-one coming out of any such place was likely to have noticed what its ceiling was like.

"Papà?"

"Yes?"

"Did they take all the money Mamma left for us?"

"Not all of it."

"How much is left?"

"What I had in my pocket. A bit less than a hundred lire."

"That's not much."

"No. You're right."

"And the rest of it?"

"Was in the desk drawer."

"Not a great place to hide it."

"I agree."

The radio played a song in which a man and a woman took turns to describe what they could see from their window. They lived in neighbouring flats in the same building but reached by different staircases, so they had never met. They were both looking for love, but were divided by a wall seventeen centimetres thick. The title of the song was "The Seventeen-Centimetre Wall". It was not very well written, but to Leonardo the idea behind it was attractive. Thinking of the building the two must have lived in, he imagined a concrete parallelepiped shape, like the home of the protagonist in some film Kieślowski had shot for Polish television.

He got up and poured water into a small pan that had been draining in the sink.

"Herb tea?"

Lucia shook her head. Leonardo placed the pan on the wood stove and a few drops of water from its wet base ran sizzling towards the edge of the hot surface.

"You should have something hot before going to bed. Do you good."

The girl touched a small fragment of bread on the table with her finger. It was rye bread, dark enough to blend in with the doodles on the oilcloth. She turned it round and pushed it away. Her hair was nearly dry.

"We have to leave," she said. "If we stay here something nasty will happen to us."

Leonardo took a cup and dropped in a herbal teabag that had already been used more than once. The small jar of honey Adele had given them was half empty. He let a few drops slip into the cup and put the top back on the jar.

"We have enough money to last a few months," he said, sitting down, "and things are bound to be better in the spring."

"Don't be stupid," the girl said sharply. "Nothing will be better at all."

Bauschan half opened one eye and looked at them as they faced each other across the table. The stove crackled.

"I'm sorry," Lucia said.

"It's alright."

"No really, I didn't mean that."

Leonardo smiled to show it was not important. He lifted the cup to his lips and took two small sips.

"We haven't enough petrol to get to Switzerland," he said.

"We can buy some."

"We haven't enough money for that."

Lucia took the little piece of bread on another circuit, bringing it back to the place where she had first found it.

"There was some money with the permits too. I hid it and they didn't find it."

Leonardo watched the steam rising from the big green mug in his hands. It must have been the mug Elio's young son drank his milk from in the mornings. On it was the logo of a popular amusement park; until recently you could get there and back in a day.

"Are you angry?" Lucia said.

"Why should I be?"

"Maybe I've said something to make you cross."

Leonardo shook his head.

"You've been really clever."

Lucia crushed the fragment of black bread against the table, dividing it into three bits of different sizes. Two months of housework had strengthened her shoulders and little veins had appeared on the backs of her hands.

"Papà?"

"Yes?"

"I'd like to ask you something."

"Go on."

"You won't be angry?"

"No."

Lucia shifted all her hair to her right shoulder. It was soft and shiny.

"When that girl denounced you why didn't you defend yourself? Why didn't you tell people she'd set the whole thing up to blackmail you? Then maybe you and Mamma would have stayed together."

Leonardo looked away from his daughter's black eyes. Outside the window the snow had begun falling again.

"I didn't want her to suffer."

"Who?"

"The girl."

Lucia looked at him as one might look at something whose very existence one doubts even though one has it before one's eyes, then looked down at the divided fragment of black bread, and wept. Leonardo watched her for a long time and noticed that she did not dry her tears. But when she had stopped weeping, the black of her eyes was very pure, like a bucketful of petroleum which could have mirrored the sky.

"Feeling better now?" Leonardo said.

She nodded, pulled a handkerchief from her pocket and blew her nose.

"I've got to have some sanitary towels," she said. "In a day or two I'm going to need them."

Achille Conterno was buried on the morning of the last day of the year. He had been ninety-four years old and lived alone in a house five hundred metres from the square, but because of the diabetes which afflicted his feet, he had not been out for months. His son and daughter had left at the end of the summer, but he had refused to go with them. They had asked some cousins to look after him, but these people had never been seen in the village.

The person who found Conterno had been Gregorio of the public weights and measures office. Suspicious at the lack of smoke from his chimney, he had gone to pay Conterno a visit and found the door locked. After calling him and getting no answer, Gregorio had gone to find a jemmy, and when he forced the door together with Felice Gallo and Mariano Occelli, they found Achille lying under the covers on his bed with his eyes closed and his cap on his head, exactly as he must have fallen asleep a couple of nights before. The three decided he must have died of cold. In fact there was not a trace of furniture in the rooms and even the matchboard wainscoting had been stripped off and burned in the stove; all that was left was an old table too tough to be broken in pieces.

The service was short. The church had not been heated for many months and everyone was numb with cold, forcing them to keep shifting their weight from one leg to the other. In his homily, Don Piero reminded them that in these difficult times everyone must gather round the church as a centre both spiritual and physical, giving help as well as expecting to receive it. He also noted that soon the last batteries for the church clock would be used up, and that without the clock in the tower everyone would be plunged like wild beasts and dumb animals into a world of approximate time divisible only into day and night. Most people were aware of a hidden agenda in his sermon but no-one felt like trying to work out what, and for the moment even Don Piero seemed to prefer to pass over the details.

Four men lifted the coffin and carried it down the nave to Mariano's pick-up truck which was waiting on the church forecourt, after which a good half of the fifty-three mourners Leonardo had counted in the church made their way to the cemetery.

Mariano's vehicle was the only one in the village big enough to carry a coffin. It had already been used for Cesare Gallo's burial, and also for removing the bodies of the two outsiders to the forest, where they had been buried in a place known only to the four men who dug the grave. When Leonardo looked at it he was reminded of the hearse in Ottavio's yard and remembered that before leaving Ottavio had repainted it as best he could and had loaded it up with his property. Leonardo had not seen him since the beginning of November when he had come to say he was going, and to leave him a Toma cheese and some eggs. He had also asked Leonardo that day if he would like to buy one of his cows, but when Leonardo politely declined, he said it didn't matter because two had died and he had slaughtered two more, and he was discussing terms with a dairy for the others. Before leaving he shook Leonardo's hand and told him his daughter really was pregnant, and that things were back to normal with his wife, so Leonardo shouldn't worry about the planes.

At the cemetery Don Piero pronounced a final blessing over the body and the sexton began to seal the tomb. A light dusting of snow had begun to fall again and the village was barely visible through the low mist.

As the mourners began to disperse, Leonardo decided on Elvira Rocca, a tiny woman of about forty with short hair, with whom he had never exchanged a word. All he knew of her was that she lived with her ancient mother and had taught Chemistry at secondary school in A.

He followed her to the lane where she lived, and approached her when she was about to put her key in the lock of her gate. Suddenly aware someone was behind her, she started, dropping her bunch of keys in the snow. For a moment they stared at each other without moving, as if awaiting the arrival of a third person to explain the situation; then the woman bent down and picked up her keys. When she stood up again she curved her lips in a tentative smile. The large eyes in her small face were a Carthusian grey. Her nose was neither hooked nor bent, but somehow irregular, and her short hair was sticking out from under her cap in a girlish way.

"Good morning," she said.

"Good morning," Leonardo replied. "I need to have a word with you."

"Would you mind if we went in? We've already been exposed to so much cold."

As she opened the door, Leonardo looked at her little green shoes which had a bit of leather sticking out of them. They were like a travel souvenir or a present from a friend who had been abroad. Her heavy red jacket entirely hid the shape of her body.

They crossed a yard that contained nothing but an empty dog basket and went into the house by a glass door. The room they came into was warm and carefully furnished with a desk, a stove, a sofa and some books on a low table. On the wall was a list of the elements which had probably been printed early in the twentieth century. There were two windows and a stair leading up to the next floor from the corner on the right. There was a smell of recently cut firewood and medicines. The total effect was restful.

"Do make yourself at home," Elvira said. "I'll be back in a few minutes." She disappeared up the stairs. Leonardo heard her footsteps cross the ceiling, stop and cross again more quietly. He moved a chair up to the table and sat down, unbuttoning his jacket but keeping it on and pushing his wet cap into his pocket so as not to mess up the room. There were four books by Thomas Bernhard on the table.

Strange, he thought.

He had known two other women who read Thomas Bernhard. One had been married to the publisher of nearly all his books, and the other was the agent who represented his novels on the American market. They had been of different ages, one married and one single, one an early-morning whisky drinker and the other abstemious, but they had been very similar. Both liked to wear waistcoats winter and summer and both loved cold but not lonely places. They were both attractive, but in a way very different from most attractive women. They did not make a man think of sex and sheets or a mountain chalet surrounded by snow, but rather of a strip of leather and a freshly painted wall into which no-one would dare to hammer a nail. Neither had the slightest vocation for maternity and no-one would have ever dared entrust them with a child even for a few minutes. Both found tea poisonous and held the muscles of their necks in a constant state of tension, but slept very well and to a late hour.

Considering their professions it was hardly surprising that both often talked of books, and when they did the conversation would turn to Thomas Bernhard. Leonardo's impression when he first met Danielle, years after he first came to know Kate, was that both women had first read Bernhard at a time in their lives when they were looking for a reason to hate the world. Yet they were too intelligent to hate at random: they needed a plan, a rule, some way of avoiding the risk of missing something they should detest. Bernhard spared nothing. There had been a time when Leonardo had read him eagerly, just as one might marvel from a safe distance at a huge vortex produced by marine currents. For the two women it had been different; they had dived into the vortex and allowed it to throw them about so long as it suited them. He had often heard one or the other make an innocuous comment on a journalist, on the colour of a fitted carpet or on food made with soya, only to develop it into a long and deeply thoughtful monologue against journalism as a profession, fitted carpets as a choice of furnishing, or healthy food in general.

He had only seen them together once, when he had been awarded a prize in Argentina, followed by a celebratory dinner at the embassy. The two women smelt each other out among the two hundred guests and spent the whole evening deep in conversation against a background of gloomy tapestry, grabbing a succession of martinis and non-alcoholic fruit juices respectively, all delivered by waiters in topaz-coloured livery. Seeing the two together against that eighteenth-century background had made Leonardo think of two halberds.

"Here I am," Elvira said, coming down the stairs.

She had changed into a hand-knitted wool sweater. Without a hat her face looked longer, her nose less prominent. Her short hair had been combed with a parting.

"Would you like some tea?"

"Thank you, but I shall only take up a few minutes of your time."

"How strange you should come here today of all days. I've so often seen you in the village and wanted to talk to you about your books."

"Why didn't you?"

Elvira sat down at the end of the table.

"I imagined your coming back here must have been some sort of voluntary exile, and that you wouldn't want to talk about your earlier life."

Leonardo looked at the covers of the books on the table. They were very early editions with images of the Viennese Secessionists on them. It was warm in the room, but the stove seemed to have gone out and the open fire had not been lit.

"Why did you say 'today of all days'?" he asked.

"In what sense?"

"You said it was strange that I came here today of all days."

"Did I say that?"

"I think so."

Elvira shrugged.

"Maybe I was referring to the fact that I can't even offer you a coffee, and that once we could have said things like 'I've been to T. to see this exhibition or to hear that concert' while now we can't. Are you sure you won't have some tea? I'd be happy to make it."

"Thank you, but I must get home soon."

Elvira looked at the clock on the wall. It had stopped. She smiled and waved a hand in the air as if to say "I'm always making that mistake". She touched one of the books on the table.

"I expect you like Bernhard," she said.

"I do."

She picked up the book and looked at the misty countryside on the cover.

"It's like watching a volcano erupt, don't you think? It can be a wonderful sight, but it all depends how near you are to it."

Leonardo nodded. Elvira put the book down on top of the others and smiled.

"I'm wasting your time with my chatter. I think there was something you wanted to say to me?"

Leonardo shook his head.

"Just something to do with my daughter. Two weeks ago our house was burgled. My daughter's sixteen and . . ."

"There's a boy there with you too, isn't there?"

"Yes, my ex-wife's son. His name's Alberto."

"And your daughter's?"

"Lucia."

"Such a lovely name. So luminous."

Leonardo nodded and opened his mouth to resume his prepared speech, then stopped. On the wall behind the woman, at the point where the stovepipe entered the chimney, a small brass ring had been fixed to seal the opening. Most people would have been satisfied with silicon or stucco, but this woman had thought of something more precise and attractive, a little piece of work wrought with devoted attention that must have taken some time to create. The ring had been fixed in place with care, avoiding rough incisions or dents. Leonardo was sure Elvira had done it because everything in the room was as simple and exactly appropriate as she was herself.

"My wife left the children here," he said. "She should have been back within a week, but by now two months have passed."

The woman looked at him closely with peaceful eyes. She had three small moles on her face, but if he had closed his eyes Leonardo would not have been able to say exactly where they were.

"The children must be worried," she said.

"Extremely."

"And you?"

"I used to spend most of my time reading; now I've left my books in an old cellar where the mice will eat them and I don't give a damn. I suppose that means I'm worried."

The woman smiled.

"Maybe," she said. "Still, I think I've guessed why you've come."

Leonardo pushed back his hair which had begun sticking to his forehead as it dried.

"Really?"

"Yes. Come with me."

There was a door under the stairs that Leonardo had not noticed. The woman walked straight through it while he had to bend low. Strip lights came on revealing a garage with a small blue car in it. It was very clean and almost new. There was also an old wardrobe and a couple of shelves on the wall with a neat collection of jam jars and vegetables preserved in oil.

Elvira took a green package out of the wardrobe. It was one of many such packages, carefully stacked to make full use of the interior.

"Maybe not quite what your daughter has in mind, but in an emergency they'll do."

Leonardo looked at the package: large sanitary pants for adults.

"Take as many as you like. For years the health authority supplied us with a packet a week."

"Won't your mother need them?"

"My mother will die today," the woman said, "or at the very latest tomorrow."

Leonardo noticed how light the package was in his hands.

"I'm so sorry. I've disturbed you at a bad time."

Elvira shook her head. She seemed incapable of looking solemn for long.

"My mother's been ill for a very long time," she said. "There used to be a drug that helped her, but now it can't be found. We said goodbye ages ago, before she fell into a coma. I'll get you a bag to put the packets in."

Leonardo, left on his own, looked at the shiny, well-kept car. He could hear piano music from the living room. Elvira came back with two large plastic bags. They managed to get three packs into each bag.

"Is that Glenn Gould?" Leonardo asked.

"Yes," the woman answered. "Do you like it?"

"Very much."

"It seemed to me that the *Variations* would be the right music to play while rereading Bernhard. My mother loves them too."

Elvira had thrust her hands into the pockets of her trousers, which were velvet and stuck closely to her thighs and buttocks, revealing the musculature of a walker. She had high breasts.

"I'll be off now," Leonardo said, embarrassed by what he was noticing.

In the courtyard they stopped in front of the gate that opened on to the lane. Leonardo put on his cap. The falling snow was very light, but he could feel it touch his cheeks. Elvira was in a sweater. The heavy sky could hardly hide the luminosity of midday.

"Thank you so much," Leonardo said, "and again, excuse me for coming at such a time."

Elvira shook her head.

"I'm glad you came. Now we know each other, we'll be able to meet for a chat sometimes."

"Yes."

Before he went into Elio's house, Leonardo stopped to look at the backdrop of houses covered in white snow round the square. The silent, motionless village seemed beautiful in a way that only seems possible for things which have nothing to do with humankind.

In the evening, when he was sure the children were asleep, Leonardo went into the lumber room and took the box of letters out of his suitcase.

He spent half an hour sorting them according to the dates on their postmarks. Those he had posted before the trial were missing, evidently because the lawyers had advised Clara to keep them as evidence to be produced in court. Even so, those returned to him from the first year were more than a hundred. One every three days. During the second year they had diminished to seventy or so and in the last few years to not much more than twenty.

When he had finished doing this he put a log in the stove and boiled some water. He drank his herb tea leaning against the window. The new year had arrived, but he had heard no celebrations nor seen any movement in the village: only two people crossing the square with a saucepan at supper time. He had completely given up his plan to go and see Adele. The children had gone to bed early. Alberto had not gone out at all since they moved to the new house while Lucia limited herself to accompanying him on the short walks he took to attend to Bauschan's needs.

Leonardo looked at the letters spread over the table. The idea of reading them again had never previously occurred to him, but since leaving Elvira's house he had thought of nothing else.

He remembered a film he had seen many years before when he was a member of a jury at a festival. It had told the story of a widow who kept the urn containing her husband's ashes on her living-room table, the same place as where she sat and read, watched television, chattered with her women friends or made love with the elderly gardener. One day, for no particular reason, she had been seized by the idea of opening the urn and looking inside. She realized there was something not quite right in this idea and for the whole hour and a half of the film was torn between her urge to open the urn and the obscure inhibitions that held her back. In the end, giving in to temptation, she discovered that her grandchildren had long been using the urn as somewhere to hide the aniseed lollipops she gave them every Sunday.

The film director who headed the jury, ignoring Leonardo's positive vote, had dismissed the film as "slight". The winning entry had been a Spanish film about a seventeen-year-old drug pusher who, to escape some loan sharks, flees to Tierra del Fuego, where he climbs a mountain and starts a small ranch in the middle of nowhere. He marries a woman older than himself with only one leg and decides to import a couple of yaks from Nepal. To pay for his journey to go and fetch them he mortgages the ranch and bets the parish priest of a nearby village that he can succeed in bringing two such animals all that way, keep them alive and above all get them to reproduce. In the end the boy wins. Throughout the film Leonardo had asked himself how anyone could live for years in Tierra del Fuego and then walk on the glaciers of Nepal in one single pair of trainers.

By the time he put the last envelope back in the box the church clock had just struck four. He went into the bathroom and spent a long time in the silence of the night on the toilet without managing to defecate, which is what he had thought he wanted to do. He was ashamed and surprised. He had always scoffed at other people's faith, both faith in reason and faith in the hereafter, and then like all the faithful had gone for years to the same place to recite the same litany to a God who did not want to listen to him or even hear him out. Boredom was what he had experienced rereading those letters. The same boredom as he felt faced with the genealogies of Old Testament prophets, or people who mistake persistence for devotion and blindness for perseverance.

When he came out of the bathroom, the dog looked at him as if to ask if he was feeling well.

"Let's go out," Leonardo told him. "A little fresh air will do us both good."

They walked round the square. Under the moon the open space looked like a new sheet and both were afraid of soiling it. The sky, furrowed with great storm clouds, bore no relation to the season.

A figure appeared at the corner of the square. Leonardo recognized Adele's walk and called the dog to stop him barking. The woman approached, cutting across the whiteness of the square. When she was near, Bauschan ran to sniff her feet which always smelt of chickens, dog and camphor. Her cheeks were red with cold and she wiped a drip off her nose with her sleeve.

"I like coming into the village at night," she said with such simplicity that Leonardo found nothing strange in it.

For a while they talked of the cold and about one of Adele's hens that was laying eggs with brown yolks. When she had exhausted these topics, she asked Leonardo if he was tired or sleepy. Leonardo said no.

"Good," Adele said, "because I've got important things to say to you that I won't be able to repeat."

Leonardo kept his gaze on her calm eyes.

"You must get strong shoes and warm clothes for yourself and the children, because you're going to have to do a lot of walking and it's going to be very cold."

Leonardo looked at the surface of the snow which the night frost had turned to crystal. A bird bigger than a sparrow, but smaller than a dove, was sitting on a cable above them. The bulk of the church rose above the roofs, both imposing and somehow ephemeral.

"As soon as the roads are clear I'm taking them to Switzerland."

Adele shook her head.

"Get yourself good shoes, you won't get far with the ones you're wearing now. And watch that boy."

Leonardo realized his hands were numb with cold. He put them in his pockets.

"Why should I watch him?"

Under the high black clouds Adele looked like a small talisman carved in wood.

"Because there's evil in him."

He dreamed he was climbing the stairs to his old apartment. Not his home with Alessandra, but where he had lived as a student, in the mansard roof of a building without a lift; a block of flats from the 1970s overlooking the river and a factory that made laboratory instruments.

Even so, as he climbed the stairs, he had known it was Alessandra and Lucia he would find at home waiting for him. In fact, in his bag he had a present for the little girl who would be four the next day: a book in Dutch. He had bought it in Nijmegen, where he had gone for a conference on Dostoevsky and where he had skated on a frozen river which linked seven towns that participated in a competition. This contest was eagerly awaited all year long, as used to be the case with the Palio of Siena and the Pamplona bull run. He also seemed to have spent several nights with a blonde woman with a thin body and big buttocks, but he could not be certain this had happened even though he could smell her sex when he sniffed his fingers, a scent unpleasant yet also attractive, like a shirt spread out to dry in a lightless place. None of this bothered him; that evening, after putting the child to bed, he would talk to Alessandra. For some days she would refuse to make love, but that would be an entirely reasonable price for casting light on the matter, and he would pay it.

The stairwell was cold and badly lit, but he knew every step of the way and was not at all disturbed by the fact that he had already been climbing for several hours. Rather, he felt rested and free from anxiety, entirely confident that he would very soon arrive at the entrance to his home, a door like all the others, with no name on the bell, no umbrella stand and no doormat. An anonymous door facing the landing, identical to the hundreds of others he had already passed, but he would recognize it.

For this reason he was not disturbed by the cold air rising from below and bringing with it small dried leaves, or by the man he could see behind a bathroom window on each landing. As he passed the window, the man, busy shaving or engaged in some sort of irremediable action, would turn and fix infinitely tired eyes on him. Leonardo knew that he was shaving with his left hand because he had just come back from a war in which he had lost both his right hand and a childhood friend. He had himself buried his friend, digging the grave with his only remaining hand. He had dug it at the foot of a hill from where his friend would have been able to see a group of *izba* log cabins round a mill. Then Leonardo climbed on and forgot everything until he reached the next landing, where a man shaving with his left hand was waiting for him behind a bathroom window. Hearing him climbing the stairs the man turned and looked at him with infinitely tired eyes. Every time Leonardo looked away to continue climbing the stairs it occurred to him that there was nothing about the man which reminded him of his own father, though it was almost certainly him.

He was woken by Lucia calling from the kitchen.

"What is it?" he asked without pushing back the bedclothes.

She did not answer. He dressed in a hurry and, without putting on his socks, came out into the corridor.

"What is it?" he said again, entering the kitchen.

"They've gone into the grocery shop."

"Who?"

"I don't know. Four of them."

He went to join Lucia at the window. The snow on the square was opaque and still. It must have been nearly noon. The only signs of life were a few smoking chimneys.

"Are they local people?" he said.

Lucia shook her head. She was staring at the square like a child watching a dying animal, afraid to bat an eyelid for fear of missing the secret of the moment of death. Leonardo raised a hand to smooth his hair, but a shot rang out, stopping him abruptly. Nothing moved in the square.

They heard a second shot, then a third, causing the window to vibrate a few centimetres from their noses with a sound like a fly trapped between the pages of a book. Then four figures hurried from the shop and headed for the road leading out of the village from the far side of the square. They were in heavy jackets and hats, but Leonardo could tell from her walk that one was a woman. They were carrying shopping bags.

By the time Norina's husband came out on the balcony they had reached the middle of the square. Wearing blue overalls, he watched them struggle through the snow for a few seconds then, as casually as if taking a comb from his pocket to tidy his hair, he raised his rifle and fired.

The first man collapsed face down on top of the bag he had been hugging to his chest. The woman, behind him, tripped over his legs and fell. As she struggled back to her feet, another shot hurled her back a couple of metres. Her hat fell off and long red hair spread like a handkerchief round her face.

Of the two remaining men, one kept running but the other stopped beside the woman. He did not bend over her or pick up any of the things strewn on the ground, but just gazed intently at her. When he had enough he put down the bags he had been carrying in both hands and slowly turned back towards the shop. After a few steps he took a pistol from his jacket pocket and began firing at the balcony where Norina's husband was reloading his rifle. Leonardo saw a spark as one of the bullets hit the rail but Norina's husband took no notice. When he had finished reloading, he closed the rifle, pointed it at the man who was by now some twenty metres away, and fired. The man's head exploded like a pumpkin hit by a stick and was scattered about, forming a coloured semicircle on the snow. His body continued to stand for a moment as if unable to believe what had happened, then bent double at the pelvis and fell, burying its neck in the snow. Anyone arriving at that moment would have thought they were in the presence of a penitent who was required by some ritual to spend part of the day meditating with his head buried in snow.

Norina's husband lowered his rifle and studied the three bodies in the square; they were lying apart in different but equally bizarre positions, like three letters spelling a word. The fourth intruder had vanished, but a few seconds later shots were heard some distance away, then silence. Norina's husband turned, leaving his wet slippers on the balcony, and went back into the house.

Leonardo looked at Lucia. A thread of saliva had appeared between her open lips and her eyes were still but without tension. He led her to the divan and made her sit down, stroking her hair until she took a deep breath and started weeping.

"Wait here," Leonardo said.

Leaving the room, he made for Alberto's room at the far end of the corridor. The boy was sitting on his bed staring at the whiteness outside. His window faced the back yard. He did not turn when he heard the door open.

Leonardo called him by name.

The child went on sitting with his back to him, his red shirt making his back look smaller. His hair was unkempt and his hands were resting with their palms upwards on his knees. Leonardo looked round the room: covers and clothes in disorder all over the place. It was only then that he noticed Bauschan.

The dog was stretched under the table with a jumper over his head, the sleeves knotted round his neck to prevent him getting it off. Alberto had tied his paws to the legs of the table with string.

"What have you done?" Leonardo said.

No answer.

Leonardo knelt down by the dog and freed his head. No sooner did Bauschan see the light again than he yelped and tried to lick Leonardo's hands. While untying the dog's paws Leonardo looked at Alberto and for the first time saw him smile.

Norina's funeral was delayed to give her husband time to find a coffin. The last one available in the village had been used for Achille Conterno and the only alternative was to make one from whatever wood could be found around the place. But her husband would not hear of it and set out early in the morning for A. in his off-road vehicle.

He came back late in the afternoon. Leonardo heard the car in the square, and getting up from the table where he was peeling potatoes, saw the Land Rover parked in front of the shop door. A large dark wood coffin was sticking out of the open boot, secured with a couple of elastic cords. It looked big enough for two people.

Next morning the bells rang out and some seventy people gathered at the church to pay their last respects. Leonardo looked for Elvira among them, but she was not there.

Studying the faces, Leonardo realized no children were present. Then he realized he had not seen any for a long time. Where were the young people? It was as if they had disappeared gradually without anyone noticing. The sound of motor scooters, the voices when the coach unloaded them onto the square on their return from school, their crabwise walk, their satchels, their smart clothes, their earphones; all these seemed images as far off in time as his own childhood. He felt a small pain between his shoulders, and felt he was very close to understanding something which required courage to accept and that offered no return to what had been before.

Realizing the distress it would have caused him to pursue this idea to the very end, he leaned back in the pew, vaguely sleepy. For a few minutes he drifted off into an innocuous beyond, an island in the middle of a river where holidaymakers and weekenders were picnicking in the fields, calling their children to come quickly and eat food they had spread out on chequered cloths. Several rowing boats were moving on the river, which at that point was as slow and still as a lake. The rowers were city men with sleeves rolled up to their elbows. Their companions and friends, female and male, were sitting in the bows looking at the vegetation on the banks and the peaceful activities of the holidaymakers. Several of the women were holding parasols. The voices that reached him were speaking French; French men directing French women and children playing French games. Through the leaves of a willow he glimpsed a motor car, one of the first, as elegant as an inkstand.

The smell of incense recalled him to the cold church and the seventy tired-looking mourners. Norina's husband was standing in the front row in his National Guard uniform, with his garnet-red beret, well-polished shoes and riding breeches, on his chest a medal as big as a breakfast cracker.

When Mass was over, Don Piero asked him to say a few words in memory of his wife. He walked with firm steps to the lectern, and declared in a loud clear voice that his wife had been the best companion a man could ever have and that he was proud of not having submitted to the crime with bowed head as most people did these days. Even when he lowered his voice to recall their habit of bathing their feet together in the same bowl each evening, he still glared disdainfully at the faces in front of him.

The coffin was so large it took eight men to carry it out of the church.

While the cortège was making its way to the cemetery behind Mariano's pick-up truck, Leonardo looked up at the windows of their home and recognized Lucia's pale face behind the curtains. He raised his hand and she waved back.

In the days after the shooting a veil of silence descended on their gestures, expectations and fears. They exchanged a few comments about food, about the books Lucia was reading and about the shower in the bathroom that was about to give up the ghost, but only as a way to avoid talking about what they had seen. Leonardo said nothing about what Alberto had done to Bauschan. They spent most of their time in the kitchen with the stove and radio. They ate what little food they had without complaint, washed themselves and their clothes, kept the fire burning and slept a little more than strictly necessary.

"We're dying," Leonardo told himself, replacing his hands in his pockets as they processed towards the cemetery.

On the way he heard that the evening after the murder there had been a long discussion between the parish priest, Norina's husband and the men who had killed the fourth bandit. Don Piero had maintained that the four intruders, though thieves and murderers, were not outsiders so a funeral should also be arranged for them; whether anyone attended it or not was another matter. But the others argued that the four should be treated the same as the outsiders shot in November.

Apparently the decisive opinion had been Mariano's, who had said he was not willing to have his car used to transport the thieves to the cemetery, and if the priest wanted a funeral, then he must bury them in his own garden himself. Faced with this, Don Piero gave way and the four were taken out of the village and buried in the forest before the ground froze at night. Papers had been found in the pockets of one of the men and the woman. They had been husband and wife and from a small village near V.

She had been a radiologist, he an artisan. The youngest carried no documents, but was probably their son since he had red hair like his mother. The third man may have been a relative or just someone who had joined their gang. He had no papers and his face had been disfigured by bullets.

Not much time was spent over prayers at Norina's interment. It was beginning to snow again and everyone seemed on the point of collapse from exhaustion and hunger. Three men, including her husband, placed a heavy slab of marble over her grave to close it, then her husband added a silver frame with a photograph of her and set off back to the village followed by the others.

Leonardo spent the afternoon in the kitchen listening to old songs and adverts for furniture manufacturers and car dealers on the radio. At about four he heard voices in the square and saw a dozen armed men gathered in front of the shop, all locals. When Norina's husband came out, they went with him on the road leading to R. and while the light lasted shots could be heard, only ending when dark fell and the group returned. The men went up into the flat over the shop and Leonardo could hear drunken singing till late at night.

Next morning the company came out at about ten and again stayed out all day. Leonardo carefully searched through the electronic croaking noises of the radio for a news bulletin, but in the end was forced to admit defeat. For a little he listened to a French station whose programmes had nothing to do with what was happening: there was a public phone-in on the suitability or otherwise of having sex with one's work colleagues: seventy per cent thought it would cause tensions and reduce productivity. For lunch they had cauliflower and potatoes. Neither Lucia nor Alberto showed any sign of noticing the explosions that reached them from time to time from the hills, but Lucia got up and switched on the radio which she had turned off as soon as she came into the kitchen. At the end of the meal they each retired to their own room.

Leonardo had a nap, brushed Bauschan and put some apples on to cook. While the pan bubbled on the stove giving off a fragrant steam he reread the whole of Flaubert's *A Simple Heart* and felt he was beginning to understand something of the woman's meekness in the face of pain and sorrow that he had never previously grasped.

That night he was woken by a smell of burning, and going out onto the balcony which faced north, he saw a huge fire on the plain, possibly in F. or a town of similar size.

In the morning he saw Norina's husband, rifle on shoulder, head for the hills. But he did not return in the evening.

Those with him on the previous days went out to look for him, but finding no trace, gave up the search. On Monday, in the presence of the priest, they forced open the locked door of the grocery and divided what was left on the shelves among the inhabitants in equal parts.

Leonardo's share was a packet of biscuits, a savoy cabbage, some mints, some prunes, a cheese past its sell-by date and some mahogany hair dye. Not seeing Elvira in the queue at the grocer's, he went to the lane where she lived.

They had tea together in the room where they had chatted before. Bernhard's works were no longer on the table, replaced by several books of poems and a catalogue of local nineteenth-century painters. Leonardo asked after her mother. She answered with her usual gentle smile that nothing had changed. They did not discuss the disagreeable events of the last few weeks in the village; Elvira simply admitted that she was aware of them, then they discussed two authors, one American and the other Chilean, that they had both much loved. For half an hour Leonardo talked about these books just as he would once have done when such things were a vital part of his life and the person he then was. As they chattered they ate some of the biscuits that Leonardo had brought and Elvira made a second pot of tea. This time the stove had been lit and a pleasant heat warmed Leonardo's right side and Elvira's left; she was wearing a cork-coloured jumper and her face looked rather more tired than the week before.

Then they talked about painters and Leonardo, listening to her, became convinced that if he had met her sooner the last seven years of his life would have been brighter. In their rare moments of silence they were

145

caressed by the *viola da gamba* of Jordi Savall.

Realizing it was getting late, Leonardo revealed the reason for his visit. Elvira said she was sorry, but that she did completely understand his decision. When they kissed each other goodbye on the cheek, Leonardo realized how soft her skin was and wanted to take her face in his hands. But he resisted the urge.

Alone once more in the street, he started for Adele's house, but as soon as he was out of the village he stopped. For about ten minutes he looked at the grey plain where leaning towers of black smoke were rising from burning villages and the air was full of tiny fragments of ash. The distant mountains seemed to be looking on with indifference.

After gazing at the mountains for what seemed a short time, but during which darkness fell, he turned on his heel and went back to the village.

For supper he boiled the cabbage and added some spaghetti to the same water, producing a sort of Vietnamese soup that the children claimed they could not eat. But when Lucia tried to put the cheese on the table he told her to leave it in the fridge.

"We'll need that tomorrow for the journey."

They watched him pour out the last spoonfuls of soup. When they realized he had nothing more to say, they dropped their eyes and hurried to finish what was left on their plates.

The only signs of life they saw in the first hour of their journey were smoke from the chimneys of a few houses and a couple of cars heading in the opposite direction. As he approached them, the man driving the first car slowed down to give them a long calculating look. Leonardo answered by raising a hand in greeting, but the man did not respond and the car vanished in his rearview mirror. In contrast, the second had been an ancient Fiat in metallic paint. Its middle-aged driver could have been a priest, or just a man who loved black pullovers and Korean-style shirts. There was an elderly woman beside him, and a single bed, complete with a mattress and a turquoise quilt, was tied to the baggage rack.

Leonardo often had to slow down and move into the other lane to avoid colliding with cars abandoned on the roadway. There were lorries too, their doors open and stripped completely bare. Some had been set on fire and reduced to black carcasses on which the white snow had settled as if in mockery.

The houses, sheds and bars lining the main road had open doors and broken windows, and looked to have been uninhabited for a long time. It was a cold, overcast day, but an occasional ray of sunlight filtered through the clouds and the rich brown of turned sods could sometimes be seen in the fields.

They had packed the boot tightly with two suitcases, a box of blankets, the radio, medicines, books and a bag with provisions to last several days. Leonardo had calculated that if he went no faster than 80 k.p.h. they would have enough petrol to reach M. Beyond there it would be at least another two hundred kilometres, during which he counted on being able to refuel. They would then head for Switzerland. Even though one of their permits was in Alessandra's name, Leonardo hoped to be able to cross the border with the children. Once in Switzerland, they would go to Basel, where Lucia had the address of some relatives of Alberto's father. They planned no further ahead than that.

After the ring road at C., they entered the main highway. On their right they passed the old foundry, which had been closed for fifty years already and was now merging perfectly with its surroundings. Alberto, sitting at the back, was gazing at the countryside and ignoring Bauschan curled up at his side.

"Stop!" Alberto shouted suddenly.

"Why?" Lucia said.

"A sheep!"

"Oh shut up," Lucia said. "We've only just started."

"You shut up! We must stop, I said."

Leonardo pulled over, and before the car had completely stopped the boy opened the door and got out. By the time Leonardo and Lucia followed, he and Bauschan had already rushed off, leaving a trail of footprints. The sheep was standing alone in the middle of a field, about a hundred metres from the road. Leonardo studied it from a distance to make sure it was real, then looked back at the main road disappearing towards the city. The city had once been his home and it was a long time since he had seen it, but looking towards it now he felt nothing.

"No-one seems to be about," Lucia said.

Leonardo looked at his daughter, smiled and nodded. The evening before, he had heard her weeping in her room. When he had come back from the garage, where he had been using new tape to fix the sheet of nylon that served as a car window, the girl was asleep. On her bedside table was a photograph of her mother and a notice for the door to say they had left for Basel and the Ritch family.

"Best not stray too far from the car," Leonardo said.

Lucia looked right and left as if about to cross a busy road, then jumped over the small ditch and went into the field. Leonardo followed.

In fact it was not a sheep but a long-haired nanny goat, tied to an irrigation pipe by a cord three or four metres long. The animal must have been there for some time because she had marked out a neat circle in the snow. Bauschan, stopping outside the circle, contemplated her with a thoughtful air. Alberto had already tried to approach her, but though showing no signs of fear, she kept moving with little jerks to keep out of his reach.

"Why have they tied her up here?" Lucia asked.

Leonardo studied the animal's black, brown and white coat. Her long beard looked like tow and her black eyes reflected the fluorescence of the snow. Behind her neck, right under her horns, she had been bitten by some animal, perhaps a small or elderly dog not strong enough to overcome her. Leonardo looked about; the shape of a farm could be seen in the distance. He calculated that it was much further from the farm to them than from them to the car. The surrounding plain, if you excluded the ditch by the road and a line of stumpy and graceless mulberry trees, offered no hiding place.

"We could set her free," Lucia said.

"What are you talking about!" Alberto exclaimed.

"You want to leave her tied up here? There isn't even any grass for her."

Alberto made a lunge for the goat which leaped sideways and bleated. Alberto slipped and fell on the mud, but immediately got up again, wiping his hands on his trousers. His shirt looked like a sort of short skirt under his jeans jacket.

"We've got to kill her," he said.

Leonardo and Lucia looked at him. There was something adult and cruel in his face.

"Is that supposed to be a joke?" Lucia said.

Alberto held his sister's gaze.

"We'll kill her and cook her, like Indians."

"What Indians?"

"Hunters in the forest."

"There are no forests here, and we have other things to eat."

"I don't want to eat other things, I want the sheep."

"But if we can't even catch her . . ."

"You must help me, we can catch her together."

"And then?"

"We'll kill her."

"Who'll kill her?"

"Leonardo!"

Leonardo looked at the boy who was staring at him with his upper lip slightly raised. It was the first time he had ever heard Alberto say his name, and it seemed a word full of angles.

"I'm not capable of killing her," he admitted.

"Not with your hands."

"Then how?" Lucia asked.

"With a knife."

"We haven't got a knife."

"Then we hit her on the head with a stone."

Lucia took a couple of steps towards her brother.

"You can't be serious!"

149

"I could do it, I'm not a bit scared."

Lucia pushed the boy aside and went towards the pipe where the cord was tied, but before she could get there Alberto flung a handful of earth at her.

"What's that you've thrown at me?"

"Shit!"

"Stop it or I'll slap you."

"Bitch! Black bitch!"

Lucia slapped him. For a few seconds everything was suspended, as if they were at the bottom of a swimming pool filled with formalin. Even the goat stood still and watched with slightly lowered head, apparently distracted by other thoughts. Then Alberto started running towards the car and after a few steps fell to the ground, thrashing about with his arms and legs.

They ran to him. Lucia knelt down and tried to hold him still and received a kick on the breast that knocked the breath out of her, but she finally managed to calm him, holding him close for several minutes. He was struggling for breath, his face marked with mud. He was not weeping. Leonardo, standing over him, became aware of a warm smell of urine and realized he had pissed himself.

"Come on, we'll get in the car now," Lucia said.

The boy allowed himself to be helped up and set off towards the car with his sister.

Leonardo and Bauschan, left behind, looked back at the she-goat. She was exploring the ground with her snout. She could probably tell the field had once been sown with *granoturco* or maize and hoped to find traces of a cob or two under the mud.

People think it's a plant the Turks brought us, Leonard mused as he tried to untie the knot restricting the animal, but the name is simply the result of linguistic confusion. In fact *granoturco* reached us from the Americas where the English called it "turkey wheat", i.e. grain suitable for turkeys to eat, but assonance caused the term to be translated into Italian as *grano di Turchia*, "grain from Turkey".

This reflection occupied him for the five minutes he needed to untie the tangle of wet cord, then, fingers numb with cold, he returned to the car.

Alberto was stretched on the rear seat; he had changed his trousers and seemed to be asleep. Before starting the car, Leonardo looked once more at the goat; she was exactly where he had left her and seemed to be gazing at the grey sky above the mountains as if waiting for a signal. Her leash was hanging loosely from her neck, like a permanent umbilical cord linking her to the earth.

They filled the car at a service station on the bypass.

Even though there were only two cars in the queue, this operation took more than an hour. The cars had to wait in a parking area at the side of the enclosure until a siren and an announcement by a man with a megaphone stationed on top of a small tower called them to the gate.

When it was their turn the gate opened and they drove into a narrow space closed on three sides. Then the gate shut behind them and the man on the tower ordered them to get out of the car, place their money on the bonnet, open both bonnet and boot and move back several paces.

Lucia gave Leonardo the banknotes; the man checked them through a telescope, then told the children to stay where they were. Lucia and Alberto put on their jackets. Once they reached an area marked by four yellow stripes a second gate opened and the Polar was allowed through.

The sum that Leonardo had to pay to fill the tank up would have been enough, a few years before, to buy a low-powered car, but it was obvious that in the last few months the money must have lost a great deal of its value. The man who served Leonardo had a pistol in a shoulder holster. Despite the fact that the right side of his face was missing, his look was alert and sharp. Even the men on the tower were armed. One pointed his rifle at Leonardo, while his colleague with the megaphone controlled the children in the narrow enclosed space.

Behind the corrugated iron hut, where the man operated the pump, Leonardo could see a full clothes line and behind that two toy cars and a plastic tractor. A family business, he thought.

"We're on our way to Switzerland," he said. "Have you any information that may be useful for us?"

The man looked as if he had been asked for details of his sexual habits.

"No-one knows anything," he answered.

Ten minutes later they were back on the bypass. They drove alongside several cars, but all eventually exited to the city and when they reached the entrance to the *autostrada* they found themselves alone again. The barriers to the tollbooths were open and there were several empty cars at the side of the road. One was a spray-painted Audi and Leonardo saw a body in it when he slowed down.

After a couple of kilometres he pulled over. It must have been about two o'clock, but no-one had a watch that still worked.

"Let's have something to eat," he said.

Lucia divided the cheese in three and Alberto, who normally bolted down everything as quickly as he could, began chewing with exasperating slowness. He seemed to be having trouble keeping his eyes open. On the other hand, Lucia seemed completely calm. The crackers were stale and insipid, but the cheese had a strong flavour. When they had eaten they went off one by one to urinate behind a container with German words on it, then resumed their journey.

They covered about eighty kilometres without seeing a human soul up to the exit to N., after which a barrier blocked the road and Leonardo was forced to slow down.

"What's going on?" Lucia asked.

"Just a checkpoint, don't worry."

Behind the barrier were three men in the uniform of the National Guard. Two of them were armed. When the Polar stopped, the tallest man approached, in an airforce pilot's helmet. Leonardo had to open the door because the nylon "window" was opaque.

"All get out, please," said the soldier.

He had several days of beard growth and yellow stains on his uniform.

"Our papers are in order."

"All get out, please," the man repeated.

While the man in the helmet opened the boot and rummaged about inside the car, Leonardo, Bauschan and the children formed up on a white line and were guarded by the second man, who looked about thirty and had a large tommy gun on his shoulder and his eyes fixed on the asphalt. A cigarette rolled from maize paper was hanging from his chapped lips. The third man, hardly more than a boy, had stayed behind the barrier. He had no hat or helmet, and his hair was a dazzling blond.

"Have you any money with you?" the man in the helmet asked after he had finished searching the car.

"Not much, we've just filled up with petrol."

"Bring it out."

Leonardo took out his wallet and asked Lucia for the permits. She held them out to him and he passed them to the guard. Meanwhile the young boy had moved the barrier and had gone to sit in the rear seat of the Polar. He was not armed.

"I have to take these children to Switzerland," Leonardo said. "Their relatives are waiting for them."

The man stuck the money into the pocket of his camouflage jacket and dropped the wallet and permits on the ground.

"Have the kids got anything?"

"No," Lucia said.

"If they have, they must give it to me," the man said, still addressing Leonardo; then he pointed the barrel of his gun at Bauschan. "If not, I'll start with the dog."

There was no anger or resentment in his words, even if he clearly must have experienced both in equal measure in the past. But his eyes were now like parched earth where grass had difficulty growing. Two large veins ran below his temples.

When Leonardo touched Lucia's shoulder she pushed a hand inside her trousers and pulled out a roll of banknotes. The man added them to the rest of the money in his pocket. His reddened eyes softened for a moment, perhaps remembering something, but quickly returned to their earlier blankness.

"We need your car," he said in the same expressionless tone he had used from the start.

Leonardo told him the keys were in the ignition.

Without another glance the men got into the car and started the engine. The man in the helmet said something to the one with the tommy gun, probably that it was an old car without automatic gears.

Leonardo took advantage of this by walking up to the Polar and knocking on the window with his knuckles.

"What do you want?" the man with the tommy gun said. His eyes were an intense cinematic blue but his teeth were those of a man from the Middle Ages.

"I'd like to ask a favour."

The man suddenly grabbed Leonardo by the ear and pulled it, simultaneously raising the window. When the glass hit Leonardo's neck, the man let go of his ear and smiled. Leonardo could smell alcohol on his breath.

"We haven't raped your daughter or killed your son. That's what you can expect these days, you know." Leonardo tried to nod but the edge of the window made it impossible. Behind him, Bauschan let out little yelps of distress.

"Please," Leonardo mumbled.

The man in the driving seat signed to the other to lower the window. Released from the pressure, Leonardo put a hand to his throat and gave a long sigh, but stood his ground.

"Thank you," he said.

"You must be stupid. What do you want?"

"There are things in the boot of no use to you but very precious to us."

The two men looked at each other, then back at Leonardo, who nodded as if to confirm his own words. The man in the helmet half turned to the boy behind him.

"Check what the bugger takes," he said.

The boy got out and tried to open the boot but failed. Leonardo asked if he could do it and the boy moved aside.

"It's defective," Leonardo apologized, raising the door of the boot and showing the boy the bag with Lucia's sanitary pants. The boy nodded that he could keep it.

"Can I take the clothes too?"

"Can he take the clothes?" the boy asked his colleagues.

"Only those for the children."

Leonardo took the children's suitcase, then removed the box of letters from his own case and opened it to show what was inside.

"Keep them."

"I'm sure you'll be able to use the food."

The boy said yes without asking the others.

"That leaves the jackets."

The boy took them from the back seat and gave them to Leonardo, closed the boot and was about to get back into the car but stopped. His face, despite his frozen nose now reduced to a black lump, still had gentle Teutonic features. The skin of his cheeks was peeling under his faint trace of beard.

"At the border they shoot at everyone," he said.

Leonardo smiled.

"We have our permits."

The boy shook his head and was about to say something more, but one of the others called him by name: "Victor."

Shortly afterwards the car vanished at the point where the grey of the *autostrada* met the more luminous grey of the sky. Leonardo looked at the children. Lucia was crying. Alberto had crossed his hands on his chest and was staring at the permits being blown open by the wind on the wet tarmac.

"Put these on," he said, holding out their jackets to them. "We'll make it."

They walked till evening along the *autostrada* towards T. in the hope of a lift, but in three hours or so only two cars passed. The first had only one person in it but didn't stop; the second, a white delivery van with blackened windows, slowed down and pulled up about fifty metres further on. Two men got out and beckoned to them.

"No, Papà," Lucia said.

The two men continued to indicate that they should come nearer. One, very fat, had a cowboy hat on his head. The other, taller, was in fur with black gloves.

"I don't like them, Papà. Let's not go."

Leonardo raised an arm to indicate they had changed their minds, but one of the two, the one in the hat, started towards them. It only took them a second to vault over the safety barrier and start running across the snow-covered field beside the *autostrada*, with their bags and the suitcase banging against their legs. They did not stop till they were sure the man was not following. Turning, they saw the van put on its lights and move forward again. A moment later it had vanished.

They spent the night in a nearby ruin, a house abandoned long ago when none of what had happened since was even imaginable. Maybe for this reason the desolation of this building was of a very different quality from the one they had most recently been concerned with: it had more the atmosphere of an ancient Roman temple and the children were happy to go in without making a fuss.

It had wooden floors and a falling tree had broken through the roof and its branches reached into a couple of the rooms. But they had left their matches in the car and had nothing to light a fire with, so they ate three sweets from the pocket of Alberto's jacket and crouched in a dry corner, out of reach of the snow that had gently begun to fall again.

"What are we going to do?" Lucia said.

"Go back home."

For a few seconds no-one spoke.

"I don't want to hitchhike," Lucia said.

"We can walk along the railway."

"It'll take a hell of a long time," Alberto said.

These were the first words he had spoken since the morning.

"Three or four days," Leonardo said, "but with any of luck we'll get a lift with someone we can trust. Feeling cold? Sit between me and Lucia."

"No."

"Then call Bauschan and keep close to him. He'll warm you up."

Alberto did not move and Bauschan stayed curled between Leonardo's legs. After a little they heard the boy's breathing get slower, broken by little hisses, and knew he was asleep.

"Papà?"

"Yes?"

"Can't you sleep?"

"Not at the moment. Are you cold?"

"My feet are."

"Is there a sweater in your case?"

"Yes."

"Then take off your shoes and wrap your feet in it, that'll warm them up."

He had read this in a story about gold prospectors in the far north.

"Better?"

"Yes, better now."

Leonardo looked at the patch of sky above them. There were orange reflections in it, as if somewhere nearby a volcano was erupting, casting a glow of lava on the clouds. An occasional snowflake settled gently on parts of his cheek unprotected by his beard. He was fifty-three and had never slept in the open before.

"Papà?"

"Yes, Lucia."

"You've been very brave," she said, taking his hand.

Leonardo closed his eyes the better to feel the perfection of her fingers.

All the next morning they followed the railway track. They could sense the regular geometry of the rice fields all round them, but apart from this the countryside seemed to have thrown off all trace of humanity. The occasional farms in the distance seemed deserted, and the only thing that passed on the *autostrada* was a tanker escorted by two army vehicles. Only once, nearing a village, did they see a house burning and some men moving round it in an attempt either to put out the flames or feed them. Lucia made it clear she would not go near it in any circumstances and

Leonardo, convinced deep down that she was right, kept straight on.

At midday they sat down on the track and ate the last of the sweets. The snow they melted in the palms of their hands only made them thirstier and the surrounding whiteness was starting to blind them. Alberto's eyes were red and had begun to weep.

Leonardo promised he would go and look for something to eat at the first farmhouse they came to, leaving them to wait for him beside the railway. Neither Alberto nor Lucia raised any objection.

By the time they came reasonably near a farm it was late afternoon and the light was beginning to fail. The children watched Leonardo put the suitcase on the ground, climb down the railway embankment and set off across a field with Bauschan. They sat on the track with their hands in their pockets to protect them from the cold wind that had got up, and gazed after Leonardo till they could no longer distinguish the brown of his jacket from the blue of his trousers. Seen from a distance, with his long grey hair blending with the white ground, he looked as if he had no head, according to Alberto. Lucia told him he was talking nonsense, but secretly she was ashamed because she had thought the same.

The building dated from the early twentieth century when trains brought rice workers to the nearby stations from where they would be transported by cart to the farms. It was typical of the farms in the district, even if it must have later been converted by someone whose work had no relation to agriculture. The yard had been paved and there was no trace of the machinery and other odds and ends normally to be found on a working farm. The store had become a garage, while large glass windows had been added to the upper floor, revealing an interior of wood and brick. It looked like the home of a painter, sculptor or art critic. This explained the statue in the courtyard, a work in concrete and fibreglass two metres high that represented two embracing bodies, but could equally well have been an enormous fossil shell or a D.N.A. helix.

Leonardo could find nothing edible anywhere in the house.

He searched every drawer, box and container; there was only one small tube of condensed tomato that had already been nibbled by mice. Nothing else. Otherwise the house seemed in reasonable condition with its beds in place, its roof solid and its windows intact. It was certainly very cold, but there was a large fireplace in the ground-floor living room, and when he found a cigarette lighter behind the radiator in the bathroom, he began to think that they might be able to sleep there for the night and light a fire.

Walking down the stairs he imagined that the person who lived there there must have smoked secretly in the bathroom, perhaps an adolescent, or a sick person forbidden to smoke by his doctor. He tried to imagine the voices of the people who could have lived in the house. But they seemed remote and painful and he decided to stop.

He was about to leave when he noticed the door to the cellar. Unlike the other doors it was blue and closed. His mind filled with images of salami, wine, preserves and everything else that had to be kept in a cool place rather than close at hand.

He opened the door, throwing light on a downward staircase. He just had enough time to recognize dark streaks left by something that must have been dragged, before a powerful acid stench of decomposition hit him from below, forcing him to close his eyes and step back. When he opened his eyes again he was facing the blue door which he had instinctively closed. Until then he had associated blue doors with Greece or Provence, but from now on for the rest of his life they would remind him of that stench and what it must conceal.

He had got most of the way back to the railway when he noticed Bauschan was not with him. His first thought was that he must have gone in through the blue door before he closed it. He imagined the dog imprisoned in the putrid darkness.

"Bauschan!" he called, his voice echoing across the fields like a blow from an axe. He was about to call again when in the semidarkness he saw a shape come running from the farm gate, disappear behind a hedge and reappear in the field. Bauschan must have sensed a note of reproach in his master's voice because he slowed down in the last few metres, and would not allow himself to be touched until he had circled once or twice round Leonardo's legs, with his ears down, as if to beg for an audience. His back was cold, but his throat was still throbbing from his race. He must have been eating something because his breath smelt of vinegar.

"Did you find anything?" Lucia asked from the top of the embankment.

Leonardo showed her the lighter.

"Nothing else?"

"Nothing else," he said, climbing up the embankment.

"You're pale."

"You too. Because we're hungry. And it's very cold. We must find somewhere before dark and light a fire. Now that we can do that."

"Was that house not alright?"

"No, it wasn't," Leonardo said, picking up the suitcase.

Lucia must have understood because she took the bag of sanitary pants and headed down the track. She had only gone a few steps when she turned to her brother.

"I've found something," Alberto said.

"What?"

"Come and see."

They went towards the *autostrada* which was now almost invisible in the dusk. Alberto was walking diagonally across a field. They could detect the rustle of *granoturco* stubble under the snow. When they reached a deep irrigation channel, Alberto stopped and pointed at something in the ditch. Leonardo climbed cautiously down the snow-covered bank and studied the few centimetres of frozen water covering the bottom: imprisoned in the ice were pieces of corncob flung to the edge of the field by the combine harvester.

"Well done," Leonardo said. "Very well done."

That evening they heated the *granoturco* they had managed to retrieve on their fire. Alberto had hoped to make popcorn, but the cobs were so sodden they would only roast or turn into a mush resembling polenta. The place they had found for the night was an old hut belonging to the water board, on which some graffiti artist had drawn the impertinent face of a small boy with a cigarette stuck in the corner of his mouth. The place consisted of a single room crossed by a spider's web of pipes of various sizes. The sheet-metal door had been forced and the place had probably served as a refuge for others like themselves: the concrete floor had been insulated with rubbish and cardboard against the cold, and on the whole they could consider themselves lucky that it was clean and not too damp. It also had a high window through which the smoke from their bonfire could escape, leaving the air breathable.

Before lying down to sleep, they talked about how many kilometres they must have covered that day, and how clever Alberto had been to find the maize. The boy was the first to fall asleep, while Leonardo and Lucia stayed awake for a long time listening to him tossing restlessly and dreaming he was quarrelling with someone to whom he then tearfully apologized.

When Lucia also crashed out, Leonardo spent some time watching the fire, feeding it from time to time with more wood. He would have liked to leaf through a few pages to make him sleepy, but all his and Lucia's books had been left in the Polar, so he took the box of letters out of the children's suitcase and reread a couple. This had the effect of annoying him profoundly and he was tempted to throw the lot on the fire, but he did not do this because he had to concentrate on holding back his tears. In fact, he now felt sure for the first time that both Clara and Alessandra must be dead and that he would never see either of them again. He imagined their bodies tossed into some field with their clothes ripped apart, their trousers round their ankles and a parliament of crows conferring nearby.

He gave way to heavy tears, then dried his face and went on weeping in a more controlled manner. In the end, exhausted, he slept deeply and dreamlessly till morning.

As soon as he woke he lit the fire and moved the stale maize near to heat it, then went out to stretch his legs. It might have been seven o'clock, perhaps eight, and the day was going to be fine and very cold. The sky was a uniform blue and the light reflected from the snow was already blinding.

He sat on the railway line stroking Bauschan and removing several thorny burrs the dog had collected from the brambles he liked to bury himself in. He talked to him about writers who had written stories with snow as an essential feature and Bauschan gazed into his green eyes, until distracted by a noise from the cabin.

They had breakfast round the fire. Alberto had woken up with encrusted eyes, a sign that his conjunctivitis was getting worse, but they had nothing to clean them with. After eating his portion of maize, Leonardo wandered round the cabin for half and hour looking for a container in which to boil snow so as to get some more or less sterile water, but all he could find was an empty plastic bottle. After walking on for two hours they came across several carcasses of cows in a plantation of poplars beside the railway and stopped to look at them without going near. The cows must have been dead for some time because their stomachs were swollen and the black patches on their coats had faded almost to grey. Even so their mouths and eyes seemed to be moving. On closer inspection it became clear that the effect was created by several small birds hopping on the animals' faces. Leonardo and the children made the most of the break by taking off their jackets and tying them round their waists, then went on without discussing what they had seen.

Before noon they reached a group of houses. As on the previous day, Leonardo went off alone to inspect them and came back an hour later with a saucepan and a small bag with a little flour in it.

"We'll boil some water," he said. "Then you can wash your eyes."

Alberto said neither yes or no and went to sit a little way off on the rails. He had grown much thinner in the last two days and his legs seemed to be dancing inside his trousers like pencils in a sock. He had a red rash round his mouth that he continually scratched.

Leonardo lit the fire. This was not difficult as brushwood, ideal for starting bonfires, was growing beside the track.

As soon as the water boiled he dipped his handkerchief in it and took it to Alberto who, asking no questions, cleaned his eyes. Leonardo used the rest of the water to mix with the flour, using the suitcase as a work surface. The result was a round greyish mass that he put into the pan and left on the fire for five minutes, before stirring it and putting it back to cook for the same length of time again. The yellow disc that emerged was christened *"focaccia"*. They all ate a piece, even Bauschan. Lucia asked if they could make another. Leonardo said yes, but that they should only eat half now, leaving the rest for supper. Lucia nodded and smiled. Her face was magnificent: the sun and the cold had given it colour and her eyes had never before looked so warm and deep.

While fiddling with the fire to try and keep it burning, Lucia saw two people.

"Someone's coming!" she said, getting up.

Leonardo put down the pan and studied the figures approaching along the railway track. If we can see them, he thought, they must see us; there's no escape."

"We need to discuss this," he told Lucia who was collecting their things.

"But we don't know who they are!"

"If we want food, sooner or later we'll have to trust someone."

By now the two figures were more substantial. Leonardo was sure one was a woman in red.

"I say let's avoid them," Lucia said.

Leonardo turned to Alberto. The boy was using his hand to shade his eyes from the sun as he looked at the two people.

"What do you say, Alberto?"

"We've seen some dead cows in the fields," Leonardo said.

The man shook his head as he continued to stir the soup on the stove. Beans, cabbage and large pieces of grey meat could be seen in the pan. The smell was hot and inviting.

"This is good meat," he said, licking the spoon before returning it to his shirt pocket. "We had some yesterday evening." Then he signed to the woman to bring the plates. Until now she had restricted herself to gazing tenderly at Lucia and Alberto, but now she put on the ground the three metal plates she had been holding on her lap.

"It seems to us," the man explained, as he poured soup onto the plates, "that the planes are dropping some substance onto built-up areas. I have no idea what it is, but it's certainly not harmful to humans; I'm a doctor and I haven't noticed anything strange. It only has this effect on cows. It's extraordinary the way game and birds are proliferating."

The woman handed them their plates. The children thanked her and began eating. Leonardo balanced his on his knee and looked at the people walking about round them, about thirty of them. Twenty more were sitting with their backs against the wall of a large shed enjoying the sun. The building that was their home was in the middle of nowhere and had probably been a warehouse used by men working on the high speed trains. Even when they first arrived no-one had come up to ask them who they were, where they came from or where they were going. Those who crossed their path limited themselves to a disinterested glance.

"For two weeks we had terrible weather," the woman said. "It never stopped raining or snowing. But look what a glorious day today."

Leonardo nodded. She must once have been attractive, but her body seemed to have suffered much more than her husband's from recent events. Her double chin seemed unrelated to the rest of her tall, slender figure.

"Have you been here long?" Leonardo asked.

The man smiled. He was obviously well over fifty, but still had a slim athletic body. Seeing him approaching in his vest with his pullover tied round his waist, Leonardo had thought he might be a former tennis professional or yachtsman, but he had introduced himself as Doctor Barbero, a dermatologist.

"A couple of months already," the doctor said, "but only a few days more. Signor Poli, who owns this place, is getting permits for us."

"For Switzerland?"

The man and woman exchanged a smile.

"They won't let anyone into Switzerland anymore," the man said, "but Signor Poli has good contacts in France. His wife worked at the embassy."

Leonardo put the first spoonful into his mouth.

"My compliments," he said. "This is excellent."

"Thank you, but I can't claim any credit for it. It wasn't my turn in the kitchen yesterday."

For a few minutes they ate in silence, watched by the couple. The two were sitting on a little wooden bench they had carried out of the ware-house when they had gone in to fetch the food and the small stove. Leonardo and the children had freed several sleepers from the snow near the railway and were treating them like the lowest tiers of a stadium. Bauschan was sitting comfortably at their feet. Several of the people walk-ing round the building were now going back into it. Leonardo had noticed that no-one had gone more than about twenty metres from the building and that there were no old people among them. He had also noticed that some were smoking real cigarettes.

"Do you think it would be possible for us to spend tonight here?" he asked, putting down the spoon on his empty plate.

"I think it might be," Barbero said, "but you'll have to discuss it with Signor Poli. He comes at about six to bring food and whatever else we've ordered. He also leaves two armed men here for the night: security's included in the price."

"May I ask the price?"

"Five hundred per person," the doctor said. "Chocolate, tuna, tea and specialities extra. Gas canisters –" the man indicated the little stove – "are also extra. On the other hand heating and water are included. There are two showers and they heat the water two days a week. Compared to the rest of life out there that's a four-star hotel, don't you agree?"

Leonardo smiled back, but he thought it odd the man had not said "five-star"; why had he not automatically pushed the hyperbole to the limit?

Rhetorical exaggeration had always fascinated him. Once he had flown to New York to attend a conference organized by a famous Jewish-American writer who was soon to die of a tumour. This man, who had always previously been known for his reserve and modesty, had asked his press agents to invite five hundred writers from all over the world – a list personally drawn up by himself. He wanted to give a final conference for these five hundred colleagues, and admit no-one else other than a journal-ist he played golf with once a week, a Peruvian girl working on a thesis about him, a boy from Cameroon doing the same, plus his barber, his present companion, and a classful of children from the elementary school in the suburb of New Jersey where he had lived since childhood.

The conference was held in a Broadway theatre that had long been closed but which the writer had reopened at his own expense. This had surprised many people, since one of the most reliable rumours about him was that he had been stingy to a maniacal degree. Before the keynote speech, fixed for 8 p.m., a small buffet was on offer, so minimal that it was restricted to white wine in cartons, Mexican cheese, and pineapple. To administer these refreshments two middle-aged ladies, possibly the writer's neighbours, had been recruited. One poured the wine into glasses while the other looked after a soup tureen containing a strawberry-coloured liquid which gave off balsamic fumes.

That night, in his room in the large cheap hotel where the writer had quartered his guests, Leonardo had grieved for the imminent death of this short, pockmarked and unusually talented man. He had assumed that despite everything he had written, despite his hard-won style and the acuteness with which he had been able to thread words together making them resound like lines from Homer; that all this would be completely forgotten. The memories of those present at the conference would not be enough, and even the notes he had seen some people taking during his magnificent lecture on hyperbole, ranging from the lowest to the highest, like Glenn Gould playing Bach, would be lost in minds packed with their own stories and appointments, soon reduced to the condition of an aquarelle left out too long in bad weather.

"Would you like some more?" the woman asked.

"Thank you," the children said.

Signora Barbero filled their plates again, then put her hand on her husband's shoulder as she stood watching Lucia and Alberto beginning to eat again. She was wearing velvet trousers, a beige broad-stitch sweater and red moon boots with white laces. Her husband had a check shirt with sleeves rolled up to the elbows and trekking trousers. Everyone Leonardo had seen there had been wearing warm, well-made clothes.

"Are many people staying here?" he asked.

"About sixty at the moment," the man said. "But ten left last week. Their permits arrived just when they were about to run out of money."

The woman noticed Leonardo had finished his soup so without saying anything she took his plate and filled it again with what was left in the pan. A couple of people were still leaning against the wall; the rest had gone in. The sun had set very quickly, as happens in winter.

After another spoonful or two Leonardo put his plate on the ground and Bauschan quickly came to lick up what was left. The doctor touched his moustache without trying to hide mild disappointment, but his wife smiled and placed her hands on her heart.

"The little one," she said, "he was hungry too."

They spent a couple of hours resting on the camp beds of the doctor and his wife. These were military pallets, but after several nights on the floor they seemed very comfortable. As always, Alberto was the first to fall asleep, then Lucia, while Leonardo lay listening to the voices reverberating inside the warehouse roof. Some of the guests were lying on their beds, while others were in what Signora Barbero called the "daytime area", that is to say the two tables where they ate their meals and could sit on a dirty sofa and a few armchairs, pretending they were in the hall of a great hotel, or the waiting lounge of an airport, or more intimately, in their own homes. Everyone talked in a low voice so as not to disturb those resting or to save energy. There were also a couple of small children, one breastfeeding from his mother. The other, a three-year-old, seemed to be alone with his father.

"Papà?"

Leonardo turned. Lucia was looking at him from the next bed. She had one hand under her head and the other by her side. Apart from her eyes, she now seemed in every respect a full-grown woman.

"Do you think we'll be able to stay here for a while?"

"Maybe tonight, but tomorrow we'll have to go on. We have no money."

Lucia slipped a hand under the covers and pulled out a bundle of banknotes folded in two.

"Where did you hide those?"

"Same place as the others."

"If they'd searched you . . ."

"Would I have had to hand them over?"

Leonardo looked at her without knowing quite what to say about the two possibilities that came to mind.

"Would you like to stay?"

"They seem respectable people. Alberto says he'd like to stay too."

It occurred to Leonardo that "respectable people" must be an expression Lucia had picked up from her mother's second husband. For several days now Leonardo had been feeling a deep, if (to be fair) unjustified, resentment of this man. A sentiment he was ashamed of, but which made him feel alive. I'm getting wicked, he thought, and I've come a long way down that path.

"If we can, we'll stay a few days," he said.

"If we have enough money, we can stay."

"Are you hungry?"

"Not now."

"Alberto?"

"Asleep. We must get him to wash."

"Tomorrow, O.K.?"

"O.K."

While the central-heating pipes were starting up, they heard the sound of a car approaching.

Signor Poli was a man of primitive appearance, short-legged and with dishevelled grey hair. He had a suede jacket open on his prominent stomach, a green pullover and jeans that puckered just below his knees. On the whole, he could have passed as a shepherd used to spending long solitary summer days in mountain pastures, or the proprietor of an engineering workshop with little in the way of formal studies to his name, but an innate talent for getting others to work.

The two tall young men with him had submachine guns on their shoulders. They were not Italian, but not outsiders either. As soon as he saw this, Leonardo remembered that the man's wife had been employed at the French embassy and he felt as if he were hearing one of the more cacophonous passages in Debussy.

Poli told his men to unload the provisions from the van and pour a couple of cans of diesel into the generator, then leaning back against the door of his Land Rover, he pulled a notepad from his pocket. A queue of about ten people had formed in front of him.

Calmly, and without lifting his eyes from the pad, he made a note of what each person wanted, took their money and put paper and pencil back in his jacket pocket. Only when he had done this did he light the Toscano cigar already in the corner of his mouth and look up at the stars. By now only Leonardo and Barbero were still before him.

"Signor Chiri arrived here today with his two children and would like to stay for a few days."

The man contemplated Leonardo's bedraggled appearance.

"How old are the children?"

"Seventeen and ten," Leonardo said.

"That'll be one thousand five hundred a day. Have you got the money?"

Leonardo nodded.

"You pay at least three days in advance. No one-night stands."

Leonardo pulled out two banknotes. The man took them and gave him five hundred in change.

"Do you need clothes?"

"I could do with a pair of trousers and a sweater."

"I'll bring them tomorrow. That'll be another five hundred."

Leonardo gave him back the banknote.

"Interested in permits? Fifty thousand each, but I could try and get a 'certificate of travel in the company of a parent' for one of the children."

"I'm afraid your charges are too high for us."

The man took the cigar out of his mouth and spat something onto the ground.

"How are things going with our permits?" Barbero asked.

"A couple of rubber stamps still needed. A matter of days."

The man's face was like a lump of turf cut by a spade. On his feet were strange moccasins with leather tassels.

"Signor Barbero will tell you how things work here," he said. "I have to go now, I've got a long way to go."

"Of course," the doctor agreed.

When the internal light came on in the car, Leonardo noticed clothes thrown untidily on the seat and a small road map. The man started the engine and swerved sharply round the open space and onto the unmetalled driveway leading to the fields, leaving behind the van in which the two armed men had come. They were nowhere to be seen; they may have still been filling the generator, or have taken up sentry duty over the warehouse. The air was still and clear, with thousands of stars. Hearing a rattle of pans from inside the building, Leonardo missed the two nights he had spent in the silence and solitude of the countryside. He had never felt any fear. The rear lights of the Land Rover turned the powdery snow red as its big wheels disappeared into the distance.

"I must thank you," said Barbero.

"What for?"

"For not saying you met us on the railway."

"I don't think I understand."

"We're not supposed to go so far from the warehouse. We were enjoying a little elopement today, if we can call it that. Community life can be inconvenient and every so often a couple needs a little privacy. I think you will understand."

"That seems reasonable to me."

"Good, I have a small flask of cognac. How about we share a drop?"

"I would happily, but I'm a teetotaller."

The man went on staring at the point where he believed Leonardo's eyes to be. A strip of light escaped from under the warehouse door.

"It'll do for another occasion then," he said, "but now we'd better go in. I wouldn't like the guards to mistake us for intruders."

The next morning they had their rations of bread, margarine and tepid tea at one of the two tables in the day room.

Waking late, they had found most of the guests in front of the baths waiting to use the hot water. The Barberos had been among the first to use the facilities and had then gone for a walk round the building in the cold air to greet the morning.

When they came in, Signora Barbero said good morning to Leonardo and kissed the children on the head. Barbero, sitting down beside them, asked them if they had slept well. Leonardo said he had been disturbed by the baby crying and Barbero assured him it was merely colic, common enough in males of that age, and one had to be patient. Leonardo took advantage of the occasion to ask him about the problem with Alberto's eyes. Without examining the boy, the doctor diagnosed conjunctivitis. An antibiotic would have solved the problem in a couple of days, but with none available, the best solution would be camomile compresses.

Alberto accepted this diagnosis with utter indifference. His eyes seemed to have lost the cold ferocity Leonardo had seen flash in them and were now observing everything with apathy. It was not even necessary to insist on a shower. He washed on his own without complaining that the water was only tepid, after which he and Lucia, but not Leonardo, changed their clothes, and all three sat close to the central-heating radiators to dry their hair.

Lunch was frugal: pasta with chickpeas and boiled onions. The smell, the metal plates and the large pots and pans the food was cooked in gave them the impression of being in a resolutely Franciscan monastic settlement. Leonardo went out to give Bauschan an onion and a little pasta taken from his own ration. The dog devoured it in an instant. A minute later the Barberos joined them for a walk round the outside of the warehouse. It was a clear, windy day, though not limpid like the day before, and dark clouds from the Alps threatened bad weather.

"It's the thirteenth of January today," Signora Barbero said.

In the afternoon Leonardo slept for a couple of hours, then went to find Signor Rovitti. This man, introduced to him by Barbero the evening before, looked after the keys to the electricity generator, the heating panel and the food store. Leonardo found him snoring on his pallet, but no sooner did the man hear him approach than he opened hare-like eyes.

For a while they discussed subjects of which Leonardo knew nothing: how to insulate large buildings of this kind, how to manage food resources, and the importance of regular timetables. Rovitti was one of those men who like to show off knowledge others do not have. Barbero had told him that in his younger days he had been the head of a private school, while his wife had managed a fashionable tennis club by the Po which had counted footballers, industrialists and female television celebrities among its members. Finally Leonardo asked him if he could possibly have a camomile teabag. Rovitti said there were none in the food store, but he could order some from Poli that evening. And if necessary, given the confidence, even friendship, he boasted with Poli, he would remember to put in a good word for Leonardo.

Leonardo thanked Rovitti and went for a stroll round the warehouse. He took care not to tread on the many objects by the beds. There were no wardrobes or cupboards and everyone had arranged their possessions under and around their beds as best they could. Some were asleep, some reading and some playing cards, but all seemed to be keeping conversation to a minimum, as if afraid of reading something embarrassing or shameful in the looks or words of others.

At about seven, Poli came back with the men who were to guard them. One was a young man whose shaven head he had noticed the day before, while the other was a very tall man of about forty with a thick neck and a tattoo on the back of his right hand.

Leonardo joined the queue in front of the Land Rover, and was given the clothes he had asked for. The jeans were padded and warm, but the sweater was threadbare and shapeless. He asked if next time they could have camomile teabags. The answer was yes. He paid and went back into the warehouse where he put on his clean clothes. Lucia said they looked good on him.

Supper was potatoes and cheese, and once the tables had been cleared, some people started playing bridge. The match went on for two hours during which neither the players nor those watching said a word. At eleven Signor Rovitti announced lights out in five minutes, and everyone retired to bed.

Leonardo was woken in the middle of the night by the sound of footsteps. He assumed someone was going to the bathroom, but in the weak moonlight filtering through the skylights he saw two male figures circulating among the beds. He recognized the guards and thought they must be looking for something to steal, but they stopped beside a pallet and woke the person sleeping there. It was a woman, and she got to her feet without saying anything and moved towards the exit escorted by the two men. Leonardo heard the door slide on its rail and close again. Someone coughed somewhere in the warehouse.

Leonardo got out of bed and put on his shoes. Bauschan raised his head, but Leonardo quietly told him not to follow and the dog obeyed.

Outside there was no more than a very slender sickle of moon, but the sky was clear and the snow reflected what light there was. There was no trace of the clouds he had seen in the afternoon or of the wind that had brought them.

He moved stealthily towards the van parked a few metres from the warehouse, but there was no-one in the driving seat, and even when he put his ear to it he could hear no sound from the interior. He walked on along the wall with the intention of going all round the building. He did not know exactly what he was doing or why. The countryside was peaceful and still, so much so that he could hear his footsteps squeaking on the snow, a sound at once reassuring but worrying. He felt like a bird that knows it must break the shell of the egg that has been its only home, even though it has no wish to do so.

Walking along one side of the shed, he heard a noise from round the next corner. A mechanical sound, like something rubbing or scraping. Putting his head round the corner, he saw them.

The woman was on her feet, leaning with her hands on a pile of railway sleepers stacked against the wall, her trousers round her ankles. The older guard, his trousers round his knees, was penetrating her from behind. The young baldheaded one was sitting on a sleeper watching the scene and smoking, his own gun and his colleague's beside him.

Leonardo felt cold in the pit of his stomach and wished he had never left the warehouse.

The man extracted his penis, which appeared enormous and livid in the shadows, and tried to insert it higher up, but the woman pulled away. He placed a hand on her chest to pull her towards him but she twisted away, saying no. Then the young bald man got up, calmly took out a knife with a blade no longer than his index finger and slowly drew it across the woman's cheek. She screamed and put her hands over her face, and in doing so lost her balance and fell against the sleepers.

The older guard continued to stand there in the night, his great penis pointing at the woman like a grotesque inquisitorial finger, while the one with the knife waited a moment, perhaps to give the woman time to feel the cut and the blood running warm through her fingers, then he grabbed her by the hair and pulled her to her feet. While the other sodomized her, the young one held the knife to her throat, but with his gaze on the countryside, as if nothing interested him except the steepling mountains far away and the livid blue painted on them by the moon.

Leonardo felt weak in every part of his body and wanted to fall on his knees and call out a familiar name, but he did none of this.

When the older guard had finished, the young one handed over the knife and took his place. Leonardo drew back, and walking as if on pieces of broken glass, reached the door and went inside.

Back in bed, he listened to his heart beating at a crazy rate, wishing he could have been dead or crippled rather than proving himself incapable of stopping what he had just seen. He desperately wanted to wake Lucia and hold her close to himself, or at least to watch her sleeping, but felt unworthy of it. He was sure the shame would be with him for ever, night and day, and with the same intensity, because he would never be able to stifle it or sleep again.

When he woke in the morning his heartbeat was normal, but he felt great acidity in his stomach and realized that during the night a little urine had escaped him. He had no change of underpants, but waited his turn for the bathroom and washed carefully. During breakfast he kept his eyes on his cup. Lucia and Alberto were discussing Alberto's claim that his eyes were feeling better and that he would no longer need the compresses; an irritatingly strident note had returned to his voice.

The woman came in when everyone else had left the table. She could not have been much more than thirty, and had long, smoky-blonde hair. She had covered the wound on her face by tying a handkerchief round her head like someone with toothache. She sat down cautiously, and with reddened eyes studied the crockery and cutlery on the table, the bread and the margarine, but had trouble concentrating on anything for more than a moment. In contrast, her hands when she poured tea into her cup were firm and steady. Unlike Leonardo's hands when she asked him to pass the sugar.

"But why?"

"Because I think it's best."

"So you've already said, but why?"

"We'll have to go in a few days anyway. Better to keep the money. We may need it."

"But we have nowhere to go."

"We can go home."

"But it's not our home. And anyway, how long will it take us to get there? And we haven't even got any food."

"I've had a word with Barbero. They'll sell us a little of their own supplies."

"When did you speak to him?"

"After breakfast."

"So you made up your mind before talking to me!"

Leonardo looked at the bottom of the basin Lucia was leaning against. The bathroom had seemed to him the only place private enough for this inevitable discussion. Bauschan watched with his head round the door. He knew he must not come in.

"Please trust me when I say it's best for us to leave at once."

"No, not unless you tell me why you've changed your mind."

Lucia's blue jumper neatly fitted the outline of her shoulders and small breasts. She could have been an actress in a French film. Leonardo gave her a long look. He was afraid he could not find the words to tell her what he had seen that night, but nonetheless he did manage it, though in a partial and hesitant manner. Lucia listened in silence. As he went on her mouth took on an increasingly bitter twist, but her eyes never left his.

"You'll never let anything like that happen to me, will you?" she said when he finished.

They packed the suitcase in a hurry and collected their things. They told Alberto they could not stay another night because their money was finished; he sat on his bed and followed their preparations without moving, after which Leonardo secretly got Lucia to pass him a banknote or two and went to join the Barberos outside the building.

When he told them they were about to leave, the woman said she was very sorry because she had grown so fond of the children. Leonardo explained the children wanted to get home because their mother could be there waiting for them, and Signor Barbero offered to sell them something to eat on the journey "at the same price they themselves had paid for it". Leonardo accepted his offer and followed him into the warehouse, while his wife went to say goodbye to the children.

"Last night I saw a rape," he said while Signor Barbero was extracting from under his bed the case in which he and his wife kept their tinned food and biscuits.

The man looked at him with the half smile of someone who has not understood.

"That's not possible," he said, but something not quite frank distorted his mouth.

"Do things like that happen often?" Leonardo asked him.

Barbero looked down at the provisions, chose two tins of tuna and a packet of chickpeas and put them on the floor together with a box of *grissini.*

"We can't give you more than this, I'm afraid," he said. "We'll need the rest for our journey to France."

Leonardo stared at him. The vein pulsing below his temple was the only evidence that he was alive. Otherwise he face was waxen, his eyelids motionless.

"Do you really believe anyone who leaves this place ever gets to France?"

The man continued to stare at the contents of the suitcase. His lips were pressed hard against his teeth. Leonardo took the tins and packets and thrust them into the pockets of his jacket. He stood up and Barbero did the same.

"Will five hundred lire do?"

"More than enough." Barbero took the banknote.

When they were about a hundred metres from the warehouse Leonardo and Lucia turned; Alberto, ahead of them, walked on. There stood the grey warehouse, dominating the flat white nothingness. The sun of the last few days had melted the snow on its corrugated iron roof. Only Signora Barbero was watching them.

"What'll happen to that woman from last night?" Lucia said.

Before leaving, Leonardo had gone to the bed where the woman was resting.

"I saw what happened," he said in a low voice. "If you like you can come with us."

She merely shook her head, hiding her face in the pillow. The man sleeping in the next bed could have been her husband.

"Never mind," Leonardo had said.

Signora Barbero raised her hand for one last goodbye, then turned and went into the warehouse. Leonardo and Lucia turned their backs on the building and resumed their walk. Twenty metres ahead, Alberto and Bauschan looked extraordinarily tall against the flat horizon of the rice fields. Leonardo's feet felt wet and he noticed one side of his right shoe was coming unstitched. He transferred the suitcase to his other hand and tried to avoid the patches of snow between the railway lines. Many thoughts were passing through his mind. Thoughts of death, unworthiness, courage and how far one could change one's own nature. Not thoughts that could bring him any relief, but he knew he must think them through. Nevertheless in one small corner of his mind there was room for the small pleasure of being alone again with the children and Bauschan, and of walking in the silence of a land that had never been walked on before. He tried to hang the portrait of his life on that fragile nail, a life that had never before seemed so miserable and inept.

Part Three

I found this exercise book three days ago and took it because I've recently developed a habit of collecting everything I find. My priority is food, clothes and anything to make our lives easier and safer. But sometimes I happen to go into a home and see a divan, a chair in good condition or a picture or a set of hand-painted plates with cockerels in rustic style, and my first impulse is always to keep these objects. This is impossible, besides being pointless and dangerous, but when I leave them behind I feel real regret, as if they always belonged to me and I've been forced to abandon them.

As I was saying, I found this exercise book three days ago. My first thought was to give it to Lucia or Alberto or use its pages to light the fire. I wasn't thinking of writing. Or perhaps I was. The fact is that, when it happened, I was confused and frightened because of what had taken me to that house, which is to say my shoes.

Recently I tried to repair them with sticky tape, but they had become so worn out that they were coming open all round and my right foot was at risk of frostbite. They were not suitable for the long walks we are forced to make. I've calculated that during the last week we've covered thirty kilometres a day.

We keep well away from towns and metalled roads. We know well enough that they are best for finding food, shelter and perhaps some means of transport, but past experiences have made us mistrustful. It is the children who are most afraid. So we walk on cart tracks and over fields, in the snow and along railway lines. My shoes haven't stood the strain. A friendly woman warned me to find stronger ones, but I didn't listen. I thought things would work out differently.

That is why, after a night spent in a hut in the forest three days ago, I left the children in a small clearing and took the dog with me into a village we had been able to see since the previous evening. The day before we ran across two cars parked in front of an abbey. As we approached, we saw a large bird inside one car and it began beating its wings against the windows. There were three bodies inside the car. They had been there a long time, but it was easy to see that they were a young couple and a small child. Lucia ran away in terror. When I caught up with her she was pale and trembling, and I thought she must have a fever because she was so hot. It was the first time I had seen her out of control in that way. Meanwhile Alberto had opened the door and the bird, perhaps a blackbird, had flown away. While I was hugging Lucia I saw him take a battery from the dashboard. I shouted at him not to touch anything. He obeyed, but as if he hadn't heard me and it had been his own decision. I don't know who or what may have been in the other car. We hurried away, almost running.

Next morning the village seemed completely deserted; the closed houses showing no sign of having been raided, as if the people had simply gone away before anything happened. This was not necessarily a good sign, so I told the children to wait for me in the clearing.

When I reached the square I looked for an open door, and not finding one I forced one that had seemed more fragile than the others, using an iron bar I'd collected a few days earlier in a railway depot. Even now it's in my jacket pocket. It's the nearest thing to a weapon I've ever had. It makes me feel secure, though I know I could never bring myself to use it against anyone.

The place seemed to have been the home of an elderly woman, or of two elderly women, because there were two single beds in the same room. There was a bath with two handles and in the bathroom cupboard medicines for diabetes. The house had not been trashed, but everything else had been removed. Bauschan sniffed at a basket where a cat may have slept. I called him and we went to look for another door.

It is extraordinary how easy it can be to effect a break-in even for someone weakened by hunger, exhaustion and little aptitude for manual action, like me. This is one of the few resources I've managed to discover in myself at this time. A discovery that gives me little comfort compared to the irremediable losses that every day brings.

I found what I was looking for in a flat on the second floor of a newly redecorated block. The man sitting in the armchair looked as if he had dozed off while contemplating a wall papered with photographs, postcards and small maps.

The only dead bodies I had seen before last summer were those of my father, an old aunt, a Latin scholar and my mother. Only in the last case was I present at the moment of death. My mother had been a practical woman, composed and not much inclined to frivolity, yet her exit had taken place with the lightness of fresh air replacing stale in a well-aired room. My impression as I watched her last breath, and the immobility that followed, was one of delicate inevitability. Something like the closing or opening of a flower. The darker feeling that came over me beside her lifeless body had been one of nostalgia; I believed no-one would ever love me unconditionally again. I would never again be able to make someone happy with so little effort. What a pity.

The bodies I have seen recently affect me quite differently. Their lives have not slipped away, but been snatched from them. Not like a child's milk tooth, that after dangling for days drops out to make room for its successor, but like healthy teeth needlessly ripped out with cold forceps and no anaesthetic. I can't get used to seeing these bodies and I am always disturbed by them.

For this reason I immediately looked away from that man sitting in his armchair studying the opposite wall. The small maps traced the stages of many itineraries, probably journeys he had made with the young woman featured in the photographs. The maps were recent ones, with the surrounding countries shaded grey and neither their borders nor their cities marked.

I looked at the man. He was short and fat, with a thick black moustache and a large mole under his left eye. When I approached, the mole flew away and I realized it must have been a fly.

Apart from its pallor, there was nothing unseemly about his face. The bullet had entered his temple cleanly. The hand holding the pistol had fallen back on the arm of the chair, while his other hand was decently covering his genitals. Only one earpiece of his glasses had slipped off.

I carefully took off his right shoe and measured it against my own: size forty-three. I put it back on him and I went to look for a more robust pair. Some hiking boots in the lumber room fitted me. There was also a camping stove, a sleeping bag, water bottles, a rucksack and fishing equipment. I took the rucksack and filled it with whatever I thought might come in useful, then went to look for food.

The larder contained flour for making polenta, freeze-dried soup, some bars of muesli and powdered milk: more than we had eaten for a week. I gulped down one muesli bar and gave another to Bauschan, who had not eaten since the previous day.

In the bedroom a dozen exercise books with hard covers were piled on a desk. The man had used them meticulously to record means of transport, times of departure, alterations of travel plans and places visited. He had also stuck in vouchers, air and rail tickets, and photographs featuring the young woman from the living-room wall with an open, friendly smile.

It was not easy to imagine the two meeting and beginning a relationship.

She looked like a woman open to new things who needed a certain dose of unconventional romance. He, until he met her, must have been a man who had happily survived the usual time of life for passion unscathed. Someone who had probably found in his work, and his love of fishing, ample justification for his existence, just as I had been satisfied with books, teaching and parenthood. But we had both made an error of judgement, and this realization had at first seemed a miracle. Though in the long run, in different ways, we had both paid for it.

I was rummaging in his drawers when I found the unused exercise book I am now writing in. Without a second thought I shoved it in the rucksack together with some underpants and socks and left the house.

Writing had once been my profession, in the sense that I had been technically defined as a novelist, but that was now closed behind a solid wall in the distant past. What had first got me started had probably been the need to create a world on my own modest scale, a world of relationships, meetings, public gardens, shops, memories, gestures and feelings that I could inhabit without feeling inadequate, just as I did in the real world. "Stories of courage always come from the basest part of ourselves, poetry and profundity from the most arid part," in the words of an elderly writer I happened to meet early in my career. I know now it was his way of putting me on my guard against the path I was beginning to follow.

Now for eight years, apart from several unanswered letters, I have not written a single line, but that hasn't stopped me still living in a world of books, both my own and those written by others. Continuing to cut myself off from life.

Now death, fear, cold, hunger and the children I am responsible for have forced me to return to real life, and the world I have found waiting for me is far more ferocious and degenerate than the one I ran away from. How did we come to this? Did the evil germinate in our hearts or have we been the victims of infection? And in either case, how can the germs have fallen on such fertile ground? I can't offer a single word of explanation. I simply wasn't there.

Days earlier we had left a warehouse where we had been well received; a place that at first had seemed safe, but had soon shown itself quite otherwise, and after a day's walk we had reached the outskirts of T. We decided to circle the town to the east rather than the west. I had been convinced of this by the sky, always clear in the east but blotted out by great grey clouds to the west.

Passing some hills, we ran into a pack of dogs. The setting sun perfectly outlined their shapes on some high ground. At first I took them for horses, they were so still and solemn. We were walking into the wind so they had not yet scented us.

Lucia and Alberto slowly began to retreat. Even Bauschan stopped. Whereas I continued down the cart track, my eyes fixed on those animals so sharply silhouetted against the indigo of dusk. A moment later, as if responding to a trumpet call, the dogs turned their heads towards me and, starting from a gentle trot rushed down the hillside at full speed. The pack dodged the trees and reformed like drops of water attracted to its own substance.

Magnificent, I thought.

Only then did I notice Lucia was calling my name. I turned. The children and Bauschan were about fifty metres behind me. They had reached the gate to a farm. Only then did I understand and start running.

Thanks to a wooden ladder we were able to climb up to what had once been a hayloft. A few seconds later the dogs entered the farmyard and stopped, panting, to look at us. They showed neither disappointment nor ferocity, but it was clear that if it hadn't been for the ladder they would have torn us to pieces.

The children threw a few tiles in an attempt to drive them away, but the dogs merely moved to avoid being hit. After a while a few crouched down. Others went to drink from a pool of melting snow. Two copulated.

We ate supper with our legs hanging down and the dogs watching us. It was very cold, but with hay around it would have been dangerous to light a fire. Bauschan stared at his fellow creatures and whimpered. He knew we were trapped.

"Go away, *merde*, you shits!" Alberto shouted, but all I could think was that they were perfectly adapted for what they had been created to do. And to me that made them piercingly beautiful.

During the night, listening to Lucia shivering with cold beside me, I realized I was utterly unsuited to the task entrusted to me, and wept. When we woke in the morning, the dogs had completely vanished.

As I write this, Sebastiano is watching me from the divan with Bauschan stretched out at his feet, stroking him as if polishing a violin. He's a tall man with a long thin face. I have been familiar with this house for many years, it is where I used to come for massages from his mother.

When we arrived this morning we found Sebastiano in the kitchen, his cowhide over his shoulders and his suitcase ready packed. I don't know how long he had been there. He certainly didn't seem surprised to see us.

I greeted him, then asked him who had reduced the village to such a state and where everyone had gone. He didn't answer. Then I asked him where Adele was.

He gave me a serious look, as if the answer must be utterly obvious. Then he took me to the room where her body was stretched on the couch, sewn into a sheet as used to be the custom in these parts. When I asked for an explanation, he pointed to a note on the bedside table. It had been written by Adele.

You refused to take any notice of what I said about the shoes, now stop being so stupid. I was perfectly happy to die; it was time and I had other things to think about. Dig a hole under the hornbeam and leave the children indoors so they don't catch cold. If you can't do it, just forget it. I haven't been able to dream clearly whether you still have your hands or if you've already lost them. But whatever happens, don't let anyone even think of burning my body. Do as I ask, then head for the sea. Take Sebastiano with you, you'll find him useful. Best wishes for the future.

This afternoon I was digging her grave under the hornbeam when it began to rain. It was like a summer storm, so much water came pelting down. Sebastiano helped me carry the body to the foot of the tree, then he went in, and he and the children watched from the window as I filled in the hole. I had never before even dug a trench, yet it seemed as natural to me as accepting a plateful of food from a neighbour and giving back the empty plate the next day washed and clean. While I shovelled that earth so heavy with rain, I thought a lot about my mother.

Then we all rested for an hour or two and dined in silence on soup and cheese.

Now the children are sleeping in Adele's double bed, and soon Sebastiano will go up to his room. I shall stretch out by the stove on the divan, with Bauschan on a towel I've laid out for him nearby. Tomorrow we have to get everything ready for our journey. It's unbelievable how long it takes to make preparations when you have nothing. Tomorrow morning I shall go into the village. I must find a small map and some eye drops for Alberto.

21 January

The village looks as if it has been hit by a retreating army blinded by hunger and defeat. Everything that could not be carried out of the houses has been smashed or burned. A lot of furniture has been thrown out of the windows into the street, and on the outer walls are graffiti in spray paint or charcoal. "It's us / you can't avoid / even if you want to / or else look out." "I can't sleep, I can't sleep, I can't sleep and I'm in grief." "Wings, needles, ideals and bonfires." "Supremacy." "Nothing comes of nothing." They were like lines written by someone who has glanced through Nietzsche and then decided he's too much trouble. The writing is in large shaky capitals, with errors of grammar and syntax. Some are slogans in basic English, as if written on a school excursion that got out of hand. I also came across syringes, empty bottles of strong drink and nylon bags into which some-one had poured what looked like glue. In the church the pews have been piled up and set on fire and windows broken.

There's no trace of the inhabitants or even of their bodies. All I found was a cat feeding four kittens. I heard them mewing from the road and went into what used to be the hairdresser's salon. Jars of cosmetics had been overturned and an enormous penis drawn on the mirror. The cat was sitting in the armchair where customers once waited their turn. When she saw Bauschan she hissed without moving so as not to disturb the kittens' feeding. Bauschan pressed himself against my leg. He seemed sorry to have caused any distress. I picked up a bottle of what looked like shampoo and we left.

At the chemist's house I found eye drops, but no food. Whoever had turned the house upside down can have had no interest in medicines because these had been left all over the cellar and attic. I helped myself to some preparations for the relief of influenza and inflammation as well as some vitamins. In the car in the garage was a map of the Côte d'Azur which also included this part of Italy.

When we passed back through the square, Bauschan stopped in front of Elio's house and looked at me. The note on which we had written that we were leaving for Basel was still on the door. When I saw it I was moved to pity, as if for something from my earliest childhood. I stroked Bauschan and told him it was no longer our house, then turned to go where I had wanted to go from the start.

The gate had been torn off its hinges though one of its uprights was still chained to the post that had been uprooted with it. The door of the house had suffered the same fate.

What a lot of trouble they've gone to, I thought.

The table where we had talked over tea about Glenn Gould, Marin Marais and early eighteenth-century painting was lying sawn in two among books, pots and pieces of foam rubber. Flour had been strewn on the floor, but there was a smell of game in the air as if a large wild boar had been living there. Two cushions had been ripped apart and were hanging from the chandelier.

Climbing the stairs to the upper floor, I noticed my heart beating fast and realized I had never listened to it properly before. The bedrooms were a mess and an item of clothing or curtain had been burned in the bath but, as I had hoped when I went into the house, there was no trace of either Elvira or her mother.

I picked one of Bernhard's books up from the floor then, before leaving, went into the garage, sat down in the red car, lowered the seat and closed my eyes. On the back seat was a dressing-gown belt. I dozed for a few minutes and dreamed I was stroking the prominent vertebrae of Elvira's naked back. My dreaming hand moved clumsily, not like caressing a woman, more as if running along a railing. Yet what I was doing gave me great pleasure and I knew it was the same for her. The nape of her neck was moving gently. I felt sexual excitement. Something I had not expected from my body for a long time.

Then I walked through the village streets. The children and Sebastiano were waiting for me, but all I wanted was to feel the weight of Bernhard's book against my leg as I walked.

In the old house I used to spend hours in a room I called "the book room". A place where I had collected thousands of novels, essays, treatises and books on art. I had read many of them more than once, underlining, annotating and dissecting them to extract instruction for myself and my students. Some had become bastions to shore up the walls of my city, and others had served as passports to my far-off lands. Syllogisms of what life was or should have been.

I haven't the slightest wish to know what has happened to them. Unless someone has burned down the house I assume they are still there feeding mould and mice. I have infinite love for those stories, although I know they have been to blame for what I am: an inadequate man.

22 January

Lucia and I have divided the food and clothes between my rucksack, Sebastiano's knapsack and a small bag the children will take turns to carry. We have made an omelette with four eggs and some polenta. When we have eaten that, we will still have the soups, the powdered milk, the muesli, some tins and the fruit in syrup we found in Adele's larder. These will last us for a week at least.

When we had finished getting ready we sat down at the table. Alberto and Sebastiano had gone to their rooms, and the gentle breath of the wind that had been pushing around the tops of the trees all day could be heard from beyond the windows. There were no animals around: I presume the chickens, geese and rabbits that had once lived in the yard had been eaten, while the dogs must have gone off in search of food. The donkey could have met with either fate.

I asked Lucia if she was sleepy. She said no. So I put another piece of wood in the stove. It could have been nine o'clock. The church clock no longer strikes and we've grown used to telling the time by the course of the sun. In any case, once the sun has gone down the time is not very important since all we can do is to find a place to retire, light a fire and sleep.

Lucia told me she and Alberto had quarrelled while I was in the village and said some very ugly things to each other. Hearing this, Sebastiano had taken refuge in his room and they hadn't seen him all morning.

"I went up to see how he was," she said. "I wanted to apologize to him but he put his hand on my head in that way priests do."

"Were you afraid?"

"No. It felt like being inside an egg, then I got sleepy."

I am surprised anew, every day, by how she manages to live through all this without losing her grip. By the fact that her first impulse is always to create order, to heal and to work for the best. Despite appearances, there is nothing fragile or dreamy about her. Lucia's a soldier: her sweetness is pugnacious and her gentle eyes have more of justice than charity in them. She's a Joan of Arc without visions or armour. A delicate asphodel protected by spiky leaves that not even starving animals can manage to devour.

When I asked her why she had quarrelled with Alberto, she told me he would rather not have gone away again. I asked her if she felt the same. She said no. When I asked her if anything else had been involved, she shook her head, got up and planted a kiss on my forehead and went off to bed.

*

It very soon became clear that walking through the vineyards and woods, as we had planned to do, was impossible and cost us the whole morning. In fact, the snow was already above our knees and an hour after starting out we had to stop, light a fire and wait until our shoes and trousers dried out. When we set off again it was after midday and we decided to take the main road. The snow has almost completely gone from it and even where it remained we saw no trace of tyres. The houses along the road are empty and the few shops already stripped bare, and we saw no smoke or anything else that might indicate human presence. Only towards dusk did I think I saw two figures in the woods but by the time I asked the others whether they could see them, they had already vanished round the corner of the hillside. Apart from that, the mantle of white is marked by many animal tracks but no human ones.

When the light began to fade we looked for somewhere to spend the night and light another fire; there is plenty of wood, and we have matches, paper and a certain expertise. Lucia is better at lighting fires than I am. She doesn't use so much paper and lays the twigs in a way that encourages the flames to leap up quickly. In this too she shows her aptitude for learning and her love of things well done.

It only took us a few minutes to devour the omelette and some of the polenta. We'll reheat the rest tomorrow morning before we leave. I showed the children the map. It should take us two days to reach the pass leading down to the sea. I've calculated five days' walk altogether. When Alberto asked why are we going to the sea, I said with a bit of luck we might find a ship, or else we can follow the coast to France. To tell the truth I don't know how many opportunities we have to leave the country in one way or another.

Alberto took my answer with indifference, going back to where he'd left his cover and lying down to sleep. In any case these were the first words I'd heard him speak since the morning. During the day he walks without complaining or asking questions. When he raises his eyes and looks ahead, he does it as if he has already made the journey any number of times. Sometimes he seems like an old man. Times when the young body that contains him seems nothing but a joke in bad taste.

Today, seeing him sitting with his head between his knees, I felt tempted to reach out and stroke his hair but, as if he knew what I had in mind, he looked up and glared fiercely at me for so long that I thought he would never stop. His eyes were two mirrors of restful brown water that seemed to have something terrible in them. At night I feel he must be awake and staring at me, but if I wake with a start I see him wrapped in his blanket, breathing deeply in his sleep, his eyes sealed by little yellow crusts.

Sometimes the silence round us is so profound I find myself longing to meet someone to rescue us in some way from our solitude and uncertainty. Often I move away with the excuse of needing to attend to my physical needs and spend a few minutes weeping, crouched among the trees. Sebastiano can't help me. I'm not even sure he's fully aware of our situation.

The only thing that cheers me is that for the moment the cold has stopped tormenting us. The sky is overcast and even at night the temperature doesn't fall below freezing. The sun may warm us for an hour or two, but once it has set, we have to face much more severe nights.

The place where we are camping now is an old road-maintenance building. Its façade is the colour of burgundy, divided in two by a broad white stripe that separates the lower floor from the upper. It has a sharply sloping roof, in the Nordic style. None of its windows face the valley, which means it cannot be easily seen, and what windows it has are covered by wooden shutters that prevent the glow of our fire filtering through to the outside world. Features I've learnt to value.

24 January

On the first afternoon we were walking halfway up the woods that entirely cover these hills, following a path formerly used by shepherds and mushroom hunters, keeping one eye on the road a hundred metres or so below us, when a voice from behind us ordered us to raise our arms above our heads. We did as we were told. I heard a rustle of dry leaves as the man approached, until he came into sight on my right, a metre or two above us. In the cold shadow his face looked severe. He might have been thirty-five years old, with long untidy hair. He placed himself in such a way that he could keep all four of us within range of his rifle, then asked us what we were doing there.

I said we were heading for the pass and our plan was to go down from there into Liguria. The man looked closely at the baggage on our shoulders and asked the children if they were with me of their own free will. Lucia said yes.

"You too?" the man asked Alberto.

The boy must have nodded because the man slightly lowered the rifle which up to then he had been pointing at my chest.

"Have you any medicines?"

"What sort of medicines?" I asked.

"Something for fever."

"I think so."

"Please check."

I took off the rucksack and opened the side pocket where I had stored the medicines. While I checked the instruction leaflets, Bauschan went over to sniff at his feet. The man let him do this.

"I've got an antibiotic here, and this is some kind of aspirin."

"They'll do. Throw them over to me."

I did as he asked. He picked them up and stowed them in one of the many pockets of his hunter's jacket. He had mountaineering boots on his feet. He seemed well fed and equipped.

"Now go," he said.

We stood looking at him in uncertainty.

"Which way?"

"Leave the path and go down to the road," he said, indicating the way for us with his rifle, "It's not far to G."

We began going down through the forest. Brambles and brushwood sometimes forced us to change direction and climb back up. On one of these occasions I looked up and saw the man still standing where we'd left him. He had lowered his gun, but was still watching us, as though pondering what he might have done but hadn't done, or the other way round.

Once we reached the road we walked on in silence until the trees behind us formed a thick curtain. Then I announced that we could stop. I pulled out one of the two bottles of water we carry and passed it to the children. They drank, their eyes still on the forest. I told them that if that man meant us any harm he would already have done it. Lucia nodded, but just as she did so I saw him reappear among the acacias at the end of the field.

We stayed sitting motionless on the safety barrier, staring at him as he approached. When he was about ten metres away he stopped, put his rifle over his shoulder and looked towards the sun which was disappearing behind the hills. I noticed his face was sunburned and clean shaven. His eyes were a peaceful hazel colour.

"I can offer you food and shelter for tonight," he said.

During the half hour we walked behind him he never spoke or turned to check if we were following. When he got to the top of the hill he went down the other side, crossed a stream and made his way to a house in the middle of a small clearing. A woman was waiting on the terrace. When she saw us she lifted her hand to her brow as though the sun was in her eyes. The man greeted her. She did not respond but went back into the house.

"That's Manon," the man said.

"I'm Leonardo."

"I know."

Manon had cooked a piece of deer and greens for supper. These seemed to be the herbs we had seen her washing earlier in the sink. There was home-made bread too, and a dessert made with milk and cocoa. Manon's fair hair had been given a basic cut. She is of Dutch origin and at first sight her beauty looks banally Nordic, but once you take in the exact colour of her eyes and their almond shape one feels one is in the presence of something religious. She and Sergio live in this house with their two sons. The elder, Salomon, is eight and has his mother's fair hair and his father's taciturn nature. The younger is called Paul but he is out of sight upstairs with a fever.

Their house is half Alpine hut and half farm. Its walls are stone and the lintels of the doors and windows are made of wood, but the rooms have high ceilings and are well lit. The house uses solar panels to produce electricity and has a wood-burning boiler, and the rooms are well heated. Before supper we were able to have a shower and rest in the room where we will spend the night.

In the bathroom I was afflicted by another fit of weeping. I had not seen myself naked in a mirror for a long time: in the last few weeks my body has become leaner, my shoulders broader and my back straighter. My leg muscles are again like when I used to run ten kilometres or so every day as a student. The whole effect is of a tired man who has grown several years younger. A tense, nervous man such as I have never been before. Lucia heard me sobbing from our room and asked if I was alright; I said fine, I'm just singing.

When they came to call us for supper I woke Alberto and Sebastiano who had fallen asleep on mattresses on the floor. Sergio waited at the door for us to put on our shoes, then asked if we were doing anything for Alberto's conjunctivitis. I said we had some eye drops and asked if he was a doctor. A vet, he said.

During supper no-one said very much. Sergio and Manon do not want to know where we have come from or where we are going and why. Nor did they ask us about the world round us in general, nor talk about what life was like before and what the future may hold now. Clearly, having guests is a new experience for them. This was obvious from the way Salomon studied the children during supper, as though until yesterday he had thought himself the last child left on earth.

While Manon was washing up, Sergio whispered something in her ear to which she replied in the same manner, then he told me he wanted to talk to me and we went out on the pretext of taking something to eat to Bauschan. I had realized at once that they preferred to have the dog left outside, so this is what I had done. They keep no animals in their house or yard. Not far from the main building is a wooden shed that I think Sergio must have built. As we walked round it I noticed the humming of a freezer coming from it. I think it must be their larder. Its door is secured with two large locks.

We sat down on the terrace steps. The air felt very cold and one or two stars could be seen in the sky. It was only then that I noticed the windows were sealed so that no light filtered out from the inside. If I had moved a few metres away the only way I could have found the house again would have been by bumping into it. Hearing our footsteps, Bauschan came up to us. Sergio offered him the piece of meat we had saved for him.

"Are you still teaching?" Sergio asked.

"No, I left my job eight years ago."

"To concentrate on writing?"

"Not entirely. I got caught up in something disagreeable. You probably heard about it."

"I've been living here for ten years. We have no television or radio and don't read the papers, so I've no idea what you might have been up to."

"Were you one of my students?"

"I was."

"What course were you on?"

"The one specializing in Leopardi."

"But then you became a vet."

"It was the exam at the end of that course that made me want to change. Till then I saw myself as having a brilliant mind."

"I'm sure that was true. Exams can always get things wrong."

"No, no. The only reason I chose Leopardi was to annoy my father, who was a vet. Changing over was the best thing I ever did. Otherwise I'd never have met Manon."

I realized from the smell of tobacco that he must have lit a cigarette, but I could see no red glow. He was holding it in the hollow of his hand like soldiers and sailors do.

"I've been trying to think of a polite way to say it but I couldn't find one, so I'll say it straight out: tomorrow you must continue your journey. We can't keep four extra people."

"Of course. It's been extremely kind of you to look after us this evening."

"It has nothing to do with kindness. When I let you go today I was afraid you might come back with someone else to rediscover the path and find our house. So I either had to shoot you or put you in our debt. At the university you seemed to me a decent sort of person. So I chose the second alternative."

"Are you always so honest?"

"We have no choice. The only reason we're still alive is that everyone else round here has either gone away or is dead and no-one even knows this house exists. If some stray person or one of the gangs were to find us, we'd be finished."

"Gangs of outsiders?"

He shook his head and for an instant I caught a glimpse of the red glow of the cigarette.

"Youngsters. A hundred, two hundred of them. Some my age, but younger too. With cars and lorries. I don't know where they get the petrol. Luckily they always play loud music and never leave the main road. If you hear them coming, keep clear."

"We will."

"Tomorrow I'll give you some salted meat for the journey and some coffee that you'll be able to reheat."

"Thanks. We do have a little money."

"Money means nothing to us. It'll be more useful to you on the road. Now I'm off to bed."

In some ways Sergio reminds me of Elio. The same control of himself and of everything round him. The same awkward determination. If I had to bet on anyone to survive all this, I'd bet on those two. If I had to trust anyone else with the children, it would be them.

Sergio walked a little way with us. He said he could help us avoid the main road by taking us a short cut through the forest, but I had the impression that what he really wanted was to disorientate us, to make it impossible for us to find the house again. When he took his leave he squeezed each one of us by the hand, after which we saw him retrace his steps and vanish into the forest. A little later we heard a rifle shot. He had told us he liked to hunt at some distance from the house so as not to attract attention to it with the sound of his gun. Bauschan was walking between my legs looking cautiously around. In the end I had to carry him in my arms so as not to trip over him. I had not done this for some time and I became aware how tough and elastic the skin under his grey-black coat had become. There is nothing left in him now of the puppy he was. He is like a flute cut from a cane. A strong hollow length of wood. Or one of those architectural creations of metal and glass I used to love so much.

Skirting an unknown small village, we heard the church clock strike four. The time corresponded with the light. Smoke was rising from a couple of chimneys but we did not go near them.

Following Sergio's advice we have kept to the fields beside the road so as to be able to take refuge in the forest at the first sound of a car engine. In our bags we have salt meat, a bottle of coffee and what's left of our provisions. The sky is clearer than in recent days though short gusts of cold wind hit us in the face and bring tears to our eyes. Despite the sunshine we have buttoned up our jackets and pulled scarves and caps from our pockets. Walking like this makes us sweat, but we can't afford to risk falling ill.

This evening, after the children had gone to sleep, I talked at length to Sebastiano about Clara. While I talked he looked steadily into my eyes without nodding or shaking his head. When he saw I had finished he lifted one of his great hands and laid it on my head. I felt my ankles and knees and my other joints stop hurting and melt with warmth.

Then he withdrew his hand and lay down under the cowhide he uses as a cloak by day and as a blanket at night, and his breathing told me almost at once that he was asleep. I settled a branch on the fire. A mass of sparks rose to skim the ceiling of the stall where we have taken refuge. Watching them fall back and go out, I ask myself whether I am being subjected to an act of purification. Or whether sentence has already been passed and a bizarre judge has placed the scaffold a long way from the cell.

26 January

A day of full sunlight. The snow has been thawing and we have had to leave the fields to walk on the road.

We had been walking on the asphalt for about an hour when a car appeared from nowhere. We were aware of it at the last moment and dived for cover as it rounded the corner behind us. The youth who was driving it looked at the clump of birches where we had thrown ourselves. He didn't slow down and I'm not sure he saw us, but I can't be sure he didn't see us either. I got the impression of a painted face and blond hair. The car was a little urban two-seater painted yellow in an amateurish manner with flames on the bonnet. The bass notes of a stereo could be heard from behind its closed windows.

Afraid the youngster might come back, we left the road. I was pretty sure we weren't far from the pass, but it was dark when we reached the hillside. A slice of moon lit the last stretch of the climb.

Where the road descends the hill into Liguria we found a hotel, a bar, a children's holiday camp and a few houses, all these places abandoned. Even so it seemed risky to stop there for the night because anyone coming over the pass would be able to see or smell the smoke from our fire. Of course we could do without a fire, but we need to eat something hot and dry our shoes. So I told the children and Sebastiano to shelter from the wind, and set off by myself along the crest of the hill where great revolving wind turbines stand. After a kilometre I came across a small building with two floors. I think it must have been a base for the installation engineers. On the ground floor it has a kitchen and a room with a computer and other instruments, and on the upper floor two small bedrooms.

I went back for the children and we settled in. We lit our fire in the most sheltered room, the laboratory, and Sebastiano went to look for wood. Some of the equipment seems to be in working order and two red indicators go on and off intermittently on one of the consoles. We ate some salt meat and then, while the soup heated, I told the children the road would be downhill the next day and within two days we'd be at the sea. Lucia said she had been to A. on holiday with her mother. For a few minutes the only sounds were the crackling of the fire and the chomping of Bauschan's jaws.

"I want to go to Switzerland," Alberto said.

He spoke with none of the usual arrogance; it was the voice of a terrified child I had not heard before.

"Perhaps we'll be able to get there from France," I answered.

He looked at me across the flames of the fire. It seemed to me his mind must still be working on one of those decisive questions I have only read about in books, never experienced in real life, like crossroads crucial to a man's destiny. His eyes were gentle and full of grace; for the first time, they were like Lucia's eyes. Then suddenly his mouth hardened and he looked away. I understood he had made his choice.

When everyone was asleep I went out to urinate. Tonight the sky is covered with a thin gauze that magnifies the moonlight. The wind is cold, but carries the smell of trees and of something unfolding.

I sat on a stone and searched the sky for some deficiency or excess that might explain what is happening. But the sky was the same as it always is, offering no signs. The powerful steel turbines were turning with a sound like enormous bicycles struggling uphill. I could see the red lights on their towers delineate the watershed between two valleys. I imagined this land after our own time, with the turbines still revolving and filling the silence with their powerful humming, cradling sleeping animals and driving them to mate as the sound of water does.

I am writing these last lines by the weak light of the dying fire. This act of writing that I had put behind me has returned to be part of me again, emerging from the dark place into which it had slipped. Before pulling my cover over me I kissed Lucia's brow. I have a daughter, the night outside is deep and indifferent and everything seems destined to last longer than us. Yet I see beauty.

27 January

The snow has gone. The vegetation has changed. We haven't yet seen the sea, but we've come across the first olives and can already feel the warm and pleasant wind rising from the coast. We walked all day at a good pace and after lunch allowed ourselves an hour's sleep with our faces turned to the warm sun. There are no villages in the valley, only an occasional group of abandoned houses along the constant curves and hairpin bends of the winding road. No problems to report except that Bauschan has trodden on a tin can or a piece of broken glass and cut his paw. It was Lucia who told me he was limping and leaving bloodstains on the leaves. I disinfected the wound and tried to put a sticking plaster over it, but as soon as we began walking again it came off. I've tried a handkerchief, but he rips it with his teeth. This evening I repeated the medication. But it doesn't seem anything serious. For the first time we've decided to sleep in the open. The *marin*, the wind rising from the sea, warms the air, and inside a ruin or other building it would be colder.

We've lit a small fire, screening it with stones. We're tired but calm. It's been a good day. I don't know what we'll find tomorrow when we reach the coast, maybe only other people like ourselves who have got so far and hope to be able to leave the country. Even if they haven't so far succeeded, they will probably have organized themselves somehow and will be able to accept us. And if some have succeeded it means it must be possible for us to find a ship and leave too; we do have a little money. If not we'll walk to France. I've copied the address Elio left me into this exercise book.

Part Four

It was not the sharp pain that woke Leonardo, but the sound of his nose being broken: a clean snap without an echo, like a stick breaking. Stunned, he opened his eyes, but barely had time to recognize the leaden first light of daybreak between the branches before something hard and hollow hit him on the cheekbone. As he sank into darkness he heard Lucia cry out. Opening his left eye, he saw her on all fours being dragged along by a man with an antique-looking rifle in his free hand.

"Lucia!" he tried to yell, but blood filled his mouth and turned her name into an incomprehensible choking sound. Then someone grabbed him by the collar. He kicked out in an effort to break free, but with the speed of someone who has done nothing else all his life, the man tied his head against the tree behind him with two turns of wire, forced his arms behind his back and bound his wrists together. Leonardo felt his shoulder pop out of joint. He shrieked. Someone kicked him in the mouth, breaking several teeth.

When he opened his eyes again, a youth with blond hair was crouching beside him, his face a few centimetres from Leonardo's. His hair was divided by a central parting and he had the nut-coloured eyes of a young dog. Two glossy black marks on his cheeks looked as if they had been made with pitch or tempera. He had no eyebrows.

Leonardo began to say something, but the boy was too quick for him.

"Take it easy," he said in a friendly voice.

When the boy got up, Leonardo saw Sebastiano and Alberto still lying where they had fallen asleep the night before. Raised on their right elbows, they were looking at him in astonishment. Sebastiano was holding Bauschan firmly under his arm; the dog was barking but could not drown Lucia's cries.

The blond youth went to sit near them in front of what was left of the fire. He rubbed the bare, nervous arms emerging from his green leather waistcoat, then taking a plastic pouch from his pocket, opened it and lifted it to his nose to inhale violently, before looking without interest at Sebastiano and Alberto. Nor did Bauschan's barking seem to bother him. The parting dividing his hair continued down the back of his neck, giving his head the appearance of a fish cleft in two on a serving dish. He had a large pistol stuck in his jeans.

Leonardo spat out his loose teeth and watched them disappear in the pool of blood forming in his lap. His nose felt enormous and shapeless and his right eye was throbbing as if trying to expel the eyeball. He began praying. The first thing that came to mind was the Act of Contrition, and he recited it straight through without hesitation even though he had not heard it for at least forty years. When he reached the end he realized Lucia was not shouting anymore. He looked at Alberto, whose eyes were fixed in spellbound terror on the boy before him.

"That's enough," the blond youth said, indicating Bauschan. "If you don't silence him I'll shoot him."

Sebastiano covered Bauschan with the cowhide and he stopped barking. In the enormous silence this created, Leonardo heard a sound from his right, like the sound of a garment being rubbed on a washboard. Weeping, he tried to turn his head, but the wire round his neck stopped him. He looked down. The grass round him was dark with his blood.

The noise stopped and footsteps could be heard among the dry leaves. A thickset dark-skinned youth went to sit next to the blond one. Leonardo recognized him as the man who had dragged Lucia away. He had the sawn-off antique rifle in his left hand.

"Have you left her on her own?" the blond youth asked.

"She's passed out and in any case I've tied her up. And the others?"

The blond boy looked at Alberto who was staring at him without moving.

"Push off! Move! Get lost!"

Everyone stayed exactly where they were.

"See? He's not moving. He's shitting himself. And the one with the dog is bonkers."

"Have you looked if they've got any food?"

"No."

"So what have you done?"

The blond youth turned to glance briefly at Leonardo. He said nothing. On the other hand the dark thickset youth went on staring at the tall man before him, the child without shoes and the dog under the cowhide. He seemed little enthused by what he saw. At the base of his skull was a round tattoo representing the Tao.

"Do you want to fuck the girl?"

"Course I do."

"Take her from behind then, that's what I did. She could be a virgin."

"Who cares if she's a virgin or not?"

"But if we bring Richard a virgin he'll maybe take us back again."

The blond youth got up decisively, but once on his feet, stopped to stare at the tattoo on the neck of the other. The thickset youth, still sitting on the ground, reached for Sebastiano's bag, pulled it over and began rummaging through it. The blond one spent a moment in thought, then thrust his hands in the pockets of his jeans and moved away. Leonardo heard his steps getting more distant. He counted to ten, realizing Lucia could not be far away. The light had changed: a pale sun had risen and the trees were beginning to produce vague shadows.

With a furious jerk he tried to get up, but the wire smacked into his Adam's apple, threatening to make a shelled bean of it and taking his breath away. He began weeping or at least thought he was weeping, since all he seemed to have left for a face was a shapeless mass of flesh.

The dark youth, hearing his struggles, stopped inspecting their luggage and turned. His forehead sloped down in steps like that of a primate, and his gestures were graceless, but his little black eyes were evidence of an intelligence which was far from crude.

Leonardo wanted to kill him; kill him and then walk over to the blond boy and kill him too. It was a wonderful sensation, a revelation that lifted him and freed him from pain. Despite his dislocated shoulder and his smashed nose and eye, he knew his hands would have no difficulty in squeezing the necks of those two youths until they were dead. And he knew it would bring him joy and satisfaction. Guilt seemed something for others but not for him. Everything he had thought, done, written and loved up to that moment meant nothing compared to this naked urge to kill.

The shaven-headed youth gave the other a smile as if welcoming someone who from now on will be a member of the family.

"What have you found?" the blond youth asked, fastening his trousers as he returned.

The dark one showed a package he had found in Sebastiano's bag.

"What's that?"

"Dried meat."

"And the other one?"

"Coffee, I think."

"Is it coffee or do you just think it is?"

"It is coffee."

"Where did they get it?"

"How do I know?"

"Let's ask them."

"O.K., let's ask them."

The thickset youth picked up the rifle and pointed it at Alberto.

"Where did you get this stuff?"

Alberto and Sebastiano stared at him in silence.

"Well?"

"In a house," Alberto said.

"What's this mumbling? Get up and speak up properly!"

Alberto stood up carefully. Once on his feet he looked down at the ash in the circle of stones. He had his hands between his legs as though he were naked.

"Some people in a house gave it to us."

"What?" shouted the blond youth.

"They . . ."

The shot echoed through the valley and two huge birds rose from nearby bushes and passed close over their heads. The bullet must have hit a branch because something could be heard falling through the leaves and hitting the ground, but no-one could see what it was. Bauschan started barking again. Alberto was crying and trembling.

"In a house!" he shouted.

"Where?"

"I don't know! A long way off."

"How far off?"

"Three days back," Alberto shouted.

The thickset youth smiled at his companion.

"Do you believe him?"

The blond youth laughed. The thickset one lowered the gun and indicated to Alberto that he could sit down again.

"O.K., O.K.," he said. "Take it easy. Just joking."

Alberto sat down with the same care as when he had got up and wiped away some snot hanging from his chin. Leonardo thought he could detect the shadow of a smile on his face even though it was contorted with terror.

"What now?" the blond youth said.

"Let's move. Can the girl walk?"

"I think so, we just have to wake her up."

"So go and wake her then."

"And the others?"

"We'll take the kid, to hell with the others."

"Don't we kill them?"

"I've only got one round left; I'm not going to waste it. You?"

"I've got two. We could kill them with the knife."

The thickset youth passed a hand over his head. He had blue overalls over a short-sleeved shirt. His olive-coloured arms bore little circular scars.

"I don't feel much like it."

"What if they follow us?"

"Their problem. Get the girl. You, nitwit, empty your knapsack."

Sebastiano released Bauschan. The dog, once free, looked round uncertainly, then walked with his ears down to Leonardo and began licking his face. Sebastiano emptied the knapsack on the ground. A sweater, a pair of trousers, some children's clothes, the exercise book with the brown cover, medicines, gloves, hats, powdered soup, two pans, a plastic bottle, two knives, a shoebox, a comb, some gauze. The thickset youth examined each item carefully, then told Sebastiano to open the shoebox. Seeing the contents were only letters, he launched a kick at one of the stones round the bonfire. A cloud of ash danced in the air and was pierced by a ray of light before settling again.

"Haven't you any money?"

Sebastiano went on staring at him in silence. His long thin face seemed on the point of giving way to an emotion but he stayed serious and distant.

"The girl had the money in her pants," said the blond youth, who had disappeared to Leonardo's right again. The thickset one looked at Alberto.

"Is there any more?" he asked.

Alberto shook his head.

"O.K., put on your shoes."

The blond youth came back, supporting Lucia with an arm round her back. She had lost her shoes and her jumper was torn. One foot was blood-stained.

"Make her put on her shoes," the thickset one said.

"Why?"

"Because I don't want to carry her over my shoulder. Where's the money?"

The blond youth took it from his pocket and handed it to his companion, then made Lucia sit down and looked about for her shoes. While he was putting them on her feet, Leonardo shooed Bauschan away with a sudden movement of his head and looked at his daughter's face. She seemed to have aged by many years, years in which she had neither slept nor eaten nor seen the sun, just wept in the dark, until in the end she had forgotten life itself and what the experience of living can be. She had a bruise on her chin and her trousers were stained with earth. A leaf had settled in her dishevelled hair.

"Shall I untie that one?" the blond youth asked when he had finished with Lucia's shoes.

"Of course not! Take the food and let's go."

They filled a knapsack with the food and coffee, then the thickset youth signalled to Alberto to come over and put it on his back. The blond youth helped Lucia to her feet and supported her under the arms; she accepted this without protest. Leonardo watched them start off. After a dozen steps the forest swallowed them. All that remained was the silence of branches moving in the wind.

Feeling himself about to faint, Leonardo bit his lips with his broken teeth. Sebastiano had begun collecting things from the ground and putting them back in the rucksack.

"What on earth are you doing?" Leonardo said.

Sebastiano seemed not to hear.

"Set me free, Christ!" Leonardo yelled, and felt the words resound in his head like a ball of wet rags. Even his left eye was misting over.

Sebastiano folded the children's covers and Leonardo's and put everything in the rucksack. When he had finished he put his cowhide round his shoulders, then went to Leonardo. He freed his neck, then his hands. Leonardo felt atrocious pain when he moved his arm. Bauschan licked his ear.

"Please give me some water," he said.

Sebastiano took the bottle and helped him to drink. When Leonardo touched his face it was like stroking a leather bag full of stones. A huge tear crept out of his left eye. Sebastiano supported him while he got up.

Once on his feet, Leonardo took a few steps holding his right arm, but quickly realized he would not be able to go far like that. He told Sebastiano to take a sweater from the bag and explained how to immobilize his limb. As soon as the weight of his arm was no longer pulling at his shoulder he felt relief.

"You stay here," he said. "I have to go."

Sebastiano nodded, but when Leonardo set off with difficulty in the direction in which the children had disappeared, he picked up the rucksack and followed. They began walking down towards the road. Leonardo fell a couple of times, once on his dislocated arm, but managed to struggle up again and go on. Bauschan walked a few paces in front. He seemed to be following a scent, but Leonardo was not sure. Nonetheless, he put his faith in the dog since there were no paths and he had no other clues, and after about ten minutes he noticed a leaf with blood on it. They continued downwards with the forest thinning out and came to a thicket of bushes. The sky was not entirely clear but the sun was beginning to warm them. Leonardo stopped to drink because his throat felt full of dust. Sebastiano helped him. Then, weeping, he started forward again. He had no idea what he would do if he caught them up, but he did know if he did not find them now he would lose them for ever.

Emerging from the thicket they came into a field that must once have been cultivated. On the right the slope was studded with olive trees, turned grey with winter. The ground between the trees had been disturbed by wild boar.

It was then that he saw them, about fifty metres lower down, walking along the path beside the river. The blond youth was in front followed by Alberto, then Lucia and bringing up the rear the other youth carrying the rifle. Lucia was managing without help, but limping. As if he had called them, the two children turned towards him and gave him a brief glance that showed no surprise.

For a while Sebastiano and Leonardo followed the path, keeping at a distance of about fifty metres, then passed a bridge and found themselves on the road. They walked for an hour, perhaps much less, losing sight of the group round sharp curves and seeing them in front again on the straight sections. Leonardo knew perfectly well that they could have hidden round a bend and shot at him, but the danger was nothing compared to his need not to lose sight of Lucia's white sweater and black hair.

As the valley grew narrower Leonardo heard distant music that gradually got louder. It seemed to come from some kind of industrial machine, like a press with a regular beat. The four left the road for a lane with a sign pointing to a camping site. Following, Sebastiano and Leonardo found themselves on the other side of the river. The trees here formed a thick roof through which light filtered, depicting bizarre animal forms on the asphalt. The further they went the louder the music grew, drowning the noise of the river, until the path opened on a grassy clearing. Then they saw the camp.

Cars, lorries and caravans were arranged in a circle like wagons in the old Wild West. A motor coach, a lorry bearing the logo of a removal firm, and a large cage on wheels completed the circle. In the centre was a large fire at least partly formed from tyres. The smoke from it was black and rose very high before dispersing. Impaled on stakes round this bonfire were whole headless animals: roe deer, foxes, possibly dogs.

Leonardo studied the few figures hanging around inside the circle. They were confused-looking and half naked, moving slowly without any obvious purpose, climbing over the bodies of others still lying on the ground. The incessant musical racket was coming from amplifiers and loudspeakers on the roof of the coach.

"Take Bauschan with you," Leonardo said. "Go by road and you'll be in A. before evening."

Sebastiano looked him attentively in the eye, then took off the rucksack and offered it to Leonardo.

"Best you keep it," Leonardo said.

Sebastiano put the rucksack on the ground, took off his cloak and draped it round Leonardo's shoulders, lacing it up carefully, then took

Bauschan in his arms and set off. When Leonardo turned they had already passed the bridge. Bauschan was staring back at him, his snout over Sebastiano's shoulder. He barked, but the din of the music drowned everything.

Leonardo looked at the encampment. He realized he was face to face with the heart of the new world, one of those places where madness was first created and then spread around. He was conscious of its presence and its attraction.

When he took a step he felt about to collapse, but stiffened his back and stayed on his feet. This is nothing, he told himself as he moved on, nothing compared to what you are going to see.

For a long time he sat with his back propped against one of the great wheels of the lorry without anyone noticing him. Every now and then one of the youngsters got up, climbed over the bonnet of a car and, without deigning to look at him, went into the forest, presumably to urinate or vomit among the trees. They had all lost their eyebrows and had coloured signs on their cheeks. Some, when they came back, opened the door of a white van and took out a beer which they drank standing up before going back to lie down under their covers or letting themselves drop to the ground wherever they happened to be. Others did not come back. Leonardo imagined Alberto and Lucia must be somewhere in the forest; he imagined the two youths with them, the blond one and the thickset one, waiting for the camp to wake up before making their entry. He told himself there was no point in going to look for them and that it was better to wait where he was and where sooner or later they would come. Using his left hand, he tightened the knot on his bandage. His face was still swollen and painful, but his arm worried him more; he had to find some way of setting his shoulder, or he would stiffen with ankylosis.

He was very thirsty, but had no water and could see none anywhere near him. The fire which had been burning fiercely when he arrived was now just a great patch of smoking embers. The sun had climbed up into a contourless sky. It must have been halfway through the morning.

A figure rose from the ground and took a few steps towards a cappuccino-coloured caravan, then suddenly changed direction and came towards the lorry. It was a girl. Leonardo thought she had seen him, then realized her eyes were closed. She was about Lucia's age, wearing army trousers and a flannel shirt. She dragged herself on another few metres, then tripped over a cover with two kids sleeping under it and fell down in the dust. On the ground she simply cuddled up to the other two bodies and fell asleep again.

It was past midday when a small individual, older than any he had seen so far, came out of the cab of the lorry and, descending the three steps from the platform, trod on Leonardo's lap. As soon as he regained his balance, the man looked at him with lively little metallic-grey eyes. Unlike the others he had no coloured signs on his face and seemed to be in full and conscious control of himself. Leonardo noticed a hump under his jacket. Although his face looked no more than thirty he was bald at the temples, and what was left of his hair shone with brilliantine and hung down to his shoulders.

Leonardo raised his hand in sign of peace, but the man leaped back as though threatened and started jumping about, crying out and waving his arms. A sharp continuous scream issued from his mouth, that reminded Leonardo of one he had heard many years before from an Arab woman when her bag had been stolen in a market in Marrakech. The scream was louder than the din of the music and within a few seconds Leonardo found himself surrounded by dozens of youngsters kicking him and covering him with spit. He took what cover he could and protested his innocence, but someone grabbed him by the hair and began dragging him towards the middle of the clearing, where thin coils of smoke were rising from the patch of ashes. Other young people, woken by the noise, emerged from the cars and coach and other vehicles. Realizing what was about to happen he dug his feet in. A lock of his hair was ripped out and for a moment he lay face down in the dust before other hands grabbed him, pulled off his shoes and socks and pushed him on to the embers.

Feeling the soles of his feet begin to burn he tried to turn back but the kids surrounding the fire closed off every escape route. He ran to the other side but was again hemmed in. Then he hurriedly took off the cowhide cloak, threw it down and stood on it. The kids, who until then had been laughing and shouting, were struck dumb, until a tall young man with a square face and big tattooed arms, uprooted one of the stakes on which meat had been roasting, shook off the scorched corpse of a dog and began to goad Leonardo with it, trying to drive him off the cowhide.

While he was trying to evade the blows, the hunchbacked cripple suddenly leaped through the circle and pulled the cloak from under him so that he fell. The kids greeted this with thunderous applause. Leonardo quickly got up again and tried to push away the hot charcoal with his feet to reach the ground beneath, but the soles of his feet, smoking and giving off a nauseating smell like burned chicken, no longer had any feeling in them. He howled and wept and hurled himself at the wall of children, who kicked and punched him. Forced back into the fire, he began leaping about.

"A dancer!" a girl screamed. "*Ballerino!*"

Someone started a chant: "*Bal-le-ri-no, bal-le-ri-no, bal-le-ri-no,*" and Leonardo found himself shifting the weight of his body from one foot to the other to the steady rhythm of a chorus. He could no longer feel any pain, aware only of a smell of roasting fat. He assumed his feet must have melted and that the fire would gradually climb his legs until it reached his balls and belly and then he would be dead. The last thing he knew before losing consciousness was a refreshing liquid heat running down his legs.

The next thing he knew he was in a cage. Opening his left eye, he could see the sky through rusty bars with the leafy branches of a tree waving gently above him. The sky was a pale blue and the sun was sinking. He touched his face. By now the deformity of his nose and eye had become familiar and it was reassuring to recognize them under his fingers. The monotonous deafening music was still thumping the air, its bass notes vibrating inside his chest like a shout in a closed fist.

He tried to raise himself up on his good arm with his back against the bars. The floor was wood and had been covered with straw. He looked out through the bars into the clearing. The young people, sitting, squatting or lying down, were enjoying the evening sun. Many, in dark glasses, were chatting in small groups as if in a public park. Then he saw them.

They were sitting some way off, behind the big cappuccino-coloured caravan. The blond youth was on his back with his hands behind his head and his legs crossed, one foot swinging. The thickset one seemed to be dozing, propped up with one hand supporting his head. No guns could be seen. Lucia was sitting between them, staring at the ground with a vacant expression. Alberto was beside her. It looked to Leonardo as if his cheeks had been marked with black.

He tried to stand up, but when he put weight on his feet it felt as if someone, for a joke, must have fastened them in a block of concrete while he was unconscious. He looked down and saw two enormous pieces of dark livid meat. He told himself he would never walk again and his left eye filled with tears. For a while he could see nothing. In the darkness inside him he struggled to reassemble his thoughts, to keep them separate from the despair that, despite himself, was overwhelming him. When his tears had dried and he could see again, the young people were still there.

"They're alive," he said, and saying this with his toothless mouth seemed to make the words more real. For a moment he forgot his feet and his shoulder and all the other parts of his body that were no longer what they used to be. He had to wait. To stay alive and wait.

The floor vibrated as if someone had started the engine of the van to which the cage was attached, but neither the trees nor the young people nor anything else round him was moving. Turning to the right he saw a huge dark wrinkly mass on the floor of the cage. When his eye got used to the dark he realized it was an elephant. The animal was sleeping curled against the wall like a great hairless and wrinkled cat.

Cries from the young people drew his attention to the clearing. They had all got to their feet and were shouting excitedly at a man who had just come out of the caravan. The blond youth and the thickset one hurriedly made Alberto and Lucia get to their feet, and when the man, advancing slowly towards the middle of the clearing, passed close to them, they threw themselves on their knees and bowed their heads. The man stopped and gazed at the necks of the two penitents with a benevolent smile. Leonardo realized this must Richard.

It's Christ, he thought, or someone doing his level best to seem like Christ.

The man had a light-coloured cowl of unbleached cotton and high tight-fitting leather boots. His long light-brown hair and his several days' worth of beard completed the priest-like effect.

Richard took his hands out of his pockets, moved forward and knelt down between the two youths like a confidant, an informer, or a father about to play with his children. Leonardo saw his lips pronounce some word with his eyes fixed on the dusty ground, then rest his chin on the shoulder of the thickset youth to listen. The youth took a little time to react, then turned his head and spoke to the man as if kissing him on the neck. The kids in the clearing watched the scene in silence.

The confession took only a few seconds, after which the man got up and placed a hand on Alberto's shoulder. He asked him something, perhaps what his name was, and nodded at the answer. Then he moved to one side and took a long look at Lucia's face, before pushing her hair slowly behind her ear like a lover. Returning to the two youths who were still on their knees he placed a hand on the head of each to impart a silent benediction, then held up all ten fingers, twisting to left and right so that everyone could see. For a time the savage cries that greeted this even managed to drown the thumping of the canned music.

The two youths took off their waistcoat and T-shirt respectively and the cripple took up position behind them, in his hand a short whip with many tails. At the first blow struck between the shoulder blades of the blond youth everyone cheered and shouted "One". The man in the cowl smiled and embraced the whole scene with a benevolent gaze, then took Lucia by the hand and led her to the caravan, turning his back on the flogging he had ordered. Alberto, seeing them go, took a few steps forward but, as if he had a third eye in the back of his neck, the man raised a hand without turning and, with a complicated movement of his fingers, gave him to understand that he must stay where he was and carefully watch what was happening, because it would be extremely useful to him.

Leonardo watched the man who looked like Christ enter the caravan followed by Lucia, and shut the door.

The cripple's whip came down twenty times on the backs of the two youths who did not flinch or emit the slightest protest. The blond one, before the last three blows, merely put his hands behind his neck to assure himself that the blows had not disordered his hair. When the youths got up, their backs were marked with red stripes but not bleeding. Several of the other young people ran forward to congratulate them. Leonardo imagined that the booty they had brought home and the whipping they had received must have made up for some fault and sanctioned their readmission to the clan.

Beer was brought, and while the two youths drank, a girl passed a wet rag over their backs. Alberto was swallowed up in the celebrations and Leonardo could no longer see him. The sun was sinking and soon it would be night, and night would bring him dark, silent hours for thinking.

He moved his weight to his left buttock because his right one was going numb. The music formed a constant background but he no longer noticed it. Turning, he became aware of a black shiny point no bigger than a button, staring at him in the twilight. The elephant was scrutinizing him sadly, perhaps sorry to be no longer alone.

It can crush me whenever it likes, he thought, as if this were an everyday observation. Nothing to do with life or death in general. Still less his own.

The animal struggled to its feet; it was like being backstage in a theatre and watching weights and counterweights rising and falling to raise the curtain. A complex operation, completed by the elephant with a long sigh. He had never seen an elephant so close before; it took up as much space as a large motorcycle but was twice as high. It was presumably Indian rather than African because its ears were small and its tusks barely visible, and a bump on its forehead gave it a worried look.

It moved towards him making the floor of the cage shake, touched him lightly with its trunk, then turned its face to one side and regarded him with compassion through the little eye in its wrinkled socket. Leonardo could feel the hot breath from its mouth and a smell like bark being steeped in water.

When the elephant had finished inspecting him it drew back. Leonardo watched its little tail swinging artfully as it moved away. Returning to its place, the beast fixed its gaze on his eye and bent its back legs to assume a position that seemed both comic and painful before discharging from its anus a huge mass of dung that spread across the floor. Leonardo smiled, supposing himself to be mad.

In the rapidly falling dusk a dozen kids had collected branches and dry wood in the place where the great bonfire had been. They doused them with petrol and kerosene and soon a new fire was lighting up the encampment.

Leonardo started counting the young people. There are about a hundred, he told himself, without any clear idea of why it could be of any use to him to know this.

There was a group of small boys beside the fire, staring at the flames and at the bigger boys he had seen dancing round the earlier fire. One of these was Alberto.

Leonardo dreamed he was copulating on the sofa in the middle of the book room with a woman in vulgar make-up, who was insulting him for his impotence. In the dream, his rage grew, feeding on thoughts related to his childhood and his mother, until he began to slap the woman, whom he finally discovered to be Alessandra. So he apologized and went to have tea in a bar under the house where he was called professor by the elderly proprietor whose walls were papered in photographs of the celebrated Torino football team whose club doctor his grandfather had been.

He was woken by the cold and by his feet which had begun to throb and send stabs of pain up beyond his knees. His arm had gone to sleep, leaving him no feeling in his fingers. He thought he should move it, but the moment he touched his shoulder he was torn by a lacerating spasm. His throat was dry but he was not hungry. The elephant was standing at the other side of the cage. The cart under the cage may have been six metres long, not more than seven. The animal was gazing at the flames in the clearing, its trunk hanging outside between the bars.

Leonardo had no idea of the time. The animals impaled on the stakes had been eaten and the youngsters were writhing in time to the tiresome music. The smoke and glare from the fire was giving a rusty tinge to the sky and neither moon nor stars could be seen. There was a light on in the window of the caravan.

He dragged himself to the bars and looked right and left. Several of the young people had detached themselves from the throng and lain down not far from the cart. They were smoking and staring at the sky as if waiting contentedly for some explanation. One of them, sitting up, inhaled a couple of times from a pouch, then let himself fall back among the others who laughed. Two bodies clasped together inside a car were knocking against one another.

He tried to find Alberto in the crowd. For a moment he thought he recognized him, but the boy was too tall and his hair too short.

He needed to urinate. He unbuttoned his trousers and lay down against the bars in such a way that the urine would fall outside the cart. This operation took him at least ten minutes because his feet were not only unable to support him but were so heavy that he had to move first one leg and then the other with his only good hand. Maybe I should have drunk it, he thought, as the urine fell to the ground in a small shower.

Once, long ago, he had heard of a man stuck for two weeks in a rubber dinghy without food or water at the mercy of the ocean and who had survived by drinking his own urine. He looked at the elephant, on whose eye the yellow flames were reflected like the corolla of a flower.

It took him a long time to get back to the other side of the cage and settle himself again with his back against the bars. He put on the sweater, but was shaken by shivers, apparently of cold, and his trousers, hardened by dried blood, were no comfort to him. Behind him were only the night and the forest and the wind they generated. The shoes and socks taken from him were probably burning in the fire.

"Lucia," he called, just to hear the sound of his own voice.

For a long time he watched the young people dancing, drinking and drugging themselves by inhaling from the small pouches. He saw some of them mate on the ground like dogs and others sit in a circle renewing the colours on their faces. At one point a brawl broke out between two girls. One was captured and carried bodily into one of the cars and three boys shut themselves in with her. As the night went on the young people began to collapse one after another, covering themselves with blankets or sheets taken from the cars. The last to stay awake sat round the fire half naked, their bodies shining with sweat, their heads swinging to the beat of the music. They did not speak, but gazed at the dying embers, and at the darkness advancing over the camp and cars and their recumbent companions. Their faces were full of grief and pain, as if at the extinction of life throughout the entire universe. Then they too lay down huddled close together against the cold and nothing moved anymore. After a while even the music stopped. Perhaps the generator had run out of fuel. Everything was buried in darkness and silence.

This was the hardest moment for Leonardo. He was shivering with cold and pain, but worse still, was tormented by thirst which stopped him giving way to fatigue. The elephant was lying down. It had let itself crash heavily and gracelessly to the floor, tormented like Leonardo by the need to eat and drink.

Dawn was breaking when he heard steps approaching. Afraid to look round, he simply listened to the rustling of branches behind him and the abrupt blows with which they were being hacked off. After a while a man came up to the cage and began pushing branches through the bars. He had grey hair, and round spectacles in a round face. He was small and plump, and could have been sixty or even much younger. He went on with his work for a few minutes, completely ignoring Leonardo, until the cage was half full of shrubs and leafy branches and smelt of resin. Afraid he would go away again, Leonardo called to him.

"What do you want?" the man asked.

"I'm thirsty."

The man stared at him for a moment, then turned without speaking and vanished.

Leonardo was overcome by discouragement, but the man came back. Leonardo leaned one side against the bars the better to see him. He was wearing a blue blazer with a crest on the pocket. A blazer which in any other situation would have looked elegant, but which now seemed to have been put on specially to mock Leonardo. The man offered him a half-litre plastic bottle.

"Drink and give me the bottle back," he said.

Leonardo had difficulty opening his lips and some of the water ended up on his sweater.

"Can I have some more?" he asked, giving the bottle back to the man.

"Not now."

Leonardo stared at his little grey expressionless eyes. Clearly life had been lived behind those eyes, but now all that was left of it was a weak reflection. To Leonardo, he looked like an old two-storey house that had somehow survived among skyscrapers.

"My name's Leonardo," he said.

The man nodded, but did not introduce himself. He rested his hands on the edge of the cage. He was holding a small hatchet in his right hand and had lost three fingers from his left: little finger, index and middle.

"My daughter's here. Have you seen her? Is there a young boy with her too?"

"The boy's in the lorry with the others," the man said. "He's fine."

"And Lucia?"

The man went on staring at the clearing where the light of dawn was getting stronger, giving everything a livid tinge and covering it with a patina of frost.

"Your daughter's with Richard," he said.

"What does that mean?"

"That she'll stay with Richard until he gets tired of her."

"And then?"

225

The man looked at his shoes. He seemed to be drawing something in the dust with the toe of one foot.

"Then she'll be common property, like the other girls you see around."

Leonardo began sobbing. The man did nothing to comfort him. He just remained silent and watched.

"Who are you?" Leonardo said.

"A doctor."

"Were you captured?"

"Yes."

"And your family too?"

"No. My wife and daughter are dead. I don't know where my son is."

"Why don't you escape?"

"Where would I go? At least I'm safe here and get fed."

Leonardo studied the calm face and closed eyes before him. He realized fear and despair were so deep inside the man that nothing and nobody could reach them and pull them back to the surface.

"Tomorrow," the doctor said, "if Richard allows it, I'll give you something to stop your feet getting infected. But it all depends on Richard and what he has in mind for you."

They listened in silence to the slow steady breathing of the sleeping elephant.

"I think I've got a broken shoulder too," Leonardo said.

The doctor looked at him with dull eyes, then stretched out a tired hand to it.

"It's dislocated," he said.

Leonardo, who had held his breath because of the pain, breathed again.

"Can you fix it?"

"Tomorrow."

"Can't you do anything now?"

The man turned and disappeared behind one of the wooden walls that closed off the two ends of the cart. Leonardo thought he had gone, but the door opened and he came in, dressed in his ridiculous crested blue blazer.

He was wearing moccasins with a little tassel at the back of each foot. He grimaced as he approached, perhaps because of the smell Leonardo was giving off.

"You mustn't cry out," he said. "Not for any reason at all."

"I promise I won't."

The man looked towards Richard's caravan: the light was off and everything in and around it was silent.

"Put something in your mouth."

"What?"

The doctor broke a piece off a branch and gave it to Leonardo who put it between his teeth, then, untying the bandage and using his foot as a lever under Leonardo's armpit, he pulled his arm upwards with a sharp jerk that made a sound like a nut being split. Leonardo collapsed whimpering.

"Quiet!"

Leonardo, his face squashed against the floor, nodded. He had clenched his teeth so hard that his mouth had begun bleeding again. The doctor left the cage and reappeared outside the bars. Leonardo was still lying on the floor, his good eye full of tears.

"Put the bandage on again. You can take it off tomorrow and pretend the arm has cured itself. Now I must go."

But the man stayed, gazing at the dark bulk of the elephant asleep at the other side of the cage.

"Don't be afraid of David," he said. "He's the only decent thing in this place."

Leonardo struggled to a sitting position.

"You'll help me?"

The man looked impersonally at him.

"I've already helped you. I can't do anything more."

"Then help my daughter."

"I'm sorry, there's nothing I can do."

Leonardo heard him going away. He turned on his back and looked up at the wooden ceiling. It was painted blue, with the words "CIRCO BALTO" written in gold letters inside an oval border. The faces of an elephant, a hippopotamus and a clown had been drawn inside the O.

I'm cold, Leonardo thought, I've never been so cold in my life.

He crawled as far as the pile of branches, lifted some and crept underneath. Closing his eyes, he inhaled the smell of resin hoping it might stupefy him, but when he opened his eyes again he was still there, in the dark, in a newly prepared wooden coffin.

They stayed in the clearing another four more days during which no-one except the doctor came near the cage or said a word to Leonardo. In his solitude he studied the rhythms and habits of what he was beginning to think of as a clan or tribe.

When the young people woke after midday, they spent a couple of hours wandering about the camp or going down to the river, in an attempt to work off the effects of drugs and alcohol. After this, the cripple would distribute the weapons, which were kept locked up in one of the vans, to the older boys, most of whom went out in groups of two or three to hunt or carry out raids. They left behind in the camp a dozen armed youths, the children (including Alberto), the cripple and the girls. When the groups returned from the hunt, they would place on a great blue cloth in front of Richard's caravan not only deer, foxes, dogs and cats but also the clothes, tools, weapons and everything else they had managed to find in the surrounding area. They would all be home by dark, when the bonfire was lit and the captured animals were skinned and stuck on the stakes to roast. Apart from the animals, the booty would not be touched until Richard came out of his caravan. This happened in the evening, after nightfall, when the bonfire had been lit. He would open the caravan door and raise his hand to acknowledge the ovation with which the young people would greet his appearance. Then he would come down among them and speak intimately to each as if he knew all about their hearts and their secret thoughts.

One evening Leonardo saw him take Alberto by the hand and go for a long walk with him but without ever going outside the circle of the camp. Alberto listened to him and answered his questions. Finally Richard embraced him and kissed him on the cheek, and Leonardo had the impression that, beneath its black markings, Alberto's face swelled with pride. It was the first time since they had come there that the child's eyes had searched behind the bars for his own. Only a moment, but enough to make it clear to Leonardo that Alberto would not return from the world he was now in and where perhaps he was destined to stay for ever.

After Richard had exchanged a word with everyone he would inspect what had been brought in. If there was not much booty, or if it was of little value, his face took on a bitter expression, but Leonardo never heard him reprove anyone or show any sign of anger. More often he would clap his hands to arouse the enthusiasm of the young people. Then he would address them with a few words that Leonardo, deafened by the music, never managed to hear, give the cripple a little urn containing the substance the youngsters inhaled, and withdraw into his caravan.

During those four days Leonardo never saw him eat or drink or join in the partying, which always went on in the same way until first light. He would spend all day in the caravan with Lucia, whom Leonardo never managed to glimpse despite keeping his eye fixed on the vehicle's two windows.

The only person he had any contact with was the doctor, who came each morning at dawn with food for him and David. In his own case this would nearly always be potatoes cooked in the embers and very tough meat which, with his broken teeth, he could not ingest until he had sucked it for a long time. During his second visit the man sprinkled his feet with a yellowish powder before binding them up with care; to prevent infection, he said. Leonardo decided he must have been told to do this by Richard, and when he asked about this, the man confirmed it. But when he asked about Lucia the man would only say that she was well.

"Why does she never come out of the caravan?"

"She can't."

"Is she tied up?"

"No."

Before leaving, the doctor would sweep the cage clean of both Leonardo's excrement and the elephant's, after which he would go to David, who was nearly always lying stretched out in his corner, and spend a long time stroking his head and whispering in the animal's great ears words like those he must once have spoken to his wife, and to his daughter before she went to sleep.

Leonardo too, as the days passed, became fond of the animal. Sometimes, in moments of depression or loneliness, he would call to him by name and the elephant would come over to be stroked.

At night, on the other hand, it would be his turn to crawl on all fours to the end of the cage to shelter from the cold next to the animal. David's skin was rough and his stomach noisy, but his huge body gave enough warmth to help Leonardo fall asleep quickly. At first he was afraid of being crushed, until he realized that David, even when asleep, was extremely careful of the fragile companion whom he had found sharing his cage. Sometimes, when David's little eyes lit up and his trunk began swinging to left and right and turning over backwards, it seemed the elephant was laughing. This would happen when Leonardo squatted in a corner to attend to his physical needs. David seemed amused by the bizarre position his human companion had to adopt to perform this function.

On the morning of the fifth day Leonardo woke to find the youngsters sitting in two lines facing the caravan. There was no music and an unreal silence reigned over the camp, broken only by birdsong. He shuffled on his knees to the bars to look for Alberto, who was sitting with the others with his face painted and his dirty hair tied in little bunches.

They waited an hour, perhaps two; Leonardo no longer had any sense of time and was even uncertain about the rising and setting of the sun. Finally the door of the caravan opened and Richard came out accompanied by a young woman. It was immediately clear to Leonardo that this was not Lucia, because she was shorter than her and several years older. She had a very beautiful face and was wearing a ball gown with a wide belt. Her hair had been completely shaved off.

Richard led her to face the youngsters who were watching in silence.

Then he called "Enrico!"

It was the first time Leonardo had heard Richard's voice; it was deep and, to Leonardo, full of mysterious overtones.

The cripple got up from the front row and ran forward, took a sheet of paper Richard held out to him, tore it into little pieces, wrote something on each piece, then screwed them into little balls before distributing them among the young people.

When this operation had been completed, Richard said something in the ear of the woman at his side, after which he kissed her forehead and turned to go back into the caravan. She looked astonished, like a bride abandoned at the altar. She watched the door close behind Richard, and when a youth with curly hair got to his feet in the second row, she understood and began weeping.

The curly-haired youth handed the cripple his scrap of paper, then went up to the woman.

Without looking her in the face he took hold of one arm and pulled her, but she shook herself free violently. Then he grabbed her with both hands but she threw herself on the ground and dug in her heels. The boy seemed discouraged; he was thin with very small bones. His eyes must be the same black as his hair, Leonardo thought.

The boy kicked the woman in the side; she gave a shrill scream but still resisted. Then he started slapping her, but his hands were small and weak and she managed to kick him in the groin. He collapsed swearing.

"Number two," shouted the cripple.

"No," yelled the curly-headed youth, trying to struggle back to his feet. Everyone watched, but no-one spoke.

"That's enough, you stupid bugger," the cripple said. "Go back to your place."

The boy went and sat down again with his head bowed. Another got up: about eighteen years old.

He leaped over the front row to the woman who was sitting with her knees drawn up to her chest, weeping. Crouching beside her he said a few words, at which she shook her head. Then, when he leaned closer to her ear, she moved sharply away so that he lost his balance and fell. Someone laughed. Then he got up and stood for a few moments staring at the woman's hips, as if he had heard there was something precious there, but was not quite sure. Then, without warning, he punched her face, knocking her backwards into the dust. After a moment of astonishment she tried to scurry away on all fours, but the boy threw an arm round her waist and dragged her towards the coach. When they got there the woman pushed with her feet against the steps at the door, making them both fall backwards. This time nobody laughed.

Showing no emotion the boy got up, twisted the woman's arm behind her back and banged her head three times on the step. Leonardo saw a wound open on her forehead and blood pour down her face. For the first time since he had been hit himself, he managed to open his swollen eye: he felt tears gush out of it and soak his face down to his chin. Getting to her feet, the woman climbed into the coach without offering further resistance.

A few minutes later the boy came out, raised his fist in triumph and and was received with shouts and applause. Then a third youth got up, handed his ticket to the cripple and made his way to the bus.

Leonardo spent the rest of the morning huddled in a corner of the cage without raising his eyes from the floor, while David, beside him, watched with his sad little eyes the procession of boys and some girls coming and going from the coach. This continued till afternoon, by when the air had already grown cold and the sun had vanished behind a cloud just above the mountains. Then the fire was lit and the monotonous and deafening music started again. Leonardo, from his corner, watched the youngsters dancing and wondered if Alberto had climbed into the coach.

Bringing him food at first light, the doctor found him crouching like a dog.

"We'll be off soon," he said.

The man had changed his trousers and had a clean shirt on under his blazer. Leonardo took the plate the doctor had left near his feet and threw it at the wall. A potato fell on David's head; he started in his sleep without opening his eyes. The doctor went away without saying a word or sweeping up the excrement.

The procession of vehicles set out in the early afternoon and when it got dark stopped right in front of the hotel Leonardo had walked past with the children a week earlier. The climb had been slow because several of the cars were out of petrol and had to be towed by the lorries and the coach. Leonardo noticed that many of the vehicles had been riddled with bullets. Even the roof of the cage was peppered with holes through which the sun filtered in blades of yellow-blue light. Noticing this, Leonardo got to his feet for the first time, and holding on to the bars moved to the far end of the cage, from where David was placidly contemplating the countryside beside the road. He saw several round scars on the elephant's body that could have been bullet wounds.

When they were into the hills the vehicles were parked in a circle and the fire was lit in the middle of a little amphitheatre once used for children's shows. The amplifiers were set up and the stakes impaled with animals, and the youngsters began drinking and dancing as usual. Alberto, sitting on the concrete steps with other children, was sharing a pouch from which each inhaled in turn. Every now and then one or other of them would throw a pine cone at the bald girl, who was tied by a short chain to the bumper of one of the cars. The woman kept her head bowed, and even when hit did not react in any way. Her dress had been torn to shreds and her face was a dark stain the fire seemed unwilling to illuminate. A three-quarters moon appeared from time to time from behind the clouds, but its light was lost long before it could touch this part of the earth. The strong wind blowing from the sea brought nothing mild with it. All was cold and tense. Leonardo could see the great wind turbines rotating and the red lights above them marking the escape route along the crest of the hills.

He lay down with his head against David's stomach and closed his eyes. He imagined Bauschan and Sebastiano sitting at the entrance to a cave, a fire behind them and their eyes fixed on the sea, waiting for something to come from far away. His feet could only just support him, but they did not hurt anymore and the pain in his shoulder had faded to a slight numbness. Only thirst still tormented him.

Even though he tried to ration the water he was given, the bottle would already be empty by mid-afternoon. The elephant would drink his two bucketfuls and eat though barely awake, spending the rest of the day with nothing. Leonardo wondered how he managed to survive.

With sleepiness beginning to confuse his thoughts he heard someone fiddling with the lock on the door. He thought the doctor must have come early, but when the door opened, he saw a boy in black trousers and a yellow shirt, with painted face and no eyebrows like all the others.

"Come," the boy said.

Leonardo struggled down the short ladder and followed the boy across the field. His bandaged feet trod uncertainly on the damp grass. The boy walked ahead, knowing Leonardo could not escape. He gave off a strong feral smell as if he had just emerged from an uncured bearskin, and his hair was cut in a triangle with its point between the tendons at the back of his neck.

The young people were waiting on the steps of the little amphitheatre while below, facing it, Richard was sitting in his pastel-shade tunic with Lucia at his side. When Leonardo came before them she continued to look at the ground. The boy who had brought him made him kneel and went off to sit with the others. Leonardo looked at Lucia's white shaven head, wishing he could weep on it and then dry it with his hands. She was wearing a decent blue frock and long earrings Leonardo had never seen before. Her face and body were intact, yet seemed lifeless as if they had disintegrated or been contaminated.

"They tell me you're a dancer," Richard said.

Leonardo studied his straight nose, thin lips and long hair, and the honey-coloured beard framing his light smile: every part of his face expressed beauty and gentleness, yet its light and warmth, like those of a will-o'-the-wisp, somehow had more to do with the extinction of life than its creation. Leonardo looked at his calm blue eyes and found them utterly insane. There was nothing human there. They were more like the eyes of a majestic bird of prey or a great creature from the depths of the sea, infinitely solitary and universally feared.

"I'd like you to dance for us," Richard said.

There was no mockery in his voice. Leonardo noticed the cripple was sitting a little higher up behind them. Armed with a pistol.

"I can't dance," Leonardo said. "I'm not a dancer."

Richard smiled.

"You're too modest, dancer," he said, offering his hand.

Leonardo dropped his eyes and felt the man's fingers slithering through his hair, loosening the knots of congealed blood that glued it together. Keeping his eyes on the ground he saw little pieces of straw falling and shining in the shadows. The fire was warm on his shoulders. It was many days since he had felt such heat. Richard pushed Leonardo's hair back one last time and withdrew his hand.

"From now on you will dance," he said, "and you will be delighted to do it, because that will give us pleasure."

Leonardo looked at the man's neat feet, at his long, well-proportioned hands and perfect teeth. Christ in our time, he thought; a Christ generated by the times we live in and thus certain to make converts, and to build a church and sow his word throughout the earth.

He was made to get to his feet and led towards the fire. A couple of youths with spades had spread a circle of embers across the concrete which glowed red in the wind.

"Take off your bandages," the cripple said.

Leonardo's eyes searched for Lucia, but she was still looking down as though the whole world was confined to the few centimetres of ground between her feet. But Richard's predator eyes were staring at him, revealing neither malice nor amusement, only an infinite power of concentration.

Leonardo breathed in the smell of meat, bodies and burned fur weighing on the air. The unskinned snout of a small boar impaled on one of the stakes had caught fire. He sat down and began to unwind his bandages.

"Get up," the cripple said as soon as he had finished.

He moved unassisted towards the embers. The usual hypnotic music was coming from the amplifiers. He placed his right foot on the embers, then his left. At first all he felt was a light tickling, like walking at midday on a sun-warmed beach, but when the first pangs rose up his legs he began to dance from one foot to the other. The audience drove him on with cries of "Dancer!", stamping their feet on the steps.

He began waving his arms, leaping and gyrating. A mad exaltation filled him and the pain in his feet faded.

He closed his eyes and danced faster, more frenetically, then opened them again and saw Richard's light but penetrating expression, which brought back familiar dreams from his childhood of warriors with matted hair and women huddling in caves. Nightmares involving dogs, bones, cold and bodies burned on high flaming pyres in faraway villages. Recurrent visions from which he woke terrified and certain there would never be a place in the world for him.

In his mind he passed down a corridor opening on to rooms with no floors. If he had gone through one of those doors he would never have been able to get back and his body would have been degraded to a shell capable only of killing and violating and, in the end, opening his own veins with a shard of flint and waiting for death with his eyes turned up to the moon.

In some hidden corner where it had been hidden for goodness knows how long, the memory came back to him of a spring morning many years ago. He and Lucia had woken late, as often happened on Saturdays, and had breakfasted at the kitchen table, listening to a radio programme that Lucia did not entirely understand and that Leonardo only loved for the voice of the female presenter. Then they had washed and started to get ready to go out. When Leonardo had laid out Lucia's clothes ready for her on the divan, the little girl had taken off her pyjamas, pulled on her pants, and begun to leap about on the bed, calling out that she was like Tarzan, Mowgli and Jesus.

"Jesus too?" Leonardo had asked.

"Jesus died with torn pants, didn't you know that?"

He remembered that while Lucia had finished getting dressed he had listened to the sound of cars on the wet road and realized he had now come really close to the secret, no matter how close he may have been before. He must preserve that perception, he told himself. Not the perception of what he himself was, but of what that child had been, what she was now, and what she would become.

He recalled his mind to the present. She turned to look at him with the eyes of a dog that has escaped to run free along the safety barrier of the *autostrada*, but has finally agreed to return and come back. He was aware of this because he felt new pain in his feet and humiliation for what he was doing. The youngsters were whistling, cheering and throwing pine cones and bits of wood at him. Then Richard raised a hand and all was silent, except the music, which continued to vibrate against the immobility of the bodies and the natural world all round.

Leonardo took a step forward and felt cold concrete refresh his ulcered feet. The wind had dropped. An elongated cloud was fleeing to the east leaving the moon behind, like a reptile that has laid her egg and wants to be far away when it hatches.

Richard stood up, and taking Lucia by the hand helped her to her feet. She was tiny beside him, as if small enough to fit into the palm of his hand.

"We are grateful to you, dancer," he said. "Now you can go back to your cage."

Panting, his mouth parched although full of saliva, Leonardo looked at him. There had not been the slightest note of derision in the man's voice. He turned and hobbled through the surrounding silence to the wagon. No-one followed to make sure he went to the cage. He climbed the stepladder, entered and closed the door. David was watching him in profile.

"It's nothing," he said. "It's nothing."

He sat down with his back to the partying in the arena. The shouts and the music, the smell of meat and the crackling of branches thrown on the fire reached him; then he realized the smell of meat was coming from himself. He looked out at the night before him, so inexorable and ancient, and wept tears quite different from the tears he would once have wept.

*

After that evening, the young people started coming to see the cage where David and Leonardo spent their days. Only Richard could give the order to open it, but that did not stop them goading Leonardo to dance or prevent them from throwing stones and food at him through the bars. When he saw them coming, he would crouch in a corner or hide behind David, trying to make himself invisible. Sometimes, having tried to provoke him with sticks and stones in the useless hope of getting him to react, the kids would stay there to study him in silence as though Leonardo were the unusual creature and not the elephant, for whom they seemed to feel little or no curiosity. As soon as they were bored they would go away and Leonardo would be able to emerge from his hideaway to collect the food. It usually turned out to be something his teeth could not cope with: bones, such as the skull of a hare or a badger, or the paws of a wild boar or fallow deer, but sometimes he was lucky and found an onion, some potato peel or a rabbit skin that he could chew for its fat before laying it out to dry.

One night, while he was asleep, they threw a live trout at him. When the youngsters stopped laughing and went back to dance, he watched the fish struggling on the floor, opening and shutting its gills, until he was sure it was dead, then spent a long time rubbing it on the bars to remove its scales before eating it.

His feet hardly hurt him at all which, according to the doctor who had treated them again and bound them up, was not a good sign. In fact, an extremely hard black calloused crust had formed under the soles, which allowed him to move about the cage as if in rubber-soled shoes, and to cross easily from the side he used as a toilet to the side where he ate and slept beside David.

During the days they spent on the hillside and those passed in a new encampment some thirty kilometres into the valley, Leonardo was able to assemble a more detailed picture of the tribe whose jester he had become. Most of the young people were between fifteen and thirty years old, leaving aside the cripple who was evidently Richard's trusted right-hand man, and there seemed no hierarchy in the group. All the males had equal access to weapons, drugs and alcohol, while the females were excluded from the distribution of weapons and never left the camp. There were no fixed relationships and the females coupled with anyone without preference or exclusion. This could happen in public or in the cars or coach at any time of the day or night. The group of children that Alberto had joined was held in high esteem, especially by Richard, and Leonardo never saw anyone maltreat them or make fun of them. They were involved in the partying and were given alcohol and drugs, but when the older males went out to hunt, they stayed in camp with the girls. One of the youths who had captured them, the dark thickset one, busied himself with skinning the animals after hanging them from a hook that stuck out of the cab of one of the smaller vans. Then the skin and entrails were thrown away and the rest of the animal was impaled on a stake to cook by the fire. A small fibreglass cistern had been installed on another lorry for water. This was kept at a certain level by a pump that drew from the river running beside the road or from the streams that carried quantities of water down the hillsides. Even so, Leonardo never saw any of the youngsters drinking from the cistern or using water to wash in. Their only form of bodily care concerned their hair and eyebrows, which the boys shaved every two or three days. Some of the young people had longer hair than others and wore rings and earrings, or had metal pins in their ears or other parts of their faces, but this seemed to be a matter for individual choice. The only things that clearly identified members of the tribe were their shaven eyebrows and the coloured markings on their cheeks and foreheads. There were no uniforms; they all dressed as they liked and sometimes the boys returned wearing garments they must have found while out plundering. None of them had anywhere to keep their clothes. What they had taken was either left lying about or thrown on the fire, and despite the severity of the weather no-one possessed a jacket or any heavy clothing.

The scraps of conversation that Leonardo could catch above the thumping beat of the music were nearly always connected with challenges, squabbles, songs or direct invitations to sex. Their vocabulary was basic, approximate and stuffed with expletives. Even so, it revealed presence of mind and alertness. It would not be accurate to say they lacked intelligence, but it was as if the electricity had left some parts of their brains to concentrate on areas related to aggressiveness and the pure pursuit of pleasure. There was no distinction for them between wanting to do something and actually doing it; the inconvenient processes of thought had dissolved to make way for untrammelled need.

Leonardo noticed they were incapable of feeling remorse or regret for anything they did, or of remembering what had happened the day before or wondering what would happen the next day. He even began to doubt whether they could remember anything of their past, or of other people who had once been close to them, or of the places they had come from.

Richard seemed to be their only law. Every evening when the hunters laid out their haul of dead animals and knick-knacks on the cloth, he would emerge from his caravan and walk among the young people, talking to them like a father, confessor or servant.

As the days passed, Leonardo noticed that Richard was beginning to look increasingly disappointed when it was time to examine the booty. On one occasion he went back into the caravan without imparting his usual benediction or handing the cripple the urn with the drug in it. This caused an icy silence to fall over the tribe, and once he was out of sight the young-sters stared in astonishment at the door that had swallowed him up. This made it clear to Leonardo that what Richard really wanted from the raids was not the sort of food and trinkets the boys regularly brought back but petrol, women and other prisoners, and he decided that until the boys found him a new girl, Lucia would be safe from the fate of the woman with the shaven head.

The evening the drug was withheld a brawl broke out and one youth was wounded in the stomach by a knife. The dancing continued but some-one went for the doctor who examined the boy, spread a sheet on the ground and stitched the wound by the flickering light of the bonfire. It looked to Leonardo as though the lad was weeping during the operation.

That night he asked the doctor where he had been captured.

"Near M."

"You were living there?"

"No, I was on my way to Austria."

"With your family?"

"My wife and daughter were already dead. I was on my own."

The man continued going backwards and forwards to the thicket where he was cutting branches for David.

"Where do they come from?" Leonardo asked.

"Who?"

"These kids."

"When I first saw them they were wearing swimsuits; I think they must be from the Adriatic coast."

"And now? Where are we going?"

"Why are you asking these questions?"

"Don't you want to know yourself?"

"I know where I stand. I won the finger-cutting, I have my place in the group, no-one will hurt me. Also, I'm a doctor, and they need a doctor."

Leonardo looked at the man, with the yellow light of the last flames of the bonfire dancing on him; as always his face was expressionless, yet infinitely sad.

"What's the finger-cutting?"

The doctor walked off. It seemed to Leonardo that he was away for hours, but it was only a few minutes later when he came back and the morning light had grown no brighter. He threw a last handful of twigs into the cage, then looked at Leonardo.

"I could give you an injection. You won't feel a thing and tomorrow they'll find you dead."

Leonardo shook his head.

"I can't leave Lucia."

"Then keep dancing and try to stay alive, there's nothing else for you."

"What do you know about Richard?"

"You're asking meaningless questions."

"Who was he before he started this madness? That I want to know."

"You're not in a position to want anything. You're full of resentment, drawing conclusions from what you see. But what you're seeing and judging is only a façade, a necessary evil. Richard is above all this. Respect him. He's bringing up his children far better than you would have been able to. You would have made them into victims destined for suffering and nothing more. I know because I did the same. Just now they are being tested by fire; they'll get burned but it'll make them stronger. I used not to believe it either, but there's a logic in it all, a new logic. Your son has understood it, children understand much more quickly than we do. Richard has read this in him which is why he wants to keep him close. The only person for you to worry about is yourself. It's not easy for people like you and me to change our skin. We are too old and too firmly locked into what we used to think was right."

Leonardo shook his head, dismissing these words.

"I'd like you to speak to Alberto and tell him to come to me."

"Why not call him yourself?"

"I have, but he pretends not to hear."

"He won't come, even if I ask him."

"But ask him all the same."

"He'll only come if Richard tells him to."

"Then tell Richard I'd like to speak to Alberto."

"No-one speaks to Richard unless Richard himself wants it."

Leonardo leaned back against the bars and looked at David. Since they had started sharing the cage, he had never seen the elephant angry or showing any sign of impatience.

"Do you ever speak to the kids?"

"No."

"If I'm the only person you can speak to, why is it so difficult for you to do it?"

"Your questions are out of place. They come from a concept of the world that no longer exists. Though being a writer, you must have got used to imagining other worlds. That's what this is."

"I'm trying to understand what sort of a world it is."

"Understanding belongs to the old world. I also studied and had a home, profession and family. That wasn't very long ago, but it no longer makes sense to think about it. These things don't mean anything anymore. There's nothing to be said and still less to understand."

Leonardo nodded.

"Why are we always on the move? What are they looking for?"

The doctor put his hands on the edge of the cage, the left hand with three fingers missing hidden under the other. The stakes facing Leonardo were stuck with black sculptures of desiccated flesh.

"Fuel for the cars," the doctor said, "and for the generators."

"Only that?"

"And prisoners, especially women and children. Richard wants them educated according to the new law."

Leonardo tried to understand whether the man believed what he was saying or was just repeating it automatically, but the doctor's face was expressionless, his eyes like cold ash.

"What are those bullet holes on the cars?"

"An aeroplane machine-gunned us. We'd gone too close to the frontier."

"Is that where Richard's trying to go? To France?"

The man did not answer. The camp, with its recumbent bodies and stream of coarse smoke from the bonfire, was reflected in his glasses. The wind had begun to shift it to the west.

"What if we run into another gang?"

The man stuck his hands into his jacket pockets.

"If it's smaller we attack it, if it's bigger we keep our distance or try to twin with it."

"Twin with it?"

"Exchange prisoners."

Leonardo studied the man's face. The strengthening light was tingeing their faces blue.

"You say you don't know where your son is. Which means he may be alive. Why don't you go and look for him? You may find him again."

The doctor shook his head.

243

"Do you care about anything at all except David?"

The man took his time before answering.

Finally he said, "No," then turned and slipped into a pocket of darkness among the trees where the morning light had not yet reached.

He recognized the field beyond the ditch and the safety barrier where they had sat down for a drink and Sergio had met them again. During those two weeks the snow had melted, but the ground was still hard and wintry with a thin layer of ice.

As soon as he heard the squeaking of brakes on the lorry he understood. It took them about ten minutes to sort themselves out, after which the cripple and some twenty youths cut quickly through the field and disappeared into the forest. The music had already been off for a couple of hours. Leonardo had thought the generator must have run out of fuel. Now he knew that was not what had happened.

The first shots rang out an hour later. At first few and far between, then more frequent.

David, hearing them, began to move nervously round the cage. He never did this when the youths went out on a normal hunt, but now, for many hours, explosions could be heard echoing from the hills. He called to the elephant who came to rest his head against Leonardo's chest. He scratched under his ears and talked to him for a long time, asking him many questions about his past to distract him and chase away the black images passing through their minds. David curled his trunk round Leonardo and held him close. Neither moved until Leonardo heard the animal's huge heart slow down so that it was beating in time with his own. Then they sat together with their eyes turned to the hills and waited. The afternoon slipped away and, as the sun sank, darkness emerged from the woods and besieged the road. An opaline mist lifted from the fields.

When the first raiders reappeared it was already night and they headed for the bonfire at the head of the convoy, which was normally led by a couple of cars used by scouts, the van where the guns were kept and Richard's caravan. They were carrying two chests full of tins on their shoulders. The next to arrive had a can of petrol and another full of a dark liquid that might have been wine or kerosene. A roar of shouts and shots greeted their arrival, but Leonardo did not lean out to see what was happening at the head of the column; he kept his eyes on the forest, from where the cripple and the main party had not yet appeared. He did not have to wait long. They were somewhat spread out, each carrying something: one had an animal that had already been skinned, some had weapons and some a box or large piece of dried meat. Four of the lads who had originally left the caravan were missing. The cripple was gripping the arm of Salomon, the elder son. There was no sign of Manon or Sergio or their younger son.

Leonardo heard the cries of excitement at the head of the column get louder, followed by a chorus of "Alberto, Alberto, Alberto . . .", then the usual music started up again, drowning everything else.

He knelt down, took a piece of David's dry dung and some straw and mixed them together to make two small balls that he stuffed into his ears, then lay down on the floor and, with the muffled noise filling his head, looked inside himself. He found himself in an empty church, stripped of all trace of the thousands who had once prayed there so earnestly. Vetch had climbed the pillars and water dripping from the roof had formed stalactites of red lime that hung down like scraps of ulcerated flesh. A wooden candelabrum was the only altar fitting. There were no pictures on the walls, only shirts, trousers and dresses fixed up with old nails. There was a door into the sacristy from the aisle to the right. It was open, and a rocking sound emanated from the room.

When he opened his eyes, Leonardo could see shadows projected against the wall of trees that marked the edge of the forest.

"Once people used to read your books, and now you dance for kids and suck bones like a dog."

"That's how it is."

"But why do that?"

"For her."

"She's not here."

245

"She'll come back."

"Are you so sure?"

"I shall dance and suck bones till she comes back and I shall be here for her."

He turned his back on the dancing shadows and closed his eyes. The church was dark and he could hear footsteps wandering in the aisles; the footsteps of Manon and Sergio and their child. "I'm here," he said. Don't be afraid."

In the morning, when everyone was asleep, the cripple opened the door and ushered the little boy into the cage.

"You'll stay here for a bit," he said, then went away without a glance at Leonardo or the sleeping elephant. Leonardo looked at the child: he had some sort of soft encrustation in his hair but did not seem to have been injured. But he was clearly very tired. Tired and dirty. Infinitely tired, dirty and depressed.

"Do you recognize me?"

The boy's eyes ran over him, but he said nothing.

"I've been in your house. With me there was a girl, a boy your age and a dog. Also a tall gentleman."

He noticed that Salomon was looking at David. The elephant was sleeping with his head propped on his front feet. He looked like a pious person mumbling prayers into cupped hands.

"Don't be afraid of him," he said to reassure the boy. "Sit down, you must be tired."

The child did not move.

"You can sit by the door. I'll stay here. Are you thirsty?"

Salomon nodded. Leonardo, without moving from the branches he was leaning against, sent the bottle rolling in his direction. Salomon grabbed it before it stopped. After drinking he stood it on the floor and stared at it with his hands hanging by his sides. He was wearing a pair of jeans, a light pullover with horizontal stripes and felt slippers. The colour of his eyes reminded him of the water of a fjord seen from the top of a

Nordic cliff. They were the same shade of blue as his mother's and required the same strength of character to sustain it. For a couple of hours now a crystalline silence had rested over the whole caravan. The croaking of a crow was deafening.

"Do you really not remember me?"

No answer.

"We had a meal together and you asked me the name of my dog."

Salomon stepped two paces back till he came up against the wooden wall and let himself slide to the ground. Leonardo realized he would soon be asleep. So as not to disturb him, he turned away to look at the forest. A tired sun was struggling from behind a thick blanket of cloud, as the darkness grudgingly retreated to leave the grass veiled with mother-of-pearl.

"That's an Indian elephant," the child said.

Leonardo looked at him. His face was very pale and his hair had been cut pageboy style.

"Are you an expert on elephants?"

"Not really, but I've got a book that tells all about them."

"It must be a book with lots of photographs."

"Yes, but it has drawings too and a sort of puzzle."

"His name's David."

The child nodded.

"Does he eat those leaves?"

"Yes."

"It says in my book that elephants are always on the move because they have to eat so much. They have intestines thirty-seven metres long."

"He doesn't eat much."

Salomon studied the animal. In the cold, troubled air the elephant looked as if it were made of slate.

"Is he also here because he tried to escape?" the boy said.

Leonardo touched his nose: the break had healed leaving it crooked and hooked.

"Have you tried to escape?" he asked.

"Yes, but I twisted my ankle."

"That was very brave of you. But now you should have a rest."

The child rubbed his hands together. It looked as if he hoped he might create fire or light that way.

"I'm afraid to fall asleep in case the elephant tramples on me." He interrupted himself: "Elephants can be aggressive."

"This one's very docile."

"What does 'docile' mean?"

"That he's gentle."

"Yes, but he doesn't know me."

Leonardo studied his hands.

"I'll stay awake and keep an eye on him, and when he wakes up I'll tell him who you are."

They looked at each other for a while in the silence of the new dawn, then the child closed his eyes and let his chin fall on his chest.

For three days, the shouts and music of partying, lasting till dawn, reached them from the head of the procession of vehicles. During those two days no-one, except the doctor, came near the wagon to see how the child was or to annoy Leonardo. Salomon, when not asleep, was content to watch the youngsters coming back from the forest carrying the food, bottles, pans, furniture and other objects that had once been part of the only home he had ever known.

Watching him, Leonardo wondered where the boy could be hiding what must be a desperate need to be alone and his grief over what had happened. In fact, he never mentioned his parents or brother or referred to their fate. He never asked any questions about the future or showed any sign of missing all the things he had had till the previous day. It was as though nothing had come to him as a surprise.

At dawn, when the doctor came, he woke and ate the food the man brought. Leonardo left the tenderest pieces of meat for Salomon and waited till he had had enough before eating the rest himself. Then Salomon would sit with his back to the wall in silence, except when he suddenly began to talk about animals he knew about, particularly his favourites, which were horses and foxes.

One afternoon he told Leonardo about the leafcutter ants of South America; and how they built nests eight metres deep with a room in the middle big enough for a man to stand upright. He explained that these ants got their name not because they ate leaves but because they cut them and carried them into their nest where they made them into a litter on which they could grow mushrooms. In fact, they had such a passion for their favourite mushrooms that they not only ate them, but used their own shit to sow the spores in the nest where they would grow and could then be eaten in comfort and fed to their larvae.

At dawn, with the child still asleep, Leonardo asked the doctor what had happened to his parents. For a while they listened in silence to Salomon's breathing as he snored through a blocked nose in the way small children do. Then the doctor told Leonardo they had barricaded themselves in their house and the father had killed four youths before he was hit in the neck. Only then had they been able to break down the door. The woman and the younger child had fled to the attic where, judging all was lost, she had shot her son and then herself. When Leonardo asked where Salomon had been at the time, the doctor said he had been found hiding under the trap door to the secret room his father had dug beneath the house as a store for provisions.

In those two days Salomon came to trust David, though he never went near him except when Leonardo was at his side. The elephant showed himself even more gentle with Salomon, giving short moans of pleasure when the boy's small hand touched his thick hide, and turning away when the child retired into the corner to attend to his physical needs.

On their last night together in the cage the child woke Leonardo to say he had had a bad dream.

"A very bad one?"

"The worst I've ever had."

"I expect you'd rather not tell me about it."

"Better not."

"Yes, perhaps that's best."

Leonardo felt his forehead to see if he was feverish. It was the first time the boy had let himself be touched. His forehead was cool.

"You can go back to sleep. You can't have two bad dreams in one night."

"Can I sleep here?"

"Of course you can. Are you cold?"

"Yes, very cold. Will David be good?"

"Of course he will."

The child lay down beside Leonardo, both with their backs against the elephant's belly. Leonardo slipped his left arm round Salomon's shoulders.

"Warmer?"

"Yes, but David has a bad smell."

"That's probably me. I haven't changed my clothes for such a long time."

"And I haven't washed for three days. If Mamma knew all hell would break loose."

"Your mother would understand the situation."

They fell silent, feeling the bass notes of the music thump against their ribs.

"What have you done to your feet? Why are they black?"

"I'm a dancer. A dancer who sometimes dances on hot coals, but one evening I didn't concentrate properly and burned myself. But they're getting better now."

"Sure?"

"It's normal for people who dance on hot coals to have black feet. It's a professional risk, like a tennis player having one arm musclier than the other."

"What's tennis?"

"Have you never seen a tennis match?"

The boy shook his head.

"You will one day, and maybe you'll even be able to play. Let's get some sleep now. In a few hours the doctor will be here and bring us something to eat."

"Can I ask you something else?"

"Of course you can."

"Where's your daughter?"

Leonardo looked into the child's eyes, which were fixed on him.

"When they brought you here, did you talk to a man with long hair and a beard? A man in a long robe?"

"Yes."

"Can I ask you what he said to you?"

"That I was one of his sons and he would teach me many useful things. That I must love all the guys round me because they were my brothers and sisters, and apart from that I could do what I liked."

"Was there a girl with a shaven head with him?"

"You mean bald?"

"Yes, a bald girl."

"Yes."

"That's my daughter."

"Is she his fiancée?"

"No, she's not his fiancée."

The child closed his eyes as though he had decided to go to sleep. Leonardo knew this was not the case and continued to watch him. In the darkness his skin was pearly white, the profile of his nose a work of art.

"Salomon?"

"Yes."

"I want to say something very important to you. Something you must remember. Will you be able to do that?"

"Alright."

"In a little time they'll let you join the others. There are some things you must promise me not to do."

"Alright."

"The first thing is don't try to escape; if they catch you doing that they could hurt you, and even if you got away you'd have nowhere to go. There are lots of bad people around. O.K.?"

The boy looked uncertainly at him.

"O.K., Salomon?"

"O.K."

"Good. Once you're out of here they'll paint your face and shave off your eyebrows with a razor. That will mean you've joined the tribe. Let them do it but remember you don't belong in their tribe. The family you had before, even if it doesn't exist anymore now, will always still be your tribe. These people here will make you breathe in from a pouch and give you something to drink, you must pretend to do it but really not do it. Those things can harm you. If you touch them you'll forget your mamma and your papà and your little brother, and if you forget them there won't be anyone left to remember them."

"You're scaring me."

Leonardo hugged him.

"Don't be scared. Are you listening to me?"

"Yes, but stop scaring me."

"I don't want to scare you. But do listen and remember what I'm telling you: they'll put you with other children. One of them is called Alberto. He was the child with me the day we came to your house. He's two years older than you and has reddish hair. Don't listen to what he tells you, O.K.? He and the others do very nasty things and will want you to join in . . ."

"What kind of nasty things?"

"Nasty things to people and animals. You love animals very much and people too and you know things like that mustn't be done. You know your mamma and your papà would never have done such things and I know you won't do them either. But don't run away from the camp, O.K.? Here you'll get food and drink and be safe. You must do like people in the theatre, you must act."

"What's the theatre?"

"Never mind, it's not important. Just pretend to be like the others. You and I and David know you're not really like the others at all. O.K.? Shall I repeat what you have to remember?"

"No. Are you pretending too?"

"Yes, I am."

"Is it difficult?"

"It is to begin with, but it gets easier. Now let's get some sleep, O.K.?"

"O.K."

Leonardo closed his eyes and felt the child snuggle against him. He could hear something moving inside David's stomach.

"Leonardo?"

He felt his eyes grow moist and kept them shut. Weeks had passed since anyone had called him by name.

"Yes?"

"Are teeth also a professional risk?"

"How do you mean?"

"You said black feet are a professional risk. But must a dancer on hot coals also have broken teeth like you?"

Leonardo smiled.

"It's not essential, but it helps. Now go to sleep, O.K.?"

"O.K."

At midday, the cripple came to retrieve the boy and not long after that the whole procession moved off. For several days they drove at walking pace along secondary roads, not stopping until nightfall; the provisions found in Salomon's home made hunting expeditions unnecessary. Sometimes the car sent ahead on reconnaissance came back to warn them they were getting near a village or group of houses. The column would then halt and the music be turned off, and a band of about twenty youths would break away to take the place by surprise. They would nearly always come back empty-handed or with rubbish that would have to be left behind. The land they were passing through seemed to have been already stripped of everything. Here and there, in the fields, they would come upon the rubble of past harvests, or find some item of agricultural machinery like a relic of a now extinct civilization. Fallow deer, red deer and wild boar fled from the fields and roadside ditches to seek refuge in the thickets. No thread of smoke cut across the continuous grey of the sky.

In the evening, the procession would be arranged in a circle in a clearing or dry field and a fire would be laid and lit. Richard would emerge to inspect the booty and talk to his people. He was always alone and Leonardo never managed to see Lucia even through the open door of the caravan.

After he had walked about and listened to each of the young people, Richard would give the cripple the drug to distribute and go back inside. The only people he never looked at, or spoke to, were Leonardo and the bald woman huddled against the ancient Opel, to which she was now tied by a rope a couple of metres long. When they were on the move she had to walk barefoot on the asphalt, struggling to keep up so as not to be dragged along, while at night she huddled against the boot of the car for warmth. As the days passed she had lost a lot of weight and her skin had taken on the malarial colour of dried clay. When pieces of meat or other food were thrown in her direction she pushed them away with her foot and asked for water which was nearly always brought to her.

Leonardo was not allowed out of the cage, but the youngsters started going near it again to torment him and scoff at him.

At first, he reacted as before by hiding in the most inaccessible corner, but realizing that this merely attracted more and more spectators, he began jumping about, dancing and writhing to the music every time he was asked to. The young people would be amused and egg him on for a few minutes by clapping their hands and then go away after throwing him something to eat as a reward. In this way he got two tins of sardines and one of tuna which he ate at night, using the oil to massage his feet and face where he was deeply scarred.

When no-one was disturbing him, he tried to concentrate on the roads and signposts so as to be able to memorize their movements; it was clear they were heading for the mountains, perhaps in the hope of finding a pass and reaching France, but at the same time they were taking the greatest care to avoid main roads, cities and towns. At first, Leonardo thought there might be troops of the National Guard about, but he eventually came to the conclusion that Richard was well aware that the main centres of population had already been looted and so wanted to search isolated areas in the hope of finding people and fuel, as at the home of

Sergio and Manon.

The temperature had dropped and each morning powdery flakes that never quite became snow floated down from the sky. The mountains, when the clouds lifted to reveal them, seemed coated with snow and misery. The cold hit Leonardo hardest during the daytime, when there was no fire to give a little heat and David had eaten the branches he liked to use for shelter. So he pressed himself close against the elephant, and when David defecated, hurried to push his hands and feet into the faeces to seek out a little warmth. His sweater had grown stiff with blood and dirt and the seat of his trousers had come apart from so much sitting. He asked the doctor for a blanket but was told no-one could bring him anything without orders from Richard.

One day the children came near; there were about ten of them, including Alberto and Salomon. It was the first time he had seen Salomon since he left the cage. Now he was only centimetres away, his face painted green and his eyebrows shaved off, his eyes like ceramic fragments.

The children collected mud from the edge of the road and began throwing it at him in handfuls. Leonardo, as usual, started dancing. Alberto laughed and ran with the others to find more ammunition in the ditch. But Salomon stayed close to the wagon, staring at him.

Leonardo signed to him to go with the others, but he shook his head.

The others came back and continued their attack. He was hit in the throat and wiped himself clean before the mud could slip down inside his sweater. The floorboards creaked as he leaped about.

"Theatre, theatre, theatre," Leonardo chanted. The children laughed. He winked at Salomon who unwillingly went to pick up a piece of turf and throw it in Leonardo's direction without hitting him. The game went on a little longer, then the procession halted and the music was turned off. Knowing what this meant, the children ran excitedly to the head of the column. Salomon stayed a moment longer by the cage, then he ran away too.

Camp was set up nearby, on the asphalted area in front of a sanctuary chapel that must once have been the object of Sunday pilgrimages. On one side were the remains of a hut with a sign saying "Souvenirs and Panini" and a powerful jet of water pouring into a basin lined with red tiles. The chapel was white and very small.

The usual fire was laid on the asphalt, but the wood was damp and slow to catch and had to be sprinkled with kerosene. A cold drizzle had started to fall while the mountain peaks were hidden by amorphous clouds.

The older youths left in the camp collected more wood, inspected the chapel and wandered about a bit in the open space, then shut themselves up in the cars and coach with the girls. Two untied the woman with the shaven head. She offered no resistance, and they led her into the cab of the van where the cans of petrol were kept. The children, left on their own, pulled blazing branches from the bonfire and began fencing with each other, raising showers of sparks that leaped impetuously up into the sky only to be suddenly extinguished like faithless prayers. One or two of the children went up to the cars to watch the bodies cavorting inside on the seats, then ran away laughing. Salomon every so often turned his eyes towards Leonardo. His hair, wet from the rain, was stuck to his head. He looked as if he had just emerged from his mother's womb. Leonardo put a hand to his lips and smiled at him. He ran off with the rest when Alberto called them to destroy their enemies hidden in the chapel.

The raiding expedition returned at nightfall. Leonardo, who had stuck his hands and feet out of the cage to get them nearer to the fire, first heard a confused sound of shouting, then saw the group appear from the ramp leading up to the space before the chapel.

The young people left in the camp, hearing the shouts, leaped out of the vehicles. The two who had been using the bald girl tied her back to the fender with her trousers still round her ankles and ran to meet the others. Even Richard emerged from his caravan, helped Lucia down the steps, and moved without hurrying towards the raiders who were approaching in a compact group. It was days since Leonardo had seen her; she seemed neither thinner nor suffering, just infinitely distant. He called her name twice, but she continued to follow Richard with tiny steps, as if unsure whether the earth could hold her weight. She was wearing the same blue

256

dress as the last time he saw her and had small and livid round marks on her neck.

The youths came into the open space. In their midst Leonardo could see two men; their faces swollen and bloodstained; he guessed one must be about forty and the other about twenty years older. The older one, thin and curved, was looking about himself with imploring eyes. Leonardo was reminded of a watchmaker, a printer or a manufacturer of dental prostheses; someone who had spent most of his life bent over work that required great patience and love of detail. He could imagine him with a cup of *caffé americano* permanently on the workbench beside him and a cigarette on the edge of a saucer, reduced to a precarious tube of ash.

But the other man advanced confidently, grimacing with contempt. Three lines tattooed on his shoulder represented a man with a shield in one hand and some terrible weapon in the other. He also had several tribal markings, some letters and a stylized mouse. Both men were in singlets and underpants, the elder with a red sock on his left foot. Leonardo felt sorry for them, but also felt he must not waste on others pity he would need for himself.

Once in the open space, the group fell back and the two men found themselves face to face with Richard. The elder dropped to his knees and began sobbing softly, but the other smiled when Richard traced the sign of the cross in the air.

"Give them something to drink," Richard said.

The youths went quiet and one ran to fetch a bottle. He was back in a few seconds, but in the meantime the kneeling man seemed to have aged by ten years. He took the bottle, drank a mouthful and gave it back, nodding thanks. He had a huge haematoma under his armpit, and his hair, when not stained with blood, was a dull white. In contrast, the tattooed man had a nervous body and recently cut black hair. He was losing a lot of blood from wounds on his face and wrists, but seemed completely in control of himself. When the boy offered him the bottle he did not even deign to glance at him.

"A path is decreed for each one of us," Richard said. "God has brought you on to our path to make clear the direction of your own. His hand can sometimes be harsh; he is a shepherd not afraid to strike his sheep when they depart from the way, but . . ."

"Just kill us, you bastard, and get it over," the tattooed man said, then spat, smearing Richard's tunic with a red stain.

One of the youths lifted his rifle to hit him with the butt, but Richard gestured to him to stop and stared without resentment at the man who had insulted him.

"I take your point," he said, "but you'll be surprised what the Lord has chosen for you." For a moment nothing could be heard but the crackling of the fire and the jet of water striking the basin of the fountain. The youths watched the scene without moving, mouths half open and their breath rising in a cloud towards the grey sky. Lucia, at Richard's side, stared at the bowed head of the kneeling man. The rain grew heavier.

"Enrico!" Richard called.

The cripple came forward. The prisoners looked at him; the rain gluing his clothes to his stunted body gave him the appearance of a child with a very large head. But his face was that of an adult, keen and ruthless.

"Would you be good enough to read the rules?" Richard asked him.

The cripple pulled a black wallet from his jacket pocket, and took out a piece of paper.

"You will sit down at a table," he read, "facing each other with a knife. One of you will be given two minutes to cut off one of his own fingers. If he fails he will be killed. If he succeeds, the other will then have two minutes to do the same. The survivor will be the one who cuts off one finger more than the other. If you both cut off all ten of your fingers, you will both live."

The cripple folded the paper, put it back into his wallet and slipped the wallet back into his inside pocket. The older man looked up at Richard. He was weeping; Richard smiled at him.

"Have you understood the rules?"

"You filthy fanatic," the man with black hair said.

Richard nodded benevolently and gave the sign to begin. Three youths unloaded from one of the lorries a table that must have come from a restaurant or some other business premises. Its formica surface was marked by deep cuts and was stained black. They set it a couple of metres from the bonfire. Night had surrounded the camp, dividing each figure into light and shadow: the brightness of the fire danced warmly on each face, while each back merged with the darkness of the forest.

The two prisoners were untied and made to sit facing each other at the table. The young people settled cross-legged in a circle. Leonardo could see Alberto and Salomon. He could also see the two youths who had captured them. The blond one had his arm round the shoulders of a very thin girl with an aquiline nose and long hair, while the thickset one, who had been involved in the capture of these two new prisoners, was now staring at them with curiosity. The bald girl was huddled under the car out of the rain. Richard blessed the two men one more time, then taking Lucia by the hand, went back into the caravan. The cripple had set a small hourglass in the middle of the table beside a knife with a wooden handle. The hourglass was of a kind once used for parlour games. Leonardo remembered having one when playing Latin Scrabble with a fellow student. The knife had a curved blade ending in a double point, of the type often used for cheese.

The cripple tossed a coin in the air, caught it and covered it with the palm of his other hand.

"Choose," he said.

The white-haired man stared at the knife and the hourglass, his head shaken by small jerks that seemed to mean no. Rain was still cutting across the circle of light from the bonfire. Apart from the flickering flames and slowly rising spirals of grey smoke, the whole world seemed to be holding its breath. The tattooed man wiped his forehead to stop the blood still running into his eyes.

"Tails," he said, in a voice that seemed to come from the far end of a long corridor.

The cripple lifted his hand.

"Heads it is." He put the coin back in his pocket, turned over the hourglass and taking his pistol from his belt, pointed it at the head of the tattooed man, who looked at the other prisoner.

"Can you do it?" the tattooed man asked in a firm voice.

The white-haired man's eyes were fixed on the knife in the middle of the table, while tears continued to fall freely down his badly shaved cheeks.

"Stop crying and look at me."

The man looked up for an instant, then dropped his eyes to the table again. His curved back was racked by sobs.

"Look at me and tell me you will do it."

"One minute!" the cripple announced.

The tattooed man wiped blood from his eyes with his forearm. He looked at the white head of the other who was staring at his hands abandoned on his knees. A thread of mucus was running down his chin to his stomach.

"Do you want to live, or will they be doing you a favour by killing you?"

The old man shook his head.

"Thirty seconds!" the cripple said.

"All you have to do is cut off one finger. Can't you do that?"

"Twenty seconds!" the cripple said, cocking his pistol.

"Can't you do it?" shouted the younger man.

The old man looked up as if, Leonardo thought, in final farewell, like someone saying goodbye to his country or to a woman he knows he will never see again.

"Ten seconds!"

The younger man grabbed the knife and lopped off his own little finger.

The young people exploded in applause.

Putting down the knife, the man looked at his finger lying on the formica table top. A small pool of blood had already formed round his hand.

"You fool," he said, looking at the man with white hair.

The cripple picked up the bloodstained knife, wiped it on his trousers, placed it in front of the older man and turned over the hourglass. Leonardo closed his eyes.

*

It was already well into the night when they took the tattooed man to the cage. They opened the door and he walked in. Then for a while he stood beside the bars, watching the young people dancing and passing the body of the man with white hair over their heads, like the corpse of an ancient rock idol. Then, when they threw the body on the fire, he went to sit down against the wooden wall, at the exact point where Salomon had huddled when he first came into the cage.

Leonardo watched from the other side of the wagon. The man's face was thin and lined and his cheekbones prominent, but the general impression he made was still one of compact solidity. In the shifting light of the bonfire his eyes were like wrought iron.

"A doctor will come and treat you," Leonardo said.

The man did not move. He was sitting with his arms round his knees. The wound where his finger had been was bleeding profusely. A red stain had already formed on the floor.

"Have you played this game too?"

"No," Leonardo said.

The man swallowed.

"Why are they keeping you here then?"

"To dance."

"They make you dance?"

Leonardo said nothing. The man seemed to be smiling.

"Was that man your friend?"

"No. I found him hiding in a cellar a few days ago. I should never have taken him with me."

"Where were you heading?"

"For the coast. They say there are fortified villages there where you can live. All you have to do is pass the quarantine. But we stopped at that house, there was a stove and we'd found some sunflower seeds. It was a mistake."

They stopped to listen to the music as it spread over the bodies, the cars, the lorries, the coach, the caravan, the flight of steps and the façade of the building picked out by the flames from the darkness. Apart from these things the world was black and inscrutable.

"Where are you from?"

"R."

"Did you walk from R.?"

The man did not admit it, but Leonardo understood this to have been the case.

"How is it down there?"

"Same as here. Plus deserters from the National Guard who shoot at anything that moves. I had a bicycle, some blankets, a water can, food; they took the lot. On the Apennines I ran into an army camp. They had tanks, lorries, armour, everything, all unable to move. No fuel. They hadn't been able to communicate with their H.Q. for months. Every day one or other of the soldiers disappeared, taking his weapons with him."

Leonardo saw Salomon standing still, a few paces from the bonfire. He was looking at the body of the man with white hair, by now reduced to a blackened puppet. About thirty youngsters were still dancing round the flames; the others had gone to bed. A cold rain was still falling. He looked back at the man with him, who seemed to have dozed off.

"I could tear off a piece of singlet to bind up your finger. You're losing a lot of blood."

Without opening his eyes, the man shook his head.

"More to the point, have you got any water?" he said.

"No, but at first light the doctor will bring you some."

"Who's the doctor?"

"Someone who got captured like us. I think he must have played the game and is now free to come and go. Maybe you'll be able to join the tribe in a few days too."

The man laughed, then coughed, spitting out a black clot. His legs were lying in a dark pool of blood. For Leonardo, the smell of his blood blended with the smell of the body burning on the bonfire and the smell of David sleeping behind him.

"What were you? A teacher? The director of a museum? A journalist?" the man asked.

"I used to teach Literature in a university."

The man laughed again, then wiped his face with his bloody hand.

"After everything they've done to you, you should grab the first one who comes anywhere near this cage and strangle him with your own hands. Instead of just sitting there trembling with fear. Don't you agree that madman must be the Antichrist? The incarnation of evil? He didn't even have the courage to watch while we were cutting off our fingers. He's just a bastard."

Leonardo contemplated his own bruised, cold and blackened feet. When he looked up again the man was dead.

At dawn, taking care not to dirty his shoes, the doctor approached the body and placed a hand on his neck. His wounds were dry. The great patch of blood had reached the middle of the wagon where it vanished down a wide crack between the floorboards.

"He was a haemophiliac," the doctor said.

"There's nothing you can do?"

"Nothing."

The procession started out again, leaving behind the ashes of the bonfire which still contained the visible remains of the man with white hair. They continued all day along narrow roads between woods and fields marked by snow, passing ruined houses, a farmers' union building and a couple of shops that had already been looted. When several youngsters came to the wagon, and Leonardo told them the man was dead, they just threw a couple of stones at the body to see if it would move, then went away. The jolting of the wagon had made the man's body fall on its side in an entirely unnatural position. Leonardo got to his feet, grasped it under the armpits and dragged it to a clean part of the floor. Then he used a little of his water ration to wash the face, and closed the eyes. Doing this comforted him, like digging Adele's grave. Maybe this is my vocation: burying the dead, he thought. Then with his finger he traced the man's tattoo marks: the skin was hard, cold and smooth, like a Nordic warrior killed in battle, Leonardo thought, or an apocalyptic Old Testament prophet ready to be placed on a pyre of fragrant wood and burned in the middle of the desert. The man's badly shaved beard looked like gold dust.

It began snowing, but before the snow could settle on the asphalt, two youths with spotty faces came into the cage, pulled the corpse out and threw it down at the side of the road. The man's left foot remained visible above the edge of the ditch and Leonardo continued to stare at it until it was too far away and everything was absorbed in the whiteness precipitating from the sky.

They spent a few days in a large industrial building waiting for the roads to become usable again; the snowfall had not been heavy, but it was so cold it formed a firm crust the sun could not penetrate.

That evening Leonardo was taken to the fire, and without being forced to, danced to amuse the tribe. Lucia, sitting beside Richard on a sofa, followed his clumsy movements with her mouth half open and her eyes expressionless, and when Richard gave the order for Leonardo to be returned to the cage, she got up and let the man take her back into the caravan, where a light stayed on all night.

The youths resumed hunting, catching mainly hares, dogs and small wild animals. It was a district of sparse woodland and occasional vineyards, the plain could not be far away. One night Leonardo heard a plane pass overhead. The youths put out what was left of the fire and kept still with their eyes on the ceiling of the building. Then, as the sound of the twin-engined plane disappeared in the distance, they started dancing again but did not relight the fire.

Leaving the warehouse, they found themselves on roads in the foothills, searching deserted villages where they found nothing but a can of motor oil, some bottles of wine, and black potatoes that had spent all winter in the earth. Then, one evening, Leonardo saw three church towers rising in the distance above the considerable expanse of a town with a square castle in the middle.

The next day, they kept to the foothills and skirted round the inhabited area; Richard must have been afraid of something since the youths carried their weapons all day and no-one went near the villas they passed.

Nightfall found them on a muddy track between fields marked by irrigation ditches and the occasional farm. The sky had been heavy and leaden all day.

Hearing the sound of motors, Leonardo got to his feet in time to see four cars travelling slowly down a parallel road not more than two hundred metres away. As soon as the youths saw the cars, they leaped into the field separating the two tracks, and, gun in hand, started running towards the cars. The leading car increased its speed but the others stopped. Eight men got out, all armed with rifles, and immediately dropped to their knees ready to fire. At this the youths, though more numerous, slowed down and stopped.

For a few seconds the two groups studied each other. The field was dark brown and it had just started raining again. The last of the light was falling obliquely from behind the mountains and painting everything an identical violet.

Richard, who had come out of the caravan, called the cripple. The man listened to what his boss had to say, then put down his pistol on the bonnet of one of the cars and began walking towards the men on the other side of the field who still had their guns trained on the boys. One of them, seeing him approach unarmed with his hands up, slung his rifle over his shoulder and came to meet him. His uniform was reminiscent of the National Guard, but by now it was too dark for Leonardo to see clearly.

The cripple and the other man met in the middle of the field and talked for several minutes without ever raising their hands from their bodies, after which the man turned towards his own people and shouted something that reminded Leonardo of a dog's bark.

Then two of the soldiers made a woman get out of one of the cars.

All Leonardo could see at that distance was that she was very fat and had a red jumper. They pushed her into the field where she slipped on the wet ground and fell. Getting back to her feet she cleaned her trousers with altogether incongruous care, before moving towards the cripple and the man in the uniform, who were waiting some fifty metres further on. When the group reached them, the cripple turned towards Richard, who nodded.

The cripple signed to the woman to follow him and headed for the caravan with the youths.

Walking in the other direction, the man in uniform rejoined his own people on the road. Leonardo saw him get into one of the cars, then the cars moved off and finally disappeared behind a group of houses blackened by smoke.

The woman was really extraordinarily fat. As she crossed the swamp her buttocks bounced in her tight wet trousers and her enormous breasts hung against her belly, like a cuttlefish with its mass of flesh centred on a single bone. The youths escorting her paid her no attention. They seemed afraid the soldiers might return and, from time to time, cast a wary eye on the group of houses where the cars had vanished.

When they got to the road two boys helped the woman over the ditch. Her black hair had once been bobbed, and she had slightly elongated eyes. Otherwise the lines of her face were coarse and unfinished, though entirely feminine. An insensitive man would have dismissed her as fat and ugly, but a closer look would have made it clear that the first adjective in no way implied the second. Watching her pass close to the cage, Leonardo noticed she had small hands, and her feet were shod in light bowling shoes.

After they had helped her into the coach, the youths went back to their own vehicles and the procession get under way again. Leonardo could hear the engine of the coach getting into gear and the heavy wheels of the wagon groaning under the cage floor. He looked at David. The elephant's melancholy eyes were fixed on the field where the exchange had taken place.

"I don't think this woman can take Lucia's place," Leonardo said, then he crouched on the branches the elephant had stripped clean the day before, and wept.

They travelled all night. It was the first time they had done so and Leonardo noticed that only the lorries, the coach and the Land Rover had their lights on; there was no fuel for the other vehicles which were all being towed. For this reason their progress had become slower and slower;

a man walking quickly would have been able to overtake them without difficulty.

They stopped at dawn in the yard of a large abandoned farmstead. As soon as the bonfire had been lit, the cripple distributed a little canned food, and several dogs which had been killed the day before were skinned and put to cook. Half the farm's roof had fallen in, but one part of the building seemed still in good shape. Still, no-one took the trouble to explore. The boys sat round the farmyard strangely silent, showing no interest whatever in the fat woman who, tied to one of the roof supports, was watching her new masters with inexplicable serenity.

For a few days now it had been as if some minor melancholy had sometimes disturbed the tribe and made them uneasy. Their nights of partying had become increasingly short and fierce, and when Richard was out of sight in the caravan, brawls constantly broke out. The cripple watched without intervening, but these quarrels would last only a few minutes and end for no apparent reason as suddenly as they had begun. Apart from meat, which was never in short supply, their food was running out. There was no more beer, only wine.

Now when Richard came out of his caravan, some of the young people still ran to surround him, but for the first time about half of them stayed under their covers, their eyes on the flames. It was not raining, but the night had made everything damp and a sterile sun hinted at another day without warmth.

Showing no disappointment in those who were absent, Richard blessed those who were there and talked to them. Leonardo was sure his mind must be working on this new state of affairs and that he was capable of doing this without his face showing any emotion at all. In fact, Richard soon told Enrico to free the captured woman and take her to the wagon for "union". This order created a ferment of excitement that quickly spread to those who had been keeping themselves to themselves. While the cripple guided the woman to the big wagon and introduced her into the cage, the youngsters gathered round with their faces glued to the bars.

"Look, dancer!" Richard announced in a loud voice for everyone to hear. "We've found you a girlfriend so you can have some fun."

The youngsters continued to make excited noises. Leonardo looked at Richard; he was smiling as serenely as usual, but Leonardo could read something in his expression that inspired contempt rather than fear.

"We're waiting, dancer," Richard sneered.

The woman, standing inside the cage door, was watching Leonardo calmly.

He guessed she must be someone who, all her life, had been used to keeping calm in situations that tended to bring the worst out of other people. But there was no sense of her holding anything back; rather her calmness seemed to take the form of acceptance. The beauty so absent from her body seemed concentrated in the oriental slant of her eyes.

"Enrico," Richard said, "please be so good as to give our dancer a little encouragement."

The cripple took his pistol from his belt and fired into the wall just above David's head. The elephant trumpeted and began tramping nervously round the cage. Leonardo leaped to his feet and he and the woman both pressed themselves against the bars to avoid being crushed. But David soon calmed down. He timidly approached the woman and his trunk gently explored her hair, arm and belly. She closed her eyes and let him touch her; face to face they were the same height. When David returned mournfully to his corner, she opened her eyes again and pushed her hair back from her forehead.

"Screw her!" someone shouted.

A stone thudded against Leonardo's chest with the dead sound of a stick striking an empty barrel. He dropped to his knees, conscious of his heart beating under the hand he pressed against his chest.

"Screw her! Screw her! Screw her!" yelled the young people.

A second pistol shot drowned their voices; it passed over Leonardo's head and was lost in the farmyard. This time David only walked round on the spot, making the floorboards shake. When Leonardo looked up he saw the woman taking off her trousers. She was not wearing knickers. Her flesh had the whiteness of fresh lime, with a tuft of black hair under her belly.

"Screw her! Screw her!"

Leonardo looked at Richard, and this time he saw no mirror image of Christ, but just a cunning, inordinately arrogant man of thirty-five. Mediocrity and fear marked him like a drop of oil on a surface of water, and they were a mediocrity and fear with no redeeming qualities whatever. His was a third-rate mind decked in feathers.

"Enrico!" Richard called out irritably.

The cripple pushed his way through the yelling youngsters pressed against the bars of the cage and came as near as he could to where Leonardo was standing. He pointed his pistol between the bars at Leonardo's head.

"Screw her! Screw her! Screw her!"

Leonardo looked for Salomon among the boys but could not see him. Instead he met the eyes of Alberto who was staring at him eagerly from the shoulders of the blond youth who had captured them. Under his green paint, he no longer had the face of the child Leonardo had known so much as the snout of a predator used to raiding the lairs of other animals among the bushes. He had pulled his hair back into a ponytail.

"Do what they want," the woman said, lying down on the floor.

Her calm voice cut through the shouting like a sword slicing through a coat of mail. She was now naked apart from her socks and a flesh-coloured bra scarcely able to hold her huge breasts. Beyond the farmyard the hilltops were a vivid white against the railway grey of the sky. Very soon it would begin raining or snowing again.

Leonardo moved towards her.

"I'm so sorry," he said.

She shook her head to dismiss this as irrelevant. Her eyes were not black, but a lively dark brown. He lowered his trousers and lay down on top of her. She smelt of earth and of something long buried. It was not a good smell, but one that gave the impression of having existed long before humanity, to have been part of this planet, and many of the creatures living on it, since time immemorial. Leonardo remembered the other women he had lain with: a fellow student, Alessandra, then Clara. The first two thin and supple, the last slender with big breasts. All had light brown eyes and smelt of paper, tobacco and dried bark. All had offered him carefully rationed warmth.

Leonardo felt his penis stiffen and slide into the woman's vulva. For a moment he lay still, lost in the simplicity of what was happening and the warmth of her belly, then the floorboards began to thump under the blows of dozens of hands.

"Screw-her-now! Screw-her-now!"

Leonardo rested his chin on the woman's shoulder and watched the leaves of a holm oak growing near the farm move lightly in the wind. Her breasts pressed against his thin chest at every breath.

"Am I hurting you?" he whispered.

"No."

He began moving slowly and soon he was standing alone in the middle of a white room waiting for someone. The shouts of the youngsters were no more than a distant hiss and their handclaps the noise of a train that had already passed long ago. The room had no windows; it was square, and on the end wall a painting had been hung. This showed a plate and a glass, both empty. Leonardo knew it had a title: "Steady Courage". It had been painted by the person he was waiting for, but the painter, when he arrived, would not be able to add anything to what Leonardo already knew about it, simply because he already knew all there was to know. So he felt no anxiety as he waited. He might wait hours, months or years; that did not matter. The room was white, its walls a regular shape and the painting concealed no secrets.

Leonardo felt a spoon scoop the inside of his belly as something escaped from it and travelled far away, then he lay exhausted, listening to his body and the light scratching of his beard against the woman's cheek.

The voices of the youngsters gradually diminished, moved off and fell silent.

Leonardo fastened his trousers and went back to sit in the place David had left for him against the wall. They were alone, and the woman was getting dressed.

When she had finished they stayed silent, each staring at their own feet. The only sound was the crackling of the bonfire on which potatoes had been put to boil. The rectangle of sky above the farmyard was an expanse of grey marble that had the same warmth as marble.

David got up, walked round the cage, then flexed his legs and crapped. Leonardo saw the woman smile.

"I've never seen an elephant do that," she said. "They're so funny!"

Leonardo looked out into the yard. Several of the young people were throwing blankets, clothes and toys out of the windows of the farmhouse. Others were eating by the fire and still more were asleep. The bald girl, leaning against the coach, was being penetrated from behind by a smallish boy with muscular buttocks. Another was inhaling from a pouch as he waited his turn.

"What's your name?" the woman asked.

"Leonardo."

"Well, Leonardo, there's nothing bad about what we've done."

He looked at her in silence.

"The important thing is to stay alive. Don't you agree?"

"Yes, I do."

"Excellent. Do you think they'll give us anything to eat?"

"Usually the doctor brings something, but today he hasn't come."

"Never mind, we won't die of hunger. What's the elephant called?"

"David."

"Can I trust David?"

"Yes."

The woman lay down on her side with her head supported on her hand and closed her eyes.

"Why don't you try to get a bit of rest too?" she said.

Leonardo continued to look at her unusual body stretched out on the floor. Soon it seemed utterly familiar to him. As though she had been with him in that prison ever since he first came there. He would not even have been able to say whether she was really fat or not.

"Do listen to me, Leonardo," she said. "Try closing your eyes."

A few moments later he heard her snoring.

The doctor came towards evening with a bucket of potato peelings among which a few pieces of grey meat could be seen. The woman asked if it was dog meat. The man said he did not know.

"Do you know where we're heading?" she asked him.

"I'm here to give you food and that's all," the doctor said, throwing an armful of bushes on the floor for David. "You mustn't ask me anything."

While the man went to and fro carrying branches to the wagon, the woman began eating the potatoes but avoided the meat. Leonardo in contrast took a large chunk of meat and broke it in pieces, using his fingers to do what his teeth could no longer manage. Behind them David's elastic lips were stripping the branches with a squeaky noise like new shoes on a rubber floor. When the doctor had finished stacking David's branches, he filled two buckets with water from a tap at the farm.

Leonardo put several pieces of meat into his mouth and began chewing.

"I think they're trying to get to France," he said.

The woman nodded.

"The first people who captured me tried that too, but at the frontier we were shot up by an aircraft. They were kids like this lot but nothing like so many, and on the plain they met those National Guard men. A few escaped into the forest, and the rest surrendered. The soldiers forced them into a ditch and killed the lot. There was another prisoner with me, a very kind elderly man. He had been headmaster of a lower secondary school. The soldiers killed him too."

The woman put another piece of potato in her mouth and chewed it slowly.

"Have you always been on your own here?"

Leonardo shook his head.

"There was a man, but he died the same night they captured him."

The children had pulled two beds out of the house. Alberto was laughing and jumping from one mattress to the other. Leonardo studied his face and gestures. For some days now he had been thinking he had never known any child called Alberto and that the girl in the caravan was not his daughter. Sometimes he felt sure he had left Lucia in her mother's home eight years ago and never seen her again. At such moments he experienced something like the serene drowsiness that is said to precede death from frostbite.

"My daughter's in the caravan," he told the woman.

She looked at the bald girl huddled against the rear wheel of one of the cars. The girl had walked all day and night without stopping. The remains of her dress barely covered her meagre buttocks and her breasts.

"When they find a new girl," Leonardo said, "this is what'll happen to Lucia."

The woman continued to stare at the bald girl; several children were trying to push pieces of wood down the front of her dress. All she did in an attempt to discourage them was to wave her hand.

"It won't happen to your daughter," the woman said.

The doctor came back with the water. He put one bucket in the middle of the wagon and took the other to David. Leonardo and the woman began to drink by cupping their hands, then she asked the doctor if he could get them some blankets. The man took the bucket emptied by the elephant and went away.

Once they were alone the woman wanted to drink some more, but Leonardo said it was better to keep some water for the next day. She asked if the elephant would drink it in the night. Leonardo reassured her that he would not. The woman went to urinate in the corner, then sat down with her legs crossed. As night fell a cold sharp wind shook the junipers beside the yard. Leonardo studied the dark clouds approaching from the east. During the night, or at the latest the next day, it would snow.

"It's nearly the end of February," the woman said.

For a couple of hours they watched the young people dancing, forming couples, and stripping the shutters from the house to keep the fire going. Leonardo read a new fury in their actions that worried him and forced him every so often to look away.

The eyes of the woman, on the other hand, showed no trace of despair or resentment. Her broad, irregular face seemed stretched as if she had long been taking in everything she had seen. Leonardo noticed two black hairs sprouting from a mole under her chin.

"What did you do in the world?" he asked her.

"I was a midwife."

As soon as the cripple saw Richard and Lucia emerge from the caravan, he jumped down from the roof of the van where he had spent the whole evening and went to meet them, climbing over the young people sitting on the ground.

"Your daughter's very beautiful," the woman said.

Leonardo watched Lucia walk as far as the bonfire and sit down on the sofa Richard had ordered to be unloaded from the lorry.

He stood up.

"Now I have to go," he said.

"Evelina?"

"Yes."

"Are you asleep?"

"No."

"Will you do something for me?"

"If I can."

"I'd like you to tell me how I am."

"In what sense?"

"Tell me what my face and body are like."

"It's a bit dark at the moment."

"Tell me what you saw when it was light."

"Where shall I start?"

"With my face."

"O.K., it's thin and hollow and where there's no beard it's been affected by the cold. You have a scar on your forehead and a smaller one on your cheekbone. I think you have some teeth missing, I don't know how many, and your eyes are a very beautiful dark green. But the whites of your eyes are a bit yellow, perhaps from what you eat. Your nose is bent, I can't remember whether to the left or the right. You have long grey hair which has grown into sort of tails. Your beard's dark grey, with occasional white hairs. I don't know what else to say."

"That's great. And my body?"

"Tall, with long legs and a very stiff back. When you were lying on me I could tell you weren't heavy for a man of your height. I could also tell your shoulder has been bound up and when you walk you hold it higher than the other. One very beautiful thing about you is your hands. In my work I have always paid a lot of attention to hands and I can tell you that yours, even if they are not in good condition now, are extremely shapely. But the first thing I noticed was your feet. At first I thought they were wrapped in rags, but when I realized they were naked I wanted to cry. When you were dancing I wondered how you could possibly do it."

"Fear's the only thing that keeps me going."

"I don't believe that."

"Now tell me about my smell."

"Do you think it's unpleasant?"

"It must be, I haven't washed for weeks."

"When we are alone for a long time without anyone touching us, our smell reverts to what it was when we were born. Rather like a piece of cardboard soaked in milk. It's not disagreeable. I often came across it in the delivery room, but it was my husband who first drew my attention to it. I'd like to talk to you about him, it's so long since I had anyone I could do that with."

"Was he a doctor?"

"A historian of the Enlightenment. When we met he was teaching at the University of Antwerp. He had come to the hospital to see his daughter who had just given birth. She lived abroad too, in her case in England, but her waters broke two months early while she was at a conference of antique dealers. Gianni arrived the next day from Germany. He was a very small man of nearly seventy; I was forty at the time. He wanted to speak to me about the birth; we talked briefly in front of the coffee machine, not more than a few minutes. Apart from his politeness, nothing particularly impressed me about that frail man with thick hair. As for me, with my physique, I didn't think any man could be attracted to me, not even one so much older.

"But a week later a letter addressed to me arrived at the hospital. Just a few lines about a boat trip he'd made the previous Sunday with a university colleague and the man's wife. I didn't know whether to answer or what to say. I didn't write back. A week later a second letter came telling me about a curious event that happened in the last century to the architect who built the Antwerp concert hall. I wondered what on earth this university professor could want from me; he was not young or good-looking, but certainly in a position to interest more attractive women. I was confused. I had never been in a serious relationship, only been pestered by a couple of men who were sexually excited by my obesity. This had made me pessimistic and diffident. I thought he must be another of these, but when I showed his letters to a woman friend she said she didn't think so.

"So I sent him a postcard. He answered and for a year we wrote to each other once or twice a week. He never suggested meeting, even though he had been divorced many years before and was living alone in a house near the university.

"He had a very sober way of writing, simple and straightforward, but filled with constant surprise. He avoided difficult words, but didn't use the simple ones he preferred in quite the same way as most other people. He wrote in tiny capitals, in the kind of writing one might expect from the first person from an uneducated family to have a chance of higher education. And in fact that's how it was: his father and mother had run a grocery shop in the Lomellina district.

"I bought myself a little chest with three drawers and kept his letters in it beside my bed. I kept a sheet of paper in the kitchen with the titles of the books he talked to me about so I could buy them in the bookshop. One day, talking to a hospital colleague, I realized that a whole day had passed without me thinking once about my unattractive appearance. That evening I wrote to Gianni and said I'd like to meet him. Are you asleep, Leonardo?"

"No. I'm listening. Where did you meet?"

"In Saarbrücken, a little German town near the French border. I don't know why he chose that place, it wasn't my idea. More than a year had passed since our first meeting. I imagined us sitting in a café and walking beside the river while we talked about ourselves in the way one would expect in an affectionate relationship between a man who had outlived his physical needs and a woman who had long believed her personal appearance could never encourage any. An alliance of deficient people. But what happened was that we had tea in silence in the station bar, then went to one of the two rooms he'd reserved in a small local guest house and spent two days there making love in every imaginable way.

"In the months that followed we went back to writing to each other without ever mentioning what had happened in that bedroom. His letters were light and full of affection, but never hinted that he'd like to see me again or do any of the things we had done together again. Then, in April, a few lines arrived in which he asked me to marry him. I answered with a postcard and three months later we met in front of the registrar. It was our third meeting, and in the meantime I'd arranged to buy us a house and he had applied for his pension.

"In the five years we lived together he continued to talk to me with the same loving kindness and care for my body, as though it was always new to him. This was how he saw everything round him: it was as if he was born again every morning and as if when he put on his pyjamas each evening he was dressing for his grave. His steps on the stairs coming down to breakfast would be like those of a boy at the threshold of life. This filled me with joy and an infinite sense of security and desire to have him inside me always."

When Evelina stopped talking, Leonardo listened to the sounds the night should have produced but they had been trapped by the cold in a compact block of silence. The wind passed silently over the bodies of the young people lying in the farmyard and made the embers of the bonfire glow. Apart from those vermilion fragments of light, and the echo of the woman's words, the world was a cold shadow with no tomorrow.

"What happened to your husband?"

He had the impression she shrugged her shoulders.

"The kids who captured us realized at once that it would be a bore having to drag him along with them. For several months he'd been having problems with his hip. So they tied him to the kitchen table and threw the lot into the river near our house. I think they did this because one of them had seen it done in a film. As the current carried him away, Gianni stared up at the sky with the same amazement that he had felt for everything. It was a beautiful sunny day. You'll think me morbid, but as I watched him drifting away, all I could think of was lying naked in bed with him again."

Leonardo rested his cheek against David's rough flank and looked at the point in the darkness where he knew the caravan to be. The wind had something minimal and cold in it. Beyond the bars it was perhaps starting to snow but beyond the bars was enormously far away. Great quantities of air and food were moving about inside David's belly.

"I should like to know which is worse," Evelina said. "To be raped a hundred times by Negro pirates, to have one buttock cut off, to run a Bulgar gauntlet, to be flogged and hanged in an auto-da-fé, to row in a galley, to experience – finally – all the miseries we all have endured, or simply to stay here with nothing to do?"

They were silent for a while, then he heard her get up, drink from the bucket and sit down again.

"Do you know the whole of that by heart?" Leonardo asked.

"Only that bit. It has always made me laugh when the old woman talks like that after all they've been through. Gianni was crazy about Voltaire. He used to say *Candide* was the cruellest thing ever written by anyone while laughing."

One of the lads in the farmyard got to his feet and walked a few steps, then they heard the dull thud of his body hitting the concrete.

"Do you think we'll die?" he asked her.

Evelina scratched her leg.

"Something like that."

A week passed during which it snowed for at least an hour or two every night.

The procession, coming in sight of the town, had veered to the east and begun skirting the approach to the valleys. Leonardo asked Evelina where her home had been and she pointed to the white mountain hovering above the town and named a small village clinging to its foot.

At night the snow turned the countryside and the roofs of the buildings along the road white, while by day a milky sky presided over the silent progress of the procession. From time to time, the youths would stick rifles out of the windows to shoot at the deer, dogs and white hares that populated the areas where they parked, then would run and retrieve the carcasses and throw them onto the lorry without the procession stopping. Along the main road they passed abandoned cars and empty heavy goods vehicles as well as houses, but the only tracks in the new snow were those they made themselves. The days were getting longer, but the cold still made their breath visible and gripped their hands in its bite.

During the daytime Leonardo and Evelina would cuddle together, stupefied by the rocking of the wagon. The shots would wake Leonardo from dreams in which he was talking to animals and being nourished by their milk. Evelina, in contrast, dreamed about beds too high for her to climb on to. At evening the tribe would camp in buildings that had once hosted car dealers and furniture showrooms, and gut the animals captured during the day and cook them round the fire. When Leonardo was not called out to dance he would stay in the cage with Evelina and David. They spent the nights talking, pressed up against the elephant, until the doctor brought them their food at dawn. Mostly they discussed places they had visited in the past and familiar events, but there was always a moment when they remembered that the places they were talking about did not exist anymore and that the people whose faces and actions they were trying to describe were dead. Then they would interrupt themselves and lie in each other's arms listening in the silence to their own breathing, which deafened them like the squeaking of a bicycle on a dark road.

Two lads had managed to retrieve a canful of diesel from the tank of an old combine harvester; but even so, by now the only vehicles still capable of moving under their own steam were the van and the coach. Nearly all the cars had been abandoned and the young people collected in the coach. Their empty eyes peered out through the windows at the mountains on one side and the desolate and apparently endless plain on the other.

Leonardo felt he could detect for the first time a belief in the young people's faces that there might be a tomorrow, and that if this was so it was something they could lose. This perception must have seemed to them like an object just dug up from under the ground, something to turn over in their hands in an attempt to understand what it was and who had buried it and why. The effort seemed to make them very tired.

That evening, when the music was switched on and the fire had been lit, they paired off without enthusiasm and after dancing for half an hour fell into a sleep like death, from which no-one woke to feed the fire.

Richard seldom appeared. When he did, his face looked as serene and cheerful as ever, even if very pale. Lucia followed him as he passed among the young people, talking to them and blessing them, and she sat with him to watch Leonardo dance. This was the only time the tribe seemed to recover their savage innocence.

"I'll never be able to get her away from here," Leonardo said one evening, returning to the cage.

Evelina stroked his cheek.

"Of course you will!"

"How?"

"Don't underestimate yourself. Soon you'll be stronger than he is. Perhaps you already are."

Leonardo looked at her. In the weak moonlight the innocence of her face was enough to send him to sleep. In the afternoon the sky had broken, showing a section of the heavenly vault.

"What will you take with you when you go?" she asked

This seemed an absurd question to Leonardo.

"Lucia, you, David, Salomon, the bald girl and my exercise book," he said.

"What exercise book?"

"A book I was writing in. I think it must be in the caravan."

"And Alberto?"

Leonardo said nothing.

The next day a series of shots broke several windows on the coach, hitting one boy in the throat and wounding another in the arm. The van towing the caravan stopped and everyone ran for shelter. Only Leonardo and Evelina stayed exposed inside the cage.

The shots had come from a large fortified building perched on a spur half a kilometre from the road. Dating from the fifteenth, perhaps sixteenth century, it must once have been the seat of some minor feudal lord, and was now surrounded by modern villas of shoddy design. When some of the youths fired back, it provoked a burst of return fire, more concentrated this time, that pierced the surface of the coach, the van and the caravan. Richard, who had got out to take shelter with Lucia, called the cripple who hurried over with his head down. They talked together for about ten minutes, a discussion punctuated by silences during which they stared at the sparse patches of snow on the asphalt. Leonardo knew they were weighing up the pros and cons of attacking the fortress, and whether to wait for night or try to negotiate. In the end the cripple got up and came to the cage, after first taking a rifle from one of the boys and tying a white shirt to the barrel. When he opened the door, Leonardo squeezed Evelina's arm.

"Move," the cripple said to Evelina from the entrance. The expression on his face was as blank and ferocious as ever.

Evelina turned to Leonardo with a smile.

"Don't let yourself down. O.K.?"

"I won't."

Leonardo got to his feet and stroked her arm.

"You are dear to me," he said.

"So are you to me," she answered, then went to David and rested her head against the elephant's forehead for a moment before following the cripple out of the cage.

Leonardo watched them make their way up the little road leading to the fortress: the little cripple bent over, with the white shirt hoisted on the barrel of his rifle and Evelina with her bulk enclosed in her dirty trousers and red chenille jumper.

As he watched her, Leonardo was aware of the existence of a form of beauty he had never previously known in things. It was a wonder that was not to be found on their surface or even in their depths, but that fluttered round them, nourished by a time that was not the present, but the recent past or a future soon to come, at any rate not the present, or no longer so.

An hour later the procession came to the first road signs announcing the pass, and veered off the main road heading for the valley. The surrounding whiteness was untouched. The few houses on the two still high sides of the valley had been abandoned but were in good condition. There were no signs of fires or wrecking and everything was steeped in the kind of silence one might expect after a dignified exodus.

Leonardo inhaled the cold air to clean out his lungs.

We'll never make it to France, he thought, watching the setting sun turn the white snow deep cobalt blue. There's too much snow and the frontier will be guarded. We shall all die.

None of these thoughts affected his heartbeat in any way at all.

The next day they managed to climb the valley as far as one of the last villages before the pass, but on reaching a hollow cutting where the road forked, they ran into a deep snowdrift out of reach of the sun and had to stop.

They parked the vehicles on a village square, where a century earlier holidaymakers had stayed in a comfortable pale-pink three-storey hotel more recently converted into a customs post and then sealed up by the military. On the other side of the square were the civic centre, a bar, a haberdasher's and a furniture store, though all that was left of any of them was their shop signs.

The coach was parked in the middle of the square to form an L with the caravan and the van, while the young people scattered round the village, which had a single main street with stone houses, to search for wood and something to eat. It was still early afternoon and several others went to hunt in the forest immediately above the houses. The frontier cannot have been more than twenty kilometres away, but the surrounding mountains were deep in snow and a steady wind was shifting great masses of cloud like a roof over the valley. Leonardo stuck his legs out through the bars to enjoy the warmth of the sun. He had seen Alberto and others head for what had once been a grocery shop with a petrol pump next to it. Only two were left to guard the square. The caravan stayed shut. As usual during the day, there was no sign of the doctor. Suddenly he heard someone calling him. He turned and saw Salomon's face just above the floor of the cage. Leonardo sat down with his back to him so that no-one should see him talking to the boy.

"Are you well?"

"Yes," said the child.

"Do they give you enough to eat?"

"Yes, but when are Mamma and Papà going to come for me?"

Leonardo adjusted his back against the bars.

"I'm sorry to have to tell you this, but I don't think they will be coming."

"Not at all?"

"No. We have to try and manage by ourselves."

Salomon mulled over this idea, staring at the floor deep in excrement and broken branches. Each morning, after the doctor's visit, Leonardo had once been in the habit of clearing both out of the wagon, but had not bothered after Evelina left.

"It's very dirty here," the child said.

"You're right, I really must clean the place up."

The child nodded.

"I'm sorry the lady has gone."

"So am I, but she'll be fine where she is now."

"But she was a bit of company for you."

"I've still got David."

Salomon was playing with a twig sticking out of the cage, then snapped it off and let it fall to the ground.

"Alberto has told me some very nasty things about you."

"What has he said?"

"That you're worthless and if he'd stayed with you he would've died, but that now he's the children's leader and Richard loves him very much."

"You know what to believe and what not to believe."

Salomon picked up the broken twig and joined it to the branch he had broken it from, fitting the two parts together again. His nails were dirty.

"I don't want to do any more theatre," he said.

"I know, but you must be patient a little bit longer. O.K.? Now go away, I don't want them to see you talking to me."

"Will you be dancing this evening?"

"I don't know."

"I don't like it when you dance, but it's funny too."

"Just remember I'm dancing to make you laugh. That it's what I do. O.K.?"

"O.K."

"Now go away."

"I don't know where the others are."

"Wait for them in the coach. It must be nice and warm behind the windows."

"There's a seat covered with blood. Where Giampiero was sitting."

"Then sit on those steps over there. Close your eyes and think of something nice."

"Can I think of Mamma, Papà and Paul?"

"Of course you can."

"So shall I go?"

"Yes, go now."

Leonardo heard his footsteps rounding the wagon. As he made his way to the steps, Salomon waved a hand behind his back without turning. The bald girl was lying on the ground taking a little sun on her wasted body. One of her small white breasts was peeping out of her dress.

In the evening it began snowing again and by next morning twenty centimetres had fallen on the square, transforming it into an unwritten page. The young people had spent the night in the great hall and ground floor of the hotel, where the previous day they had piled clothes, mattresses, stoves and wood collected from the houses in the village. The place had two glass walls and the stoves had been arranged in such a way that their chimneys led through several broken panes, which had then been resealed with nylon and old curtains. Leonardo had watched through the glass as they ate and then threw themselves onto the mattresses and drifted off into deep sleep.

He had spent all night watching the snow falling without ever wanting to close his eyes. There was no moon, but the square was lit by a photovoltaic street lamp and the snow emerging from the black sky was tinged a deep fluorescent blue that turned to pewter as it settled on the ground. It was not cold, or at least it was not as cold as the night before, when the sky had been full of stars.

In the morning, when he emerged from the caravan, Richard's face was twisted with rage: now they could go neither forward nor back. They were stuck, under the grey still sky. Looking round himself, he found Leonardo's eyes staring at him. He held his gaze for a moment, until Lucia appeared with a blanket round her shoulders and both moved pale and trembling towards the hotel. Leonardo realized the caravan's heating must have failed.

That evening he was taken to the great hall where the mattresses had been pushed aside to free a circle in the middle of the room. The atmosphere was warm and comfortable, but the young people seemed restless and disappointed, and even while Leonardo was dancing some preferred to look out at the snow which had begun falling again on the parking place below them.

Richard and Lucia watched the dancing from behind a desk with a black leather writing surface, then Richard took Lucia by the hand, and without bestowing his usual blessing on the tribe, climbed the stairs and disappeared to the floor above.

Before the cripple sent him back to the cage, Leonardo had a chance to study the faces of the youngsters. Their old naïve ferocity had given way to something still terrible but more human, and though he did not know their names, he felt that for the first time he could tell them apart. Before leaving the hall he noticed Salomon sitting pretending to smile stupidly at nothing.

Two days later a donkey appeared in the square with her foal. Leonardo saw them emerge from the road leading from the country; they were thin and in very bad condition. Noticing them from the hotel windows, the youngsters ran out and surrounded them; the she-ass, who must have been searching for food, let herself be caught without putting up any resistance.

A squabble then broke out between those who wanted to tell Richard and those who wanted to kill the two animals without telling him. During the ensuing brawl Leonardo noticed that the aggressive indifference that had previously characterized their actions was dwindling into petty malice.

The cripple came out pistol in hand and fired a shot into the air. Leonardo saw a second-floor curtain move aside and Richard's face appear behind the glass. Then he opened the window and stared for a while in silence at the panting youngsters in the square. He was bare to the waist, with a few blond hairs on his gaunt chest.

"Only eat the little one," he directed before closing the window again.

It snowed every day of the following week. Showers that lasted only a few hours but were enough to preserve the depth of snow on the ground and prevent the procession moving forward despite a rise in temperature and the gradual lengthening of the days.

Leonardo waited every evening for the young people to fall asleep, then went over to Circe and spent a long time sucking her rough little teats. It had not occurred to anyone that the donkey was in milk and Leonardo tried the keep this little source of nourishment to himself. For her part, Circe seemed happy to be relieved of the burden and stood still while Leonardo massaged her teats to make the milk descend. He called her Circe after a fable he had written for Lucia when she was little, in which a donkey called Circe decided she only had to puff out her cheeks to be able to fly. The other animals on the farm mocked and scorned her, but in the end she succeeded.

One night he woke up to find his thoughts as still as crocodiles under the moon, all motionless below the surface of the water as they waited for their prey to come down to drink. Basic thoughts without frills, stretched taut and ready for action.

This reminded him how much his mind used to be agitated by an infinity of imprecise ideas wriggling about like eels in a bucket. He was ashamed of this busy lack of purpose, but since this guilt too belonged to the past, he let it go.

When the doctor came that morning Leonardo watched him moving from one side of the cage to the other to give food and water to the two animals. Since Circe's arrival, David would no longer leave his side of the cage. The two had tacitly agreed to divide the available space and limited themselves to exchanging an occasional glance. Leonardo would sleep next to one on one night and the other on the next night. When the doctor had finished he stroked David and began to leave.

"Push the door to, but don't close it," Leonardo told him. The man stopped.

"Do you want to run away?" he said, studying Leonardo's impassive face.

"No. But I need you to do something else for me."

The doctor noticed Leonardo was looking at the hatchet he used to cut branches for David.

"What are you hoping to do?"

"Leave it on that window ledge over there," Leonardo said, using his chin to indicate the bar on the other side of the square.

"You're mad. You'll only get yourself killed. And then what'll happen to your daughter?"

Leonardo looked at the man and the entirely rational expression he always wore on his face.

"Where's your son?" he asked him.

The man raised an eyebrow.

"What do you mean?"

"One day you told me your wife and daughter were dead, but that you don't know where your son is."

"That's true."

"When did you lose him? Where did it happen?"

The doctor wiped his left hand on his side. A very slow movement. Then he looked through the windows at the several young people circling lazily in the great hall. The sky was overcast, but with a strip of lighter clouds stretched across it.

"Who did you play finger-cutting with?" Leonardo asked him.

The man half opened his lips but said nothing. His eyes were very tired.

"You played finger-cutting with your son, didn't you?"

The doctor shook his head, his face overcome with weariness at this reappearance of something he had loaded with ballast and sent to the bottom of the sea. Then he turned for the door. When he left, Leonardo could hear that he had not bolted it. He got up and went and stroked David's head first, then Circe's.

"This evening," he whispered to them both.

That afternoon Leonardo slept a calm, restful sleep, of the kind that normally follows rather than precedes an event that may change the course of one's life.

What woke him was the lighting of the lamp in the square; day had already retreated behind the mountains, though a trace still survived in the blue profiles of the highest peaks. Thawing snow was dripping softly from the roofs.

He looked at the hall where the young people were dozing on the mattresses. They had already cleared a space in the centre of the room; soon Richard and Lucia would come down and someone would fetch him to dance.

He got to his feet, pushed open the door left unbolted by the doctor and climbed down from the wagon.

Crossing the square to the old bar with bare feet was like crossing the middle of an immense space, big enough to walk through for days without ever reaching a destination. This did not dismay him in the least.

He picked up the hatchet left on the window ledge, stuck it into the back of his trousers, and started back to the wagon. But before he got there he moved aside from his footprints in the snow and headed for the caravan instead; the door was ajar.

It was like entering the office of a methodical clerk who was able to rest for an hour or two on a camp bed between jobs. There was nothing formal, just a narrow space decorated with pornographic photographs and a great ceiling mirror that reflected a dirty green bedcover. The floor was rubber, and pans on the gas cooker had been used for cooking rice. From an iron hook over the bed hung cords, chains and other improvised sadomasochistic contraptions, including a machine with rubber tubes designed for milking cows.

Leonardo went to the desk. Propped on its surface were several charcoal sketches and a Bible with a fabric cover. The sketches showed Lucia naked and bound. There were others in a filing cabinet above the desk. Leonardo assumed they probably featured other girls and did not open them.

He found what he was looking for in the second drawer of the desk. He took the exercise book, slipped it into what was left of his back pocket and left.

Once back in the cage, he closed the door and began waiting. Two lamps fed by an electrical generator feebly lit the hall where the bodies of the youngsters were moving to music which was increasingly drowned by the sounds of the thaw. The mountains were hidden by a black cloak though it was obvious they were still keeping a watch on everything.

When he saw Richard and Lucia appear at the foot of the stairs, Leonardo took his hands out of his pockets but did not move. Not yet. The dancing stopped, and he watched them circulate among the young people in the hall. Lucia was in a red dress that must have belonged to a larger woman who had been a mother, while Richard was wearing a beige tunic, with a woollen scarf draped artistically over his shoulders. When he saw Richard have a word with the cripple and sit down at the desk, he knew the moment had come for him to get to his feet.

The boy who had been sent to fetch him saw him approaching the hotel and briefly stopped dead at the door to stare at him in astonishment, as if he were watching the flight of an animal that cannot fly. He was young and blond, with a high forehead and a chin that seemed borrowed from someone else's face.

When Leonardo entered the room the young people did not move, their eyes fixed on him. The music was far away and the only noise was the sound of the fires burning in the stoves. The air smelt of sweat, thunderstorms and youth.

He came up to the desk behind which Richard and Lucia were sitting. No-one did anything to stop him. Passing among the youngsters, he saw the doctor sitting near an antique stove, Salomon standing on a raised counter, and the bald girl crouched between two boys. During the last month or so her hair had begun to grow again in a confused manner, leaving great bald patches.

When he reached the desk, Leonardo looked first at Lucia, then at Richard, and finally at the cripple standing a couple of paces behind them. He realized this small, deformed and cruel man had been waiting for this moment from the first.

"What do you want to do, dancer?" Richard said. "Cut off my head?"

Leonardo realized he had pulled the hatchet from his trousers and was grasping it in his right hand. He stared at Richard who was watching him with amusement, placed his left hand on the desk, and with a neat stroke cut off his own thumb.

Raising his eyes from his hand, Leonardo met the pale face of Richard, who was staring at the amputated thumb as blood began to spread over the desk. Richard's smile had hardened.

"What are you trying to prove?" he said, avoiding Leonardo's eye.

Leonardo struck again, chopping off his index and middle fingers.

The two fingers rolled off the desk and fell into Richard's lap; he leaped back, his tunic stained with little bright-red drops. Leonardo looked into Lucia's lukewarm eyes and smiled at her, for a moment joining her in the far-off world where she was living, then he turned to stare at Richard, who looked as colourless and fleshy as a funeral bloom, his lower lip visibly trembling.

Leonardo raised the hatchet a third time and cut off the remaining fingers of his left hand. One fell from the table to the floor but the little finger swivelled round and ended pointing upwards. Leonardo then extricated the hatchet which had stuck in the wood, and still grasping it in his fist, lowered it to his side. The young people were paralyzed. He could hear their breath cutting the air like the great strings of a cello reverberating to the tiniest movement.

He looked into Richard's blue eyes: he had turned white, with red patches appearing on his cheeks. He placed his hands on the arms of his chair and tried to get up but his arms gave way. Leonardo waited patiently. His hand felt as if it was in flames but he was also conscious of a sense of relief.

"Do you think you can impress . . ." Richard began, but his words ended in a gurgle.

Leonardo smiled at him, lifted the hatchet again and brought it down on his left wrist, cutting off the whole hand.

This time the blood spurted everywhere, hitting the cripple who did not even bother to wipe his face. The sound of splintering bone echoed from the walls like the crash of a falling tree.

Leonardo put the hatchet down on the desk and looked at his severed hand lying in his own blood. Electricity was rising up his arm to form a circuit round his body in which he felt as well protected as he had ever been in his life. It was as if his father and mother were with him, and also his brother who had died at three months and only once even been mentioned by his mother. A child not him but very like him, who would never now feel alone again. Then he remembered Richard.

He picked up his severed left hand and threw it into Richard's lap. The man tried to struggle to his feet, but his eyes turned back in his head and he crashed to the ground, hitting his head on the edge of the desk as he fell. Leonardo glanced at the body curled on the floor.

"Come on," he said to Lucia.

The girl took the hand he held out to her and stood up.

"Salomon," Leonardo called.

The child joined them and together they headed for the door. No-one tried to stop them and when Leonardo released Lucia to offer his hand to the bald girl on the mattress, the two boys on either side of her moved to let her go.

Once outside they made for the wagon, Leonardo leaving a trail of blood that turned lilac on the snow. The young people, who had followed them onto the square in a line, watched them lead the elephant and the donkey out of the cage like a chorus silently watching the passing of a coffin. Then Leonardo told Salomon to see to the animals and turned back to the hotel.

"Fetch your bag," he said, stopping in front of the doctor.

The man seemed even older and more resigned among all the adolescent faces.

"You'll be able to go back later," Leonardo added, "but for the moment I need you to come with us."

When the doctor went back into the hotel to fetch his bag, Leonardo looked up towards the full moon and studied the great clouds with fluorescent edges being pulled rather than pushed by the wind towards the valley. He could feel Alberto's eyes on him and saw the boy standing on a great concrete bowl. Leonardo held his gaze without feeling any need to ask questions of himself, or any indecision faced with Alberto's hesitation. In the past he would have let other people, circumstances or timing make up his mind for him as he took refuge behind his characteristic meekness, but that past did not exist anymore, just as the men and women who had inhabited it did not exist anymore. Now everything was terrible and simple, like his warm blood carving its way through the snow.

"The haemorrhage must be stopped," the doctor said.

He had come out of the hotel with a leather bag, several blankets over his shoulder and a pair of shoes under his arm.

"Later," Leonardo said. "First we must get going."

Reaching the corner of the square with Salomon, Lucia, the bald woman, the doctor and the two animals, he turned to look back at the young people for the last time. They were standing still where he had left them, bewitched by the blood and cruelty they had witnessed. Among their perfect slender bodies he recognized the deformed shape of the cripple. Under the perpendicular rays of the moon his face was as composed as a funeral mask.

They left the foot of the valley by a lane that seemed likely to lead to a few isolated houses. The doctor had controlled the haemorrhage with a bandage, but Leonardo could feel blood running down his leg again. They had been walking in the snow for hours and needed to find somewhere to rest and light a fire.

After a couple of hairpin bends the road became less steep and they came to a group of houses round a small church and a little square that would not have been able to provide parking for more than three cars. It was a tiny village that would have been inhabited a century ago but which had then been abandoned before being partly restored by city dwellers looking for a peaceful retreat for their weekends.

They took the main thoroughfare, obstructed by compressed snow. Leonardo walked in front, followed by David. At points where the lane narrowed the elephant's sides rubbed against the walls and he let out long melancholy sighs. Salomon, the bald woman and Lucia followed, having taken turns on the donkey the whole way. The doctor brought up the rear. The doors of some houses had been made fast with rusty old padlocks and their glassless windows revealed grain-processing machinery, ploughs, furniture, old sledges, hay and wood piled up haphazardly. But the recently reconditioned houses showed clear signs of having been broken into and looted. Leonardo stopped at the end of the village in front of a large building resembling an Alpine chalet in stone with an oddly shaped terrace. The roof of the little loggia was supported by a pillar set with a large blue stone on which someone had carved a cross and the date 1845. In front of the house, level ground stretched to a bank marked by a line of beeches. Beyond these were presumably the road and the river.

"What do you hope to find here?" the doctor asked.

Leonardo examined the half-open door of the house, then took off his shoes and, after placing them neatly on the bottom step, limped towards the door.

They spent the morning on the terrace, faces turned to a weak spring sun that had risen uncertainly as if seeing the world for the first time.

No-one, since they left the camp the previous evening, had asked where they were going and when they would find food. Salomon had been the only one to talk during the night. Walking beside Leonardo, he had expounded all he knew about creatures that could see in the dark, explaining how certain deep-sea fish were able to see by polarized light and so could detect their prey even in the darkness of the depths. Now and then Leonardo had turned towards Lucia, but his daughter's eyes remained remote and blank. The bald woman, whenever she met his gaze, looked down. The doctor, at the back of the procession, contributed only a laboured panting.

"They won't escape, will they?" Salomon asked.

David and Circe were wandering round the field below the house eating the bark of several cherry trees.

"No, they won't," Leonardo said.

"Because they're fond of us?"

"Exactly."

Salomon looked at the girls and the doctor sleeping on the disjointed boards of the balcony, their hands red and swollen with warmth after the night's frost. Then he stared at the mountain facing them, and the leafless trees punctuating the brilliant white of the snow.

"Yesterday evening I was scared."

"I know, but that's over now."

"Doesn't it feel sore?"

"No. Are you hungry?"

"A bit."

"Only a bit?"

"Very hungry."

Leonardo woke the doctor and together they went down into the field where he showed the doctor how to milk Circe, then they went back and put the pot of milk to warm on the stove. The house had been uninhabited for many years, but it was in good shape and despite the fact that others had been there before them some dishes and cutlery had survived; also a table, a kitchen range, three beds with mattresses and blankets, a sofa, a wardrobe with men's clothes in it and a cellar containing a lot of tools. Leonardo and the doctor inspected the house from top to bottom without finding anything to eat, but in the attic they found some firewood and a few bales of hay that would be useful for the animals.

The doctor told Leonardo to sit down and began unwrapping his bandage.

"Don't rest it on the table," he said when the wound was revealed. Leonardo studied the dark flesh and white bone. His arm felt cold, light and incomplete, but was not painful. It just felt as though the limb was filling with air and sooner or later would fly away, detaching itself from his body.

"What's that?"

The doctor was spreading on the wound a yellow cream from a jar.

"An ointment I've made from tobacco. Very basic, but it'll prevent infection. The best I can do."

The doctor went to wash his hands at the sink, then sat down to bind up the stump.

"You'll have to dress it morning and evening. This is the only bandage I've got so try to keep it clean. If it does get dirty, you can make another by cutting up a piece of clothing or a towel, but make sure it's cotton and that you boil it before use. If there's no infection, your temperature should return to normal in a couple of days and the wound will begin to heal."

Leonardo looked out of the window. He could see the river and part of the bottom of the valley. The sun, beating all morning on the road, had revealed a few patches of asphalt.

"Do you really want to go back to them?"

The doctor looked at him as though the question was entirely meaningless.

"You only have one hand and no weapons," he said, knotting the bandage. "The child and the girls can only get in your way. If you're lucky, someone will kill you all; failing that, you'll die of hunger."

The milk began hissing. Leonardo got up and took the pot off the stove using an old towel with a printed picture of Mickey Mouse dressed as a chef, and poured the milk into some containers he had found. There were two cups and a glass, and two metal containers intended for salt and coffee. He offered one to the doctor, who accepted it and put it on the table.

"I don't care what you think of me," he said.

Leonardo stared at him for a moment, his eyes calm and lacking in resentment, then took one of the containers out to the balcony. When he got back to collect the rest and take them to the girls, the man had vanished.

Before dark Leonardo and Salomon checked the houses in the village, gleaning a local map, a parka, some sunflower seeds, a pencil, a little seed oil, a piece of soap, a pack of cards, an old snare and a handful of sowing potatoes.

On their return, they found the stove had gone out; the house was dark and the girls were asleep in the bed behind the wooden partition. Leonardo and Salomon went down to the cellar, where Leonardo showed the boy how to make an oil lamp using an empty drinks bottle, a piece of rag and the oil they had found. The boy followed the instructions carefully without getting impatient even when he had difficulty rolling the wick in the right way, and he was finally able to watch the lamp with pride as it lit the low ceiling of the room. Leonardo pocketed the lighter the doctor had left with the ointment.

"Now I feel calm."

"Why?"

"Because I know when I ask you to do something I can't do myself, you'll do it well."

Salomon looked down. Leonardo placed his hand on the boy's head. His fair hair was smooth and shone like new grass. His blue eyes collected light, absorbing something from inside himself and releasing it again very slowly.

"I have to ask you one more favour."

The child looked up.

"Let's keep to ourselves what we saw in that house."

"You mean the skeletons?"

"Yes, better not tell the girls about that."

"I only cried out because it was such a surprise."

"I know, but it would frighten them."

Salomon stared at the flame.

"What happened to those people?"

Leonardo had found tufts of hair; the man and woman had died of hunger or cold, and dogs and wolves must have found some way of getting into the house.

"I don't know," he said, "but best keep it to ourselves."

"I'd already decided not to say anything."

"I can believe that."

Salomon looked at the refrigerator and the washing machine against the wall. Apart from a pile of planks thrown down in the middle of the room, the cellar was in perfect order. There was a well-stocked tool shelf, a rack for garden tools and a workbench with a vice and grindstone for working with metals. When he had come in there that morning and seen that equipment and the planks, he had imagined someone dreaming of an imminent flood and seized by the urge to build a barge. Someone who after buying the wood had suddenly become less confident about trusting his dreams.

"I wish Lucia and the other lady would say something," Salomon said.

Leonardo slid his hand down his face.

"Sometimes people are happier keeping silent."

"But they will talk in the end, won't they?"

"It may take time. We must be patient, O.K.?"

"O.K. Will they be happy we found the potatoes?"

"Yes, they'll be very happy about that."

They lit the stove and put a pan of water on to boil, then prepared one of the beds in the upstairs room and left the door open for the heat to rise and warm it. They washed plates and cutlery and cleaned the surface of the dresser, then put everything they had found on it, which at the moment was their whole fortune.

When the potatoes had boiled, Leonardo went into the bedroom next door and touched the bald woman's shoulder to wake her. She opened her eyes at once, as if she had only been pretending to be asleep. She looked serious, attentive and confident, with no trace of the terrified girl Leonardo had led out of the hotel by the hand.

"We've found something to eat," Leonardo said, then interrupted himself and looked at Lucia, who was fast asleep, with her mouth half open and one hand under her cheek. Her breathing was calm and regular.

"Let her sleep," the woman said. "That's what she needs at the moment."

They sat down at the table and the woman peeled the potatoes. She had on a man's sweater they had found in the wardrobe and a pair of trousers rolled above her ankles, but Leonardo noticed that she had not taken off the torn and dirty dress in which she had come. She told them her name was Silvia and asked Salomon what he was called. The child told her, then they ate in silence.

Salomon occasionally looked at the rope marks on the woman's wrists and the cold sores on her face. He seemed less impressed by the way her hair had grown back in tufts over her shaven head. Their meal only took a few minutes, and they left two potatoes on a plate for Lucia when she woke up.

"Do you know what I'd like now?" the woman said.

Leonardo shook his head. She smiled, her teeth shaded by an opaque film.

"Some coffee."

They sat on in silence, watching the flame of the lamp bending towards the empty side of the table in the draught from the door. From time to time Salomon closed his eyes and his chin fell on his chest.

"Go to bed now," Leonardo told him.

The child looked at the stairs, then started playing with a piece of potato peel, shaping it so that it looked like a whale. Leonardo wrapped the base of the lamp in the towel and offered it to Salomon.

"You take it," he said. "I'll blow it out when I come up."

Salomon said goodnight and climbed the stairs to the upper floor. The light he was taking away surrounded him like a cloak. Left in the dark, Leonardo went to open the door of the stove; the fire inside cast light on the walls. He began clearing the table, carrying the plates one at a time to the sink.

"No, I'll do that," the woman said, getting up. "You sit down, we haven't done much to help you today."

She rinsed the plates and glasses in the sink, then poured a little of the water used for boiling the potatoes into the two cups. Then she sat down again. Anyone walking in at that moment would have seen a man with thick grey hair and a woman with a badly shaven head sitting facing one another by the weak light of the fire with two cups in front of them, as if about to embark on an existential conversation. But on closer inspection, he would have seen that the man's face was deeply scarred and that the woman's hands were damaged and incapable of keeping still for more than a few seconds at a time.

"How old's your daughter?"

"Seventeen."

The woman stared at her cup.

"Now I'm going to tell you something you might think rather impersonal and insensitive, but it's the only way I can be useful to you. Would you like to hear it?"

Leonardo nodded.

"I worked as a psychologist with an international organization and travelled in a war zone where rape was used as a weapon for ethnic cleansing. My job was to convince the women to report the rapes and to help organize assistance for them. So I know what I'm talking about."

The woman took a sip of hot water and put the cup down over a small mark on the table.

"Lucia's in a state of shock. It often happens to girls who suffer violence, especially if they are young and their ordeal goes on for a long time. The fact that she doesn't speak or react to external stimuli is part of the picture, but don't be misled into thinking she isn't feeling anything: there is certain to be enormous anger inside her. She feels responsible in some way for what has happened to her and hates herself for not having been able to extract herself from it. She has suffered very deep humiliation."

Leonardo met her eyes without moving a muscle in his face.

"It may take a long time before she emerges from the shell inside which she has closed herself, and it's even possible she may never emerge from it, or not entirely. All you can do is keep close to her without trying to hurry things on. Act as if you are waiting for her to return from a journey and in the meantime are looking after her home for her. Talk to her, even if she seems not to listen. Touch her hands and feet but not any other part of her body and never hug her however much you want to, because that could make her feel imprisoned. It could even make her unconsciously superimpose you on the image of that man. In any case it's likely she can remember little or nothing of what you have been to her and done for her in the past. You mustn't feel hurt by that, it's only a defence mechanism. I know you love her very much and that you will know how to do what is right for her."

"How old are you?"

"Twice your daughter's age."

"Have you anyone yourself?"

"No, not any longer."

Leonardo looked out of the window; the moon had turned the trees to stone.

"We'll wait till the snow melts, then make for the coast. You could come too."

The woman got up and put another piece of wood in the stove, then filled a pan with water at the sink and placed it on the hot cast-iron cooking surface.

"Now we'll have a little warm water to wash in tomorrow morning," she said.

Leonardo realized his thoughts would stop functioning long before dawn and that there was nothing he could do to stop it.

"Till tomorrow, then," the woman said.

"Till tomorrow."

When she withdrew to the other room, Leonardo went to take a little hay to Circe and David, and talked to them for a long time about what he was afraid might happen.

The elephant and the donkey gave him their full attention, chewing great handfuls of dried grass. A full moon lit the valley and in the silence of the night Leonardo sensed life quivering under the snow as the earth softened and opened.

He urinated.

Then he went up to the bedroom, extinguished the lamp Salomon had placed on the floor well clear of the bed, and lay down beside the little boy who was wheezing lightly like a sleeping rodent. In the dark he felt Salomon's forehead; it was warm with exhaustion but he had no fever. On the other hand Leonardo felt himself to be burning hot. He closed his eyes but tried to stay awake so as not to miss any sounds from the floor below.

A few minutes, or perhaps a few hours later, he was woken by hearing steps. He made his way downstairs without lighting the lamp but the kitchen was empty and silent. Nor was there any sound from the room where Lucia and Silvia were. He went back to bed and slept.

When he woke again it was light. The room had a small window that was reflected in a mirror on the wall, making it look as if two suns were rising from opposite points of the compass.

Salomon was sleeping curled against him. It was the first time for a very long time that he had smelt a good smell, and he lay staring at the cloudless sky and the outline of the mountains beyond the faded curtains, reflecting that the scent, the colour and the shape were all one. When he delicately extracted his arm from beneath the child's head he realized it was completely numb from the shoulder down, so he massaged it until he could feel the blood beginning to circulate again and his wound starting to throb inside the bandage. Only then did he get up and head for the stairs.

The first thing he saw when he got down was that the pan was no longer on the stove.

He found it in the bathroom with the woman's dress and pants. He could smell the cake of soap which was still on the basin. He picked up the clothes, threw them into the stove, lit it and went out.

It did not take him long to find her. She had chosen an out-of-the-way spot that Leonardo was certain to find. A solitary holm oak in the middle of a pasture.

By the time Lucia and Salomon woke, Leonardo had already milked Circe.

The child and the girl sat at the table sipping milk from steaming cups. Leonardo rubbed his nails on a sponge at the sink, trying to clean them of earth. Then he joined the others at the table.

"The woman who was with us has gone," he said. "Her family is not far away and she wants to join them."

Salomon looked at the muddy bandage that Leonardo had not yet changed and the scratches on his right hand, lowered his eyes and said nothing. Lucia went on staring at the stove, chewing a potato left over from the night before.

In the afternoon, while they were busy in the cellar, Salomon and Leonardo heard music from the road. They ran to the beeches at the edge of the field, and hiding in the bushes behind the great trees, they watched the familiar procession pass on the main road. The Land Rover was leading, followed by a car they had not seen before, and the coach, towed by a tractor. Most of the youngsters were lying on the roof of the coach or on an agricultural trailer that had been attached to it. The cripple, sitting on the bonnet of the first car, was wearing a bizarre piece of headgear and inspecting the road ahead. He was holding a pike on the end of which Leonardo recognized Richard's head, blond hair waving in the wind like a ragged flag.

When the music faded in the distance, Leonardo and Salomon went back to the cellar where they had been struggling with the snare for a couple of hours already, trying to replace its old spring by another one taken from a sofa.

"What was the name of the lady who went away this morning?" Salomon asked.

Leonardo realized that Salomon had not recognized Richard's head.

"Silvia," he said. "Now let's try again."

He grasped the cord that he had attached to one end of the spring while Salomon tried to fasten a hook to the snap mechanism connected to the framework.

"It's gone in!" Salomon said at one point.

Leonardo opened his eyes which he had closed with the effort he was making.

"Good."

The child placed the trap carefully on the floor. He studied it for a long time: it looked like the jaws of a fish, but also like a great dried flower.

"Will the lady be able to find her family?" he asked.

"Yes," Leonardo said, not feeling he was telling a lie.

That evening, when the boy was asleep, he went down the stairs to the room where Lucia was. Placing the lamp on the windowsill, he sat down at the foot of the bed. Lucia was staring at the ceiling, a slight smile on her lips. She was still wearing the red dress and had not washed since they arrived.

Leonardo slipped off her shoes, took her little feet in his lap and began massaging them with his remaining hand. She went on gazing at the ceiling as if her feet belonged to someone else.

"I'll do this every evening," he told her, "for as long as I live."

He stopped talking and massaging her feet because it was dawn. Then he put out the light and, by the feeble light of daybreak, climbed the stairs to bed. Salomon was asleep, but some dream must have disturbed him because his mouth was twisted in a grimace and his hair, usually so neat, was in disorder. Using his fingers as a comb Leonardo tidied the boy's hair, then lay down beside him and shut his eyes.

Part Five

With the coming of May they reached the hills from where they planned to begin their descent to the sea.

It was a clear evening and the sky was bright in the east, as if the sun setting behind the mountains was already about to appear on the other side of the world.

For twenty days now they had been trudging through the woods, avoiding roads, villages and even hamlets with only a few houses. When Leonardo noticed the youngsters were tired, he got them to climb onto David's back. The elephant accepted this burden without protest and proceeded at a slow, solemn pace. Circe, bringing up the rear, was saddled with two large panniers they had constructed from wicker baskets. These contained blankets, clothes, knives, the lamp, tools and a little food collected before they left, including a pumpkin, some nuts, a handful of flour, a bottle of wine and two onions. Along the way they had found the bodies of a woman and a man in a hut and the carcasses of cattle devoured by dogs, deer, wild boars and other game, but no-one they could exchange a word with.

One morning they saw from a distance an old man running on the road and disappearing into a factory building, but neither Leonardo nor

Salomon wanted to go and find out who he was and whether there might be anyone else there.

A little before dusk Leonardo would decide where they would spend the night, and after lighting the fire would go out and set the snare.

"We'll reach the sea tomorrow, won't we?" Salomon would ask while they waited for the rabbit or hare caught the previous night to cook on the flames.

"Not quite yet."

"But it can't be very far now?"

"No, not far."

They would eat in silence, Lucia and the child with a good appetite and Leonardo less hungrily, then he and Salomon would sew the animal's skin together with other skins from which they were making a cover. If the day had been wet, and the skin was not dry enough, they would stretch it out by the fire and postpone their work till the next day. While he was sewing, the boy's eyes would sometimes close so that he pricked himself with the wire they used for a needle, but he would refuse to go to sleep till the job was finished. Then when he put the cover down he would go and greet David and Circe, who would be browsing in the circle of light cast by the fire; the elephant polishing off newly sprouting leaves while the donkey concentrated on young grass. Salomon would stroke them and thank them for carrying him when he was tired, then go back to the fire, say goodnight to Lucia without ever looking her in the eyes, and lie down under his cover.

While they chatted before going to sleep the boy would talk about his father and mother and other people he cannot have known. Leonardo would listen without interrupting because he knew true things were spoken in those words, and would stroke his head until he fell asleep, then get up and go to Lucia.

Sometimes the girl would be staring up at the immense vault heavy with stars above them, and sometimes she would be asleep. Leonardo would take her feet in his lap and caress them lovingly, talking to her about her childhood, places they had visited and things they had loved doing together, but never about things that had frightened them. David and Circe, attracted by his voice, would come near and listen spellbound, their round black eyes reflecting the fire.

Lucia would breathe softly, her expression never changing: even in sleep her body seemed wrapped in a shroud of stillness and distance.

By the time Leonardo lay down it would be nearly day and the air chill, but even without covers he would quickly fall asleep and not feel the cold.

He would walk all day in bare feet, eating and drinking very little, sleeping two hours a night, defecating when he woke in the morning and urinating three times a day, yet he would never have claimed to be hungry, tired, cold or tormented by any great physical need. The months spent in the cage had toughened his body, paring him down to the essential; his arms bundles of nerves with prominent veins and his leg muscles like sheaths of leather. His eyes, half hidden behind a curtain of hair and beard, shone sea-green. The skin of his face was brown and wrinkled. The scar of his amputation had healed well, and looked as if his hand had been not so much cut off as reabsorbed into his arm.

In the morning, by the time the young people woke, he would have already milked the donkey and retrieved whatever had been caught in the snare. Often a rabbit or hare was attracted by the potato bait, but once he was surprised to find a badger and another time a fox. The animals were nearly always dead and if they weren't Leonardo would finish them off with a stick, and take them to the camp, where Salomon would tie them to a branch to skin and gut them. When Leonardo had told the child that this must be his job since with only one hand he could not do it himself, Salomon had been reluctant, but as the days passed he had proved an able and meticulous butcher.

When they had cleaned the animal they would go back to the water and wash their hands, arms, face and feet, drying themselves on a large beach towel they had found. Lucia would wait for them by the fire. She showed no fear of being left alone and when they were on the march she would sometimes disappear into the woods – Leonardo imagined to attend to her physical needs – reappearing at the exact point where they had stopped to wait for her. With time the red dress got torn and one of the flat shoes she wore began coming apart, but she seemed to have no interest in the change of clothing Leonardo had brought for her.

"Will we see the sea today?" Salomon asked. The airy valley below them was of such a dazzling green as to force them to look away. These were the first steps they had taken downhill for a long time.

"A few days more."

"How many?"

Leonardo looked towards the far hillside where the wind turbines were revolving silently. This time he had decided to take a route to the south, where the map had shown an ancient series of military trenches that, as he hoped, had turned out to be overgrown with brambles and impassable for cars.

"Three," he said.

Late in the afternoon they saw the roofs of a village beneath them and the ruins of a castle high above it. All that was left of the castle was a shell of walls covered with ivy, but the village looked to be in good condition if deserted.

Leonardo sat down on a stone and studied the castle for a few minutes, with Salomon crouching at his side. Lucia stood behind them. David and Circe, as always when they stopped, went off to eat. Nearby, a sorb tree blown down during the winter was still putting out toothed oval leaves.

"Do we absolutely have to go there?" the boy said.

"No, we don't have to," Leonardo said.

"Then why do you want to?"

"I don't know."

The hot sun was piercing the roof of leaves above them and marking out patches on the surrounding grass. Leonardo was thinking about a man he had never seen or known, but who he knew to have lived in one of those houses. He could smell his clothes. For days he had been having similar visions, and clearly remembering everything he had read or heard in the past. Even so his mind was light and free, as if his immense archive of stories could fit into a suitcase in an empty house.

"Can we come too?" Salomon asked.

"Better not. I'll be back soon."

He went down to the village through the woods, reaching the backs of the first houses: tall, narrow stone structures in the Ligurian style, but solidly built in the way that things are in the mountains.

He found an alley and walked down it as far as the main lane, which was no wider than his extended arms and paved with round cobbles. The shutters of the houses were closed, their doors ajar or wide open to empty rooms. After some fifty metres the main street opened into a space with a fountain, a small play area for children and the terrace of a bar. A cat dozing on a low stone wall was the only living creature to be seen. Up a flight of steps was the church.

Leonardo went in. There were no pews or fittings. High up, a great wooden crucifix was watching over the empty aisles like someone casting a final glance over his home before closing the door and leaving for a new life elsewhere.

Leaving the church, he wandered through the village until he found the house. Access was by a set of stone steps, but the door was hidden by a vine which had spread over the whole garden. Above it a Japanese persimmon extended its branches, and in front were olive trees and what had been a terraced kitchen garden but had now been taken over by wild boars.

First he came into a small room with a high ceiling and then the kitchen. The house had been built vertically with small rooms one above another linked by steep stairways up to the top floor, which from the outside looked like a small turret covered with ivy. There was no trace of the man who had lived there, or of the woman Leonardo knew to have shared most of his life: no garment, book or furniture, only the great cloths and sheets of paper on which the man had traced designs in ash, anticipating what the world would become.

In the space under a roof that must have been his studio, Leonardo found jars of burned earth, sand and dust, each with a small label written in pencil. Also fragments of wood smoothed by the sea and strangely formed stones. He picked up one of the stones; it was grey, interlaced with white circles of a different mineral, and as he held it he could feel the man's warm, bony hand in his palm. He could see him, small and white-haired, moving through the rooms in a pullover and bending for hours over his artwork of ashes, the work of a man who knew that all things begin in poverty. Leonardo spoke to him.

By the time he left the garden of the house, the sun had lost its heat. He climbed back up the main lane to the square, but before reaching it he heard singing and stopped. A cheerful song sung by a woman.

He followed the music to the door it was coming from and found himself in a bare kitchen with a table laid for three. From the stairs leading to the floor above came two female voices, one responding to the other. They were singing in old French.

He climbed the stairs and even before he reached the top step, met the eyes of three women sitting together in the middle of a room. All the furniture, consisting of a sofa, sideboard, wardrobe and double bed, had been moved to one side as though someone had tilted the floor to make it slide, while the other walls were hung with carpets giving it a peaceful and Arab feeling.

The women stared at Leonardo for a moment without interrupting their song, then turned round to face the window beyond which the sun was sinking and tingeing the colours of the valley with yellow. The thin woman in the middle was about fifty and her black dress would not have looked out of place under a raincoat on some suburban street in Amsterdam or Paris. Her mulatto face was beautiful, even if tired and bloodless, sparse hair framing it like a veil. The other two were younger but infinitely more resigned. All three must have lost something; in fact, their eyes clashed with the frivolity of their song, clearly intended to raise a smile. The mulatto woman was conducting, raising and lowering her hands from her knees. When the song ended she got up and walked towards Leonardo.

"Did you like that?"

"Very much."

She was just as tall and slim as he remembered her.

"You really mean that?"

"I do."

The woman returned to the others, complimented them and took her leave of them, making an appointment for the next day. Then she went back to Leonardo.

"It's such a lovely day," she said. "Shall we sit outside for a while?"

Leonardo followed her into the street and towards the bar. There were still two tables and a few chairs on the terrace. They chose two that still had unbroken seats and sat down, facing the hillside behind which the sun would set. The door of the bar at the back had been smashed and one could imagine excrement and screwed-up waste paper inside on the floor. Small skulls could be seen in the shadows. On the other hand, the terrace was clean and full of light. From the acacias came a good smell and the buzzing of wasps.

"Have you ever been here before?" the woman asked.

Leonardo remembered her face surrounded by curly hair, of which hardly any now remained.

"No," he said.

She looked at the terraces rising above the houses and the two lanes, one coming out behind a swing and the other beside the church. A notice said "Go Slow, Children Still Play in the Street Here."

"I first saw this place thirty years ago. I'd come to Europe as a backing singer for Leonard Cohen and the day after a gig in Nice a lighting technician brought me here on his motorbike. I was twenty-five then, and thought sooner or later I'd come to live in this village, especially if I had a child."

"I often came to your concerts."

"Mine or Leonard's?"

"Yours."

"I read your books. Do you remember the lecture on Bolaño you gave in the theatre in Nantes? I came to hear it and nearly asked your agent how I could meet you."

"Why didn't you?"

"Because I thought if you came to one of my performances you would never have done that."

"But how did you recognize me?"

"Do you think you've changed much?"

"Yes."

"Quite wrong, I knew who you were at once. But how did you recognize me? I've lost all my hair."

"I knew your voice. What was that song I was listening to?"

"Provençal, very old, great fun. It's about a bailiff who tells his wife he's being tormented by a mosquito buzzing in his stomach. She sends him to the doctor at Cavaillon. The doctor agrees it's a mosquito and suggests a natural remedy: the frog is the sworn enemy of the mosquito so all the man has to do is to eat a live frog to hunt it down. The bailiff does this because he's afraid of what people will say if they hear the mosquito buzzing, and after a few days the buzzing does indeed stop, but now he can't sleep because of the frog croaking. So his wife sends him back to the doctor, who this time makes him eat a live pike because the pike is the sworn enemy of the frog. Returning home, the bailiff is happy because the croaking stops, but now the pike is turning his stomach upside down. Then his wife says there's no point in going to the doctor again because the sworn enemy of the pike is the fisherman, so all her husband needs to do is to lower a hook and line into his stomach. The bailiff agrees and his wife is able to lead him round the village by the hook and line for days. The last verse reveals that she is the lover of the doctor at Cavaillon and had sewn the mosquito into the border of her husband's pants."

"A good story."

"The two women you saw with me have lost their children and husbands. They need songs to distract their thoughts. They have never sung before, but now we do an hour or two every day. They've become very good at it."

"Are you the only people in the village now?"

"Yes, only us."

"Why don't you go down to the sea?"

"This is where our homes are, and even if we no longer have our men and children, we still like to sleep in the beds we used to share with them. We saved enough food to get us through the winter, and now we have the kitchen gardens and orchards."

"Aren't you afraid?"

"Why should we be? We've already lost everything."

Leonardo pushed back the hair the gentle wind had blown into his eyes.

"Are they with you?" the woman asked.

Leonardo turned to see Salomon and the animals standing in front of the church, and Lucia sitting a little way off on the edge of the fountain. Salomon was looking at Leonardo but pretending not to, as though afraid of getting into trouble. Leonardo raised a hand in greeting. The boy said *ciao*. David and Circe were standing meekly to his left and right as if in a bizarre Nativity scene. Lucia was staring at the rectangle of water into which the jet of the fountain was falling with a hypnotic gurgling sound.

"Are these your children?" the woman asked.

"Only Lucia. The boy's been with us for several months."

The woman nodded.

"May I ask what happened to your hand?"

"I had to renounce it."

"In exchange for something important, presumably?"

"Something extremely important."

They watched the young people. The leaves of a lime tree were still glowing in the last of the setting sun. The cat had moved to a window ledge higher up, from where it was presiding over this unusual movement of humans and animals.

"When is your daughter due to give birth?" the woman asked.

"At the end of the summer."

They spent four days in the village. On the first night he caressed Lucia's feet, then left the house, and as Clarisse had asked him to, went to the house where the youngest of the women was waiting for him, while on the second night he went to the other.

In the morning he got some sleep in the shade of a sycamore, while the young people supervised David and Circe grazing among the olive trees. In the afternoon he went back to the house with the Japanese persimmon in the garden and studied the ash pictures on the walls, holding a long conversation with the man who had created them. The man was very old, and when he said he was tired they sat in silence at a little table in front of the fireplace. On these occasions Leonardo still had his left hand and used it to hold the stones the man showed him, stones he had collected over the years for their shape or colour.

During these days Leonardo ate the polenta, vegetables and fruit Clarisse prepared for them and never set the snare. Towards evening he would sit with the youngsters in the room on the upper floor and listen to the women singing. Clarisse had washed Lucia's hair and she now had an ample yellow dress that left her shoulders bare. Her breasts had developed and there was something new and lively in her eyes.

On the last night, after seeing Salomon and Lucia to bed, Leonardo went down to the kitchen where Clarisse was waiting for him by the light of the oil lamp. David and Circe were moving about in the garden under the window, between the slide and the swings. They could hear the branches rustling as the elephant pulled them within reach with his trunk.

"That time at Nantes," Clarisse said, "you said that in the Cabala, unlike Genesis, God initially fails by creating other worlds that are soon extinguished like sparks. Do you remember?"

"He fails because he only uses the feminine principle, the principle of will and determination. When he also brings in the masculine principle of compassion and mercy, he creates a spark that is able to survive, and that spark is the world we're living in now."

She smiled. Her teeth were white, her eyes like black leather.

"But what if this too is just another attempt on his part? That he's still learning and that the successful world is still to come? Wouldn't that be wonderful?"

"It would be, but I don't think that's how it is."

They were drinking an infusion Clarisse had made from mint,

hawthorn and dried medlar leaves, then with an imperceptible movement of her hips she shifted her chair closer to the table.

"The others are still young and with a bit of luck they may still have children. I'm not well, and in any case I'm too old for pregnancy. But I'd like to ask you something."

Leonardo waited in silence.

"I've engraved some lines of Rilke on my husband's gravestone and one of Leonard's songs on my son's. I'd like you to advise me what to put on my own."

Leonardo looked at Clarisse's smile, her perfect nose, and the hands round her cup, and he knew for certain that her hands had touched tears, seed, earth and blood and never hesitated to respond to the feelings that had moved them.

"A little while ago I tried to start writing again," he said, "but I know now I shall never be able to."

She took his hand. The light from the lamp began to flicker; the oil was running out.

"You've read so many stories," she said. "Find one that would do for me. It doesn't matter if it's not one of yours."

Leonardo stared at the surface of the table. From the dark marks of tears on the wood he realized he was weeping, and understood that his eyes like every other part of him now belonged to the outside world, and that he would never be their master again. This caused him no regret. The draught from the window was bringing in the smell of the animals and the cold scent of flowers at night.

"When I see minds that have no pride," he said, "no anger, no passion, finding nothing to give them pleasure; when the absent-minded and care-worn never venture under the sign of fire; when I see sluggish brows, empty spirits, and promises of love weakly sustained, and voices and eyes that hold nothing of the universe in them; then what good fortune that I have made all of you, who have known me, a present of the whole world including the stars, just because you have known me!"

"That's so beautiful. Who wrote it?"

"A woman," Leonardo said. "A century and a half ago."

"Say it again slowly, I want to learn it by heart."

Leonardo recited it again more slowly.

"Thank you," Clarisse said. Then she got up and moved towards the stairs. At that moment the lamp went out.

"I've got some food ready for your journey, and a couple of dresses for Lucia," she said. "Soon the one she's wearing won't fit anymore."

The beach, at the point where they reached the sea, consisted of grey, blue and white pebbles the size of eggs, but the winter storms had swallowed most of it, only stopping a few metres short of the embankment that carried the Aurelia *autostrada*.

They walked a little way along the deserted path that skirted the road. It was a stretch of coast in between two built-up areas and there were few buildings, only wooden structures facing the sea that had once been bars and bathing establishments. There were still a few abandoned deckchairs on the beach, among abraded pieces of wood and flotsam.

When they found a place with no steps to the water, they led the animals down. Faced by such a huge expanse of water David stopped dead, and they had to wait for many minutes for him to take in what he was seeing. The donkey on the other hand went off at once to nibble at the woodwork of a fence.

"Can I go in the water?" the child asked.

Leonardo looked at the deserted beach and a distant village.

"Can you swim?"

"Yes," said the boy.

"Alright then, but keep close to the shore."

"O.K.," the child said, taking off his trousers.

Leonardo watched him go into the water. The elephant had followed him as far as the edge of the surf and stayed there to watch over him with his great feet immersed in the foam. Salomon splashed him and cried out with joy. Lucia, at Leonardo's side, watched the sun sink beyond the promontory to the west.

"Let's go and have a look inside there," Leonardo said.

The restaurant had a large terrace, a kitchen, a bathroom with running water and a storeroom whose shelves had been emptied and tipped over. There were no beds or electricity, but in a hut next to it Leonardo found a few sunloungers and a solar-powered battery. He carried the sunloungers up one at a time, then remembered Salomon.

By the time Leonardo got him out of the water, the boy was shivering. Leonardo wrapped him in the towel and took him in his arms. Salomon leaned his head on Leonardo's shoulder and put his arms round his neck.

"Please can we stay here for ever," he said.

Sitting on the terrace they dined on Clarisse's rice and carrots. The restaurant's windows were still unbroken and even though they found nothing to eat in the place, no-one else seemed to have stayed there before them. Salomon, what with all the excitement and exhaustion, ate little and asked Leonardo endless questions about the origin of waves, the depths of the sea and how they could be reached. The lamp spread a laboured, leaden light over the table, but the sky was clear and a fragment of moon lit the coast, sharply defining sea, beach, sky and rocks.

It was very late when the child finally fell asleep; Leonardo crossed the road to cut some branches and grass for the animals and carry them back to the beach because he did not want to spend much time away from the restaurant; then he filled a bucket with water and gave it to them to drink while Lucia sat on a deckchair on the terrace.

"Do you like it here?" he asked, taking off one of her shoes. Her ankles were swollen and her skin had a new smell. He remembered how when she had come to him only a few months earlier she had smelt of new paper whereas now she smelt of milk and blood.

He answered his own question. "It's a nice place," he said, starting the massage.

Two days later, having finished the food Clarisse had given them, they set the snare in bushes by the road.

It was not necessary to go very far because hares, foxes and badgers came near the road fearlessly. Usually in not more than half an hour Leonardo would hear the trap spring and the brief cries of the animal would fill the night. Then, to prevent dogs or other predators stripping it clean, he would get up and go and remove it from the metal jaws. In the morning, as soon as he woke, he would light a fire on the beach and cook the meat to prevent it going off.

He and Salomon would spend all day in their underpants. Leonardo had persuaded the boy to stay on the veranda out of the sun during the hottest part of the day, but the skin of both had become tanned and their hair lighter, making them look like Nordic adventurers.

The boy spent a lot of time in the water throwing stones and retrieving them and trying unsuccessfully to get David to follow him. The elephant would watch over him from the beach like a timid granny, and when the waves threatened would take a few clumsy steps backwards, but without turning away for fear of losing sight of the boy. Circe, in contrast, free of her large panniers, would spend the day sheltering in the shade between the thick concrete posts that supported the restaurant terrace.

In the evening Leonardo and the child would lead the animals over the main road to where there were plenty of bushes, and afterwards would have supper with Lucia before throwing the leftovers in the sea so as not to attract dogs.

One morning, after a couple of hours away, Leonardo brought back a fishing line and several hooks. Now there were no bathers anymore, the fish had come back near the shore and could easily be enticed to take a bait of little bits of meat or small bones. As dusk fell, Leonardo and Salomon would sit on the beach near the fire while the child recounted his dreams, which were populated by the animals and fish he had killed, creatures who knew he had only killed them out of necessity.

"Sometimes I feel we must be waiting for someone," he said one evening.

His hair reflected the yellow of the fire, like a crocus in the night.

Leonardo stroked his hair.

"If we do leave here," he said, "it will be to go somewhere better."

"There can't be a better place than this," Salomon said.

"Then we stay here."

Next morning, while cooking an octopus, Leonardo saw the far-off figure of a very tall man coming along the beach with a dog, his silhouette vibrating in the heat of the air.

He took the octopus off the fire, put it on a plate so it would not get too hard, and knelt down and waited for the dog to run into his arms.

When he felt Bauschan's hot body against his chest, he buried his face and fingers in the dog's hair while the animal licked his ears and face and whimpered with joy. His scent had become that of an adult dog and his physique more compact, but with his long legs and patchy coat there was still something of the puppy about him. Then Leonardo stood up to meet Sebastiano.

During the last months his head had grown a covering of light-coloured hair, making him look like a folksinger-songwriter from the years of the great American Depression. His body was still slender though his shoulders and arms had grown more substantial. The two men embraced the way children do, turning their heads to one side with their eyes open, their hips apart, hardly hugging at all. Even so, Leonardo could feel the man's great heart beating against his own in the same rhythm as the surf. A slow and profound but weightless rhythm. The beat of a light heart.

"I have so many things to tell you," Leonardo said.

They sat down by the fire facing the sea and began to eat the octopus. Bauschan, sitting against his master's back, stared at the elephant and the donkey who were crouching between the pillars of the restaurant. Every so often he would let out an uncomprehending howl.

"Alberto's lost," Leonardo said, "but we've got another boy with us now, and soon Lucia's going to have a baby."

Sebastiano went on staring at the gentle coming and going of the waves, as if he had already heard these facts many times. He was wearing a flowered overall with a hole in place of the pocket and formal twill trousers.

Leonardo opened his mouth to say more but realized that there was nothing else in what had happened that he needed to report. He could remember a time when the past had played a great part in his life, but that seemed a remote period and no longer his.

For a little longer he stroked the dog in silence. The rising sun was softening the air and great slate-coloured clouds were rising from the sea. Then he got up, went into the restaurant, woke the young people and told them it was time to move on.

Part Six

They walked eastwards along beaches that had once echoed with the cries of holidaymakers and were now desolate and silent. Many of the villages had been raided and set on fire; others seemed intact but lifeless, like cold casts of their former selves. Empty houses, overgrown gardens, harbours without boats. Groups of cats were dozing under cars and in the shade of pittosporum bushes, taking note without interest of the passing humans. No human sound tempered the stillness; only the cries of gulls and crows and the constant lapping of the sea.

It was sunset by the time they came to the section of beach facing the island. Leonardo helped Lucia down from the elephant and went to sit with her on one of the rocks at the end of the stretch of sand. At that point the coast extended into the sea as a rocky promontory, like a hand trying to recapture something it had absent-mindedly allowed to escape. The island, a few hundred metres from the shore, seemed naked and unfriendly despite the oblique light of the sun. A triangle of opaline rock with nothing on it but a few shrubs including broom.

Leonardo looked at it: it seemed sprinkled with lime and looked like a relic from a far distant past. When he turned, he saw Sebastiano heading towards the embankment that carried the road. After a moment his figure vanished into the dark arch of a tunnel.

"Why are you crying?" Leonardo asked.

Salomon, sitting on the donkey, shook his head to indicate it was nothing, but went on glowering at the island. He had been silent all day without ever asking who the man leading them was, or where they were going or how long it would take to get there. In a cave where they had stopped for a half hour's rest he had found a woman's old handbag and spent the afternoon filling it with crabs he caught on the way. The legs emerging from his shorts were as dry and dark as sticks of liquorice. His bright yellow shoulder-length hair made him look like someone born for running over moors.

"Are you scared?"

The child shrugged and tipped up his nose. The island was all rocky outcrops and seemed to offer no landing place. On the highest point were the circular ruins of an ancient lookout tower, now little more than a pile of stones.

Leonardo reached down to Bauschan's head. The dog's hair was rough with salt, his nose cold and damp. When he looked back at Salomon, he realised the child's eyes and the dog's were exactly the same blue.

"What do you mean, scared?"

Salomon looked around as if wanting to relate this fear to something visible, then simply slid his hand down a couple of times from his throat to the top of his stomach. The elephant crapped, filling the air with a smell of rotten fruit. The sun had set, removing both the warmth and the ferocity of the day.

"I understand," Leonardo nodded, "but it won't happen."

Salomon looked Leonardo in the eye, and then at the elephant, the island, the dog and Lucia, who was holding her bump in her hands and glancing back at the stretch of coast they had come along. Leonardo realized the boy's mind was occupied by one of those thoughts we live with from the moment we are born to the moment we leave the earth. Something to do with finishing a task passed on to us by those who have gone before. He remained dumb to think of the violence and grace involved in all this.

"Now let's eat," he said, aware the boy had stopped weeping and that the crisis had passed.

Salomon jumped off the donkey, came up to Leonardo and emptied his handbag on the ground. After a moment of uncertainty, the crabs began fleeing in all directions. Leonardo grabbed one of the biggest that was about to disappear among the rocks.

"The knife from the basket," he said.

The boy caught up with the donkey which was heading for the road and took a small knife with an arts-and-crafts handle from one of her panniers. David was ripping long sprays of bougainvillea from the embankment with his trunk. This vegetable noise was the only sound in the world. The wind had dropped, silencing the backwash of surf, and the sea just a few metres away was a motionless membrane.

Leonardo opened the crabs and the young people ate their flesh, then Salomon went on a trip round the rocks and came back with some sea snails and limpets. By the time they had finished their meal the sand round them was dotted with mother-of-pearl shells. The smaller crabs, in translucent armour, circulated among the leftovers polishing off what remained.

At this point they saw Sebastiano come out of the tunnel.

He laid a series of round poles on the ground at regular intervals, then went back in and a few seconds later the bow of a small rowing boat began to emerge from the darkness. Before Leonardo and Salomon could even get to their feet, the boat had slithered towards the waterline with a thundering echo like a drumroll.

Sebastiano lit an oil lamp in the boat, and while Leonardo and Salomon loaded on the baskets, he collected the poles and carried them back to the tunnel. After a moment of reluctance, the donkey agreed to get into the boat and, as they left the shore, stood gazing ahead like an old sea hand.

The crossing took half an hour, and throughout this time Salomon looked back at the shore where the elephant was staring steadily at the little light from the lamp disappearing towards the island. Leonardo put his arm round the boy's narrow waist and felt his thin stomach shaken by sobs.

"We'll find a way," was all he said.

They landed on gravel at a little bay on the side of the island facing the open sea. A few metres from the shore, with a dexterity that betrayed long experience, Sebastiano pulled in the oars, and letting the boat bounce on the waves, guided it right up to the beach. The donkey got off by herself, and they unloaded the panniers and two large cans of water that Sebastiano had filled. Then Leonardo helped Lucia off and they were on their way.

During the last few months Sebastiano had added to the only hut already on the island, transforming it into a house with three rooms. The room they entered contained four chairs, a table made from a door placed on two tree trunks, a basin, a stove and three shelves with some dishes and cutlery and a couple of pans. Stretched in a corner, next to a prie-dieu, was an animal hide similar to the one Sebastiano had given Leonardo when they separated. The only furniture in the other two rooms was three sunloungers.

They drank a little water, pouring it into a bowl from one of the cans that Sebastiano had carried up to the house on his shoulders, after which Lucia retired to the room with a single bed while Leonardo and the boy took the other. The plastic on the beds was hard and smelt of chloroform, so they covered them with the rabbit skins they had sewn together in recent months and lay down. Leonardo had the solar battery with him but did not switch it on.

"Have you ever been on an island before?" he asked the boy.

Salomon thought.

"Yes, but I was very little. They told me about it."

"Was it a large island?"

"I think so, because we couldn't even see the sea."

Leonardo stretched out his hand and passed his fingers through the boy's hair. Bauschan was lying in the space between the two beds. Leonardo understood from his whimpers that Salomon was stroking him.

"Has it gone now?" he asked.

"Yes."

"Sure?"

"Yes."

"Then go to sleep, we've got a lot to do tomorrow."

"For David?"

"Yes, for David too."

Lucia's room was smaller; she had moved the bed against the wall, right under the window. Leonardo sat beside her, listening to her breathing interrupted by little wheezing sounds. A dream. Then he took her left foot and ran his thumb over the sole. He did this many times, then switched to her ankle and the other foot. When he got up to go he felt her lightly touch his hand. She gave him time to understand the meaning of what she had done after such a long absence, then after a minute or two she moved his hand to her belly. Leonardo felt hot firm skin under his fingers, then something press against his palm, like a little dog waking up in a sack.

For the first time he was fully aware of Good. Not like in the past, as something that burns and consumes, but as a fire you can hold in your hand and eat in small portions. A fire containing both hot and cold, both light and dark shadow, and that for this reason is more closely related to humanity than to any other creature. Because, in principle, humanity can never be separated from it, in the same way that the water of the sea, the water of the stream and the water that forms the clouds intercommunicate and belong together.

When Lucia released his hand he got to his feet and tiptoed to the door. "Thank you," he said before leaving the room.

As usual, he only slept for a few hours, and at first light went out with Bauschan. It only took him a few steps to realize that the opaline colour of the island was not due to salt or the nature of the rock, but to a covering of dogs' bones.

He climbed up to the ruins of the tower from where he could take in the whole handkerchief of land, but he could see no dogs or animal carcasses. Bauschan stayed quietly at his side with no smell to follow.

Whatever happened on the island had happened long ago.

Returning to the house, he found Sebastiano busy watering the kitchen garden.

During the months he had been here, he had been cultivating a rectangle of land about fifty paces from the shanty. His garden offered *zucchini*, tomatoes, melons and peas and, like the house, was on the part of the island not visible from the mainland.

"Do you know why these are here?" Leonardo asked him, indicating the bones Sebastiano had raked up from his garden and piled in a little white pyramid.

Sebastiano shook his head, then emptied the bucket between two lines of tomatoes and went off to the tank where he kept the water. The sun was getting strong enough to define shadows, and from the pines at the highest point of the island came the first chirping of two cicadas.

Leonardo looked back at the settlement on the western coast: in fact there was a fortified town or citadel enclosed within walls, and ugly houses built in the previous century leading down to the sea. In the clear morning air he could make out threads of smoke rising from the upper part, already turned to ochre by the sun. During the crossing the night before he had noticed fires on the walls but had said nothing because he did not want to worry the young people.

"Who are those people?" he asked.

Sebastiano went back to watering the garden. Leonardo looked at him and waited for an answer, before realizing none would come because no answer existed.

"Have they ever come looking for you?"

Sebastiano bent down to pull up a tuft of grass from among the carrots and indicated no. Leonardo looked at the house where the youngsters were still asleep. The outside of the shanty had been painted with sea-blue paint, and Sebastiano had covered the windows with large jute sacks now swelling in the wind from the mainland, giving the whole house the appearance of an enormous and complicated wind instrument.

"Thank you so much for all this," Leonardo said.

In fifteen days they managed to scrape together four empty drums that Leonardo and Sebastiano had found by pushing on as far as a service station on the main road; also about twenty wooden planks retrieved from bathing huts, a few metres of rope, some nails and tar, and two almost complete rolls of adhesive tape.

Each morning, after milking Circe and drinking a cup of milk, they left the donkey to graze on the island and took the boat back to the beach.

David, seeing them arrive, would start turning round on himself and giving long emotional trumpetings.

The first to embrace him would be Salomon, who jumped into the water a few metres from the shore, and then it would be Leonardo's turn. Sebastiano and Lucia would join in these effusions from a distance, while Bauschan would run between David's legs as if to demonstrate confidence in the elephant's slowness and gentleness. Once mutual greetings were over Sebastiano and Leonardo would begin work on the hull and Salomon would concentrate on the octopuses. Lucia would pass the time sitting with her hands on her belly and watching the sparse clouds crossing the blue sky from a little shelter of branches Leonardo had built for her.

Towards midday the two men would take the boat and the rest of the material back to the tunnel so that it would not be too noticeable, and with the young people and the elephant would go a little way inland to a stream, about twenty metres from the beach.

Under a roof of birches, holm oaks and carob trees the water had scooped out a number of pools where David was able to refresh himself and Salomon amused himself by diving from the elephant's back. Even Lucia, without any warning, one day stripped naked and slid carefully into the water in a more secluded pool, where she spent a long time floating with her eyes half closed and her great belly turned to the sky.

When he had refilled the freshwater cans, Leonardo would go off to inspect the snare he had set the day before. The prey it caught was more sporadic than it had been in the hills and the forest, but he did find a small wild boar and a doe whose meat, when salted, could last them the best part of the summer.

Lunch would consist of tomatoes, boiled *zucchini* and dried peaches; or an omelette made with gulls' eggs which Sebastiano had taught Salomon to search for among the inlets on the island. They never lit a fire and before leaving were careful to cover their traces by collecting every scrap left over from their meal.

Back on the beach, the men would work till sunset. Then everyone except the elephant would get back into the boat which every day looked more like a clumsy catamaran, and would row back to the island.

"Tomorrow can David come too?" Salomon asked as he watched the grey bulk of the elephant shrink until it was lost in the evening.

"Not yet," Leonardo would say.

When they got to the island Sebastiano would go up to the house, light the stove and put on the soup to heat, while Leonardo and the boy fished on the rocks till nightfall. It was then that Salomon would tell his dreams and ask Leonardo to tell his, but Leonardo's dreams were too obscure for a child, so he would replace them with stories from the vast library of his mind. First he told African stories about man and woman; then the exploits of Achilles, the wiles of Ulysses, the misadventures of Don Quixote, the vengeance of the Count of Monte Cristo and Ahab's obsession. Leonardo had to tie the fishing line to the child's wrist so he would not let the fish slip through his hands. Then they would take home what they had caught to be boiled, salted or eaten raw. Some of the entrails were given to Bauschan, and some kept as bait for the next evening's fishing.

After supper Lucia would withdraw to her bedroom, while Salomon stayed up to play with Bauschan. When the boy said goodnight the two men were left together. Leonardo would then put out the lamp and set two chairs on the little open space in front of the house, where they would sit in the dark, breathing the smell of smoke which came from the citadel walls where fires would burn all night.

They were good, controlled fires, but even so neither of them wanted to find out who was living there. They felt no unease and no desire to make discoveries, and even if Sebastiano had decided to speak, they would have had nothing to say to each other. In the dark they could hear Circe walking round the house, the gentle motion of the sea and the cries of gulls among the rocks. It was all they had and all they needed.

Before going to bed Leonardo would go to Lucia to massage her feet and place his hand on her belly to feel the movements of the creature she had been carrying so long inside her and which was now almost ready to come out.

If she was not asleep, the girl would keep her eyes fixed on her father in silence, as though the warmth of his hand was a long speech full of good sense she must not lose.

Coming out of Lucia's bedroom Leonardo would find Sebastiano sitting at the table, busy writing in a narrow script like oblique rainfall in the brown exercise book he had given him during the first days.

Hearing him come in, Sebastiano would raise his head.

They would look at each other for a few moments in silence, then both nod in greeting, before Leonardo went to lie down on his bed next to the boy and the dog.

He had no idea what Sebastiano was writing and he did not want to know. He no longer felt any desire for that act once so familiar to him, in which he had invested so much of himself and which had caused him such agonies in the long years after he had abandoned it. Whatever the reason that had driven him to try to compose what could not be composed, it had gone. The stories inside him would not outlive the beating of his heart. He knew that and it was how he wanted it, and this sense of impermanence would never disturb his sleep.

Two days before the boat was finished, he saw them.

There were three of them, watching from the bridge that linked the two banks of the stream, about a hundred metres up the hillside from the pool. One was a tall man, one a man with red hair, and the third was in shadow.

"There's someone there," Leonardo said.

Sebastiano looked up at the bridge, but from the way he quickly looked down again and went on filling the cans, Leonardo realized this could not be the first time he had seen them.

"We have to go," Leonardo told Salomon, who was swimming with the elephant in the lowest of the pools.

"But it's early!" the child objected.

"I know, but we must get back to the beach."

Lucia had gone upstream to bathe in a more secluded and shaded pool. When Leonardo reached her, she was standing on a great rock in the middle of the stream, staring at the men who were watching her from some fifty metres further up. Her face showed no distress. Apart from the milky whiteness of her full breasts and belly, her body was slender and suntanned, and her hair now reached down to her buttocks.

Leonardo called her. She walked to meet him and let him help her on with her dress over her wet skin; then, with the others, and moving more quickly than usual, they set out down the path to the beach.

Halfway there Salomon turned off towards a path leading to an old house with a garden where they had found two peach trees and a fig tree heavy with fruit. Leonardo told him they could not go there today.

"Why not?" the child asked.

"I'll tell you later, now go with Sebastiano, I have to stop for a moment."

The child realized this was no time for arguing and ran to join Sebastiano.

Leonardo, left on his own, took the dog under his arm and hid behind a low stone wall from where he could watch the path above. The three men appeared soon afterwards, walking unhurriedly in single file. One had white hair; the others were younger, but were not boys. They were wearing T-shirts and an overall, and knee-length trousers. They had short hair and did not have beards.

When they disappeared behind the trees, Leonardo went back onto the road and quickly reached the beach. When the three men emerged from the tunnel, the boat was already about a hundred metres offshore. Salomon, not yet understanding what had happened, ran to the stern when he saw them; one of the men had gone up to David.

"Leave him alone!" the child shouted.

The man, who was about to stroke the elephant, pulled his hand back. The one with white hair and the other one watched the boat moving away.

"Don't worry," Leonardo said. "They won't hurt him."

The boy went on staring at them, with great tears running down his cheeks. Sebastiano was rowing for all he was worth. The island was getting nearer. It was a sunny day, but white cumulus clouds were forming above the coast.

As soon as they landed, Salomon ran to the ruins of the tower from where he could see the beach. Leonardo helped Sebastiano carry the water cans to the house, then joined the boy who was inspecting the coast with his hand shading his eyes. Leonardo sat down beside him on the stones that had once been the foundation of the tower.

"I don't want them to take him away!"

Leonardo reassured him: "They won't."

He could only see one man; the others had either gone away or were sheltering in the vegetation on the far side of the road. David was standing still, like a huge sandcastle.

"But if they are good people, why did we have to run away?"

Leonardo could think of nothing to say to that.

"Let's do some fishing," he said. "Then we'll come back and see if they've gone."

That evening the child did not ask him to continue the story he had started the day before and sat with his eyes fixed on the point where the fishing line disappeared into the dark water, agitated by the coming storm.

They caught a bass and two bream which Sebastiano garnished with rosemary and put to boil in a little sea water. While they were eating it began to rain. Sebastiano put out the basin and several cups to catch the water, then came back in and they continued to eat in silence. No-one said anything about what had happened during the afternoon or what might happen the next day.

When he had finished his supper, Salomon went out.

Leonardo caught up with him halfway up the hill and the two climbed the last bit together. The bones covering the ground seemed to be gradually releasing the light they had stored up during the day. In contrast, once they reached the top the coast seemed black and dense as if moulded in wrought iron. Amid the gloom the fire lit by the three men on the beach shone like a beacon. Even at that distance they could distinguish the figures sitting round the flames. They could imagine David not far off.

"They're still there," the boy confirmed.

Leonardo put his hand on Bauschan's head and stroked it. The wind was driving the clouds inland and, in the half of the sky reflected by the sea, the first stars had appeared.

"David's fine," he said. "They'll be gone tomorrow, you'll see."

They went back to the house. Lucia was in bed and Sebastiano was washing up. Leonardo went into the room with the boy.

"Do those men want to hurt us?" Salomon asked as he lay down on his bed.

"I don't think so."

"Why are they staying there, then?"

"I don't know, but tomorrow we'll bring David here with us," Leonardo said.

The child stared at him in the dark.

"You're not telling me lies, are you?"

"No."

"Sure?"

"Quite sure, but you go to sleep now."

"But what if they come here?"

"They won't come here."

"Maybe they're good swimmers."

"They won't come here."

As soon as Salomon was asleep, Leonardo went out to sit with Sebastiano, who was looking at the fires on the walls of the fortified town. The sky was clear and a thin slice of moon was suspended a little above the hills. The storm had disturbed the sea and a salty vapour rising from the rocks forced them to close their eyes. Leonardo stroked his stump, feeling conscious of the loss of his hand.

"Let's go as soon as it gets light," he said.

Fifty metres from the shore Leonardo signalled to Sebastiano to stop the boat.

Sebastiano took the oars out of the water and the bow pitched to the left, breaking the straight line their journey had maintained till that moment. The three men had got up and were waiting in silence. The covers they had slept on were lying abandoned round the fire like open petals round a burning pistil.

Minutes passed in which nothing happened. The elephant was lying on the sand, his belly rising and falling in his sleep. In the quiet moments of the sea's ebb and flow, Leonardo could hear the animal's breath and smell the cold stench of his dung, both brought to them on the wind.

Then the oldest man understood; he said something to the other two, who began to go along the beach in the direction of the village. It took half an hour for their figures to disappear round the jetty behind the first houses.

"Get close to the shore," Leonardo told Sebastiano. "Then go back to the kids."

The old man was standing waiting for him beside the fire, which by now had gone out. When Leonardo was a few paces from him, he nodded a greeting.

"I'm sorry," he said. "We had no intention of frightening you."

He was more than seventy, but his short, compact body was in no sense fragile. He had the strength of an olive tree grown in a pot. His black eyes must once have been formidable, but they seemed to have signed a truce with humanity and the world.

"What is it you want?" Leonardo asked him.

The man smiled weakly.

"Let's sit down," he said.

The three men had left a small saucepan on the embers. The water had gone cold but the man moved it to where the charcoal was still hot, then poured in a powder resembling coffee from a small envelope taken from his pocket. His movements were calm and precise.

"We didn't recognize you," the old man said, "but the boy who was here just now, the red-haired one, was certain he wasn't making a mistake. He said he used to work in the bank where you were a customer."

Leonardo remembered the young man with freckles who had advised him to accept the fact that he had lost his money. Ever since he had lost all sense of time, the people who had appeared in his life, even those he had only met for a few minutes, inhabited a special place in his mind from where he could recall them without difficulty. It was rather like what had happened to all the stories he had read or listened to.

The old man took a spoon from his pocket and stirred the coffee, on which a thin ivory-coloured froth was forming.

"There are more than five hundred of us in the citadel," he said, "most are from far away. This winter we rescued a lot of people who were dying of starvation on the coast. They'd come hoping to find a boat to take them to France, but all the boats vanished long ago and the border's guarded by the army. If we hadn't taken them in they would have died or become victims of the gangs."

The man broke off to taste a spoonful of the liquid, then nodded that it was almost ready.

"Inside the walls we have a kitchen garden, an orchard, a dozen cows, chickens, goats and a small vineyard. There's also an old furnace and a well we've been able to restore to active use, and what we still lack we're building a little at a time or retrieving from the lower town. Every two or three days we go hunting in the hills. We also have two boats hidden among the newer buildings, but only use them at night and without lights."

He put the spoon back in his pocket and took two glasses from the rucksack that must have been his pillow during the night.

"Some time ago a woman who came from the north told us about a man with only one hand who was travelling about with an elephant, a horse and two children. She had never met him, but had heard it said that he'd been shut up in a cage and given up his hand to be free. When you arrived we realized it must be you, but didn't recognize you at first. We haven't many weapons, and we prefer not to use those we do have, so we keep a careful eye on anyone circulating round here. We prefer them to come to us first. That's why we didn't approach you earlier."

The man filled the glasses with the hot dark liquid. He gave one to Leonardo and lifted the other to his own lips. For a while they sat in silence, watching the island slowly emerging from the darkness.

"I worked as a marine biologist in this nature reserve for thirty years," the man said. "It was I who built the hut you are sleeping in, because I needed somewhere to keep my tools and the instruments I used for surveying."

He savoured a mouthful of coffee, then swallowed it.

"Two years ago, when the dogs began to be a problem, someone thought of dumping them here. There was no building big enough to house them and it would have been too costly to exterminate them, so they began sending them here from the whole riviera. They were brought in cages by the lorryload, put in a boat and winched onto the island. They were given nothing to eat or drink so tore each other to pieces. Any that survived mated, producing puppies that were either devoured at birth or hidden by their mothers in some lair until they were strong enough to come out and themselves start killing.

"It was utter hell, but people said it was better than having the dogs in town or on the beaches. In fact there was no more economical way to get rid of them and dispose of their bodies. There's a strong current between here and the island and those that tried to swim back to the mainland were drowned at sea. One day on the beach we found a labrador that had lost a leg, the only one that made it across. I hid it, but it died a day later.

"I was living on the hillside at that time and at night I couldn't get any sleep. The dogs snarled and howled incessantly, then would suddenly stop. They knew that the cages would arrive the next day and wanted to save their strength. In the morning they would all be there on the beach.

"There was the kind of silence that makes your hair stand on end while we were lowering the cages, but as soon as we opened them the inferno would begin again. They would form bands and divide the island between them, but once the weak, the old and the puppies had been torn to pieces, they would return to fighting among themselves. There was a great deal we could learn from them, if one could face watching them. *Homo homini lupus*. What happened afterwards proved my point. I wish I could have been wrong, but I wasn't.

"The last to survive was a large white dog from the Maremma district.

"He went round for days trying to find a lair full of puppies, but there was nothing left on the island. And no more cages would be arriving, because the few dogs left on the coast had fled inland. Then he began to howl. When I went out onto the balcony at night I could see his white shape on the highest point of the island where the old tower was. It was like a kind of singing. Begging for a mate so he could impregnate her and then rip her to pieces. Then he stopped and I realized he must be dead."

Leonardo looked at the island basking in the fluorescent light rising from the east. Like everywhere else where the ferocity of life had been revealed, it seemed unrelated to the rest of the world. He turned to the old man.

"What's your name?"

"Clemente."

"Why did you come looking for me?"

The old man smiled a toothless smile, then took the full glass Leonardo was still holding in his fingers from him, emptied it on the sand and filled it again with the coffee he had been keeping warm in the pan on the ashes.

"We know you are a guardian of stories," he said, holding out the glass to Leonardo. "We'd like to be able to listen to them."

In August the days got shorter. In the morning the sky was nearly always clear, but in the afternoon cumulonimbus clouds, as black as great anvils, would bring long and quiet storms in from the sea, which left the world magnificently clean and silent.

Sebastiano had made a Chinese chess set, and while they waited for the rain to stop, he and Salomon would play, moving the pieces according to rules they had tacitly agreed between themselves. Leonardo would sit under a little awning they had built from a piece of plexiglass and two posts, and watch Circe and David enjoying the freshness brought by the squalls.

Sometimes, looking down, he noticed he had the palm of his hand turned up, as if holding an invisible book. That made him aware of a small absence, but so slight that he could cure it by moving his hand over Lucia's belly while she sat beside him with her feet up. Her eyes were fixed on the distance where, Leonardo imagined, she must have spent the long months of her absence and which still guarded her words. It had to be a place where there was no fear, and no past and future, because Lucia had come home with her eyes filled with the kind of melancholy that belongs to exiles, the old and gamblers. Sometimes Bauschan would follow her gaze to the horizon as though he thought she was watching something there, but there were no ships or lights or even land to be seen. Then he would whine with disappointment and Leonardo would take his hand from Lucia's stomach and caress the dog's head to reassure him that everything was as it should be.

If in the afternoon the sky did not threaten rain they would take the boat to the beach.

David's weight had made their journeys longer, but they had added two more oars in the bows so Leonardo and Salomon could help Sebastiano.

When they reached the shore they would hide the boat and climb the path to the bend in the river. There was nothing left on the island for Circe and David to eat, so the elephant would spend the afternoon devouring leaves above the river, while the donkey browsed on grass growing in the shade.

Lucia would bathe in her pool and, further down, Leonardo, Sebastiano and the boy would wash with a piece of soap, then lie on the rocks to get dry in the gentle afternoon sun. All except Lucia had cut their hair using the blade of a knife.

Anyone seeing them on their way back down to the beach would have imagined them penitent acolytes of some ancient earthly faith that had reverted to ritual ablutions and hair clipping. Salomon usually sat on David and sang songs he made up himself about diving and catching crabs and fish, but which also involved having a bicycle and going to school.

Some days Leonardo stayed behind and watched the boat set out on its way back to the island. Left on his own, he would build a bonfire from the dead bushes that lined the main road, then sit on the rocks and wait.

Soon the first lights would appear below the citadel, winding down like a fluorescent serpent towards the sea.

When the men and women got to the beach it would already be night. They would gather in silence round Leonardo, extinguish their lanterns and sit in silent expectation. The fire would endow their deprived faces with an unqualified beauty and transform their necklaces of tinplate and shells into precious jewels. Most of them had no idea when the stories they were listening to had been written or who had written them, but they intuited, like animals predicting the coming of a storm or an earthquake, that there was mystery in Leonardo's words, and that the mystery was life pure and simple.

When after an hour or two Leonardo fell silent, at first they would not move, searching in the air for a final echo of his words, then they would slowly get up, thank him with a nod, and take the path back to the citadel. They would leave presents on the sand: baskets of fruit, handkerchiefs, bread, a cigarette lighter, a pen, some rouge, a notepad, a shoelace, a little glass horse, coins, or a cloth made by hand from raw wool. Leonardo would collect everything that could be of use in a bag, then put out the fire and wait for Sebastiano to come with the boat to pick him up.

When he lay down on his bed Salomon was still awake.

"What are those people like?"

"How do you mean?"

342

"Are they good people?"

"I don't know."

"Then why tell them stories?"

"I don't even know the answer to that."

The child was silent.

"But we're not going to stay here, are we?"

"Soon it'll be cold and we won't have anything to eat."

"We can set the snare the way we did before, and we have fishing lines too. And the chicken they've given us."

"We'll see, Salomon. Now go to sleep."

Salomon stroked Bauschan, who was lying on the floor between the beds.

"Leonardo?"

"Yes."

"Are there children up in the fort too?"

"Yes, certainly there are."

"But older or younger than me?"

"Of all ages, I think."

"Maybe one day I can go and see them?"

"Of course you can."

"Even if we don't go and live there?"

"Even if we stay living here."

The child turned on his back and looked up at the ceiling.

"What is it?" Leonardo said, noticing he was still scratching his legs.

"I'm not sleepy."

Leonardo put his hand on the child's cheek.

"You won't die till I'm much older, will you?"

"Very much older. Now let's get some sleep."

It was halfway through September when Leonardo and Sebastiano went back to the service station where they had found the drums they had used as extra floats for the boat.

During the intervening two months someone had been to the site and

343

many of the utensils from the workshop had vanished, together with a pile of tyres and the generator Leonardo had thought too heavy to move. Whoever had taken it must have had access to a horse and cart which was a sign that people in some inland village were getting themselves organized.

They scraped the floor of the workshop with a spatula to retrieve another canful of oil for the lamp, and used a ladle tied to a pole to sound out the bottom of a cistern, something they had not had tools for on their previous visit. They found a body in it, someone who had probably fallen in and been suffocated by the fumes. Pushing it aside with the pole, they managed to fill three bottles with a sticky substance similar to petrol from the bottom. If they used this sparingly it would light them at night all winter. Then they loaded the donkey with two large rolls of linoleum to help to waterproof the roof and started back.

It was evening when they reached the island. Salomon was waiting on the jetty eager to know at once what they had found. Leonardo showed him the oil and the petrol and handed him a little bag of coloured chalks he had found under the seat of an old Opel still propped on a ramp in the workshop. Even if there was hardly anything left of the chalks, the boy was very grateful for them.

"Where's Lucia?" Leonardo asked; she would normally have been sitting on the veranda at that time.

"In her room," Salomon said. "She hasn't been out all day."

Leonardo left the bottles on the beach and hurried to the house. Lucia was lying on her bed, her face and chest covered with sweat. She was holding her belly in her hands, breathing with short regular breaths. Her face was calm and concentrated and her eyes fixed on the ceiling as if what she must do had been written there by all the women who had lived on earth before her.

"She's not ill, is she?" Salomon asked, putting his head round the door.

"Everything's normal," Leonardo said. "Go and call Sebastiano.

While the boy ran to the beach, Leonardo reached under the bed for a large wooden box once intended for quality whisky or cognac, and where for the last few months he had been storing towels and sheets to protect them from dust; then he helped Lucia up, took off the cover stained by the breaking of her waters, spread a clean sheet on the bed and made her lie down again. She grasped his hand. There was a light in her eyes that seemed to come from some far-off depths, which were filled with the same simplicity as when a flower is ready to break through the earth. Leonardo gave her a smile; she smiled back, her lips tense with effort. Another part of her had returned from that distant land. Sebastiano's footsteps were at the door.

"Please put on some water to boil," Leonardo said without turning round.

Sebastiano went away.

"Salomon, come here," Leonardo said.

The boy took a few steps into the room.

"Sit down and hold her hand."

The child sat on the edge of the bed and took Lucia's hand. She was now taking longer breaths.

"Where are you going?" Salomon asked Leonardo.

"To the next room, I'll be back in a minute."

In the kitchen, Leonardo asked Sebastiano to wash his right hand for him with soap and clean his nails, then asked Sebastiano to wash his own hands in the same way, because he was going to be needed.

When he got back to Salomon, the boy was exactly where he had left him.

"Now go and take Bauschan with you," he said. "When I need you, I'll call you." Then he sat down beside Lucia and waited.

The little girl was born in the middle of the night and cried the moment she came from her mother's body. Sebastiano, who had been sitting to one side holding the lantern, helped Leonardo clean the baby and wrap her in a towel, then they passed her to Lucia who hugged her against her full breasts.

"Please go and call Salomon," Leonardo said.

Darkness took over when Sebastiano left the room with the lantern, and the baby stopped crying. Leonardo listened to the breathing of mother and child. There was no mystery, he realized. Just time and the human beings who pass through time.

The boy returned with Sebastiano and they approached the bed together.

"Would you like to do something very, very important?" Leonardo said.

"Yes," Salomon answered.

Uncovering the baby, Leonardo took the umbilical cord in his fingers and formed a small loop in it. Sebastiano handed Salomon the knife.

"Put it in here," Leonardo said.

"Like this?"

"Yes, that's right. Now cut."

The child did as he was told and cut the cord, then lifted the knife in the air. Leonardo took it from him and gave it back to Sebastiano.

"You've done a great job."

"I didn't hurt her, did I?"

"No. Now go to bed. Sebastiano will go with you."

An hour later, after Lucia had fallen asleep, Leonardo, who had kept awake until that moment, picked up the baby and took her out of the room. Salomon was lying asleep on the animal skin in the kitchen while Sebastiano, sitting at the table, was filling the last page of the exercise book in his oblique writing. He got up and offered the lamp to Leonardo, who shook his head to show he did not need it.

He climbed to the highest point of the island where the euphorbia was beginning to put out new leaves with the approach of autumn.

When he reached the ruins of the old tower, he sat down on the pile of stones and looked across to the moonlit coast. The air was warm and there was a faint hiss crossing the night, like the overtones of a note sounded centuries ago but still vibrating in a closed room.

Leonardo unwrapped the baby and lifted her on his only hand towards the moon. For an instant she seemed to levitate weightlessly. Then he pulled her back close to him and kissed her forehead; she smelt of newly kneaded dough.

When they got back Lucia was awake. She laid the baby at her side, and by the weak light from the window, watched her agitate her tiny hands until she found the warmth of the breast.

"Papà?" Lucia called when Leonardo had already reached the door.

He turned.

"Is this the world?"

"Yes, my sweet, this is the world."

In the morning, at first light, two boats left the mainland bringing presents to the island.

DAVIDE LONGO was born in Carmognola in the Province of Torino. In addition to novels he writes books for children, short stories and articles, and his texts have been adapted for musical and theatrical productions. He lives in Turin, where he works as a teacher.

SILVESTER MAZZARELLA is a distinguished translator of Italian and Swedish literature.